The
WOMAN
IN THE
WALLPAPER

The WOMAN IN THE WALLPAPER

LORA JONES

SPHERE

SPHERE

First published in Great Britain in 2025 by Sphere

1 3 5 7 9 10 8 6 4 2

A CIP catalogue record for this book
is available from the British Library.

Hardback ISBN 978-1-4087-3143-7
Trade paperback ISBN 978-1-4087-3142-0

Typeset in Garamond by M Rules
Printed and bound in Great Britain by
Clays Ltd, Elcograf S.p.A.

Papers used by Sphere are from well-managed forests
and other responsible sources.

MIX
Paper | Supporting
responsible forestry
FSC® C104740

Sphere
An imprint of
Little, Brown Book Group
Carmelite House
50 Victoria Embankment
London EC4Y 0DZ

The authorised representative
in the EEA is
Hachette Ireland
8 Castlecourt Centre
Dublin 15, D15 XTP3, Ireland
(email: info@hbgi.ie)

An Hachette UK Company
www.hachette.co.uk

www.littlebrown.co.uk

For Barry

A Note on the Wallpaper

This novel was very loosely inspired by Christophe-Philippe Oberkampf's factory in Jouy-en-Josas, near Paris. Established in 1760, it produced wallpapers and fabrics known as 'Toile de Jouy'. Translated as 'cotton of Jouy', these designs were characterised by floral or pastoral scenes, arranged in repeating vignettes to form a pattern; a style still popular today. Many of the chapters in this novel take their names from the designs produced at Oberkampf's factory between 1760 and 1818.

Prologue

Paris, October 1793

The scene opens up before her as the tumbril rounds the corner. For a moment she imagines the view ahead could be printed, observes the way the high buildings lining the square darken the edges of her vision, creating a vignette, a pattern. She blinks hard.

She sees patterns in everything, still, momentarily wonders if this scene is real at all or simply another deception. She forces herself to focus upon it, waiting for it to vanish or change, to morph into something else entirely. But it does not.

The capital's largest square – the Place de la Révolution – is thronging with crowds so dense it has swelled to bursting point, overflowing into the surrounding *rues* as far as the river's edge. Her gaze travels beyond the mere size of these crowds, right to the heart of their common purpose. This mass of people is all sharp edges: splinters, spikes, snarls. Some break the skyline with pistols, some pierce it with pikes. Others wield a cruder arsenal: sickles, knives, shanks, items they have snatched up or quickly fashioned.

At this distance the scene might almost be pastoral, the high-held weaponry nothing more than meadow-grass, whipped and jostled by the wind. But they have gathered, she knows, to watch death come. Their hunger for it charges the air like a southerly storm.

And there, beyond them all, at the head of the square and high on the scaffold, there she sees it. Taller than two men and looming darkly in its own shadow. The Half-Moon. The Fanlight. The Machine. *Le Rasoir National*. The tocsin bell begins to toll.

The weather is strange, the woman notes, at odds with both the ghoulishness of the scene and the changing season, rendering the colours bright and extraordinary. The sky is a startling blue, as though some vast vat of indigo had upended in the heavens. In turn, the few clouds that punctuate it appear abnormally pristine. The unadulterated white of still-falling snow. Pure as a baby's first breath.

The red only comes into view the closer to the scaffold the tumbril clatters, glimpsed through the hordes. That colour is not vivid. It is dull and stale, staining the boards beneath the great contraption like blooms of rust.

When she'd first been bundled onto the tumbril, a side of meat loaded for market, every judder of its progress had travelled deep into her bones, forced her to nod along with the motion, as if in perfect agreement with what was happening. As if her hands weren't tied at her back, wrists grinding rope.

Now, as the tumbril rattles through the hemming crowds, its motion bothers her no longer. Nor does the sting of the objects people are flinging towards it: the grit and the animal dung, the rags soaked through with trough water and worse. She barely registers the mob either, their taunting, yelling and spitting skimming from her skin. It isn't so much that she is calm, more that she has the notion of not really being here at all.

Papers are thrust towards her and one flutters to rest at her feet. It is printed with rows of names, the first of the day's offerings to the Republic's cause. She stares down at the last of them in recognition, and as her eyes pass across the patterns of ink, her attention turns back to the others in the tumbril alongside her. She had almost forgotten they were there.

The first, a boy, cannot be more than seventeen. His eyes are shut tight, his face pleated with fear. The second, an older woman, is a marquise, though you would never guess to look at her. Her hair, too, is shorn for the occasion; prickly scalp masked beneath cap.

The marquise is damp-faced, grubby-frocked, reciting a prayer in desperate, rapid repetition.

The tumbril jolts to a standstill and the guards fringing the scaffold begin to beat their drums. Her eyes move to the objects positioned behind them: three straw coffins, waiting patiently to be filled.

Without warning, hands shoot over the sides of the tumbril and seize the boy, dragging him up the steps onto the scaffold. He thrashes uselessly against them, toes scuffing wood, impotent as a sprat on a line. He begins to call out, to cry, his tears hot and fast.

'Ma mère! Ma mère!'

'Maman! Maman!' the crowd parrots back.

She recalls the slogan of the Revolution, those watchwords of progress. *Liberté. Égalité. Fraternité.*

The Executioner asks for the boy's last words. *'Quelque chose à dire?'*

'Ma mère!' They are the only words his mind can find.

He is still writhing as they fix him, upright, to the bascule, secure the leather straps around his back, his legs and arms. He is still crying out as they slide him, like a length of timber for processing, into the instrument. *Madame Guillotine.* The lunette clicks shut around his neck.

When the Officiator raises one finger, the Executioner's grip tightens on the *déclic.* The signal is given and – with a terrific, echoing clank – the blade drops.

An object, taken from the basket at the foot of the guillotine, is held proudly aloft. It is so small and insignificant an article that, for a minute, she does not realise what it is. Pistols fire as the boy's head is presented to the crowd, the chant *'VIVE LA FRANCE! VIVE LA FRANCE!'* splitting the sky.

'Sauvages! Barbares!' shrieks the marquise, her voice almost inaudible above the din. Her body solidifies when it becomes clear that she is next, and she is hauled onto the scaffold, the guards' legs buckling against her weight. The marquise makes a noise, 'Oh, oh, oh,' over and over, enfeebled and birdlike, and the blade falls a second time.

3

Now it is her turn. The terrors of her final months, weeks, hours show sorely on her face.

'Quelque chose à dire?' the Executioner asks, leaning in close. His eyes slide to her dress, to the bloody stain that has blotted through the print of the fine fabric. He scowls, and she cannot work out whether it is the stain or the pattern itself that has prompted his distaste.

She pauses. Though her mouth is open, no words leave it. There is nothing left to say, she thinks, so she tilts her head to the sun and feels it warm on her face.

The Executioner huffs and ties a length of cotton about her eyes. Then she, too, is strapped to the bascule, and her breasts press sore at its surface. She tries to make out the wild thump of her heart against the wood, but cannot feel it. What she can feel is a square of something stiff against the fronts of her thighs. His letter, still unopened in her pocket-bag. Still unread. As the bascule is swivelled horizontal, the letter is released and drifts to the floor. A susurration faint, but unmistakable. The low crinkle of paper.

The paper.

The lunette encircles her neck and the Executioner's glove creaks on the *déclic.* The crowds have fallen silent, drawn a collective breath, thrilled mute and motionless at that unseen precipice between life and death.

Then, from nowhere, a scream tears the air. A torrent of words. A familiar voice.

'NO! STOP! *ARRÊTEZ!* She's not on the paper!'

They are wrong, the woman thinks, they are mistaken, for it is hard to recollect a time when she has not been on that paper, *in* that paper. Has she not identified herself, printed indelibly into its pattern, innumerable times? Does the pattern not, even now, enswathe nearly every part of her body?

She remembers what it was like inside the circle of that room, as though enclosed in an exquisitely lined box. Some might have called such paper beautiful, yes, but it was also cluttered and frenzied and tight. Airless, each finger-width of it inundated by those repeating

4

scenes. Mottled purple vignettes of figures and landscapes, tumbles of flora and fauna. Unhealed bruises from an earlier time. There had been no escaping them. Until now.

The changing patterns of those scenes start through her mind in hastening succession, in this precious, infinitesimal moment before release.

PART I

Monuments of the South of France

Marseilles, October 1788

Sofi

'Fi, if you really want to be as good a draughtsman as Pa, you will need to draw as well as observe.'

I scowl. My sketching lies abandoned on my lap and my sister has noticed. The wealthy visitors to the city have distracted me from my work. I have been watching them disembark from the packets and sailing ships, trailed by servants panting beneath the weight of their luggage like overburdened donkeys.

'Pa always says observing is two-thirds of the skill,' I return.

Lara's voice, though mild, does not miss a beat. 'You still need to practise the other third.'

I look at her, strands of blonde hair playing against her cheeks as she bends over her parchment, and consider how different we are. How all our mother's looks have passed to her and all our father's to me. How she is so fair and delicate and me so swarthy and tall. How our characters are quite the opposite, with Lara docile as Pa. I am the one marked by Mama's temper.

We have brought our drawing things to the harbour, where I have been attempting to capture the likenesses of the fishermen as Lara sketches the morning's catch. The crabs and squid, the slippery ribbons of seaweed brought up in the nets. My sister and I always set about it this way – Lara drawing the wild things she loves so much, me concentrating on the passers-by. We hope to work for our father before long, to create the designs for his sculptures and plaques, for the scrolling curlicues and Grecian heads he conjures from rough lumps of stone. We want it desperately, to see Lara's talent for creatures and mine for figures to combine in a finished piece, a product someone would be happy to part with their coin to own. Yet whenever we are out sketching, something will always snag my attention and it will be time to leave before I know it, and Lara will have made a good handful of sketches and me none.

Mama, of course, has no idea we are here at all. She would likely boil herself out in a rash if she knew we were at the harbour, even now Lara is sixteen and me fifteen. 'Too dangerous,' she carps. Heaven knows what she thinks might happen. But we dressed in stealth before dawn and tucked a supply of parchment and charcoal into our pocket-bags. Crept from the house whilst the old quarter was still quiet and tiptoed under the letters carved large above its entrance.

L. THIBAULT. STONEMASON.

We cannot stay long. It is the same when we go to the tree-lined boulevards on the city's outskirts, where Lara sketches the geckos. Or the high rocks above the coast, where red-streaked cliffs meet bright blue sky and brighter, bluer, foam-streaked sea. We time our outings carefully, ensure we are back at the house before Mama misses us and starts to make a fuss.

At the dock, a *débardeur* hacks a dusty ball of phlegm onto the cobbles and curses. He has the appearance of a wrung-out cloth, thin and spent, the grime from the coal he's just hauled from a barge deep in the lines on his face. Behind him, a portly *gentilhomme* is hoisted into a monogrammed carriage, kerchief clamped to his nose. Nearby, an old woman has passed out from exhaustion in a huddle of sack-cloth, naked from the knees down. She must have come here to beg, her small body little more than skin drawn over bone. When I look back at my lap, I see I have been gripping my stick of charcoal so tight it has crumbled onto my parchment, blackening it like the skin of that *débardeur*.

Lara regards my expression and her face falls. She sees the rest of it, too. 'I really think Pa will let us help with one of his commissions soon,' she says, forcing brightness. 'There was an enquiry yesterday from Le Roucas Blanc.' She looks at me earnestly, shading wide eyes from the sun.

Le Roucas Blanc is one of the wealthiest stretches of the city, the rock from which it takes its name as white and unsullied as the hands of the people who dwell on it, with their vast mirrors and well-stocked cellars and parterres overlooking the ocean. And although working alongside my sister for Pa is all I've ever wanted to do, the notion suddenly seems wrong. Crafting fine objects for the rich. What good is such business to the poor and the vulnerable? It might keep the wolf from our door, but it won't stop him from slinking through theirs, devouring the likes of that old, sleeping woman. The thought strikes me that she might not be sleeping at all but already dead, slipped away in the time we have been here and nobody to mark it. It makes me want to cry.

'Did I hear Pa say you would be going on the wagon with Guillaume soon?' I ask Lara, glancing at her parchment in an attempt to break my thoughts. She is drawing a duck, charcoal arching over the page to map its likeness, the motion light and precise. On my own sheet floats a disembodied head, all the progress I have made with my fisherman, peering out from dense clouds of smudged charcoal.

'Next week, I think,' my sister replies.

A pause.

I have seen the way she looks at Guillaume, cannot believe she is not counting down the days until she is on the wagon with him, the first time they will ever have been alone together.

'You *think*?' I blurt. 'Come, Lara, surely you know he is sweet on you?'

'What? No!' she counters hastily, not lifting her eyes from her parchment. But I note the hint of self-conscious mirth in her expression.

Guillaume Errard, a year or two older than my sister, is a local blacksmith's apprentice who drives Pa's wagon now and then to help with his deliveries. He's lately started to wear a short black beard, and I wonder whether this is just his way of disguising that thin scar that runs between his nose and lip, the one that seems to give him his slight lisp. If so, I think it a shame. I have never once seen Guillaume out of temper. He is as gentle a soul as my sister. In a way, they are perfect for each other.

'You like him, too, don't you?' I ask, suddenly unable to hide the flint in my voice.

She makes no reply, continuing to form the bill of the duck with her charcoal.

'Go on, admit it!' Irked by her coyness, I elbow Lara's drawing arm, turning duck's bill into elephant's trunk and regretting it immediately.

'Sofi!' There is an unusual edge to her tone and she darts a look at my drawing. 'Do not speak so when you only see half the story. Why do you always fixate on circumstances that do not concern you, when you could be improving your own? You keep saying you want to work with Pa. You have the talent. Well, now is the time to put in the practice.'

She has never spoken to me this way before and her outburst quietens me a moment. Then the realisation I must have hit a nerve hooks my anger.

'Has Mama worked out that you're soft on Pa's delivery boy? She wouldn't like it – you know how she is about such things.'

Lara's grey eyes remain focused on her parchment, but she has stopped drawing.

'There is nothing for her to work out,' she replies. 'If he didn't help Pa I should not have cause to see Guillaume at all. I do what Mama asks of me, complete all my chores. I don't see why any of that should displease her.'

I do not remember a time when Lara's goodness did not irritate me, yet neither do I remember a time when it did not make me love her all the more. But I know, too, that as good and diligent as Lara is, there is something about her which always *does* seem to displease Mama, and I find it a mystery I cannot unravel.

'I'm sorry,' I murmur and plant a quick kiss on my sister's cheek. 'I should not have spoken so.'

She smiles and continues to sketch, already managing to make the mistake in the duck's bill look as though it was always meant to be there. 'That head's very good, you know,' she says, nodding at my parchment. 'You should finish it.'

I contemplate my work and try to locate the fisherman I'd been drawing, when out of nowhere, a shape swoops down on us, seizing Lara's arm.

'I knew I'd find you here!' Our mother's face is sheeted steel. 'What is all this? What are you doing?'

'Drawing—' I start.

'Drawing?' Mama flares. 'Loitering, more like. What kind of impression do you think that gives these . . .' her lips twist, 'these *men*.' She spits this last word, eyes flicking to the dockers. 'Men don't need any encouragement where young girls are concerned.'

'Mama,' Lara begins, 'we did not mean—'

My mother's grip tightens on my sister's arm, and I sense people starting to stare at this bony woman wrestling her daughter by the wrists, seething and scolding over nothing. 'I presume sneaking to the harbour was *your* idea?'

The question, directed only at Lara, pins my sister like the sharpened end of a pike.

Carving in Stone

Sofi

Back at the house, Mama steams silently for the rest of the day, waiting for Pa to stop work like a dog straining at its leash. She presumes he will punish us, but I already know she is mistaken.

'Surely they were doing no harm,' our father says when he finally appears. He goes to put a hand around Mama's shoulders, but she steps out of reach.

'I do not want them sprawled at the harbour like street girls,' she cries. 'It isn't decent!'

Pa rubs the dark shadow of his chin. 'Decent?' he repeats wearily. 'Come, Margot. They've done nothing—'

'I don't like them lingering there alone, you know that,' Mama flares. She pauses, straightens her back. 'Too many gulls for one thing. Peck your eyes out sooner than look at you.'

I wonder why Mama will never say what she really means when Pa is present. That, as she has made clear to Lara and me, it isn't the birds that worry her.

'Any drawing to show me today then, girls?' Pa asks. 'Shells, scales and lobstermen, perhaps, if you've been at the harbour?' He attempts to hide a smile from Mama and lays our parchments over the dining table.

'Not now, Luc,' she snaps. 'I need to set for supper.'

'At least we *have* supper, Mama,' I snap back, annoyed by her chiding.

I remember that old woman at the harbour, the things Pa has told us over the past months. About the country's droughts, the failing crops, the hunger. About the people he sees along the roadsides, begging for work and for food. So thin they look like they might have been hollowed with spoons.

Pa hushes me. 'Very well, Margot, we'll take this to the workshop and out of your way,' he says. 'Just for a few moments.' He scoops up our papers, winks and shepherds us to the door, and we are down the stairs before Mama has the chance to object.

Whenever he has a moment to spare, and often when he does not, Pa will sit patiently with us in his workshop, teaching us everything he has learned himself. How to observe in minute detail the exact line needed to capture the tone and form of a thing, how to scale up images in squares, create a repeat and use negative space to a design's advantage. Sometimes he will make a mark upon the page and ask us what we see in it, tell us to transform his random scribble into a drawing or a pattern of its own.

Pa's workshop is my favourite place in the world. Situated below the parlour, it takes up the entire lowest floor of our house and is dominated by his huge working table, each nick and dent on its surface a slip of one of Pa's tools, the rest worn smooth as sea-stones beneath his hands.

He unfurls my parchment first, the sketch of a fisherman with the rough outline of a body I'd added like an afterthought. 'Very good!' Pa remarks as my cheeks redden guiltily, unworthy of such praise. 'You've captured the movement just right, *alsghyr*, he leaps from the page!'

Even though I shall never tire of his nickname for me – 'little one' in Arabic, which was his father's tongue – I am already certain he will have more praise for Lara. He always does.

'Well indeed, exceptional work once more,' Pa tells my sister. 'Carry on like this and you'll make a fine draughtswoman for me before long, I've no doubt.'

It is my sister who colours now, pride large on her face, while I feel the same keen swell of hurt I do whenever Pa tells Lara she will work with him, but never says the same to me.

I cross to Pa and put my arms around his waist, despite myself.

He laughs and squeezes me back, and I take in the peculiar smell of him. Apron leather, cut stone, a hint of sandalwood. And as I stand there feeling the solid beating of his heart, the breath strong in his chest, I think, *This is all I need.* There is no cause to worry about any of it, about Mama and Lara, or the people starving in the streets. About the fact that it feels like something huge and ominous is just over the horizon and it is impossible to see where it will begin or end. As long as Pa is here, everything will be all right.

A sudden clip of footsteps sounds from outside.

'Luuuc!' The man stretches Pa's name long, making it creak. It is not a voice I have heard before.

'Baron de Comtois!' my father says with surprise. 'Please, come in.' He makes a hasty attempt to clean a chair, wiping the dust away with a cloth.

I recognise the name then. De Comtois. Not just our landlord, but landlord of almost the whole region, his pockets lined thick with his tenants' coin. I wonder why he has come here himself and not sent a clerk. He has never done so before.

De Comtois smirks at Pa's invitation, as though my father had said something embarrassing, his gait as he enters absurd. He takes such pains to avoid the dust and stone flakes on the floor, it is as though he is trying to pick his way across a sewer.

'May I introduce my daughters, Baron,' says Pa, pressing our shoulders into a curtsy. 'Here is Lara and her sister, Sofia.'

De Comtois, dressed from head-to-toe in the pale blue of a pearl, studies Lara for longer than is decent. I have seen other men do the same. This one's eyes are just as beady, but a flat grey, as though someone had sucked the colour from them like marrow. His face is tapered, chin pointed as an arrowhead. As he appraises my sister, a muscle quivers in his cheek.

'Charmed,' the man drawls, gaze falling from Lara to our drawings, still spread across the table. 'And what do we have here?'

As he picks up the parchments, his thumb smudges our work and I know he is doing it on purpose. I try to shoot out a hand to snatch the papers from him, but feel my father's preventing it.

'Hmm,' de Comtois muses, 'a little practice required, I think.' He flicks a finger at Lara's drawing. 'That is, after all, a rather strange-looking rabbit—'

De Comtois discards the pages carelessly and my forehead prickles with anger. 'That's a duck,' I say. 'Are you blin—'

'Baron, might I help you with anything?' Pa cuts in.

De Comtois' lip curls in irritation. Mine does the same.

'I regret, Thibault, that I come bearing some ...' he hesitates, 'unpalatable news.'

My father's face drops. 'I see,' he replies. 'Girls, go and find your mother, I'm sure she'll be in need of your help.'

Reluctantly I trail Lara to the stairs, lingering at the threshold. On the other side of the door de Comtois' voice is sticky as treacle. My father's questioning, disappointed.

'I'm afraid so,' de Comtois is saying. 'I have no choice but to raise your rent by twenty *livres*. With immediate effect.'

'A *month*? But Baron, that is over a third of what I earn in that time—'

'You are doing well enough, though, are you not? You will surely be able to make the extra work up, somehow.'

It is now that I understand why the man came himself instead of sending a clerk. The amusement in his voice is plain. He is taking pleasure from this, from watching his tenants fret and squirm.

My father does not answer, and there is a long moment of silence before de Comtois speaks again. 'You know, Luc, I heard only last week how prisons like the great Bastille are filling up with men unable to pay their way—'

'Sofia!' my sister hisses from the top of the staircase. 'It is rude to eavesdrop!'

I do not have time to object before Lara has dashed downstairs, taken hold of my hand, and pulled me up to the parlour.

I strain for more, but hear nothing.

The Lights of Marseilles

One week later

Lara

It's been a strange sensation today, riding up front on my father's wagon. Everything has looked clearer, somehow. The colours more intense, the sun warmer on my face, the sky more dazzling, a vast, enveloping blue.

Perhaps it is because I am sitting next to Guillaume, who is helping with Pa's deliveries, steering the ponies along the track. Every bump and dip in the road sends our thighs momentarily pressing together, something which neither of us mentions. I have never been this close to him before.

'So *his* father came here before he was born?' Guillaume asks.

He is talking about Pa, who is back home, labouring in his workshop. Despite the lateness of the hour, he will remain there for many more yet. Since the rent was increased, he has had little choice.

'Yes,' I nod, 'from Algiers. He met my grandmother at a dance, they married a few years later. Her family has lived in Marseilles for generations.'

'I never realised that Luc was short for anything,' Guillaume comments. 'Luq-man.' He sounds Pa's name out carefully. 'But your last name is French?'

'Pa's father changed it not long after he moved here. He thought it best to have a family name that sounded French. Before the war, my grandfather had a good job in Algiers. That changed when he came here, of course. But my grandfather taught Pa to read and he us.'

'I'm impressed,' Guillaume says. 'I wish I could read and write.'

'You can shoe a horse,' I reply. 'That's just as good. Better, even.'

I think of Guillaume helping his uncle in the smithy every day, beating out the metal from the furnace, helping to craft many of Pa's tools.

'So, how did your parents meet?' He turns to me and, as he does, the wheels on his side of the wagon drop into a rut, sending me sliding towards him. We part quickly and both look away, making a show of admiring the view in opposite directions.

'They met when Pa was a mason's apprentice, coming from the quarry one night. He saw Mama walking home. She used to work at the soap factory.'

'The one de Comtois owns?'

'That's right.'

I think of Mama, making her way back with the other factory girls, in a cloud of lavender-scented air from the flowers they poured in the soap mix. I remember the hints Pa has dropped over the years, without meaning to, about how different Mama was then. Softer, freer, laughing easily. When Pa spotted her at the edge of the woods she had been singing with the others, petticoats hoisted, tanned legs skipping beneath. It's hard to picture her like that now.

'She left her job at the factory when she knew she would be having me,' I say. 'Then Sofi came along not two years later.'

'I like Sofi,' Guillaume says amiably, 'very much.'

'She can be headstrong,' I reply. 'But she means well. Remind me, how many brothers and sisters do you have altogether?'

He laughs. 'Too many.' His fingers flick out from the reins he holds, as though counting them off. 'I'm the oldest at home. Five younger there as well . . . two boys, three girls. Then there's my eldest sister, Agathe. She was like a mother to me growing up, since Mama was always busy with the littler ones. Agathe lives up near the capital now with her own family. Her husband's a clerk.'

'Goodness,' I say, 'so many. I've an aunt near the capital too.'

We proceed around a bend in the road, about a mile or two from home, and the lights of Marseilles twinkle thickly ahead. We are not far from the tavern, and hear the noise of its patrons long before we see them. As we draw closer, the men clustered at the entrance come into view, conversing raucously, laughing into the dusk and clanking drinking vessels.

'They're having a fine time,' Guillaume remarks, and for the briefest second transfers his attention from the road to me.

'Careful!' I cry, my hands flying to the tops of his, to seize the reins. Ahead of us a man, heavy with drink, has stepped out right before the animals, making them jump and whinny.

'Whoa!' Guillaume calls. 'Steady!' He brings them to a halt not two paces from where the man is reeling.

I see from his clothes that the reveller is a gentleman, though why he should be drinking here I cannot guess. He takes off his wig and bows mockingly, making no effort to remove himself from the road. This goes on for many moments, before he teeters to the side.

'You should be careful, Monsieur,' says Guillaume as he gets the horses moving again. 'You should not be walking on the lane in your state. Specially not after dark.'

The man only laughs, a wet, disdainful sound, and staggers into the night.

'Good job the wagon was empty,' Guillaume says. 'We mightn't have stopped so easily otherwise.'

When we arrive back in the old quarter, there is still a light showing in my father's workshop.

'Might he be able to finish soon?' asks Guillaume, inclining his head towards it.

'I don't think so,' I answer. 'I should go and see if he has eaten.' I squint at the house, notice Mama's slender silhouette flickering against the parlour window.

'Right then,' Guillaume remarks, securing the wagon in the outhouse. 'I'll be heading home.'

As he says this my sister appears, greeting Guillaume and noticing the manner in which we are standing, faltering and awkward. 'You're welcome to some food, you know,' she tells him.

My cheeks tingle with shame. 'I'm sorry, I should have offered—' I do not know if there is enough food even for us, but I know for sure that with his father gone and mother left with so many mouths to feed, there is less to go around at the Errards' table.

'No, I must go,' Guillaume replies cheerfully. 'Do not worry.'

He starts off along the lane and I suddenly remember. 'Wait!' I cry. 'You haven't been paid!'

Guillaume stops, glances at my sister and slowly moves to face me, hands clasped shyly before him. 'I do not want money for today,' he says. 'Tell your father not to worry.'

'But—' I begin, confused, still sensing Mama's gaze boring into me from above.

'Company was enough,' he mumbles and turns quickly away. '*Bonne nuit.*'

He heads off along the cobbles and down the next street, but before he does, dark though it is, I am sure I see him blush.

That Wallpaper Factory in Jouy

Several days later

Sofi

I should have known when my mother sent me to the market alone that something was amiss. Fetching the day's bread is normally an errand my sister and I complete together. But Mama declared that I should be the one to go, straight there and straight back, telling Lara in the same breath she was needed for some vague-sounding task at home.

The house is unusually quiet when I return. I call out, enter the parlour to find Mama and Lara seated silently at the table. I drop my basket between them.

'That is the best I could get,' I announce. 'I swear it gets blacker by the week.'

Neither Mama nor Lara respond. The loaf stares back at me from the bottom of the basket, looking foul. Several of Lara's drawings, I see, lie a little to the side of it, together with a letter addressed to my aunt.

Mme B. Charpentier
The Oberst Wallpaper Factory
Jouy-en-Jouvant

Last time I saw my mother's elder sister I cannot have been more than two years old. Aunt Berthé, a widow now, works as housekeeper to a factory-owner in the north. She and my mother aren't especially close, but Mama will have Lara reply to Aunt's letters from time to time. Unlike Pa, Lara and me, Mama never learned to read or write.

'What news is there for Aunt Berthé?' I say. 'I did not know she had written to us recently.'

Mama does not answer.

I look at Lara, expecting her to break the ominous quiet, but her fingertips are blue-black with ink and her eyes red with tears.

'Why have you written to our aunt, Mama?' I ask, confused. 'Is it urgent?'

Lara stifles a sob and my pulse begins to rise. I squint at the letter but, in a flash, Mama pushes back her chair and plucks it from the tabletop.

I think of stepping forwards, snatching it off her. 'What is happening?' I say instead. 'Tell me, Mama!'

My mother shifts. 'If you must know now, well . . . I've written to your aunt to ask her to find Lara a place.'

'A place? What do you mean, a place?'

Mama clears her throat. 'Your sister is sixteen now, Sofia. It is only proper that she find work. It is vital, in fact, given our landlord's . . .' her voice trails, lips pursing as though the words were too sour on the tongue, 'rise in rent last week.'

'Find work? Why can she not find work here?'

Mama's face hardens oddly, like this decision has been a long time in the making and her expression a long time in the rehearsing. Across the table, Lara hurriedly swabs her eyes.

'*I* am nearly sixteen,' I add, more feebly than I intend. 'Does that mean next year I will be sent away too?'

'Of course not, Sofia,' Mama returns, too quickly. 'And there is no need to worry about your sister, your aunt will look after her.'

'But, why—?' I rush to Lara's chair and crouch beside it, gathering her hands into mine. 'What is going on?' I ask her, my voice lowered.

My sister glances nervously at our mother. 'You heard what Mama said,' she croaks. 'I am to be sent away.'

'I heard what Mama said, but not what she meant. Why should she do such a thing?'

Lara shrugs and shakes her head, dislodging a patter of tears onto her apron.

'Is this something to do with Guillaume?' I whisper, casting my mind back to the other night. How awkward yet intimate he and my sister looked, standing about in the street, with Mama watching from the window. 'I told you she wouldn't like it.'

'It is nothing to do with any boy, man or anyone else,' Mama clips.

I can tell that she is lying.

'It is certainly nothing to do with Pa,' I return. 'For he would never consent to it!' My gaze again lands on my sister's sketches spread upon the table. 'Why are your drawings out, Lara?'

'I am sending a few of the best to your aunt,' Mama answers for her. 'A wallpaper factory is in the business of design, and it's not as though Lara's work isn't accomplished.'

My mind starts to swim. This wallpaper factory is miles and miles from Marseilles, all the way up near Paris. If Aunt Berthé does find work for Lara there then I would not see her from one year to the next. There would be no more drawing together, no more of Lara's calm words of encouragement. Worst of all, we would never be able to work for Pa as we always wanted.

'It was a nice idea that you could both design for your father one day, but it would never have worked,' Mama says, as if teasing the thoughts from my head. 'People just don't buy the work of girls. And by people I mean rich men, the ones who make decisions as they please, hold the purse strings and everything else besides.'

I want her to be wrong with every bone in my body. 'So why can Lara and I not both find work here?' I ask. 'Why can't you go back to the soap factory—'

Mama cuts me off in an instant. 'Enough! If your sister can secure work in Jouy there will be no need for any of that.'

'You cannot do this, Mama!' I cry, blood roaring in my ears. 'Why do you always have to be this way? It's like you don't love Lara at all.'

24

I am immediately seized by remorse, even though it is true. Mama's face freezes as if I had just slapped her. There is a brief moment of quiet.

'How ... dare ... you—'

'What on earth is going on?'

I look up to see Pa standing in the doorway, rubbing the stone dust from his hands, his face tensed.

'You had better ask her,' I cry, jabbing a finger in Mama's direction.

My mother draws herself rigid as the poker at her back, saying nothing.

'She is sending Lara away!' I go on, tears prickling my eyes. 'To work at that wallpaper factory in Jouy where Aunt Berthé keeps house. She has the letter all written. She's sending Lara's drawings along with it!'

Pa's mouth falls open. 'Is this true, Margot?'

I was right, Pa didn't know. I shoot Lara a look.

Mama bristles. 'The extra coin Lara's wages would bring is needed, is it not?'

'Oh, Margot,' Pa murmurs, and there is a strange crush to his voice that implies he had seen this coming. 'We do not know for sure that we will not make the rent. It has hardly been a week.' He sighs heavily. 'Let us discuss it later. When I have finished my work.'

Moving to the table, Pa examines the bread in the basket. 'Listen, how about you girls come out on the wagon with me this afternoon?' he says. 'I've just had word that my order is ready to collect from the quarry and should be glad of the company.'

'You may take Lara,' says Mama, fixing me with a glare. 'But after her outburst Sofia will be going nowhere today. She will stay here. With me.'

I go to make some remark about what a terrible punishment that will be, but feel Pa's hands on mine.

'Be kind,' he says, kissing my hair. 'Stay here. Help your mother. Look after her for me.'

25

'Yes, Pa,' I whisper, but I know that my father is wrong, that my mother is the last person who needs any looking after. And I make up my mind to slip from the house and meet his wagon when he returns. Whether Mama likes it or not.

The Gathering Dusk

Lara

As the limestone-weighted wagon groans around the bend in the lane, the tavern and the old horse-pond down the hill hone into view. It is strange to see so little water in the pond. I remember marking last week how depleted it was, reduced by the droughts to hardly more than a puddle. I'd been with Guillaume then, and have the sudden urge to be with him again and put my head upon his shoulder. I lean on Pa's instead, feel the warm, safe mass of him beneath my cheek. He has promised that he will speak to Mama, try to find work for me here in Marseilles. But he has so little time at the moment as it is. My throat tightens, threatening tears, and I do my best to disguise them with a yawn.

'Nearly home,' Pa says, laying a hand on my knee. It is still there a few seconds later, when I see movement in the gathering dusk ahead of us.

I start, bolt upright. 'Careful, Pa!' A gaggle of men is idling on the lane. 'One stepped out in front of the ponies the other evening.'

'Whoa!' my father calls, managing to slow the heavy wagon.

There are more of them tonight. Two sway unsteadily towards us, two more lingering closer to the tavern.

'Look here!' one of them guffaws. The smell of something sour and strong comes off him in waves as his eyes wander lazily over my father.

'*Bonsoir*,' Pa replies politely, attempting to move the wagon around the men. But one of them lurches at the horses, grabbing at a bridle.

'Not so fast,' he slurs. 'Let us have a better look at you. And your pretty Mademoiselle. 'Tis not every day we see such a sight.'

I feel for the ponies. They shy at the men's closeness and clumsy, unpredictable movements. Like the man Guillaume and I encountered, the voices of these strangers, though proper, are as unsteady as their bodies.

The figures obscured in the entrance shuffle together, snatches of their words drifting towards us. 'I did,' one is saying, the tone strangely familiar, 'lost it all, every last *sou*!'

'You and your card games, Édouard,' the other replies, spluttering into laughter. 'When will you learn?'

'Ah well. 'Twas good sport, all in.'

I realise it is him, the man who came to Pa's workshop, and see that my father has also recognised the voice of our landlord. The Baron de Comtois comes forwards then, swaggering into the low patch of light near the wagon. He blinks and presses a hand to his chest. 'Thibault, it is you!' he says. 'I do hope you didn't—' He stops abruptly when he sees me.

The last man joins the others, bringing with him a torch from the tavern's entrance. He holds it high, the flame cutting menacingly through the dark.

'Not too close with that, gentlemen,' Pa begins, 'I beg you. My horses will take fright.' Unease tightens inside me, more so when I detect it in Pa's voice too.

'He's begging!' the first man says, prompting laughter from the rest.

'My, the skin on him!' the second man dribbles, careening closer. 'It's as though he has eaten mud every day of his life!'

The others, with the exception of de Comtois, knock their glasses together and howl as though this is the funniest remark they have ever heard. The man with the torch staggers nearer to the wagon. He is waving the flame in earnest now, left and right, closer and closer to the ponies' eyes. The worry is plain on Pa's face and the animals are growing more agitated by the second. Their ears are flattened, heads high. They have nowhere to go, their reins and the wagon's bulk keeping them in place.

'Messieurs, please!' Pa says, his voice firmer than before. 'That is enough. Now let me pass.'

De Comtois looks on, a few paces behind the others, amusement twisting his lips. The horses begin to whinny in alarm, to contort their heads in one direction then the other.

Panic is rising in me now, the flame's sweep through the murk making it seem like ten more of them are burning. I know I must say something.

'Please, gentlemen,' I begin, trying in vain to still the wobble in my voice. 'We should be grateful if you could let us by.'

'I'll let you by my breeches,' one quips, and the others wheeze with laughter.

Pa is about to lose his temper, I can tell, shaking with suppressed anger. But before he has the chance, everything comes asunder. The man holding the torch staggers drunkenly closer and trips. As he falls, the flame catches one of the ponies on the neck. The pony screams and bolts, the second animal taking fright along with her. One of the other men is almost toppled, leaping clear of the horses' hooves just in time.

'You mongrel!' he spits after us. 'You could have killed me!'

'Whoa, whoa!' Pa shouts. He is clinging fiercely to the reins, attempting to steady the wagon and right its direction. But it is veering out of control down the hill, the great weight of its cargo rendering it more and more unwieldy. The wagon swerves, approaching the place where the lane falls away to the horse-pond. Another swerve and it will come off the track altogether.

'Lara! Jump! To the right!' Pa shouts.

The wagon and the horses are thundering, and my father is trying to save them both. I want to shout back, to tell him to leave them, to jump, too, but no sound leaves my mouth.

'NOW!'

I do as Pa says, and hurl myself sideways with as much strength as I can muster.

Plunging through the blurred and blackening landscape, it seems as though I am falling forever.

The Horse-Pond

Sofi

I have almost reached the tavern above the horse-pond when I see him do it. That man with de Comtois, deliberately putting his flame to the pony's neck.

It all happens so quickly then. One second the wagon is there, the next it is not. The noise is deafening, the wheels and the hooves, the petrified whinnying of the ponies, and then an earth-splitting crash. The next thing I know, dust clouds have billowed from the ground, swallowing everything in their wake.

As I edge forwards, a shape looms large through these smothering gales of dust, a whirring thing, high as a monument. The wagon has toppled, come to rest upended in the horse-pond, its rear wheels still spinning and cast askance to the heavens. The full weight of the wagon's load is trapping the ponies. They thrash in what is left of the water.

'Pa!' I shout. 'Pa!' I cannot see him. My ears start to ring, blind panic at what is unfolding shaking loose my senses.

I notice my sister then, a few paces away. She has an unearthly look on her face, like she cannot fathom where she is or what she is seeing, a hand held to the back of her head as though trying to free her cap. 'Lara?'

'Fi!' Lara removes her hand and reaches out to me. Her fingers are slicked and dark.

'You're bleeding!' I cry. 'You're hurt!'

'It's nothing,' she utters distractedly and wipes the blood on her

31

apron. 'I jumped from the wagon. I must have hit my head when I landed.'

'Where's Pa?' I ask. If Lara was able to jump clear of the wagon then surely my father was, too.

'I ...' Lara begins, 'I don't ...'

I become aware that a group of men is encircling my sister and me, scrambling down to the horse-pond and calling instructions between them. They must have made their way over from the houses dotting the lane, summoned by the commotion.

I don't know how much time passes before one of them steps out of the chaos and comes towards us. It is Guillaume. He takes Lara's arm, tries to guide me away with her, away from the horse-pond, but I do not want to move. Any moment, I think, Pa will emerge from the tumult. Dirty and stunned, but unharmed.

'Ready, men?' someone hollers. 'One, two ... heave!'

'Quick, *le médecin*!'

The wail of a man in agony and then the sight of five others rising from the pond. They are carrying a broken thing in their arms, the water spilling from it the colour of poppies, and only when they lay the shape across the back of a cart do I realise. It is Pa.

'Careful! Gentle, now!'

White bone glints from my father's thigh. Down in the horse-pond, the sound of a pistol firing. Once, twice.

The journey back to the house seems to take an eternity. Lara goes with Guillaume, his arm around her, her folded cap pressed as a makeshift dressing against her head. More than once he tries to hold me, too, but I shake him away. I must be as close to Pa as possible. All about me I sense a confusion of noise, of hustle. But I can hear nothing save my father's cries as the wheels of the cart snag on every stone and furrow, the way his breath bubbles in his throat.

When we finally reach the house, one of the men near the front puts his shoulder to the door. Inside the workshop, there is a tussle to light candles.

'Has *le médecin* been summoned?' someone demands.

'Where shall we put him?' shouts another.

'Here!' Amazed by the strength of my voice, I push to the front and swipe my arm across the long workshop table. Tools clatter to the floor. Several men remove their jackets and spread them out, laying Pa down upon them as gently as if he were a child. His blood eddies into the nicks of the tabletop, those marks made by his own hands for more than a decade.

'That your ma?' a woman asks.

I follow her gaze. There is my mother, frozen at the door to the parlour, pale and spectral. Her expression is more anguished than I have ever seen it.

'Here, *monsieur*! In here!' comes a call from the street.

It is only when he enters that Mama begins to speak. 'Take him upstairs, please, we must take him upstairs,' she burbles. 'This is no place for him.'

'He's in too fragile a state, Madame,' the doctor warns. 'It wouldn't be advisable to move him, not in his present condition.'

Mama falls quiet. One by one, the men file out into the street.

The doctor stays for what seems like hours, Lara and I passing him the dressings between us, the shining dishes and instruments, the tiny brown bottles with their sharp, astringent smells. Guillaume stays, too, bringing water, holding Pa as the doctor does his work.

At length, the man takes Mama to one side. 'I have done my best to set the breaks and close the wounds, though I cannot say what other damage has been done.'

He seems like he might be turning to leave when I call out to him. 'Wait! My sister is hurt, too.' I pull Lara gently towards him. 'She fell and hit her head when the wagon ...'

Embarrassed by the attention, my sister shuffles forwards while Guillaume stares at me, concerned. 'It has stopped bleeding now,' Lara mutters, 'it is fine.'

The doctor studies her head, cleans the dried blood away. 'A slight lump,' he reassures her. 'Nothing to worry about. You may have some headaches or dizziness, but that should all clear before long. A few days, perhaps, a week.' He lifts his bag from the floor and moves to the door, pausing close to Mama. 'If your husband can survive the night, we may rest a little easier,' he says softly.

If he can survive the night, we may rest a little easier. Throughout the long hours that follow, those words twist, a sickening, desperate skein of hope, through my mind.

The Rag-Doll

Sofi

I wake suddenly, my eyes starting open. I am in my bed, I'm amazed to discover, my heart racing, my body clammy beneath my chemise. I blink into the darkness. Lara's breath is warm on my neck and her arms are linked through mine as they always are when we sleep. I relax a little. What happened last night must all have been a dream, a horrible dream. But I've scarce emptied my lungs with relief when realisation rushes me like a fever. Not only am I still fully clothed, I realise, but so is my sister. It was no dream at all.

I scrabble from the bed, my heel knocking against something on the floor. When I reach down I see it is the rag-doll my father had given me a decade before. She must have slipped from her usual place on the nightstand. The doll had once been fine, adorned and clothed like a gentlewoman, but her yellow wool wig is thinning now and dress faded, the stitching coming apart, straw stuffing revealed at the seam of the neck. At this moment in time, I cannot decide whether she is a cruelty or a comfort.

I descend the stairs and enter the workshop, where Pa lies still on the table, a blanket over him. There is a shifting creak behind me and when I spin to face it I observe Mama, slumped in a pool of shadow, her eyes closed.

'Pa?' I whisper.

My father's head twitches, very slightly, and I tuck my hand into his. It is warm.

'Pa!'

'Fi,' he murmurs, his voice rasping and low. He tries to incline himself towards me, but the pain is too much. 'Ah, you have brought *ta petite poupée* to see me, too.'

The rag-doll. I had not realised I was still holding it.

I want to smile, to reassure him that everything is going to be all right. But my face feels like it is being dragged to my knees. 'Are you feeling better?' is all I can manage. A ridiculous, childish question.

Pa's lips slowly lift into a smile. 'Of course I am, *alsghyr*. I just need to rest. I'll be up and about in no time, you shall see.'

I notice a bowl of water and wonder if I should cool Pa's head, swab more of the dried blood from his skin. But the liquid inside the bowl is the colour of diluted wine and I cannot bring myself to touch it.

'What can I do?' I ask, my voice sticking.

'Go and rest,' Pa whispers. 'It will do no good if you are tired. I need you to be strong.'

I nod, kiss him carefully. But I do not leave. The smallest noise makes me turn, and I see that Mama isn't asleep, after all. She is concealing her face with her apron, her shoulders shaking with sobs.

The doctor returns within the hour to examine my father and I can hardly believe the look on his face. 'You are improved,' he remarks and my heart hammers with hope.

My father attempts a laugh and winces. 'Do not sound so surprised.'

'How is the pain? I can give you more laudanum—' Glass tinkles inside the doctor's bag. 'If you can rest now I shall return at first light. Then we may try and lift you upstairs, if you are up to it.'

Pa attempts a nod and the doctor takes Mama to one side. 'There is hope,' he murmurs. 'There is hope.'

Relief surges through me. It is only when I try to move that I feel how tired I am, how all of me aches. I do not make it further than the door to the parlour stairs before I sink to the floor behind a stack of uncut stone and drift into sleep.

*

36

It scarcely feels like any time has passed at all when I become aware of movement, of lowered voices and a single yelp. When I wake, the chair Mama had been sitting in is empty. Daylight is falling aslant through the window and onto the workshop floor, illuminating the pattern of last night's footprints on the flagstones. Rust-coloured forms, layering one over the other like fossils.

A chill hangs in the air and I see the door to the street is ajar. A sudden spike of annoyance. Why has the door been left open, with Pa growing cold upon the table? I close it and resolve to fetch him another blanket, make sure that he is warm.

As I do, I notice my father's hand has fallen over the table's edge. And not only that, but someone has drawn the blanket right up to cover his face. I stride forwards to remove it, before something stops me in my tracks. Instead of lifting the blanket, I reach for Pa's hand, to guide it gently back to his side. It is frozen to the bone. The temperature is so unexpected I stand awhile, slack-jawed, trying to work it out.

'Pa.' My fingers clutch the rough edge of the wool. 'Pa?' Shaking, I tentatively draw the blanket down and the edges of my vision crash away like a landslide. A sound fills the room, raw, like a child in pain. It frightens me. Then I sense my own mouth open, a pressure like a dagger at my throat.

'Sofi, is that you?'

Lara is calling me from upstairs. My pulse is thump-thumping in my ears and I feel faint, like I am going to keel over onto the floor and break like an egg, spill my insides all over the flagstones.

I race through the door and outside. I will not cry, I tell myself. I cannot. What was the last thing Pa said to me, the very last? *I need you to be strong.*

'Sofi?'

I look down and see I am still holding the rag-doll. Adorned and clothed like a gentlewoman, cut from the same cloth as de Comtois. I grip it tight and, with purple knuckles, I squeeze.

The Palace of the Sun King

Versailles

Hortense

'What kind of sorbet did you say it was? Inside the meringue? Some type of berry?'

Mama is putting a barrage of questions to a serving girl who is growing more befuddled by the second. She has been at this line of questioning for several minutes now, while the last course of our supper sits before us, waiting to be eaten. *Vacherin*, assorted *pâtisseries*, boiled quails' eggs and a selection of *marrons glacés*.

'Yes, Marquise, berry, Marquise,' the girl answers.

'I know it is berry, I just said as much, did I not?' Mama squawks. 'But which *kind* of berry is it, pray?'

If the colour the girl turns is any clue, I would hazard a guess at raspberry.

'Orange,' she replies.

Mama harrumphs like an affronted horse and raises her eyebrows. 'Orange? Or-ange—?'

'Yes, Mama, she is quite right,' I cut in, a gauze of gratitude sweeping the girl's face. 'Orangeberry. Haven't you heard of such a fruit?'

I smother a laugh with my serviette as the maid colours again, but Mama merely looks on, confused.

'Good heavens,' Papa comments, once the girl has gone. 'Servants these days.' He attempts to sink his fork into the pristine outer layer of his *vacherin*, but the curving segment of meringue is too hard and too smooth and so flies from his plate.

That Papa should be dining with us at all is an anomaly. His preference is to take himself elsewhere for his repasts, usually to the residences of the other gentlemen of the court, whose company he finds far more agreeable than that of his own wife and daughter. But I am well aware that he is here tonight for a reason. To raise a matter he would much rather not broach. He will finish his meal before he speaks of it, so that once he has done so he may scamper directly away for his armagnac, leaving Mama and me alone for the evening, as we have been since the last of my siblings married and left. Yes, all of them married off and out of Papa's wig now, except for me. And so I'll wager I know exactly what my father has to say to me tonight.

Across the table, Mama pushes a whole peeled egg between her lips as though trying to recreate its laying in reverse. It is a truly revolting thing to behold. In the dishes surrounding us, stacks of eggs sit upon little nests of spun sugar, which I suppose is some-one's attempt at artful presentation. The sugar mounds look as disgusting as the eggs, like shorn and discarded clumps of private hair.

As the horrible, towering aviary in her salon can testify, my mother is obsessed with eggs and their layers. The food on this table is a veritable surfeit of them – the boiled quails' eggs, the egg-whites in the meringue, the egg-laden pastries. I pick at one or two of the *marrons glacés* distractedly. They are the only part of this course I can stomach.

'Does your dear dog not want an egg, *ma petite*?' asks Mama.

Inwardly cringing at the name she still insists on addressing me by, I run a hand across the flossy russet back of the small Pomeranian dog in my lap. I might be Mama's youngest, but I am seventeen now. I have not been a child for years.

'Pépin cannot tolerate them, Mama, as well you know,' I say. 'The smallest bite and his farts are atrocious.'

'Sulphur,' Papa agrees. Another piece of meringue propels itself from his plate, this time landing in one of the spun sugar nests.

'Hortense,' chides Mama. 'Language.'

Pépin gives a whimper and smacks his jaws, so I offer him one of the *pâtisseries* instead.

'The servants were never like that in my day, you know,' Papa tells us, keen to pick up his earlier thread and make conversation about anything other than why he is here. 'If you asked them what one of the dishes was at supper, they could not only tell you but recite the rest of the week's menu while they were at it. And look at them now, complaining of their pay, claiming they need tips to survive, as well as their wage ...'

Mama purrs her assent, too busy with her eggs to offer much of an opinion.

Word reached Versailles about the situation in Paris some time ago. I have overheard the exchanges in the great marbled corridors about the King's financial crisis. Talk that the abnormally hot summers and deep-frozen winters have wreaked havoc on the harvests and caused the peasants to starve. As if that is anything to do with us, *la noblesse*. As if those in power are capable of holding any sway over the weather.

What a lot of people fail to understand is that the working classes are worse than we are. There are servants at Versailles still receiving travel allowances, as tradition dictates, even though the King and Queen no longer tour the country as they did. Yet the tradition must be maintained and, like the Bengalese tiger in the Ménagerie Royale, tradition is expensive to keep.

'It is why this place is falling apart,' Papa adds. 'The view from in here this morning! Good job the daylight is fading by suppertime.'

'Perhaps we should keep the drapes drawn,' Mama adds, as though taking every meal in the dark was a perfectly sensible suggestion. 'Or arrange to dine later.'

'Perhaps we could become fully nocturnal,' I say, but the remark does not register.

The aspect from this window has never been one of the palace's finest. The best views – of the gardens, the canals and the grand fountains – are reserved for those with purer blood. Since my father is a marquis, and neither a prince nor a *duc*, the views from our apartments leave a lot to be desired. From this particular room we are confronted, in daylight, by the ramshackle town that has sprouted up around Versailles over the years like a spurt of fungi, to house the thousands of social-climbers whose desire it is to be received at court. But it grows more deserted by the day. The Palace of the Sun King, as this place was known a hundred years ago, is now on the wane. Versailles' sun is burning itself out.

'The court is going to wrack and ruin, too,' Papa says. 'It wasn't like that in my day. This young crowd the Queen has installed, for one thing. All those confounded parties of hers.'

'I pity Antoinette,' I say. 'The King is hardly a wit. She needs every diversion she can muster.'

Mama croons in agreement as she sucks another quail's egg into her mouth.

My father glares at me. 'The King is losing support from the older generations by the day due to his wife's antics.'

'It is always the woman's fault, Papa,' I offer sarcastically, but he simply continues.

'The old guard doesn't approve of such behaviour. And if the peasants grow more fractious, as some say they might, then the King will find there are few left willing to speak up for him.'

I think of the Queen, Antoinette. Of His Majesty, her plump and inane husband. Though they were scarcely more than children when they married, their union was unconsummated for years. On account, it is rumoured, of His Majesty's impotence. Something that apparently troubles him no longer, Lord help the Queen.

If I was in her position, I would be tempted to make a midnight flit, pack up my trinkets and abscond to Venice. I have always wanted to go, and how agreeable the carnival would be. To wear a mask for extended stretches of time, to have one's face concealed behind a moulded stud of jewels.

At the end of the table, Papa, having consumed the last of his *vacherin*, dabs the corners of his mouth with the tablecloth and clears his throat. Finally, here it comes.

'Now, Hortense,' he begins. 'My man had word from de Courtemanche today...'

As I suspected. Papa is here with the latest news on his attempts to marry me off. His infernal matchmaking, although under way for well over a year now, is still yet to bear fruit.

'... I'm afraid he would not hear of the match.'

'*Another* rejection?' Mama's open mouth is a cave of partially masticated egg. 'Why, that is the fifth! How dare the man, Hortense would make his son a perfectly exquisite bride!'

I exhale my relief into my serviette.

'Which only leaves Dubois' son,' my father continues. 'For every other young man at court is either married, betrothed, or else...' He glances at Mama. 'Or else their fathers will not countenance a marriage to our daughter.' Papa turns back to me. 'Your reputation precedes you, my dear.'

My cheeks sting with frosty indignation.

'Well, I—' Mama counters, before stopping herself. 'Dubois, you say? He's been keen for his son to marry for some considerable time, you know, due to the boy's...'

Her words trail to nothing and I know exactly why. Because this Dubois' son is a well-known simpleton. The Idiot of the Vast Village of Versailles. And even if he weren't, I have no desire to be married to him or anyone else and never will. The very notion of it, of what such a union entails, turns my stomach.

As my father goes to push back his chair to leave, a crescendo of frantic twittering reaches us from Mama's salon. The finches in their enormous cage are chirping madly, screaming as though a bird of prey had been loosed amongst them.

'Hmm,' Mama muses, with little real concern. 'I wonder what has disturbed my birds?'

The stack of naked eggs closest to me catches my eye. The vile things are perspiring in the light from the candelabras, their skins greying and clammy. The food I have eaten begins to stir in my stomach. A stale, acrid swell—

Before either of my parents have the chance to speak again, I scoop up my dog and, pressing the fingers of my free hand to my mouth, hasten from the room.

Lost Time

Marseilles, several days later

Sofi

Time, since it happened, is rubber. Drawn long or else snapping by in an instant. One day might be over in little more than the blink of an eye, while each second of the next seems to last an eternity.

The void in the house is an agony. It yawns, inescapable, more of a smothering than an absence. It is as though a vast beast now dwells here, pressing its massive weight down on me and stopping my breath.

Mama ranges the house restlessly, forever seeking out a new task to occupy herself. I watch the hairpins she has been too distracted to properly secure, tinkling unnoticed from her cap to the floor. I mark the apron, still bearing yesterday's stains, fastened back-to-front around her waist.

Lara, by contrast, moves as though she is struggling through treacle, pausing every few paces to clutch a wall for support, negotiating each stair as though a valley lay between them. I wish she would rest awhile, let her head heal, but like a spirit that won't be laid she fusses me instead, brow netted with concern.

One afternoon, I enter our chamber to find my rag-doll gone, missing from her place on the bedside table. I hurl back the coverlet, tip the pillows and mattress to the floor, crawl beneath the bedstead, but still I cannot find her.

'Sofia!' Mama shouts up to me. 'What in heaven's name are you doing?'

Her question is followed by a tread upon the stairs, before Lara's face appears around the door, eyes wide. 'Sofi!'

Seeming to know instinctively what I am looking for, my sister rummages amongst a small stack of clothes, drawing the doll out.

'Why do you have her, give her back—!' I step forwards to snatch the thing, then stop. The doll is different, the seams mended, the cloth's pattern meticulously patched, her wig filled out with fresh yellow wool.

'I wanted her to be like she was when Pa gave her to you,' Lara says. 'So you can keep her forever.'

I pinch the soft back of one hand with the nails of the other, focusing hard on the sensation so I do not have to feel the stinging at my eyes.

'Sorry, Fi,' Lara murmurs. 'I thought you would like it.' She sits the doll tenderly on the window-ledge and drags the mattress from the floor, arranging the coverlet across it again as though nothing had happened. Then she brushes a stray hair from her cheek, awkward and apologetic, and crosses to the threshold so sadly I can stand it no longer. I rush over and fling my arms around her waist.

I open my mouth to tell her how grateful I am, while at the same time not knowing how to feel at all, not understanding why I am so heavy every hour of every day, so angry. I want desperately to explain to Lara how such anger frightens me. But no sound escapes my lips.

I wonder at Lara's repairs to the rag-doll. How, despite her headaches and dizziness from the accident, she managed to patch in the exact shade of linen needed to restore the small gown. But although my sister lined up the pattern so the join is invisible, it isn't the same doll Pa gave to me, isn't the same cloth his hands touched and held. It will never be the same again.

Pieces

Sofi

De Comtois does send a clerk this time. The day after we bury Pa, no less. I see him from the window, dressed in black and skulking down the lane, hands clutched to his chest as though he was the one who had lost something.

I reach the door just as the man is passing Mama a letter. She unfolds it and appraises him blankly. 'How am I supposed to know the meaning of this?'

'Ah, of course.' The clerk looks uncomfortable. Stupid, too. De Comtois employs men who are cheap, not competent. That way he has money to squander. The more he bleeds from his tenants, the more he has to gamble away, while honest folk work to their deaths, starve in the streets. What were men like him even doing, drinking in that tavern? Amusing themselves by fraternising with the peasants?

'It is your notice, Madame,' the clerk announces.

'My notice?'

'Now that your husband is . . . ' The man breaks off.

A vice grips my chest.

'Dead?' Mama spits. 'Is that what you mean?'

The man opens and closes his mouth noiselessly, looking lost for words. 'Ah, a . . . a tragic accident, Madame.'

Accident. What an insult that word is.

'What I mean is . . . the Baron de Comtois regrettably had no choice but to raise the rent on this property some weeks ago. Your husband, it seems, was not able to meet the sum.'

46

Mama's hand tightens, scrunching the paper within it.

'And now, with you finding yourself widowed . . . well, the Baron de Comtois trusts you will no longer be staying. That your needs would be . . . better accommodated elsewhere.'

Mama comes straight to it. 'How long do we have?'

The man clears his throat. 'A week. The Baron de Comtois trusts that will be sufficient.'

'The Baron de Comtois's very trusting, isn't he?'

The clerk doesn't seem to register Mama's gibe. 'He also asked me to inform you that the stock, materials and so on in the lower room are now his property, to be seized in lieu of the unpaid rent—'

'Those things in the workshop belong to my father, he bought them himself! Your master has no right to any of them, just so he can drink away the proceeds of everything Pa worked for. He has no right at all!' The words spew loudly from my mouth before I can censor them, leaving me shaking, my cheeks ablaze.

The clerk raises an eyebrow. 'Madame, might I suggest you instil some manners into your dau—'

Before he can finish, my mother shuts the door.

'What is it?'

Behind us, Lara makes her way slowly down the stairs, rubbing her temple. She had been lying down. The noise must have roused her.

'Oh, Mama,' she sighs when she reads the clerk's paper. 'What are we going to do?'

A letter addressed to Mama arrives a few days later. I catch her with it at the parlour table, recognising my aunt's handwriting at once. Something sticking out from behind the paper snags my attention. A larger, square cut of fabric-like parchment, decorated with some sort of design.

I call my sister from the kitchen and Mama sombrely passes her the letter.

'Well, what does it say?' I urge, panicking briefly that our aunt is replying to Mama's earlier correspondence, and writing to offer Lara work at the factory.

My sister scans the first page. 'Aunt thanks us for letting her know about Pa. She expresses her sympathies . . . ' Her words fade.

It had been my sister's suggestion to write to Aunt Berthé and inform her of the accident. I don't remember much of what happened in the hours after I came in off the street that morning, but I do recall Lara, feebly inking her pen and composing the message, squinting to make sense of the letters as the pain from her fall rang fresh in her skull.

Lara turns my aunt's letter over and her lips part in surprise. She reads—

'Sister, I have good news. After receiving your last dreadful correspondence, a notion came to me. I have spoken to the master, Monsieur Wilhelm Oberst, and have been fortunate enough to secure a position, not just for Lara, but for you and Sofia, too, all here at the wallpaper factory in Jouy.'

Wilhelm Oberst. The name sounds German. Austrian, maybe. Like our frivolous Queen. 'That is the man Aunt Berthé keeps house for, is it not?' I ask.

'It is,' Mama returns, staring at my sister in anticipation. 'Carry on, Lara.'

'The master was very interested to learn of your experience in the soap factory, sister, and offers you work in the dye-house with great pleasure. Monsieur Oberst is a fair man and a good master—'

Mama snorts. 'As if there is any such thing.'

'There are also,' Lara goes on, *'two positions for your girls here, if agreeable. Since the master thought Lara's draughtsmanship so accomplished, he is willing to offer her work in the print-house, where the wallpaper is designed. There is work for Sofia, too, in the dye-house, assisting with the colours used in the printing processes—'*

'The dye-house?' I interrupt. 'Why is it Lara who gets the better work?'

'Do not start, Sofia,' Mama clips back. 'We're lucky to be offered work at all, with the country as it is.'

Lara continues. 'Finally, Aunt Berthé writes that there is a cottage that comes with the position. The place is only small, but there is room for us all. She says to send word back as soon as possible and, if accepting, to arrange travel to Jouy-en-Jouvant forthwith.'

'I see ...' my mother begins and I'm astonished to observe that the corners of her mouth have started to rise.

'Wait, Mama,' says Lara, 'there is a line added at the end. *I include a sample of the wallpaper that is made here, showing one of the factory's most popular designs.*'

My sister lifts the sample out from behind the letter, the same large square I saw Mama holding earlier. The scene printed upon it shows a young woman in a room, sitting with her face turned away from the viewer. It is oval in shape, vignetted by a darkness that seems to hold the image in place.

I have never seen wallpaper this closely before and it is strange. The material is so thin that when held up for the light to shine through it, both sides of the paper can be seen together, allowing my sister and I different views of the same image. There is a grain to it, too, a warp and a weft, giving its deep red print the impression of dried blood on skin. I release my grip on the paper and push it away.

'We must start to pack immediately,' Mama announces. 'There is much to be done.'

'But, what—' I hardly know where to begin. 'What about Pa's things? What happens to them?'

My head starts to swim. The thought of those objects, the ones Pa used every day, now lying neglected. The wooden parts of the tools worn to the contours of his hands, the leather apron moulded to the form of him. The pieces of stone he had already begun to carve. They are like pieces of Pa himself, the only pieces still left.

'They will have to stay,' Mama replies. 'We cannot take them.'

'But—'

'Enough, Sofia! For goodness' sake. Why do you have to fight against everything? Anyhow, as that clerk so helpfully pointed out, everything in your father's workshop is now the property of the Baron de Comtois.' She adds something more, lost against the racket of my thoughts.

I look at Lara, wait for her to object, too. But she is studying her hands on the tabletop, her face drained of colour. She has not spoken since she held up that sample of wallpaper.

'Girls,' Mama starts, 'do you really think we have any choice? Jobs like these, and lodgings, too, they do not just grow on trees. 'Specially not nowadays. There are people just like us, all over the country, out of work, nowhere to live, no money to put food in their mouths.'

Her words, the uncharacteristic mellowness of her voice. With a clang it comes to me. She is glad to be leaving. No thought for the memories of Pa, for the life he lived with us here. No thought for any of it.

Mama inclines her head to Lara. 'We must send word back.'

Her dictation blurs to a panic in my ears. I do not want to leave. I do not want to leave the place where Pa lived, worked, laughed. I can feel my heart drumming in my mouth, I cannot catch a breath. What if I forget? Memory is slippery, like water through fingers. It spills and swirls, drains before you can catch it. What if I forget him, forget it all?

My sister seals the letter and the room falls silent. It is not only Pa's things we will be leaving behind, it is the hope of ever being able to design together, Lara and I, alongside Pa in his workshop. It is like all we ever wanted has been torn away. And that man has been the one to do it. *De Comtois*. He has destroyed everything.

I glance at Mama. She is staring at Aunt Berthé's words as though they were the map and legend of a new world.

Cobbles and Stripes

Several days later

Lara

I am in a part of the city I have never ventured to before. I am not even sure I remember the way I came. But I must be quick, since Mama does not know that I am here at all. We are leaving tomorrow, and it is the only chance that I will have.

I found the address scribbled on one of the papers in Pa's workshop. I glance at it now, turn down an alleyway so narrow it would be murky on a summer's afternoon, but with the added grime from the cobbles and the waste-streaked walls, it is almost as though day here is already tipping dizzyingly into night.

There are people begging along this cramped alley, stray dogs showing their ribs like stripes. A woman hunched in a doorway grabs my skirts as I pass, her knuckles nothing more than protruding balls of bone. I tell her I have no money and, though it is the truth, I feel wretched. The stench of human waste is overwhelming. I did not expect that he would live in such a place.

I find the building at last. It stretches up four floors at least, and at its base is a door so rotten it might powder at my touch. I knock, tentatively, and have the sense that I am being watched. Tilting my head upwards, I feel my cap press against the still-tender spot at the base of my skull. A gull squawks in the sky. A handful of the birds have gathered on a rooftop, to bicker and stretch their wings.

Suddenly, a missile shoots from a paneless window and straight at the creatures, sending them screeching into flight. The door before me grinds open a crack, catching me unawares.

A child is peeking around it, blinking in the light. She is tiny, perhaps no more than four or five. Perhaps older, but stunted from lack of food.

I greet her and smile. 'I'm looking for Guillaume. Guillaume Errard? Do you know if he is here?'

She stares at me, wide-eyed, her cheeks mucky, little nose streaming. I see that she is gripping an object in both hands, a small wooden pail containing a brownish, gritty tilth.

'Do you know Guillaume?' I ask.

She weighs the words, murmurs, 'He's my brother.'

'Do you know if he is here? It is very important that I speak to him.'

She shakes her small head. 'Only me and baby here today,' she says. 'Guillaume gone to work.'

My heart sinks. 'With his uncle?'

She shakes her head again and sniffs. 'Out of town.'

I glance around as though, at any moment, he might turn the corner and walk down the alleyway towards me. I have brought no letter, since Guillaume wouldn't be able to read it. I have only the address of the factory we're leaving for, inked on a tear of parchment. I hope he might be able to find someone to help him make sense of it.

I recall my last conversation with Guillaume, two days ago, snatched on a side street near the house. His words, the rush of understanding that followed them. I cannot leave without telling him where we are going, without giving him some hope.

'What is your name?' I ask.

'Estelle,' the child replies, her eyes opening to wider puddles of hazel, as though no one had ever posed such a question before.

'What do you have that pail of soil for, Estelle? Is it for planting seeds?'

'No,' she says. 'For mixing in the bread.'

Her answer confounds me. I have heard stories of people padding out their grain with sawdust, but never did I think such poverty had found its way to Guillaume's door. I feel an unbearable urge to scoop the child from the ground and hold her, crouching level with her instead. The action seems to take her by surprise, and for a second I think she will duck back behind the door.

'Well, Estelle,' I continue, 'my name is Lara. I need you to give your brother this.' I tuck the torn parchment beneath her hands, still tightly curled around the pail's handle. 'Give this note to Guillaume. And can you tell Guillaume something for me? Can you do that?'

She nods vigorously and I hear her stomach growl.

'Can you tell him Lara was here? Tell him Sofi and I have to leave tomorrow. That we have no choice. We are going to the address on that paper. And we do not know if we will ever be back.' I try to keep my voice steady. 'Do you understand, Estelle? Could you do that for me?'

'Yes,' she replies earnestly, and looks back at the rickety stairs.

I go to thank her, but she is already heading inside with her pail, taking great pains not to spill a single grain of its contents.

Le Miroir

Versailles

Hortense

Ordinarily I would not contemplate rousing myself at this unconscionable hour but I cannot sleep, my thoughts overflowing with my father's accursed matchmaking. Daybreak is just beginning to seep its way in around the shutters and, taking care not to wake Pépin, I sidle from between the sheets and move to the large standing mirror facing the window.

I appraise the girl who meets my stare in the glass. There is an imprint encircling her wrist where bracelet has pressed into flesh overnight, a debossed ghost of its pattern. The girl adjusts it then straightens the rest of her *parure*, the almond-shaped peridots at her ears echoing the tilt and colour of her eyes, their posts sore now after pressing into the sides of her head for so many hours. I straighten her white-blonde sleeping wig, curled like an animal around the white-blonde hair beneath. I do not recognise this girl, as pure and untainted as a new doll, and would not have it any other way.

I have had this mirror positioned here deliberately, so that whenever I look into it I am afforded a view, not of myself in my gilded cage, but of myself before the wide-open sky. Of the sun's golden diadem by day, the moon's white gown by night. Of a lavish scattering of stars, glistening like diamonds.

I turn around to ease apart the shutters, wanting to see that open sky again. Outside, as dawn dilates the horizon, a carriage approaches. The vehicle must be conveying a group of gentlemen back to the palace from a night of carousing in the capital. Even though it is still some way away, I can hear the noise of the men inside that carriage long before it finally comes to a halt. They are laughing and swearing, breaking into tuneless bursts of shouted song, something about a nubile young woman and her fine display of cantaloupes. About as witty an anthem as I would have expected to hear, given the circumstances.

Once the carriage had come to a stop a footman opens the door, causing one of the men inside to fall out immediately. He lies blinking on the ground, looking around so gormlessly I begin to wonder whether this vehicle has come to the wrong place and was intended for the asylum instead. My doubts are quickly answered when a second man steps from the carriage in such a great haste to take offence on his fallen friend's behalf that he administers the footman a swift thrashing for his trouble. There is no question, these are indeed men of Versailles. Their wigs are askance, their shirts slack and what remains of their make-up lies in streaky blotches across their faces.

As I watch, a curious sensation takes over. The men's uproar recedes, quietens as though it is reaching me through water. Before I can prevent it, my mind casts itself back to another early morning, years ago, when a very different kind of vehicle drew up outside my window. A wagon, stacked with an array of old linens and tools, brushes and wooden pails. And something else I did not recognise at first. Something that almost looked like baguettes, freshly packed into a series of baskets.

Not sticks of bread but rolls of wallpaper. The men were decorators, come to refurbish our apartments on Mama's insistence. Some German-owned company that Papa had used before. And almost everything in the whole place had been prepared for them in advance, swathed in vast sheets of linen to protect it. Even Mama's pride and joy – her *volière* – her great walk-in birdcage.

Now, as the men in the courtyard stagger towards the entrance, I turn away from the window, bile rising up my throat.

Cupid and Psyche

Marseilles

Sofi

I lay the rag-doll carefully in the packing crate, running a thumb across Lara's new stitches, tiny and even as the work of elves. It is like my sister knew when she mended it how we would have to leave everything else of Pa's behind. How it would be the only thing of his that I could take—

A knocking from downstairs makes me jump. There is someone at the door, no doubt that imbecile clerk, returned to cast us onto the street even before our notice is up. I put my face to the chamber window. It is Guillaume, tugging smooth his cuffs and clasping his hands self-consciously before him as he always does. He seems to be short of breath, as though he has been running.

Since Lara is out, settling a bill with the last of the coin, I move to answer the door. But before I make it into the passageway, I hear Mama's voice carrying up from below. She has beaten me to it.

I cannot see her from my vantage point, nor hear any details of what is being said. I can only see Guillaume's uneasy movements, the increasing droop of his shoulders. Several times he pauses to blink up at the chamber window, forcing me to dive down out of sight.

I ease the latch and pull the window open a sliver. The words are still muffled, but the unhappiness is clear in Guillaume's voice, broken only by my mother's stilted replies.

After a few minutes, I watch him turn and plod slowly away down the lane, and wonder what Mama has said to him. Whether she has told him where we were going and when. I doubt it.

No sooner does Guillaume round the corner into the next street than Lara appears from the opposite direction, missing him by seconds. I go downstairs.

'Have there been any messages left for me?' Lara urges as she enters the parlour. 'Or Sofi?'

'Why? Should there be?' Mama asks.

Lara tenses slightly. 'No matter.'

Placing the last of the linen in a crate, Mama tuts. 'If you're referring to that boy, then put him from your mind.' Her tone is false, too quick and tight. 'If he was going to come he would have done so by now. I've told you a thousand times, haven't I? Men are not to be trusted.'

I'm about to speak, to contradict her words and tell Lara exactly what has just happened, when my mother flashes me such a look it stops my mouth. I will tell her later, I decide, when Mama is not listening.

Keen to avoid Lara's eye, my mother flaps a hand for her to take the other end of the crate and help lift it to the door.

The View

Lara

It is the night before we are due to leave for the north and sleep will not come. It is odd, as since Pa's accident I have yearned to close my eyes every minute, not only to try and shut out the awful reminders of it, but also to silence the pain in my head. But tonight, something is different, and I cannot help but stare into the darkness of our chamber for what I know is the last time. An hour passes.

Taking care not to rouse Sofi from her fitful sleep, I gently unravel my limbs from hers and slip from the bed, positioning myself on the window-ledge. The view from here has changed constantly in the time I've known it. By day, the ochre streets that wind to the harbour teem with ever-shifting life. The quayside bustles, the packets come and go, a succession of fishing boats bob on the ocean beyond. By night, the casement frames a spread of pretty, quivering stars, the distant sea answering their glimmer in the moonlight. But the only thing before me tonight is a creeping, swallowing black. A featureless city and an invisible water. The sky starless, save a meagre shred of yellowish moon.

I pray that Guillaume will find somebody to read the address I left for him, maybe even have them write to the factory on his behalf. I should also have left some coin to pay that person to carry out the task. Then again, from where would such spare coin have been conjured? Surely Estelle has passed my message to him by now? I had hoped he might have come to the house already, to speak to Mama, to request her permission—

I think of Sofi, how she has tried to smother her pain in the fortnight since Pa's accident, chasing it below ground like a fox a rabbit, only for it to explode out of cover a different way. Grief dressed as anger. I think of all the things she doesn't know and wonder if there is any more I could do to help her.

My eyes fall from the window to the sample of wallpaper my aunt sent, now lying beside me on the ledge. I mark how much deeper the red appears. Too dark, even in this near non-existent light. It is like I am seeing the print for the first time. And, with the cold of a blade on the back of my neck and a sweeping, sickening recognition, I realise that I am. Something about that scene has changed.

I look back at the featureless midnight vignetted by my window, that slim hook of a moon. I bring the square of wallpaper closer to my face. The young woman is still there in the print, in a room of her own, but whilst I had assumed earlier that she was sitting before a painting, I now see that she is sitting on the ledge of a window, its casement also framing impenetrable night, the thinnest curve of a moon hanging against it. At first I think it must be some trick, the after-image of the view through my own window held in my vision, its echo stamped by my eyes onto the paper I hold. But it is not.

Though the woman is turned away from the viewer, she is as light-haired as I, and wearing clothes that are impossibly familiar. I cannot help but whisper it aloud. *She looks exactly like me.*

PART II

Broken Sticks

Jouy-en-Jouvant

Sofi

At the intersection ahead, a carved object juts from the earth like a gravestone.

'Jouy-en-Jouvant, one *lieue*,' reads Lara. 'We're almost there, Mama,' she adds, and angles her face away.

I shift closer to my sister and her hand finds mine. She has seen it, too, the stone's similarity to one of Pa's own mile-markers, its painful familiarity. I think of my father's workshop lying abandoned, hundreds of miles away now, and my whole body feels as though it is filling with lead.

Almost as soon as the wagon makes its turn at the marker, the temperature plummets, and the lane stretching before us is entirely obliterated by fog.

'It's the river,' the driver says. 'Goes by the factory. Jouy is known for its fogs.'

I recall the sea mists of the south, how they smudged the coastline to white. This fog is different, so thick it seems the clouds have grown tired of the sky and come to rest permanently on the ground. I draw my thin shawl around my shoulders, already shivering.

As the wagon lumbers on, I become aware that we must now have entered Jouy, even though we can see no more of it than fleeting glimpses of the buildings lining the lane. They emerge, they recede, as if through stirred milk. A keystone here, a door there. A front step worn by unknown feet.

The driver slows the wagon and a vast pair of iron gates loom into view. They are huge, elaborate things, forming an entrance finer than I've ever seen in my life. Metal screeches as the gates are pulled apart, but the fog blots out the men that move them. The ornamentation each gate bears is not obscured, however. Sets of initials, highlighted in gold. *W. O.* on one, *J. O.* on the other.

We come out in an expansive open area like a forecourt. The fog is clearer here, and tracks leading off from all sides of the wagon are just about visible. To the left is a flash of grass, not far from it the sweep of a tree-lined lane.

I follow the curve of the lane upwards and glimpse a building at its end. Although I cannot see the structure well, I can tell it is enormous. Even larger than the big houses in Marseilles. Indeed, this is not a house at all, but a gigantic chateau, white and smooth as though iced.

As we pass, I make out high, fine shutters patterning the facade, dormers blinking like jewels from the roof tiles. Twin stone stairways at the centre of the building arch upwards to a balconied area, behind which is a set of double doors, each capped with a lunette window. And curiously for such a symmetrical structure, the building has but a single, dome-capped tower to the right-hand corner, giving the place an unsteady, precarious appearance.

This must be where the Obersts live, I think, in all their ostentatious splendour, and the revulsion this thought kindles in me takes me by surprise.

Away from the forecourt, the wagon starts to slow before a row of small stone cottages. They are grey and squat, about a quarter of the height of our house in Marseilles. Outside the last on the row, a woman is waving frantically.

'Sister! Girls! How you have grown!'

The woman looks exactly like my mother and nothing like her at all. She is soft where Mama is hard, curved in the places where Mama has straight lines and angles. Yet I know her at once.

'Aunt Berthé!' cries Lara, jumping from the wagon.

My aunt squeezes each of us fast, not pausing for breath. 'Lara, so fair now, such a young lady! And Sofia, my, you're as tall as two of me!'

As the driver starts to unload our things, we follow our aunt the few paces down the path and into the cottage, finding ourselves in a shrunken-down version of our old parlour. There is a hearth, several battered chairs and a table. Low beams dissect the entire ceiling, all the way to the tiny yard at the rear. Boxy wooden steps groan to two connected chambers under the eaves, one looking to the front of the cottage, one to the back. And that is the extent of it. I shiver again, the place is freezing.

Mama runs a finger over the thin veneer of dust that coats every surface, and examines the results blankly.

'Been no one here for a month or so,' Aunt Berthé tells her. 'But I'm sure you'll lick the place into shape in no time. I'm only sorry I cannot stay to help you myself, but the young Master Oberst will be finishing in the factory soon, and he'll need his supper.'

'Is that the Monsieur's—' Lara begins.

'The Monsieur's son, yes,' Aunt Berthé replies, not waiting for her to finish. 'A lovely boy.'

'He is working on a Sunday?' I ask.

'He is. Likes to keep busy, all things considered.' My aunt's attention drifts abstractedly to the window. 'Anyhow, why don't you come up to the chateau later for some supper? You saw it on your way in, I presume?'

'That huge palace, you mean?'

Aunt Berthé laughs. 'Not quite, Sofia.' She gazes into the distance again. 'Well then, I shall see you later. Come to the servants' door, round the right-hand side, and we'll take food in my chamber. Oh, and if you want to get the fire going, you'll find wood in the yard at the rear.' Waving us farewell, she heads off along the track.

With Aunt Berthé gone, Mama begins shuttling between the cottage and the heap of our belongings at the bottom of the path. 'We ought to make a start. Lara, help me with these and we may clean. Sofia, go and check what needs doing upstairs. And take that with you—'

I haul the crate Mama was referring to up the wooden steps, slamming my elbows against the narrow doorway as I struggle into the chamber. When I remove the lid, my throat clenches. The rag-doll is the first thing I see, lying atop the linens. I lift her out, noticing at once how stale the room is, like it wants for air, and cross the few steps to the window to let some in.

The old latch rasps free easily enough, but when I try to swing the glass out it sticks, and I have to give the frame a shove. As I do, the rag-doll slips from my hand. She tumbles down the tiles and clean off the edge of the roof, landing with a thump on the ground.

'No!' I cry, and rush downstairs. I fling open the cottage door, then freeze.

A boy is standing on the threshold, holding out my doll. Offering her to me as tenderly as if she were real. He is around my height, though maybe a little older, and has startling, glass-blue eyes and full, wide lips that take up exactly the right amount of space on his face, with the slightest cleft to his chin below. The sheen to his hair suggests it might have started the day powdered slick, but has since sprung back to form an unruly mop across his crown, a colour more honey than blond.

It is his expression, however, that makes his countenance so striking, coloured by a haunted sadness I recognise instantly. It is like being able to pluck a fallen apple from the ground and gaze right through its skin and its flesh, all the way to the dark pips inside.

I suddenly become aware of every second that has passed since I opened the door, each seeming to have taken my tongue along with it. I try to arrange the sides of my face in something resembling a smile, but feel them stiffen instead.

A queer look crosses the boy's face, as if he is amused by me, but shy of seeming so.

'Hello,' he says. 'Is this yours?'

The doll in his hands at once seems childish, pathetic. 'Oh, well . . .' I hesitate, 'that? I suppose it must be.'

The boy smiles bashfully and the blood in my neck jumps like a cricket. He passes me the doll and I snatch her quickly away, stuffing her beneath my apron.

'Oh, sorry, I—' I take a breath. 'Thank you.'

'I saw her fall,' the boy says.

There is an odd sort of a pause and I wonder what brought him to the cottage in the first place, think I should really introduce myself.

'I'm Sofi!' The words blurt too loud, like a sneeze. 'Sofi Thibault.'

'Pleased to meet you, Sofi Thibault,' the boy replies. 'I'm Josef.'

He gives a slight bow and I wonder whether he is expecting me to curtsy, but I know if I did I would only lose my balance and end up looking stupider than I already do.

'You are new here,' he says.

'We arrived this afternoon.'

'We?' he asks, as though I should have come by myself.

'My mother, my sister and I. From Marseilles.'

Josef's light eyes scan my skin, coming to rest on the lumpy roll of hair erupting from my cap like hog weave stuffing from torn up-holstery. I press it out of sight.

'I'm to begin tomorrow, in the dye-house,' I say, taking in his clothes. They are working clothes in style and wear, but with a cut and quality that sets them apart. 'Do you work here too?'

'I do.'

'In the dye-house too?'

'In the print-house,' he says and I try not to let my disappoint-ment show. 'In fact, if your sister is Lara, then I am to show her how everything works in the morning.'

I make another attempt at a smile. 'I will let Lara know.'

'Let me know what?'

From the very moment my sister begins to speak, the boy's face changes. His eyes fix upon her, his lips part.

'Oh, hello,' Lara says, as she reaches the door.

Josef does not answer. It seems he has been struck dumb. An unseen thumb presses a thorn into my chest.

67

'Lara, this is Josef. He's very keen to show you around tomorrow.' I am unable to keep the hardness from my voice.

My sister brushes down her apron, tucks a lock of loose blonde hair behind her ear distractedly. 'Oh, thank you. That is kind.'

Mama's voice comes then, calling from the yard at the back.

'Sorry ... Josef,' says my sister, 'we must go. Thank you for coming. I will see you tomorrow.'

'Yes ... ' he murmurs, dazed. 'Yes, see you then.'

He runs a hand over his hair and backs away. He does not look at me again.

Myths and Legends

Sofi

By the time Mama, Lara and I leave for the chateau, huddled in an extra shawl apiece, darkness has fallen. Hazed by fog it hangs, thick as a woollen pall, cold as glass.

We follow the track from the cottage and attempt to retrace the way the wagon brought us, but the fog is so thick we can see little more than a few paces ahead at a time. Finally, the bottom of the chateau's approach hones into view, and we follow its sweep upwards, twin rows of poplars materialising either side of us as we go, like sentries scrutinising our passing.

The further we proceed up the approach, the thinner the fog becomes, causing the chateau to rear ahead so suddenly it takes my breath away. The building before us is a vast, blanched expanse, stone faces peering enquiringly from the carved pediments that cap each immense window, single tower soaring into black sky. It is so much larger than it had seemed from the wagon, so large I might be looking on Versailles itself.

'My, what a beautiful place,' Lara gasps, and I am surprised she is so blinkered to the monstrousness of such excess, when there are people perishing in the gutters.

'This way,' says Mama, and we follow the gravel sweep as it narrows to a much smaller, plainer door where Aunt Berthé is waiting.

Our aunt greets us as warmly as she had earlier but, as we cross the threshold and advance inside, the atmosphere changes. It seems heavier, somehow, oppressive and restless, like something had been halted long before its time. It is quiet, too, though I know from my aunt's letters that the Obersts employ a good number of servants. Yet the building is still as an ice-house.

It's also as cold as one, just as biting as it was outside, the set of stone steps before us plunging to the lower floor like the entrance to an underworld. The walls close in down here, the staircases and passageways leading off from the main corridor tight, stark burrows veering this way and that. Aside from a servants' hall, the lower floor is taken up entirely by working rooms. I wonder how the great extravagance of the rest of the chateau compares to it.

Despite its subterranean location, my aunt's chamber is larger than the entire footprint of our cottage. There is a bed against one wall, a small table set for supper beneath the high window opposite. Wine, baguettes, cheese and a little charcuterie have all been laid out ready, and the howl of Lara's stomach mimics my own at the sight of it. It is probably as much as we have eaten for the last week.

'Help yourselves, girls,' Aunt Berthé says. 'Go on, now.'

I seize a hunk of baguette and tear at it with my teeth.

'It is kind of the Obersts to share their bread with you, Aunt,' Lara says between mouthfuls.

'Ah, this isn't the Obersts' bread,' my aunt replies. 'They have different. Whiter stuff. Fluffier, too. I tried some once, it was like biting into a cloud.'

I swallow hard. What had my sister told me? That she'd heard of a child somewhere having to bulk out her bread-mix with soil. The decent flour is always kept for those with the money to buy it, the rest of the country forced to scavenge for what is left after the droughts and the hailstorms. Those mouldering, shrivelled little grains not even fit for the birds.

'So, I hear you young ladies have met Master Oberst, then?' Aunt Berthé asks. 'Wasn't that nice of him to come and introduce himself?'

'The master?' says Lara. 'No, we haven't met Monsieur Oberst yet.'

'No, the *young* master, I mean. Master Josef.'

My hands drop to the table, making the cutlery clang. 'Josef? You mean that boy at the cottage was the son of the Monsieur? You mean, *he* lives *here*?'

'Indeed he does. When I told him I had relations arriving today, he was dead set on stopping by the cottage to say hello. I've tried my best to be like family to him over the years, whenever I could ...' She pauses. 'Poor love. Master Josef has not had such an easy time of it.'

'Not had an easy time of it!' I snort, thinking of the vast building above us, the Obersts' fancy bread. 'He's had an easier time than most, no doubt.'

'The Obersts are not the nobility, Sofi,' my aunt says. 'Monsieur Wilhelm is a businessman.'

'Yet they live in such luxury. They eat the good bread, Aunt, you said so yourself!'

'Well, yes, but—'

'Nobody can choose their birth, Sofi,' Lara says softly. 'It's what they do with their privilege that matters, how they behave. It isn't right to paint everyone with the same brush.'

'Not unless they're—'

'Girls, girls,' Aunt Berthé interjects. 'Come now, let us enjoy our supper. It is such a time since we last saw each other. Let us speak of something else.'

When nobody is forthcoming with a topic of conversation, my aunt continues. 'Let me tell you something about the factory, how about that?'

'How long have you—' Lara starts.

'Your aunt has been here twenty years or so now,' Mama cuts in. 'Isn't that right, sister?'

Aunt Berthé nods. 'Came to serve Monsieur Wilhelm just after he married Madame Justine. Same year as the King and Queen married, in fact.'

'Is she Austrian too?' I say.

'Oh, the Monsieur isn't Austrian,' my aunt replies. 'He is from Germany. The Madame from England.'

71

'From England?' Lara asks, as though the country was exotic. 'How did they meet?'

'Now, that is a remarkable story,' my aunt begins. 'Monsieur Wilhelm was attending a soirée one night at the Maison des Peupliers – the chateau of his friend Monsieur Guyot. It was midsummer's evening, in fact, and he found himself alone in the gardens. Then . . . there she was before him!'

'A guest too?' my sister asks.

'Dear me, no. Madame Justine was the Guyots' governess. She'd sneaked down to the library to fetch some books for the children, going through the garden in the hopes she wouldn't be seen by the guests. Well, it was love at first sight for the Monsieur – he used to say the Madame looked just like a goddess that night. And I'm sorry to say that Monsieur Wilhelm isn't blessed with what you'd call a handsome countenance, never has been.' My aunt takes a hasty sip of wine, as if to wet her throat for the rest of it. 'So, as soon as he found this land – this was before he built this house and the factory – he brought her here to see it. Meant to ask for her hand in marriage, but got down on both knees by mistake and dirtied his stockings. But Madame Justine just laughed and knelt along with him. When they were married, the Monsieur had this very house built as a wedding present for her, an exact copy of the chateau where they met, right down to the tower. Indeed, the tower room of Monsieur Guyot's chateau was Madame Justine's chamber, when she was his family's governess.'

Aunt Berthé finally stops for breath as Lara looks on dreamily.

'That is why the wallpaper here's so special,' my aunt continues. 'The idea was that it should be a marriage also, of the papers the Madame used to teach the Guyot children – the book pages and writing parchments and so on – and the Monsieur's calicoes. He sold only fabrics back then, you see. Started manufacturing wallpaper as a tribute to Madame Justine. Even included her monogram on the entrance gates. Theirs was a rare love indeed.'

'How romantic,' whispers Lara, her fair lashes blinking fast in the candlelight. She is thinking of Guillaume, I am sure of it, and I feel a pull of guilt that I forgot to tell her about him coming to the house, the day before we left Marseilles.

'It is,' Aunt Berthé agrees, her expression changing. 'Mind you, there's no doubt Monsieur Wilhelm has his eccentricities.'

'What do you mean?' I ask.

'Oh well, I simply mean ... that he loves a bit of wordplay, for one.' She gives a low chuckle. 'Whenever he'd find himself speaking to an Englishman, for example, he would tell them, *I am in the business of dyeing*. He meant the wallpaper, of course, but ... well, they would take him to be an undertaker!' She laughs properly at this and fans her face with her serviette. 'Oh yes, he loves a good pun, does the Monsieur. Or he used to. Of course, he hasn't been quite right since his wife ...' The sentence is left there. 'But Monsieur Wilhelm's a good master.'

'And a good businessman, too, no doubt,' returns Mama. 'Must be, to have somewhere grand as this.'

'Do the Obersts have any more children, Aunt?' asks Lara.

'No,' she replies. 'Just Master Josef.'

'And what is your mistress like?' my sister goes on. 'Madame Justine?'

Aunt Berthé casts her eyes to her lap, and hesitates awhile before answering. 'Wonderful,' she says. 'Kind, full of life. Full of laughter and fun. Always coming up with games for young Josef, inventing new ways for him to learn his lessons. Whether that was teaching him English folk songs or arranging what she called one of her "winter picnics" under the dining table. Why, it wasn't unknown for her to join her son in sliding right down the baluster of the stairs, neither! There was never a dull moment with the Madame.'

'*Was?*' I ask.

'I'm sorry to say that she died, very suddenly, some years ago. I don't believe we'll ever really know what happened to her. The Monsieur hasn't been the same since. Master Josef was eleven at the time, I believe. Poor mite, it's a big loss, the loss of a parent—' She halts her speech and grimaces apologetically, as though trying to draw back her words.

73

'That's so sad,' murmurs Lara, and I attempt to swallow the lump in my throat, becoming aware again, in this moment, of how ominously silent the chateau is, like the entire building is holding its breath.

A gust of wind rises outside, enveloping it like the call of a restless soul.

Bells

Sofi

Our first night in the cottage is a miserable one. The chamber is freezing, and my sister and I sleep pressed even closer together than usual, the thin straw mattress beneath us not only lumpy, but damp to the touch.

The room is much darker than our chamber in Marseilles, and as I lie shivering against Lara, the blackness seems to draw every gloomy apprehension to the surface. I am dreading starting in the dye-house tomorrow, I realise. I know it will be harder work than any I have done before, and I worry about what the other workers will think of us, two lettered stonemason's daughters with accents of the south.

I tell myself not to dwell on it, to settle down to sleep before we must rise. But whenever I close my eyes I see the same scenes I always do, flashing before me in appalling succession. The wagon thundering, the ponies thrashing behind that choking curtain of dust, my father's broken body being hoisted from the pond, the water sluicing off it in startling red sheets. And I don't know why, but every time I try to drive my mind to something else, all it seems able to find is what my aunt said at supper. That Josef Oberst's mother had died, too, when he was just a child. I cannot seem to shake it from my head.

At some point, I must fall into a doze, as I wake with a jolt to the clanging of a bell. The darkness in the room is still thick as tar. It is well before daybreak.

'I think it's signalling for the workers to rise,' my sister murmurs. 'We must get up and wash.'

Lara pokes a foot from the bed to test the air, shivers and quickly draws it in again. Then, summoning all her courage, she seizes a jacket, pulls it about her and heads down the stairs.

She returns with a water jug, pouring its contents into the wash-bowl on the window-ledge. Chunks of ice bob to the surface as the water settles.

I drag myself from the bed, taking the coverlet with me. 'You first,' I say, eyeing the water suspiciously.

My sister bites her lip, lifts her wash-cloth and lowers it into the bowl. 'Oh!' she exclaims, wringing it out with a genuine look of surprise. 'It is lovely and warm!'

I edge closer. 'Warm? How can it be?'

'Come try.'

'I don't believe you.'

'It is!'

I frown and take another step towards her.

'See for yourself.'

Tentatively, I extend my fingers out from the coverlet, and that is when the cloth whips towards me, landing with a splat on the back of my hand.

I squeal, shaking it away. As I suspected, the water is cold as hoar frost. 'Liar!' I laugh, and the action feels peculiar.

Lara laughs too. 'I'm sorry, that was mean. Your face was a picture, though.' She finishes washing and turns towards me. 'I'm glad we're here together, Fi,' she says. 'I'm glad I didn't have to come alone.'

'Me too.'

'Don't worry about today. It'll be all right. Here—'

My sister holds out the cloth and I push my face towards her, closing my eyes as she rubs the linen across my cheeks. It is warm now from her own skin, dulling the bite of the icy water.

After we have dressed and pinned our hair, we join Mama downstairs to share the leftover bread from supper that Aunt Berthé gave us. It isn't long before the bell we heard earlier sounds once more.

'Come,' says Mama. 'We must leave for work.'

She opens the cottage door and I half-expect Josef Oberst to be there again, but the path is clear. The thought of him on the doorstep holding my doll takes my mind straight back to supper the previous night. To the building's strange stillness, to my aunt's sad tale. To a motherless boy.

As we start to head along the track to the factory, I glance over to the chateau on the hill. The lone tower rises straight as a pike in the low dawn, its single window a bald, staring eye. I just cannot work out whether that eye is looking out at me, or looking in, transfixed by whatever is inside.

The Meadow

Lara

I see the tocsin as we cross the forecourt, high in a structure standing proud of a nearby roof. It hangs between two vertical wooden posts, metal glinting in the early light as it swings out its sound, suspended so precariously it could, it seems, drop at any second.

Continuing in the direction of the factory, we pass an old stone bridge that spans the river, and the wide, meadow-like expanse of grass adjacent to the forecourt. The fog has cleared today and already the area hums with activity. Workers push barrows along trackways, some bearing mallets and buckets of spiked pegs, others bulky scrolls of coloured paper, one between two. The workers unroll this paper, shaking it free with a smack of air, their mallets thwacking the pegs to moor it to the grass. The nearer to the working buildings we go, the more grass disappears beneath paper, green giving way to a myriad of other colours.

That is when I notice him, there between the unfurling, spreading sheets. Quite invisible not a moment before, Josef is revealed, for a split-second at a time, between the billowing lengths of wallpaper like a conjuring trick.

He calls out to me, waving, 'Lara!'

As I draw close I glance at the flat slices of colour that surround us, pinned taut to the earth, the needling wind passing under and over them, making them twitch.

'They are laid out like that so the colours may bleach,' Josef says, without looking down. 'Being soaked in the dye-baths is quite intense a process. They need the open air to lighten again.'

They put me in mind of a giant display of butterfly specimens, bright wings spread, pierced and secured so they cannot fly away. My head, by contrast, suddenly feels so light it might float into the clouds, like a tatter of paper caught on the breeze.

At that moment the wind catches the back of my cap, causing several of my hairpins to tumble to the ground.

'Come,' Josef says, bending to retrieve them. 'I'll show you what to do.'

The Activities of the Factory

Sofi

Master Josef is dressed in his working clothes again this morning, finer cloth though they are cut from. His hair is slicked down and he is smiling, faint dimples showing in his cheeks. How easy it must be to smile so, when you live in a grand chateau, stacks of logs burning in its hearths, cellars stocked plentifully with food. Yet I cannot deny my spirits lift a little at the sight of him, despite the thought.

'Madame Colbert will be showing you what to do this morning, Madame Thibault,' Josef tells Mama, gesturing to a woman a little way behind him. She is slight and sunken-featured, with a stooped posture and an expression neither hostile nor friendly. Vivid specks of viridian speckle the woman's hands, the marks of her work with the pigments. I feel a stitch of shame. She must be at least sixty. I had worried that *I* might find the work too hard, yet she is employed here still, labouring every day in the dye-house.

The elderly woman nods and my mother gives us a tight smile before heading off with her.

'Now I should like to show you around, if I may,' Josef says. At first I think he is speaking only to Lara, but he adds, 'Both of you, that is. So you might familiarise yourselves with the place and understand a little more about the wallpaper-making process.'

We proceed towards the collection of structures that comprise the factory, passing cart houses, tool houses and stores for wood, cloths and other materials, before the track forks abruptly at a broad stone building. Its doors are open, and pungent, chemical fumes billow towards us. Inside, a woman is stoking a fire between two colossal copper vats, kerchief held to her nose. When she moves away from the vats and lowers it, I realise that though she cannot be more than two decades older than I, the hair revealing itself from the bottom of her cap is a pure, chalky white. Her forearms are fretted all over with pink and brown scars.

'This is the wash-house,' Josef says. 'Where we boil the raw calicoes we use to make the paper. Those vats hold the lye. If you ever have need to go in there, don't go near them. That stuff is dangerous, corrosive, if it gets on your skin.'

The woman inside notices us, and tugs down her sleeves in an attempt to hide her arms. Another worker permanently marked by her living, by products sold to people who never stop to consider the real cost of them at all.

We stop outside a much larger building next. Josef tells us it is the *papeterie*, where the paper itself is made from a mix of wood pulp, rags and fibres of calico. The doors to this building are open, too, exposing a bustle of activity. Workers turn handles on cumbersome, oversized machines or tend to steaming tanks, whilst others slop a pulpy greyish soup into vessels of varying dimensions. The musty, plant-like smell of sodden paper wafts through the doors.

From the *papeterie*, we go to the dye-house, which is every bit as large, but filled with low tables long as tracks, splashed and spotted with every conceivable colour. Rows of huge, tub-shaped dyeing vats crowd the rest of the space, the dripping lengths of paper being pulled from their tops hanging tight as wet hides.

'You will be working here, Sofi,' Josef says. 'Helping with the pigments, dye-stuffs and priming. We prepare the new sheets of paper by painting them white. Some of the colours we use for the printing start as powdered pigments, which are then mixed with water or oils. Others come from plants. Madder roots for the reds, indigo leaves for the blues. A number of these have to be made by adding in other substances too. Lime and various chemicals. And fixed with mordants, or the pattern can change.'

'Change?' I ask.

'Can lighten or bleed. Shift across the surface of the paper and alter its appearance.'

I look around. Full buckets of water, powders and salts are being hauled left and right, the huge dyeing vats holding scalding, rainbow-coloured liquids which workers are churning with chunky paddles. I see Mama near one of these vats, Madame Colbert guiding her arm to show her how much to discharge from the pail she is holding. Bound, netted bundles of plantstuffs surround them, ready to steep.

'Come,' says Josef, ushering us away. 'Let me show you the printhouse now.'

Standing at the very centre of the factory, the print-house is the largest structure of them all. It has so many windows it might be made from glass alone, and the entire lower floor is taken up by tables long enough to accommodate thirty people at a time. Above these tables, squarish blocks of wood hang suspended on chains, lengths of paper laid out below.

'So this,' Josef explains, turning to my sister, 'is where you shall be working.'

At the end of each table sits a wooden pot, bright spills of liquid dribbling down its sides. A man pours one of these colours onto a flat sponge inside a shallow tray, as another draws a wooden block down on its chain. He tamps the block onto this sponge, which oozes thick blue ink, then guides it across to a length of paper, pressing the inked underside onto its surface. The process is repeated, until I see many splodges of blue begin to multiply on the previously blank sheet.

'However do they manage to line the pattern up?' asks Lara, baffled.

'There's a metal pin in each corner of the block,' Josef says. 'Once those four points are matched, the print is aligned and it is almost impossible for it to go awry.'

He leads us up a wide staircase to a room bearing a similar arrangement as the floor below, the long workbenches here positioned tight against the outer walls, making the most of the light streaming through the vast windows.

'This is where the draughtsmen and women work,' says Josef. 'There is one in charge of every bench. They draw the designs out on parchment. Then the carvers cut the designs into the wooden blocks which, as you saw downstairs, are coated with colour to be printed onto the paper.'

At each bench, a small army works. Laid out before them are stacks of parchment and graphite, an array of wooden-handled tools of all shapes and sizes. The smell here, the sight of those parchments and tools, the noises of the carving, mallet against handle, it is all so sorely familiar yet unexpected that I have to pause, floored by it. Even the leather aprons the workers wear are the same as Pa's. My sister slips her hand into mine.

'This will be your job, for the time being,' Josef tells her. 'Fetching the blocks, papers and so on. Ensuring the tools are sharpened. I shall show you where the whetstone is presently.' He moves to face her. 'I'm sure you'll work your way up and out of these menial tasks in no time. I saw the designs your mother sent. They were very impressive.'

As my sister smiles demurely I experience a stab of envy. I wish I was Lara. I wish I could work here instead, take up those tools and close my eyes, imagine myself once more in Marseilles and everything back to the way it was. I wish we could work together, my sister and I, as we always said we would.

My eyes begin to sting and I spin away from the carving tables, incapable of looking at them any longer. I will not cry, I vow. Not here, not anywhere. I take a deep breath and mark that to the other side of the staircase is a galleried walkway I had not seen at first. A line of what looks like separate rooms borders it, rows of doors with a small window between each. The first door and window are a little more impressive than the rest, and spaced a little further apart. It must be the largest room in the row.

When Josef catches me peering at the door, his face shadows curiously. 'My father's office,' he says, lowering his voice. 'He hardly ever comes down here any more, but he just so happens to be in today, approving some new designs. He has the final say on all of them, you see, and . . . well, whether at home or here in the factory, he doesn't take kindly to being disturbed.'

With that, Josef hastens away from the gallery, signalling for us to return to the lower floor. 'I'll accompany you back to the dye-house,' he tells me. 'Find someone to show you what to do. Then I can return to help you here, Lara.'

My sister thanks him and together they start towards the stairs ahead of me, and I don't know what prompts me to do it, but I have the uncontrollable urge to turn around and look back at the first of those office windows.

A man is standing in it now, his bulky frame taking up almost the whole of the glass. I see large eyes, a long, steeply sloping nose whitened by powder, a pale grey wig resting a little too far back on his head. His lower features I can scarcely make out at all, as the rippling plane of glass he is standing behind distorts them strangely, mouth and chin mashing together in a darkened expanse of flesh.

This must be the Monsieur, I think, Josef's father. His body is perfectly rigid and unmoving, eyes fixed so intensely on something to my right that he does not even blink. I follow them to the top of the stairs. Not something, but someone. He is staring at my sister.

Déjeuner sur l'Herbe

Lara

All morning long I carry the dulled carving tools to the whetstone and the honed ones back again, bring the parchments and the wooden blocks to the design tables, sharpen the sticks of graphite and sweep the wood shavings from the floor. I cannot say they are the most interesting tasks and the morning crawls by, especially the hours after Josef returns to his work on the lower floor where he oversees the printing. He spent far longer at my side than I expected, patiently showing me what to do. It was only when he'd gone that I felt my cap gaping at the back, and realised he had forgotten to pass me my hairpins after he picked them up.

At midday the bell starts to ring once more, this time to signal the break for dinner. I look around. Everyone in the print-house is downing their things and disappearing outside. I follow uncertainly, not sure what else to do.

Despite the chill in the air, the workers perch on walls or steps, flop on the grass or draw drinking water from the well. I watch them for a few moments, deciding to cross to the dye-house to find Sofi or Mama, when I hear footsteps behind me.

'Come on,' a voice says and I turn to see Josef. 'It's time to eat.'

I haven't brought anything for dinner, not remembering whether Mama had even told us what we should do about eating. She probably had a little of the bread saved from breakfast. 'Oh, it is all right,' I reply, 'I am not hungry.' But my stomach betrays me, making a noise like a rasping timber.

Josef does not smile exactly, but his eyes brighten a little. 'I've enough for us both,' he says, lifting a bundle of brown cloth into the air, some kind of knapsack tied up with twine. 'And I know a good place to eat. If you'd like to join me, that is?' He glances tentatively towards the upper floor of the print-house, at the neat row of windows, smaller than the others. The offices.

'Thank you.' I think how kind he is to offer me some of his food, then waver guiltily. 'That is generous. But I should go and find Mama. And my sister.'

'Oh . . . yes.' Josef colours a little. 'I'm sorry, I did not think. There is enough food for them, too, of course. Perhaps I could help you find them?'

The dye-house is all but empty when we get there, so we search for Sofi and Mama in the gathering crowd outside. It seems that each and every worker in that crowd examines me intently as I pass, before clustering back together, their voices hushed. I wonder what they're saying, why they are so interested in me. It must be because I am with the son of their employer, I suppose, but then I recall them staring at me all morning, too.

Josef draws out a small brass pocket-watch from his jacket, studies the time and winces. 'I'm sorry, Lara, but we should eat now if we're to finish dinner before the bell sounds again.'

'Oh . . .' I scan the shifting knots of workers, but Mama and Sofi are nowhere to be seen. 'Yes, of course.'

Josef tilts his head towards the trackway. 'Shall we?'

I hesitate a second time. Sofi and Mama might appear at any moment, I do not want to miss them. I hope Sofi is getting on well in the dye-house and I should like to find out. 'Could we not eat here?'

'We could, but I prefer to take dinner somewhere quieter,' he replies. 'If I don't, I'm likely to be bombarded by all sorts of questions. Factory matters. Not that I mind, but I'm afraid the workers sometimes forget it is my father who is in control here and not me. What I might want doesn't really matter.'

'Oh,' I say again, as the hurt in his words registers. 'I see. Well, no

86

doubt you need a break also.' I touch my hand to the once sore place at the back of my head, and feel the flapping hem of my cap.

'Ah, I almost forgot,' Josef says, reaching into his pocket. 'You dropped this earlier.'

He passes me a hairpin and I thank him. 'I did think perhaps I had dropped more.'

'Sorry,' he smiles, heading off along the track, 'that's all I saw amongst the grass.'

The Picnic

Lara

At first I presume we will go as far as the meadow, where one or two workers are already sitting, but Josef continues around it. To my right I can hear the gush of fast-moving water, the flow of the river that supplies the factory. A little way further and the noise lessens, a dark stand of trees pitching into view ahead. They appear to delineate some sort of boundary.

Josef makes straight for them, whilst I hang back. He turns his head, notes my faltering.

'I won't get into trouble . . . coming so far from the print-house?'

His lips form a shy sort of smile. 'Of course not.'

I follow him all the way through the trees, their shed leaves skidding over the tops of my feet. A second or two later and we come out onto a large, well-tended lawn. For a moment I am disoriented, having no idea where we are. Then I see the pale rear walls of the chateau in the distance. I assume we must be somewhere near the back of the gardens.

Josef heads for the shelter of an enormous old sycamore, its branches swaying unwieldy against the grey-blue sky. The tree has a very distinctive shape, the ridges of its ancient, twisted trunk are raised as forearms, its burls bunched as fists. Crouching on the grass, Josef places his brown-cloth parcel beside him.

'Here.'

He undoes the twine that binds the cloth together and reaches inside, withdrawing a baguette, some hard sliced cheese, a cold *saucisson*, a twist of dried fruit. It is more than all four of us would have eaten for a meal back in Marseilles, and I cannot pretend I am not pleased to see it. 'Do you always bring so much?' I ask.

'No,' he says quietly, 'not always. It is a shame we could not find your mother or Sofi to share it. Please, help yourself.'

My mouth waters at the lovely, floury top to the bread, at the full, ripe scent of the cheese. I try to stay my hunger and eat at a respectable pace, but it isn't easy. The bread and cheese make my mouth tingle, salty and delicious against the tang of the dried fruit. Pangs of guilt replace those of hunger, as I picture Mama and Sofi, somewhere in that crowd outside the dye-house, finishing the remainder of last night's bread.

The food almost finished and my stomach fuller than it has been in a good many months, I thank Josef, supposing it is time to return to the factory. But he moves back towards the bundle of cloth, opening it fully this time, and smoothing it over the grass to reveal a wrap of paper. Inside are a handful of the most perfect strawberry jam tarts I have ever seen, the red of the preserve deep as jewels, their shells glazed and golden.

'Could you manage a dessert?' Josef asks.

My eyes widen and I think I must make some exclamation of delight, as he immediately offers them out to me.

'I asked Cook to bake them yesterday,' he says. 'They're my favourites. And, judging by your face, I imagine you might be fond of them, too.'

I marvel at the exquisite circle of pastry in my hand. 'Oh, thank you! I can't remember the last time I had one!'

We eat the tarts in a companionable silence, the wind stirring the limbs of the tree above us, a clutter of starlings chirruping in the distance. After a while, my gaze wanders to the paper the tarts were wrapped in, and I see it is an off-cut of wallpaper from the factory. Small pastoral scenes are printed across it, an array of people engaged in outdoor country pursuits.

The scene on the flat part of this paper parcel shows a woman. She is sitting on a patch of tussocky grass, a tree's thick trunk rising sinuous at her back, its dark and dipping branches curving to vignette her figure. And were it not for a smudge of scarlet jam obscuring a portion of the scene, I could almost imagine that woman was sitting next to an assortment of food. A picnic. It is uncanny.

I'm suddenly reminded of our last night in Marseilles, of the woman printed on that off-cut of wallpaper. The eerie similarity of the room in which she sat to my own, her eerie similarity to me. My head begins to spin, my vision speckle. Without warning, the picnic cloth recedes, sinking into the earth. It is as if a terrible chasm is opening between us, a chasm the shape of a grave. I stare down at it in horror.

'Lara?' asks Josef anxiously, touching his hand to my forearm. 'Are you quite well?'

I force a breath and rub my eyes. I am being silly. The cloth spread beside us is not a grave at all, I see that now. It is just a man's jacket. Josef's jacket.

The bell begins to ring in the forecourt and I thank Josef once more for the food, watch as he shakes his jacket free of crumbs and rolls it up. But, as I trail him to the factory, I find myself growing dizzy, and have to fix my attention hard upon him in order to make it back along the path.

Little Venice

Versailles

Hortense

I dally with the last morsels of the picnic. Sautéed salmon with watercress purée, mackerel pâté and oysters. This morning's catch, freshly prepared. Pépin settles in my lap, his little stomach full of fish pâté, and I turn my ear to the gentle lapping of the Grand Canal, the plash of the gondoliers' oars. Somewhere in the distance a man is singing, in a bass light yet rich as tobacco smoke, curling towards me on the wind.

'*Non più andrai, farfallone amoroso—*'

I recognise the piece instantly. An aria from *The Marriage of Figaro*, and the only Italian currently being spoken, here on the expansive shores of the Grand Canal. Otherwise I could almost believe I really was in Venice—

'*MA PETITE? MA PETITE!*'

A grating and familiar tone brings me back to reality with an unpleasant jolt. I open my eyes to see Pépin staring in my mother's direction, velveteen ears drawn quite flat. My lady's maid, Mireille Anouilh, a woman with more years behind her than Methuselah, is very nearly doing the same. Albeit rather more lethargically. Mama's crowing must have woken her up.

Of course, I knew I wasn't *really* in Venice, but it is still a shock to the system to be so rudely returned to reality. I am actually in the palace gardens, at one of those mock fishing villages along the Sun King's landscaping *pièce de résistance*, the Grand Canal, where local peasants are employed to wear the garb of humble sailors and serve fish to the residents of Versailles.

Pépin gives a sharp yap and I smile. I have dressed him up for the occasion. These servants ferrying fish to and fro might be wearing the costumes of sailors, but my dog is made of higher-ranking stuff. *He* is clothed in the outfit of a sea captain, complete with lace-trim cravat and miniature jacket, the gold-fringed braiding of its epaulettes shining proudly in the bursts of afternoon sun.

'*Ma petite . . .*' pants Mama, having reached us. She waves a hand to dismiss Mireille and, as my maid shuffles off, attempts to regain her breath. 'I have been looking for you everywhere!'

My mother swirls her fan as hopelessly around her head as if she were signalling from a sinking gondola. She is trying to keep the mosquitoes at bay and failing miserably, for it is a little-known fact that Versailles was built upon swampy ground. This not only results in the gardens being plagued by hordes of blood-hungry mosquitoes for over half the year but causes it to stink, too, a miasma reminiscent of rotting vegetables and piss. The King himself rarely perambulates the gardens without a nosegay.

'Well, Mama?' I arch my brows and fix her with a stare, but she does not elaborate. 'What is it?'

'Oh, Hortense . . . it is your father!' she exclaims, dropping heavily into the chair Mireille vacated. 'He has . . . had word from . . . Dubois . . . at last!'

Since she is still lost for breath the sentence is ragged, making it difficult to judge her tone. So I cannot tell whether I am about to be lifted by the wings of elation or plunged into the depths of despair.

Mama reclines and closes her eyes, the great swell of her bosom heaving up and down. It is almost as though she has forgotten why she has come. Unable to wait any longer, I jab my toe sharply into her ankle.

'Oh!' Mama jumps, her eyes springing open. 'You see, that is exactly why this Dubois has *refused* the match!'

An immense flood of relief overwhelms me. Thank the heavens. I do not have to marry that half-wit. And not only that, but this Dubois' son was the last possible match available. My dear Papa is firmly out of options.

'You need not look so pleased with yourself!' Mama returns, swatting at a mosquito on her arm.

I appraise her blankly, taking in the *retroussé* tip to her nose, her small wet lips. She is Papa's second wife and mother to his youngest five children, myself included. His first wife, a woman with a forehead as high as the ceiling in the Hall of Mirrors and a perpetually stricken expression – I have seen the portraits as evidence – produced my four older half-siblings and died giving birth to the last of them. I haven't encountered my half-siblings for years, thank the Lord. Nor do I want to.

'Have you not considered,' Mama continues, 'that since there are no suitable matches now left for you in Versailles, your father will have his man find you a husband elsewhere?'

The notion throws me a little, before I force out a derisive snort. 'Mama, you know as well as I that Papa will do no such thing.' It is no secret my father is not the most decisive of men and neither does he have the strongest backbone. He would far rather spend his time engaging in drinks and cards than continuing to engineer a marriage for me. 'He has done what he can and that will be an end to the matter.'

I assume that Mama will agree but, to my surprise, she quietens instead.

'I fear not ...' she replies, after a few moments have passed. 'I don't think you understand. Your father has become far more ... *determined* on the subject of late.' She wrinkles her brow. 'If only you were a little less difficult—'

The buzzing of an insect at my ear suddenly enrages me. I flick the wretched thing away and start to my feet, leaving my mother to the mosquitoes.

English Folk Songs

Jouy-en-Jouvant

Sofi

It has been a fortnight since we came to the factory and it has passed in a haze of labour and new routine, of rules to adhere to and instructions to remember. We have done almost nothing but work since we arrived, having neither the time nor the energy for anything else, for when our day off comes around every Sunday, there is church to attend and chores to catch up on, after which Lara, Mama and I are so weary we can scarce keep our eyes open beyond supper.

On each of the six days of the working week, the clanging of the forecourt bell wakes us before sunrise, and we trudge to the factory as the first rays of dawn are lightening the sky. We work until noon, have a half-hour's break for bread, toil again until the end of the day. It is unrelenting and monotonous. And the work is hard, as I feared it might be. Stooping to dredge the steeped leaves from the dye-baths makes my back ache. Carrying the pails and pigments up and down the stairs from one part of the building to the other turns my legs to jelly.

Of Josef I have seen almost nothing. But in the quietest moments of the night when I am somehow still awake despite the heaviness in my bones and the aching of my muscles, I find myself remembering him on the cottage doorstep, holding my rag-doll out to me.

*

Today, we haven't long recommenced work after the dinner-break when there is a mishap in the dye-house. Aveline Colbert, the elderly woman who showed Mama what to do during our first morning here, suddenly stumbles as she hauls a pail of red madder to the vats, a heavy task for a woman half her age. Most of the liquid sloshes from her bucket, soaking both the floor and her apron in the process. The woman moans and attempts to struggle to her feet, slipping repeatedly on the puddle of dye as she does. I rush over and help her from the ground.

'Are you hurt, Madame?'

She rubs her knees, wincing. 'Oh heavens, my apron ... the wasted mix ...'

I tell her not to worry, find a mop to clean the dye and guide her to a seat on a low wall outside.

'Let me help you with your apron,' I say, untying the wet garment from her waist. 'I'll run and fetch you a clean one. Do not worry, I shall only be a few moments.'

I race back to the cottage, past the meadow and the old stone bridge. Inside, I draw a half-pail of water, add a scoop of salt from the nook in the hearth and leave the stained apron to soak. Then I snatch one of my own clean aprons from my chamber and hasten back with it along the track.

Although it is still early in the afternoon, low patches of mist are already gathering above the river. The old stone bridge comes back into view, and I see that a figure is now standing upon it, almost entirely obscured by the thickening suspensions of white.

Through this dense and frigid air, notes of music begin to reach me. Slow, unexpected.

'Dum dee-dee dum, dilly dilly ...'

I am so struck by the quality of the voice, faltering and plaintive, that I nearly do not recognise the tune. I used to hear an Englishwoman sing the song, back at the harbour in Marseilles.

'For thee and I, dilly dilly, now all are one, And we will lie, dilly dilly, no more alone.'

Lavender's Blue. I stand awhile, distracted by its sadness and beauty. And then the melody stops, fading back into the fog just as it had started.

I go closer, in order to determine who was singing, but as the mist clouds shift and diminish before me, I see the bridge is deserted. Nobody is there at all.

The Royal Menagerie

Versailles

Hortense

'Wait, *ma petite*! Wait for Mama!'

I pause, more to fix Pépin onto his leash than to obey my mother's entreaty, her unwelcome assertion concerning my father still buzzing at my head as incessantly as the mosquitoes. I look back at Mama. The sight of her furiously scratching her ample chest, angry pink welts rising across it, affords me some pleasure.

'These infernal mosquito hordes are biting me to death,' she moans. 'One would think they hadn't eaten all year. They're almost as bad as the peasants.'

'You'll only make the bites worse by scratching.'

She tuts and beckons me with her fan. 'Come, *ma petite*. Let us forget all this marriage business awhile and take a turn through the Ménagerie Royale. I am being eaten alive here.'

'Then you'll be far safer amongst the lions,' I quip, as she proceeds to the edge of the water to flag down an idling gondola.

The gondolier, in his seaman's outfit, ventures the briefest of glances at Captain Pépin, and I straighten my little dog's epaulettes and feel quite satisfied. Then Mama's last words produce another immense burst of acrimony within me. *Let us forget all this marriage business awhile.* How easy it is for her to say. She has

97

no idea what goes on right under the upturned tip of her nose and never has.

Purposefully ignoring my mother for the duration of the journey, I watch the Menagerie Pavilion come into view at the far end of the canal. Octagonal in shape and built of a light-coloured stone, it is not so dissimilar to the great Bastille itself. But unlike the Bastille, the highest part of *this* building is topped with a domed roof, a cupola like an aviary—

'I see you are giving me *la froideur* now,' Mama pipes up, breaking my thoughts. 'I was merely trying to warn you, that was all. If your father is still as intent on your marriage as I fear he is, and there are no suitable young men left at Versailles, then he will start looking for one *outside* of the palace.'

I prickle with ire. 'Mama, you told me not a minute ago that we were to forget the matter, yet here you are, raking it over once again.'

'Tush, Hortense,' my mother scolds, her fan quickening. 'All I'm saying is this. If your father has his man find you a suitable beau elsewhere, then you must see – you shall have to leave the palace!'

Leave the palace. I cannot imagine such a thing. No matter how many times I try, I can never decide whether Versailles is an oppressive cage or a gilded sanctuary, and it is a dilemma that unsettles me even more than the notion of leaving it.

The gondola comes to a halt, and I immediately clutch Pépin tight and leap onto the grass. I have a mind to turn directly around and head back to the apartments, but the thought utterly stifles me. At my back, Mama huffs and puffs as she tries to extricate herself from the boat. I turn a deaf ear to her pleas for assistance and advance directly to the Menagerie Pavilion.

The building's interior is decorated in *rocaille*, encrusted with pebbles and shells like a grotto. A fountain bubbles at its centre, rivulets running around its walls in an effort to keep the place cool. It doesn't appear to work. The white bear's hair fell out some months ago. The wolf died last summer, apparently of heatstroke. Indeed, every animal within the menagerie walls seems to be ailing in one way or another, hovering on the cusp of a premature end. A few years ago an elephant drowned in the canal, having drunk its daily quota of five bottles of burgundy in quicker succession than usual. I have known some of the gentlemen of Versailles to do the same.

Pépin and I approach the cage of the Bengalese tiger. The big cat is languishing towards the back of the bare stone enclosure, its stripes dulled and dirty. It is lying with its head on a forepaw as though resigned to its fate, seeming to know that the cage is locked and escape is futile. I have never liked cats, but in that instant something about the animal's plight affects me strangely and I have to look away.

'I do wish you wouldn't fly off like that,' Mama gasps, having finally caught up with me. She stands fanning herself at my side, her face as pink as the spreading weals on her chest. 'Now, let us see these new apes they have.'

Several weeks ago, the menagerie took delivery of a group of emaciated chimpanzees, a gift from the King of Senegal. Alas, their residency at Versailles hadn't started auspiciously. One night, the worse for drink, a gentleman of the court paid a keeper to enter their cage, and the mob of apes set upon the man with such unbridled ferocity, he was pulled from the enclosure soaked with blood and half-dead.

Mama heard about the episode from one of her maids who, after communicating details of the violent encounter, was quite insistent the ringleader of the chimpanzees possessed the power of speech.

My mother edges towards the bars of their enclosure now, where a mangy-looking ape with a woebegone expression sits rocking pathetically on its heels. I beat my fan at my nose to mask its stink.

'Say *Bonjour*,' Mama croons at the animal. 'Say *Bon-jour, Marquise*.'

It does not move a muscle.

'See, I knew it was a nonsense,' my mother trumpets, imagining herself vindicated. 'Apes cannot talk.'

'That one's not very lively, I'm afraid,' a nearby man offers. 'The creature's parents were . . .' he pauses awhile, as though weighing up whether to continue, 'brother and sister. It was a fact sadly forgotten

99

by the animal's custodian, who permitted them to copulate. That unfortunate beast is the result.'

The man who is talking to us is an oaf. Siblings have been permitted to copulate in palaces like Versailles for centuries. Royal dynasties have been founded upon it.

I consider the act itself, urgent and bestial, the laboured grunts and bellowings not unlike those sounding from the cages that surround us. A shiver passes across my scalp.

The Fables of La Fontaine

Jouy-en-Jouvant, several days later

Lara

It must be gone seven when I step into the darkness and find Sofi, waiting alone outside the print-house door.

'Mama has been kept at work,' she tells me. 'She shouldn't be longer than an hour.'

'In that case we ought to go and get the fire lit.'

'Go and get the fire smoking, you mean,' Sofi returns, slipping her arm through mine.

We walk down the track and away from the factory, a few scant groups of other workers going in the same direction. The bell stopped some time ago and most have left already, returning to their cottages on the Oberst estate or the village at the bottom of the hill.

It is another frigid night, and Sofi and I huddle together as we negotiate the path bordering the meadow, its grass the pile on a dark stretch of velvet in this light. As we approach the forecourt we become aware of several pairs of footsteps behind us, keeping step with ours exactly, tread for tread. Sofi and I exchange a glance, and as if deciding what to do without a word passing between us, we stop walking and slowly turn to see who is there.

Behind us stand two women and a man, all three of them meeting our eyes boldly. The man is maybe forty, the shorter of the women close to his age, with the other not that much older than I. The man is tall, stringy but strong-looking, carrying a knobbly stick and drumming it intermittently against his thigh. The younger woman glances at the older and sniggers quietly. I wonder what on earth they could want. Whether down to our friendship with Josef or the fact we're outsiders, the other workers have hardly gone out of their way to be sociable since we arrived. I begin to worry that these three, having followed us almost all the way back to our cottage in the dark, seem decidedly unfriendly. My grip stiffens on my sister's arm.

'You Sofi Thibault?' the older woman says. The hair at the hem of her cap is a pure chalk white, and I realise I have seen her before.

Doing a fine job of steadying her nerve, Sofi lifts her chin. 'I am.'

There is a pause, filled by the ominous sound of the man's stick against his leg. When the older woman reaches into the front of her jacket, both Sofi and I tense. To my surprise, the man begins to laugh.

'My, don't look so worried,' the older woman says, drawing out a flat parcel of cloth. 'I just wanted to thank you for helping my ma, was all. Return your apron. The dye-house isn't easy work for a woman of her age. It's nice to know someone's looking out for her.'

Sofi breathes her relief as the woman extends a hand.

'I'm Bernadette Durand, by the way. I work in the—'

As she speaks, I suddenly recall where it is I have seen her. Stoking the fire beneath the copper vats when Josef showed us around the factory. Her forearms are covered tonight, the furrowed pink scars caused by the lye tucked beneath her shawl.

'In the wash-house!' my sister cuts in, having had the same thought as I.

The woman nods. 'This is my husband, Pascal. He drives one of the Monsieur's drays. Collection and delivery.'

Pascal removes his hat and bows.

'And this is Sidonie. Sid to her friends. She works in the *papeterie*.'

Sid, lively eyes glittering beneath a head of tight, light curls, raises a hand in greeting.

'Anyhow,' Bernadette goes on. 'Feel free to pass Ma's apron back to her when you get a moment—'

'Unless you want to exchange it for a couple of good loaves of bread,' Sid interrupts, nudging her friend.

Bernadette snorts.

'As if there is any good bread to be had in exchange for anything!' says Pascal.

'You may have the apron now, if you like,' says Sofi. 'It is clean.'

'Yes,' I add, pleased to have unexpectedly made three new friends we didn't have an hour ago. 'Would you like to come back to the cottage? I think there is a little wine.'

Pascal raises the brim of his hat with his stick. 'That's very kind. Don't mind if we do.'

Back in the cottage Sofi gathers together the chairs. We find a few cups, sharing the small remainder of wine between us, and I try my best to kindle a fire in the hearth, but thick grey smoke immediately starts funnelling straight into the parlour.

'Allow me.' Pascal kneels at the fireplace, and for the first time in weeks I'm amazed to see the wood burn fast and hot, with every last shred of smoke drawn straight up the chimney.

Bernadette asks how we are finding the factory and we make small-talk for a while about the work each of us does. Conversation drifts to where we have come from, to life in the south, our father's profession—

'What do you think of the Monsieur?' Sofi blurts abruptly and I know she is trying to change the subject.

'Monsieur Wilhelm?' says Bernadette, wrinkling her nose. 'Never see him. Spends most of his time holed up in his chateau. The workers didn't think anything of it at first, but as the years go on they're losing patience with him, is my opinion. Once upon a time, if there was an issue in the factory the Monsieur would put it right. Nowadays everything has to go through his under-manager, Monsieur Marchant. Or Master Josef.'

'But he still approves all the designs . . . for the wallpaper?' Sofi asks.

'About the only thing he does do,' scoffs Bernadette, taking a sip from her cup.

Sensing a kindred spirit, my sister makes a noise in agreement.

'And what about his wife?' she says. 'We heard Monsieur Wilhelm hasn't been the same since she died?'

Bernadette narrows her eyes. 'Madame Justine?'

'She died suddenly, did she not?'

'About five years ago now, wasn't it?' offers Pascal.

'It was,' Bernadette confirms. 'Cal and me hadn't come to the factory then. My mother was here, though. Said it was all very bizarre, how the Madame died. Disturbing.'

'I heard she was found,' says Sid, 'in the middle of the night. Dead as you like.'

'Don't suppose *she* liked it very much,' Pascal replies. 'Maybe that's why she haunts the place. Eh, Bernadette?'

'*Haunts* the place?' asks Sofi, agog.

'Well, we have seen odd lights up in the tower at times,' Bernadette says. 'Haven't we, Cal?'

Her husband nods. 'We have indeed.'

'One day Cal was coming back late with the wagon, well after midnight, and the shutters were open and—'

'And one second the tower was completely dark, the next there was light moving about.'

'Someone had taken a candle up there, you mean?' I ask.

'Nah, it was stranger than that,' replies Pascal. 'The light just suddenly appeared, from right by the window. It was almost like it had floated straight out of the wall of its own free will.'

'Like a *feu follet*,' adds Sid, curls bouncing across her forehead. 'A will-o'-the-wisp. A lost soul in purgatory.' She shivers.

'And all that by the by,' Bernadette continues. 'Madame Justine *was* found in the middle of the night. In the middle of a storm, too. She was outside, so my mother heard, lying on the ground. Skirts and petticoats right up over her head. Well, as a result there was nothing left to the imagination. From the waist down, that poor woman was naked as the day she was born.'

The idea sends a shaft of ice speeding right through me.

'There were also marks, don't forget,' says Pascal. 'On the Madame's neck.'

'Marks?' asks Sofi.

'Deep lines. Cutting right into the skin. The Madame's face was purple.'

My sister and I are both stunned into silence. Nobody speaks for a minute or two.

'There was also the matter of who found her,' Pascal adds eventually, draining the wine from his cup. 'Man by the name of Emile Porcher.' He leans forward conspiratorially and crosses an ankle over his knee. 'Lives with his mother outside the village. You'll see him up here, from time to time. Monsieur Marchant pays him to keep down the rats. Though ask yourself what he was doing laying rat traps in the dead of the night. Ask yourself how he just happened to find the Madame's half-naked body. If you were to ask me, I'd say it was all too much of a coincidence.'

'Oh, vicious rumours,' snaps Bernadette. 'There was no evidence to suggest he had anything to do with it, as well you know, but people still talk about the man as though he were the Devil himself.' She gets up from her chair and grasps Sofi's hand. 'And, on that note, I think we ought to get going. Thanks again for helping my ma.'

We say our goodbyes at the cottage door, and I realise our own mother will be back any moment. Indeed, there is already a figure hovering at the end of the track. But before I have the chance to see who it is, Sid seizes my arm.

'Speak of the devil,' she hisses, flicking her eyes to the place where they stand. 'You want to watch that one, never mind what Bernadette says. He ain't right in the head.'

I lean around her. A thin, sallow man is there, older than Pascal and darkly dressed, greasy strands of hair combed back over the crown of his balding head. He looks at me for some seconds, a jarring, unblinking stare, then tugs his jacket collar high, jams his hands into his pockets and hurries away.

'*That's* Emile Porcher,' says Sid.

'The man who found the Madame's body?'

She breathes the words. 'The very same.'

Midnight

Sofi

A thin bar of moonlight cuts through the drapes, coming to rest on my sister's sweep of already light hair, giving it an other-worldly glow. Her breathing is steady and deep, she has been asleep for some time, and every so often I think of lifting my hand to nudge her awake, for a plan is forming and fattening in my mind that I cannot seem to ignore, no matter how hard I try.

It must be almost midnight, and despite my body aching with exhaustion, I haven't been able to sleep a wink, the earlier conversation with Bernadette, Pascal and Sid playing over and over in my head. Madame Justine, Josef's mother, found dead so suddenly and in such a horrible way. The lights Pascal said he observed coming out of the wall of the tower room in the middle of the night.

I finally do it, move my hand and gently prod Lara awake.

My sister stirs. 'Mmm?'

'I can't sleep.'

Lara's brows dip, concerned. 'More nightmares?' she asks, tucking the coverlet around my shoulder.

'It's not that,' I return, pulling it down again. 'I've been thinking about the chateau. You remember what Aunt Berthé told us. That the tower room used to be Madame Justine's chamber, at the Maison des Peupliers, when she was a governess to the Guyot children. And you heard what Pascal was saying. About seeing those ghostly lights? Do you not think it all peculiar? As peculiar as the way in which Madame Justine died?'

'Peculiar? It's tragic.'

'But don't you wonder what might be up there?'

'No.' Lara says the word as though it was a full stop, and closes her eyes.

'Liar,' I needle. 'I saw your face earlier when I was asking Bernadette about Madame Justine. You're as intrigued as I.'

'It is none of our business,' Lara responds, flicking open her eyes again to fix them reproachfully on mine.

'But don't you think we might see it after supper tomorrow, somehow? The tower? Perhaps I could ask Aunt Berthé to show us?'

'That would be taking advantage of Aunt's kindness, Sofi. She has invited us there to eat. She's not going to betray her employer's trust like that.'

The fact that my sister is always so principled is annoying even when I know, deep-down, that she is right. But something in me has been tweaked at over the past weeks like a pulled stitch, and now I cannot put that tower room from my mind.

'Tomorrow . . .' I start drowsily, closing my eyes, and before long I am asleep. For the first time since Pa's accident, I do not dream of thundering wagons or thrashing ponies or bloodied water. I dream of that tower, hanging apart from the rest of the chateau in the dark sky.

Secrets

Sofi

'Shall I refill your cup, Aunt?' I ask, as Lara eyes me suspiciously from across the table.

'*Non merci*, Sofia,' answers Aunt Berthé, draining the last of her wine. 'Else I shall never be able to get up in the morning!'

I try not to let Lara mark my brow tightening. I've been waiting for an opportunity to question my aunt from the moment we sat down to supper. I glance at the empty plates, knowing that if I don't ask now I never will. All those things Bernadette, Sid and Pascal told us of Madame Justine's death seem to be burning a hole in my gut.

'Aunt Berthé,' I say suddenly, 'how do you find the Monsieur?' I spit this sentence out fast, avoiding my sister's gaze.

My aunt looks confused. '*Find* him? Well, as I told you before, he can be awkward . . . strange at times. But he's a good enough master.'

'Yet he doesn't concern himself with the factory much any more?' I press. 'He keeps his distance from the business, does he not? Apart from overseeing the designs of the wallpaper?'

Lara gives my thigh a gentle warning dig beneath the table. My sister may disapprove of my nosiness, but my mother does not. I regard her now, awaiting Aunt Berthé's response to my questions with interest, always keen to learn the failings of a man like the Monsieur.

My aunt discards her serviette, a gesture of surprise tinged with the faintest air of annoyance. 'Who told you that?'

'Oh,' I answer, not admitting it was Josef, 'it was just something the other workers said.'

'It's all over the factory, sister,' Mama chimes in. 'I haven't so much as glimpsed the man in the weeks we have been here.'

Aunt Berthé screws her mouth uneasily, her cheeks pinking. 'Well, that is because the Monsieur has found the last years without his wife very difficult . . . going on with his business, getting out and about, interacting with others. As I have said, he hasn't been the same since her death . . . '

'We heard from someone in the factory that the death was suspicious . . . ' I press on still further.

Lara glares at me and gives a slight shake of her head.

'Well, I never,' Aunt Berthé exclaims. 'Why, they've no right to be gossiping—'

'What happened to Madame Justine, Aunt?'

A cast of sadness settles across her countenance and I regret the question instantly. As curious as I am to hear what she has to say, I realise – too late, as always – that Lara was probably right. I should not have asked her at all.

Aunt Berthé dips her head. 'I don't really like discussing it, if you must know,' she replies, patting her cheeks with the backs of her hands. 'It was such a dreadful business.'

'I'm sorry,' I murmur. 'Of course, if it is upsetting then you shouldn't speak of it.'

'Sofi is right,' Lara adds. 'Thank you for a lovely supper—'

'Nevertheless . . . ' Aunt Berthé continues, 'I don't like to think of those workers spreading rumours.' She pours a few fingers of wine into her cup. 'But if I tell you what I know of the matter, you must speak no more about it. Not with the other workers, not with anyone.'

Mama raises an eyebrow.

'And it must go no further than the walls of this room. You understand?' Aunt Berthé takes a long sip of her wine. 'It was late one Sunday. The day after the *Bal de Printemps* – a yearly springtime dance organised by Monsieur Wilhelm for his workers – and the factory was quiet. Madame Justine and Master Josef went out and didn't come back. Since that wasn't out-of-the-ordinary, it was only when the two of them still hadn't returned by supper that the alarm was raised. Then a storm got up, the worst in an age.' She takes a long, unsteady breath. 'Madame Justine was found, eventually, at the far end of the gardens. Soaked through. Unfortunately, it was too late by then.'

My aunt, I notice, mentions nothing about the man who found her. About what that man – that Emile Porcher – was doing in the chateau gardens in the middle of the night. More and more questions boil inside me. I want to ask about the things Bernadette had told us. The state in which the body was found, the Madame's nakedness—

'What about the marks, on Madame Justine's neck?' I say, heart beating hard and unable to stop myself.

Aunt Berthé purses her lips. 'Well, I never. Those workers really *have* been babbling.'

'They said a man found her?' I go on.

'That's right,' my aunt answers, reluctantly. 'But he had nothing to do with it. Official verdict was the Madame's tragic death was a robbery gone wrong, according to Monsieur Wilhelm. There'd been a spate of throttlings along *le grande route* at the time, things taken from the victims. The evil creature responsible must have found his way up to the chateau. The poor Madame was just in the wrong place at the wrong time.'

My stomach clenches. There is something about the story that doesn't feel right. 'But surely if Josef was with her, then he would have been able to tell—'

'That's just it,' my aunt says slowly. 'He wasn't with her when she was found. And I'm afraid Josef has never been able to speak of what he saw happen to his mother that night. If he actually saw anything, that is.'

There again, that foreboding silence, like a beast uncurled and tensed for the strike. Just as it was the last time we were in this room discussing Madame Justine's mysterious death with our aunt.

'When they did find him,' Aunt Berthé sighs, 'he was at the very top of the old sycamore. That big one at the edge of the gardens—'

My sister's face blanches.

'He wouldn't come down for hours, despite all our best efforts. Was so high up that it was almost light by the time a man managed to reach him with a rope and lower him to safety. And then, in the weeks that followed . . . well, he shut up like a clam, poor child. Monsieur Wilhelm could see no other option than to send him away to school. Just eleven years old . . . '

'That's . . . that's *awful*,' Lara whispers.

Nobody speaks for some moments. I find I cannot comprehend how perfect everything can be one second, then upturned by such drastic change the very next that there isn't a single soul with the power to stop it. I think of my father's tools, his apron and carvings, all those things I will never see again.

'Monsieur Wilhelm was never the same after his wife died,' Aunt Berthé goes on. 'Couldn't stand any reminder of her in the house. Found it too painful. Doesn't even use their old chamber no more, it's all locked up and the furniture sheeted. While Master Josef was away at school, his father had every one of his mother's possessions disposed of, right down to the last hairpin, right down to the wallp—' She pauses.

'What is it, Aunt?' Lara asks, resting a hand on Aunt Berthé's. 'You do not have to go on if you do not want to.'

'Well . . . it is only that Monsieur Wilhelm also instructed that the decor – every bit of wallpaper in the entire chateau, that is – be stripped out, too. Every room was papered anew.'

'That's men for you,' Mama interjects. 'Anything comes their way that they'd rather not deal with and they take things to the extreme.'

'You don't understand, sister,' replies Aunt Berthé. 'The wallpaper that was destroyed, it was *specially designed*. By Monsieur Wilhelm. Each and every scene within it . . . was taken directly from Madame Justine's life. All the things she had done with her husband and son. That is why the Monsieur declared it had to go. He couldn't stand the reminder of what had been lost.'

I have heard of men making paintings of women, of sculpting their nakedness from marble, but never have I heard of one fixing a woman into wallpaper. I cannot work out whether it is romantic or obsessive.

'She was his muse, that was the truth of it,' Aunt Berthé mutters, seeming to catch what I am thinking. 'And it is good that she was, since at least Josef does have a little of it left.'

'I thought you said it had all been stripped out—' I start. 'Aunt, do you mean that the wallpaper in every room was destroyed, apart from—'

'Apart from the tower,' she answers, nodding gravely. 'Since that room's never really been used, nobody at the time thought to re-do it. But that particular wallpaper, with Madame Justine in the pattern ... Well, what covers the walls of the tower is all that is left of that paper in the whole place.'

'All that is left?' I ask. 'Could they not make more?'

'Oh no,' replies my aunt. 'The printing blocks were destroyed as well. Also on the Monsieur's orders. By the time Josef returned from school that summer, almost nothing remained of his mother at all.'

'It's eerie ... her whole life, up there in the wallpaper,' Lara murmurs, her voice far off and echoey. 'Poor Josef. He never even got the chance to say goodbye.'

'Are you all right, Sofia?' Aunt Berthé asks. 'You've gone awful pale.'

'I ...' I stammer, not knowing where to begin. 'I'm sorry, Aunt, but I am not feeling well. Would you mind if I returned to the cottage?'

The Tower

Sofi

I only make it a few paces down the passageway before I hesitate, feeling the chateau's massive walls soaring above me. I have no idea where to start, how to even reach the floor above this one, let alone get all the way up to the tower.

I take a breath. *Think,* I tell myself with more certainty than I feel, *it can't be that difficult.* I bring to mind the chateau from the outside. Recollect that, from the front, the tower stands at the right-hand corner of the building. So all I need do is head for that same corner, and find some way upwards.

Checking there is nobody else about, I hurry back the way we came in, recalling the sight of these subterranean passageways nearly three weeks ago, the staircases and corridors leading off from the steps to the servants' door. And it is as I remembered, for just before I reach the steps to that door, I see a second set of stairs winding upwards. Voices accumulate at the far end of the corridor, momentarily tempting me to give up altogether, since I am so close to the exit. But as the servants draw closer, I dart up the new set of plain stone steps instead, seconds later finding myself at a door.

Although the steps continue past this door, I cannot resist extending my fingers to the handle, if only to try and determine where in the chateau I now am, and how many more floors I have to climb. I nudge the door open the tiniest crack and peer around it.

The sight astounds me – an extraordinarily vast and opulent room, such a contrast to the parts of the chateau I have seen so far, it is breathtaking. This room must be the vestibule, and it is a cavernous space of unending polished marble, its chequered floor dizzying in glossy squares of ebony and white. A pair of chandeliers large as globes hang suspended from the ceiling, irradiating the whole space as brightly as two suns, while a grand staircase with an intricate ironwork balustrade sweeps gracefully upwards. It is like peeking out from the small, grey and everyday at an enlarged and dazzling world.

On one wall I see the insides of the two towering front doors, capped by their lunette windows. On another, an enormous portrait hanging on chains above the imposing mantel of a carved fireplace. It is a man's likeness in oils, the subject's wig positioned a little too far back on his head. I think of Monsieur Wilhelm, staring from that casement in the print-house, the darkly varnished surface of this painting not unlike the glass of that office window, his face a smear behind it. And next to this portrait, in an odd and unbalanced area of blank wall, a second chain dangles, as though missing a portrait of its own.

I close the door softly and continue up the steps. They end at the next door I come to, leaving me no other choice this time than to steal right through.

I find myself in a maze of grand, high-ceilinged landings, bordered by fine cornices and ablaze with sconces. I check left and right, puzzled as to whether I am at the front of the building or the rear, and unable to observe any landmark through the night-filled windows with which to right myself. Then, finally, I come upon it. A spiralled wooden staircase, set quite apart from any of the others, curving tightly upwards into blackness. I move to the nearest sconce and carefully extract one of its candles.

The spiralling stairs creak as I ascend them, and more than once I have to freeze my steps, heart beating hard as my ears are straining for anyone who might have heard me. Eventually, I come to a halt on a small landing before an unassuming panelled door, my breath clouding in the light from the candle. Strangely, it is even colder here than on the lower floors.

In the second it takes me to tentatively spread my fingers to the door handle, a noise inside the room stops my blood. There is a shift, from right behind the door, as though someone is hovering at the threshold. I exhale raggedly, turn as though to race back down those spiralling stairs, before managing to summon the mettle to put my ear to the wood. I wait in this position for what feels like minutes, hours, but hear nothing. All is silent. It must have been my imagination.

With a shaking hand, I gently twist the handle, half-expecting the room to be locked. But to my amazement, the latch clicks and the door gradually gives. As I step inside I see a key, jutting out of the keyhole on the inside of the door.

My single candle provides scant light after the brightness of the upper passageways, and I blink hard, willing my eyes to adjust. Then the flame swells, and vague hints of the chamber begin to show themselves through the darkness.

The space is perfectly round, the curving wall enclosing me inside of it like the fingers of a fist. Above my head, it is just possible to discern the murky rectangles of crossing ceiling beams. The window is shuttered and the room, aside from a dark-wood armoire, its door very slightly ajar, is completely bare of furniture, objects or possessions.

And then I see the wallpaper, and the breath is snatched from my throat. The room's single curving wall is covered with it, from floor to ceiling, shrouded in a pattern printed with violet-coloured ink. As I move my candle, I see that small, vignetted scenes cover the paper's surface, sprigs of foliage, curlicues and birds weaving between them.

I realise, for the first time, that this is what the wallpaper must look like when viewed in its entirety. It is as though, while each individual scene captures a single moment of a life, this wall captures the whole of one. The whole of a woman's life. I see her there, in the print, with her sweep of light hair, her delicate, animated countenance. She stares back at me, again and again, inhabiting every last image.

A curious shiver thrills my skin. No more than one or two scenes at a time are visible in the candle's flicker, the rest dissolving to black where the light cannot reach. And yet it is odd how, when the glowing wick passes across each one, the woman in that pattern seems to pause, mid-gesture, knowing she is being observed.

Scenes from Antiquity

Sofi

Though the scenes in the wallpaper are small, it is unearthly how real they look in the candle's light. With the tower chamber so dark, it isn't unlike peering through a window after nightfall to observe the occupants of a lit room. The sense I shouldn't be watching only makes those strange vignettes the more compelling.

I bring the candle closer to the wall and move it more slowly from one part of the pattern to the next. My hand stills, the light it holds revealing a startlingly familiar building. A couple converse in a beautiful garden, a printed purple sun sinking low in the sky. I squint at the vignette, run a fingertip over the two figures within it. A man, a woman.

I recognise that man instantly, bulky as he is, with his ungainly features and posture. The scene in the paper might be small, but it has captured the Monsieur's likeness perfectly. Madame Justine, by contrast, stands slight and exquisite at his side.

The wallpaper might have captured Monsieur Wilhelm's likeness, but not his manner. For there is a distinct cheeriness to his coun-tenance in this scene, his expression a world away from the grim mask that was staring at my sister. He is happy here, transfixed by Madame Justine, gazing at the fine form of her face, her profile held as perfectly as a cameo by the lunette window behind it. I study the building again, a building almost identical to this very chateau. Almost, but not quite. It has the same pale facade, the same single tower, even the same two rows of poplars bordering the approach.

But that approach doesn't quite angle itself towards the building as I know it should, and I wonder if the house in this scene is actually the place my aunt spoke of when we first arrived – the Maison des Peupliers – the chateau where Monsieur Wilhelm and Madame Justine first met. My light drifts to the next vignette.

The same two figures are under an enormous old tree now and its shape is distinctive. The trunk is twisted and burled, the canopy broad, lower branches arcing to the earth. It looks exactly like the sycamore at the edge of the gardens, Monsieur Wilhelm smiling nervously, expectantly, as he kneels on the ground beneath. It is even possible to see splashes of mud on his stockings. Next to him, Madame Justine is laughing, pressing one hand to her chest, reaching out to the Monsieur with the other. Her pose is graceful, but utterly unchecked. She is not laughing at Monsieur Wilhelm, but with him. This scene must depict the moment the Monsieur proposed, I think, Aunt Berthé's voice chiming in my mind. *Meant to ask for her hand in marriage, but got down on both knees by mistake and dirtied his stockings.*

I shift the flame further along the wall. The next of the scenes shows the inside of a chamber, where Madame Justine is propped against a bed-head, a tiny baby in her arms. Her lips are parted slightly, as though she is speaking to her child. Or perhaps not speaking, but singing.

A melody seems to curl out of the darkness towards me, just as it had from the fog at the river. Those haunting notes, an English folk song.

'*Lavender's blue, dilly dilly, lavender's green ... When I am King, dilly dilly, you shall be Queen.*'

A creak at my back. I jump and swing my candle through the blackness. I could swear I was being observed, could swear I just caught the scent of lavender on the air. But there is no one here and the door is closed as I left it. The thought of lavender suddenly brings Mama to mind. Since working in the soap factory, she cannot abide the smell of the stuff.

I calm myself, allow the candle's light to flicker four more vignettes into life. The first of these scenes shows Madame Justine's toilette. It is cluttered with emollient pots and jewellery, powder cases and cups of pins, and she sits before it, dabbing the contents of a small bottle onto the pulsing spot below her earlobe. In the second she is at a desk, pen poised over paper and a small cage of songbirds behind. The third shows her with her son at the market, surrounded by vegetables, flowers and poultry. In the fourth they stand together on the far side of a river, skimming stones across the water.

The next scene is altogether more unusual. Here is a large dining-table, spread with *aunes* of linen, and in the tented space below, beside a heap of cushions, a latticework dish is piled high with tarts, a steaming pot and two cups set next to it. Could this vignette have captured one of Madame Justine's winter picnics? Once again, my aunt's words find me ... *Kind, full of life. Full of laughter and fun.* Pa's own laugh, warm as cinnamon, sounds in my skull. An echo from another time. Eyes stinging fiercely, I bring my candle to the next vignette.

It, too, shows a moment my aunt described to us. There is Madame Justine, her skirts tucked up, slipper swung over the top of the baluster. She seems to be about to slide right down it, while a small boy – Josef – looks on in surprise.

In the next scene they are together again, flying a kite on an expanse of grass. The same spreading sycamore stands solid behind them, and their kite is almost heart-shaped, its ribboned tail, like their clothes and hair, licked untamed by the wind. With its tiny, swirling speckles, it almost looks like the kite itself is made from a piece of wallpaper.

There can't be many vignettes left in the pattern now that I haven't seen, and the candle I took from the sconce in the passage-way is burning low, guttering and flaring two more scenes into life. In the first of these, Madame Justine and Josef are at a fortepiano, smiling once more, the pair of them playing the instrument to-gether, and it is uncanny how similar they look. The other scene shows some kind of party, at which they are dancing, mother spin-ning son, mirroring each other's laughter in a rushing, uncensored glee. The *Bal de Printemps*. The air around me stills and thickens, takes on the silence of a grave. Madame Justine died the day after one of these annual balls, that is what my aunt had said. And since Josef does not look much younger than ten in this scene, that means this paper must have been printed and hung in the very last year of his mother's life—

I freeze. I can hear something, and this time it is not my imagination. I can hear footsteps. Someone is climbing the tower staircase.

I cast wildly about. There is only one way out of this room and that is the way I came in. My frantic gaze lands on the armoire, and I rush to it and open the doors. Shelves cover the inside of the structure, from around thigh-height all the way to its ceiling, but if I curl up beneath the lowest of those shelves, there may just be enough room.

I blow out my light and crush my body onto the armoire's wooden floor, feeling it give a little. Drawing the door shut as noiselessly as I can, I clamp a hand to my mouth. The footsteps get closer.

Breath Inside a Bubble

Lara

I enter the chamber slowly, terrified I might be discovered at any moment. I told Mama and Aunt Berthé that I must go back to the cottage to check on Sofi. But I am certain this is where she has come. When I edge the door open, however, the room is empty.

I only risked climbing all this way up to the tower myself to drag my sister back down again, as quickly as I can. It was not easy, stealing along the unending staircases and corridors, realising I needed a light to see the way and taking a candle from a wall sconce next to a gap where one was already missing.

I scan that candle around the room. It is completely empty, save for an armoire. I frown, try to work out where my sister might have gone. Perhaps she has left already, I think, and I mean to do the same when the sight of the wallpaper seizes me to such a degree I cannot move.

I am utterly surrounded by a myriad of scenes, enclosed within their violet print by the room's unending, curving wall. The quivering light from my candle animates the paper strangely, making its printed figures look as though they are dancing over that wall, like memories across a closed eyelid.

The temperature drops, the chamber growing icily cold, causing my hands to numb, my candle to shake. I vaguely sense some noise to my right, but it is difficult to concentrate on anything other than those strange, innumerable scenes and the same three figures that peer back at me from every one. Monsieur Wilhelm. Josef. Madame

Justine. How desperately sad it all is, how unfair. A child missing a parent. A lost love, still immortalised after all these years. None of them had any way of knowing what lay ahead. How precious everything is, I think, and yet how fragile, merely breath inside a bubble, held within the thinnest, frailest skin. It might burst at any second—

The candle halts before the scene of Monsieur Wilhelm's proposal. I recognise the gnarled and ancient sycamore in the print – the same tree Josef was found at the top of the night his mother died. The noise comes again then, tearing my gaze away from the wallpaper and directly towards the armoire. Someone is in the room with me, I can feel it. Pulse quickening, I move to the old piece of furniture and pull open the door.

'Lara!' my sister gasps. 'Thank goodness!'

'Sofi!' I hiss. 'How could you, after everything I said about not coming up here, about us getting into trouble. How could you be so impetuous?'

I watch as Sofi scrambles clumsily from the armoire, too angry with her to help.

'I know,' she answers, 'and I'm sorry. But have you seen the wall-paper? Have you seen *her*?' She guides my candle from one scene to the next. 'Imagine if everything we'd done with Pa had been captured like this.'

The flame lights the same vignette I was looking at before my attention was snatched to the armoire. The proposal. I observe Monsieur Wilhelm's jacket, laid between him and Madame Justine and the muddy earth, then move my gaze to the picnic under the dining-table, complete with its small but perfect stack of strawberry jam tarts. And even though the print of the wallpaper is purple on a cream ground, I think I can almost see the red of the preserve that fills those pastry shells, deep as jewels.

I study the woman in the wallpaper once more. Madame Justine. It must have been her I saw in the wallpaper sample Aunt Berthé sent to Marseilles, even though that pattern was a different colour, a different print entirely. Yet it showed a woman in the same room, gazing at the very same view through her window as I had been. Surely it was too much of a coincidence? Just as it is too frighteningly familiar that the woman I see in this pattern now is as light-haired and slightly built as I. That she is sitting beneath the gnarled boughs of an ancient tree, a man's jacket spread upon the ground. Sitting next to a neat pyramid of jam tarts—

'Lara?'

My head begins to spin, my vision flux and swim as though my senses were melting. Despite the differing cut of her clothes this time, that woman in the wallpaper again looks exactly like me. How could this be? The question holds me cold by the roots of my hair, sends long claws of ice raking down my skin. I do not have the answer.

PART III

Cameos

March 1789, four months later

Sofi

Scraps of parchment are strewn across the coverlet, as if individual sections had been chopped out of the wallpaper and arranged flat. But these scenes do not belong to the wallpaper at all, these scenes are my own. They are the drawings I have been making ever since that night last November, when Lara and I stole up to the tower chamber. The way those vignettes had Josef's whole childhood with his mother stoppered and captured. Memorialised forever.

Though I have divulged to no one what I've been up to these past months, not even Lara, I have been attempting to do the same. To capture the scenes of our old life in Marseilles. The moments I cannot bear to forget, made in the moments when no one is looking. I haven't shown them to another soul. There is Pa, smiling as he sits next to Lara and me at the table of his workshop. There we are again in the parlour ... on his wagon ... high on the cliffs ... at the harbour. There are many of my sister. She is a good subject, still and serene, allowing me to take more time over her likeness. The sunlight cuts through the window and across the sketches on the bed, bisecting her portrait.

It is a Sunday afternoon, and Lara and Mama are out with Aunt Berthé, gone to pay a visit to an acquaintance of my aunt's several villages away. I was supposed to go with them, but the idea of some time alone, to privately draw more scenes from my head and onto paper, nagged at me like a loose thread.

Hungry now I go downstairs, certain there will be nothing to eat, and my eyes land on the collapsed crumble of wood barely glowing in the hearth. Keeping the fire going was one of the tasks I promised Mama I would complete if she let me stay back. Despite it being March now, the air outside is still cold as midwinter. I know Mama will never allow me to do anything again if I don't keep my word, so stuff a few more logs into the mouth of the fireplace and jab at them with the poker. Realising I shall need to fetch more in to dry from the yard at the rear, I take up the dented copper bucket and head outside.

As I go I catch sight of a silhouette, slowly receding from the front window. A man like a spindle, cadaverous and concave, his posture stooped, strings of lank hair dangling over his upturned collar. Emile Porcher, the rat-catcher. I have seen him around the factory only once or twice over the last few months and always alone. I bristle, wondering why he should be here today, and so close to the cottage. But when I look through the glass, he is gone.

In the yard I pick the top row of frost-studded logs off the stack, fill my bucket and struggle back inside with the thing, cursing as it bumps against my shin. On re-entering the dim downstairs room, however, I stop. I can see someone, moving to the staircase and heading upstairs. At first I think myself mistaken, that it was most likely nothing more than the echo of the daylight's glare after being outside. But then the second step from the top groans, and I recall Emile Porcher, moments before on the front path. My whole body stiffens.

I am determined not to cry out, no matter how hard my heart is pounding. I refuse to let that odd, solitary man hear the tear of fear in my voice. Instead, I put down the bucket as softly as I can by the hearth and seize the poker.

As I reach the foot of the stairs, I sense the faintest movement in the front chamber. Fear crests once more, then anger that such a man – a complete stranger, no less – should dare to intrude in this way, dare to let himself into our cottage uninvited and now be upstairs, creeping about our chamber. My fingers tighten around the makeshift weapon in my hand.

I keep my tread noiseless and steady on the stairs, avoiding the parts that creak, my pulse thudding as I near the chamber door. Taking a second to still my breath, I fling the door open and burst into the room.

'Get out!' I shout. 'Get out or I will strike!'

The poker is aloft, the dull metal spike hovering above my head. He turns, then, and my cheeks flood red. 'Oh!' I exclaim. 'It is you!'

'Sofi!' Josef's light eyes widen. 'I'm sorry, I did not know you were here . . . that is to say . . .'

Josef hasn't been to the cottage since that first day I opened the door to find him holding out my rag-doll. I speak to him a little during the week, a couple of times he has even brought food for dinner. And these are the times I've felt my insides strum and glow, against my better judgement.

He sees far more of Lara, of course. Working in the print-house together they see each other every day. And I try not to let it vex me, as I lug another load of pigments to the dye-vats, as I scrub the stains from another pail, my hands raw.

At this precise moment, however, I'm not irritated but mortified. Standing in my chamber brandishing the poker, I want the boards beneath my feet to swallow me whole. I suddenly remember I took my cap off earlier and unpinned my heavy hair. Coarse, dark lengths of it now bounce wildly past my shoulders like a disturbed nest of snakes. Not only had I charged into the room like a thing possessed, I must have looked savage whilst doing so.

'I am sorry—' he repeats.

'I am sorry—' I say, the exact same time.

'I'm sorry if I scared you,' he goes on. 'I did knock at the front door but there was no answer. Forgive me.' He lowers his face bashfully.

I take a step forwards. 'Of course. I was outside, in the yard. There is no need to apologise.'

Josef brushes his hands over his pockets. 'I was only in search of Lara, you see.'

'She is out with Mama and my aunt.'

'Oh,' he replies, disappointed. 'Will they return soon?'

'Possibly,' I say. 'I'm not sure.'

There is a beat of silence. Josef smooths an errant lock of hair from his forehead and gestures at my drawings, scattered across the bed. 'These are your sister's?'

My face burns, I'd quite forgotten they were there. I hastily gather the fragments of parchment between two thin sheets of board, binding them together with a loop of twine.

'Oh . . . no,' I answer, 'they are mine.'

I look back at him and see his eyes are fixed upon me, and I laugh, self-conscious at his unexpected attention.

'They are very good indeed,' he says. 'They're the reason I did not leave the chamber as soon as I realised nobody was up here.'

I clasp the papers to my chest, along with the notion that Josef is the only person to have seen my drawings since I made them. 'Thank you.'

'I mean it.'

A moment passes and a thought briefly sprouts and subsides. How indecent it is to be alone like this with a boy, how agreeable an indecency.

Josef turns to the stairs. 'I should leave.'

I go after him, combing my brain for something more to say. 'Can I offer you some refreshment?' It is the only thing that comes to mind and it is a ridiculous question, as there is next to nothing here.

'No, thank you.' He extends a hand to the front door. 'However . . .' he says, halting at the threshold, seemingly thinking, 'I do not have anything to do today.' His half-turn sees him held by the pure square of light washing in from outside. 'I should very much like to see more of your drawings.'

I am still clutching them tight, I realise. My stomach lurches.

'If you want to, that is. If not—'

'Yes, if you like,' I answer, a pathetic attempt at indifference.

He smiles a little and returns inside. I smooth down my skirts, offer him a seat at the small table, and place my folder between us.

My hands shake as I loosen the twine on the crude bindings, allowing the outer sheets to fall apart and expose my sketches. Doing so feels oddly intimate, akin to unlacing my stays. I shake the comparison away, not knowing whether I can bear to watch Josef's reaction to my work. Will he notice I have taken the tower wallpaper as the inspiration to record my childhood, as his is recorded?

Josef thumbs through the little compositions I have made of the four of us, of Pa, Lara, Mama and me. He regards them thoughtfully, eyes wandering across the elements I've drawn as decoration around each scene. The laurel wreaths and beads that encircle our likenesses, the geometric embellishments that enclose them like lozenges. For this is where my scenes differ from the vignettes in the tower wallpaper. I have attempted to make these designs my own, in every possible way.

'Sofi, they are beautiful,' he replies, 'truly. I had no notion you were so accomplished.'

I thank him clumsily as he holds up the last of the drawings. A double portrait of my sister and myself. I had drawn it in our chamber, sketching Lara unawares, recording myself by studying my reflection in the small square of looking-glass we keep there. The flowers and the foliage behind us I had added in from memory, the beaded border from imagination.

'This is extraordinary,' he says. He speaks reverently, as though in awe of it, and I feel myself flush, proud that it is a drawing of both of us he has singled out, and not a portrait of Lara alone. 'You have rendered it superbly. It is you, there is no doubt, and yet you have captured . . . another quality, also.'

He places the sheet back amongst the others and I ponder how to ask him if he might speak to his father, recommend that I work with him and Lara in the print-house, instead of mixing dye all day.

'You are very talented, Sofi. Your aunt told me your father was an artist, too. He would be proud of these, no doubt.'

I forget about the dye-house in an instant then as I have to look away, to imagine my chin is a stone so it will not start to wobble.

Josef gazes into the distance, as if again lost in thought, and

I almost open my mouth to ask what he is thinking, then stop myself.

'I wish my mother could see the things I do,' he says, as though able to hear the question. The corners of his mouth turn down peculiarly, as though half in anger, half anguish. 'I hope she would approve.'

He lapses into utter stillness and I do not know what throws me more, the fact he has brought up the subject of his mother so unexpectedly, or that he looks like he is about to cry.

'Of course she would,' I say. 'You work hard, you're kind, and you're ... well, you know.' My face grows hot.

He doesn't seem to register that I was close to embarrassing myself by mentioning the way he looks. 'I hope so,' he murmurs. 'I really do.'

Josef picks up the discarded loop of twine, absent-mindedly wrapping it around his fingers to make it tighten and knot, take on new forms.

'Cat's-cradle?' I ask. 'My sister and I used to play the game in Marseilles.' I recall the hours Lara and I spent cross-legged on our chamber floor, the single cord binding us shape-shifting into one arrangement after another as if it were magic.

The information seems to shake Josef from his reverie and he holds out his hands. 'So what can you make?'

'A bird,' I say, lacing my fingers into the twine with his, 'like this ... and a butterfly, like this ...'

He watches enthralled, lashes flickering softly as he examines the altering forms in our hands.

'Now, what can *you* make?'

Josef pauses, contemplating. 'The old stone bridge ...' he replies, as his fingers pluck and bend, 'the chateau tower ...' He moves his hands again, but in his eagerness to coax the twine into its new shape, it tightens around the bones of my thumb.

'Ow!'

Josef does not hesitate. In less than an instant and in one flawless motion, he has drawn a silver folding pocket-knife out of his jacket and is cutting right through the twine. 'I do hope you're not hurt?'

I rub my hand, the pinch dulling already. 'Not at all. It is fine.'

He holds my gaze. A beat passes. Then he turns away. I try to understand what just happened between us. Whether anything did.

I imagine that Josef will stand up and leave, but he returns to leafing through the parchments distractedly, always coming back to the same drawing and appearing absorbed by the thing anew. The double portrait of my sister and me.

'Can I keep this?' he asks. 'Would you mind at all?'

Seconds pass before I can answer. 'Please, do.'

Children's Games

April, the following month

Lara

I am standing at our chamber window. The spring sunshine, weak though it is, pours through the casement, making my closed eyelids glow the colour of sliced peaches.

When I open them again I see Josef through the glass, coming along the final stretch of the track, hair smoothed sprucely back. He glances up at me, and I move away from the window and go down to him.

Josef is midway up the short front path when I open the door, and he appraises me a moment before glancing shyly to his feet. 'I like your hair that way,' he mutters.

My hands tap the sides of my head. I hadn't finished pinning my hair when I closed my eyes to the sunshine, leaving loose waves hanging from each temple.

'Happy birthday!' I say, pulling on the cap I hold. 'The sun has come out especially.'

In truth, the weather is still unseasonably cold, abnormally so for late April. The winter has been freakish and bitter, the death grip of the season long outlasting its usual span. Over the past months, outdoor labour has been suspended, men left without their wages as a result. The mills have iced up and each day more bodies are found, frozen and malnourished from lack of bread.

The people of France are growing increasingly desperate with every week that passes.

As Josef nears me now I see that he is carrying an object wound round with ribbon and sprigs of blossom. It looks like a small *fiole*. Cut-glass and sealed with an elaborate teardrop stopper.

'I came to give you this,' he says, putting it in my hand.

'Goodness—' I say, flustered, uncertain. 'Are you sure? It is I who should be giving a gift to you today, not the other way around.' I unwind the ribbon and remove the stopper. A thick, floral scent escapes the neck. 'Oh thank you,' I exclaim. 'I've never had proper cologne before.'

I hear my sister's tread behind me, pattering rapidly to the door and, still holding the length of ribbon, I place the *fiole* in the pocket of my apron.

'Happy birthday, Josef!' Sofi shouts from the doorway. '*Joyeux anniversaire!*'

'Thank you.'

'Or should I say . . . ' She pauses. '*Alles Gute zum . . . Geb-urt-stag!*'

He says nothing, seeming to be searching for the right words. He has not expected her to have learned the greeting in German, the result of her urging Aunt Berthé for at least the past fortnight to ask the Monsieur. I wonder why Josef is here today, wonder if it means Monsieur Wilhelm had nothing planned for his son's birthday. Maybe Josef found himself in need of company.

'Oh, and I have baked you a present,' my sister announces, not waiting for him to respond. 'I was going to drop it by the chateau later, leave it with my aunt.'

He looks amused by this. '*Baked*? In that case I wonder what it could be?'

But Sofi is too distracted to notice his quip. 'What's that?' she asks, pointing at the ribbon in my hand.

I open my mouth, unsure how to answer, knowing how hurt Sofi would be if she discovered that Josef had brought me a present, but not her.

'A gift for *you*, Sofi,' says Josef hastily, apparently as awkward as I.

He lifts the length of ribbon from my fingers, offering it out to her. It is the bright green of a chive leaf.

I watch as Sofi's expression is utterly transformed. 'Velvet!' she cries with delight, and fastens the ribbon around her throat. 'What a lovely colour.'

Josef turns back to me. 'Might I interest you in a walk to the river?'

'I'll come, too,' Sofi declares, glowing now.

At that moment, Mama appears in the doorway. 'Many happy returns, Master Oberst,' she says flatly. 'And, Sofia Thibault, you will be going nowhere this morning, since you are yet to finish your chores. Unlike your sister.'

Something about Mama's tone when she says this, clipped and resentful, pulls me up short, even though I have done everything she's asked of me this morning and she has acknowledged it.

'But—' starts Sofi.

I touch my forehead to hers. 'Come, Fi, don't be sad. We'll be back soon and can all enjoy your cake together.'

Sofi's smile evaporates as my words kindle anger. 'Thank you for completely spoiling the surprise,' she says drily. 'Josef knows it's a cake now.'

'I think I worked that much out for myself,' he replies, smiling.

As we head for the track, I look back to see Mama pushing a broom towards Sofi, her expression in daggers.

'That why you've been plaguing your aunt for kitchen scraps from the big house then, is it?' Mama mutters to my sister, gripping her wrist. 'Listen to me, Sofia. Steer clear of all that or you're in danger of making yourself a laughing stock, you mark my words.'

Sofi wriggles free of Mama's grasp, rubbing her arm.

'You'll be laying your coat over a puddle for him next,' our mother adds sourly. 'You should be ashamed of yourself.'

I glance at Josef, hoping he hasn't heard, not least for Sofi's sake, but his gaze is intent on the view beyond the factory forecourt. We pass it, following the far row of poplars lining the chateau's approach. We're not far from the river when Josef stops at a tree, drawing out the pocket-knife he always carries and putting its blade to the bark. It takes me a moment to recognise this tree, the same sycamore we picnicked under last autumn. The same tree from the tower wallpaper. We are on the other side of it now, nearer the river than the chateau gardens.

Josef starts to carve letters into the trunk and I recall the sensation that overcame me in the tower room that evening last November, when I was convinced I had seen my own life somehow mirrored in the wallpaper. I had been wrong, of course, foolish to be anxious about something so implausible. It was just a coincidence. And nothing like it has happened since.

'Josef,' I say, 'were you ever friends with anyone else here? Outside of working, I mean? Aside from us?'

He squints, not removing his gaze from the blade. 'Not really,' he says, gouging the bark. 'But you're Madame Charpentier's family. So sort of like my family, too.'

At the river the water dazzles, and dainty fawn caddisflies flit about us, so fast I can feel their tiny wing draughts on my face. I extend an arm and try to coax one to land on my finger. Josef looks over.

'The baby flies, as grubs underwater, build the most beautiful carapaces around themselves,' I tell him. 'From parts of the river-bed . . . little bits of silt, tiny twigs. For protection, while they change into flies.'

His eyebrows lift as though he might only be half-listening.

I think of something else to say. 'How does it feel to be seventeen?'

'No different to sixteen.' His attention drifts to the ground. He selects a flat, oval stone from the shore and rolls its worn circumference between thumb and forefinger.

Sofi's crestfallen expression at being left behind at the cottage washes through my mind. 'I wonder if my sister will bake me a cake on my birthday?' Although it is only a few months away it will be the first since we came here. 'It'll be strange not having Pa—'

'Watch!' Josef calls, his voice sudden as a cannon, too loud in the brisk air. He flicks his stone at the water, where it glances the surface and moves in a series of diminishing bounces before sinking. 'Can you do that?'

I stare at the river. Josef is so earnest, so diligent in the print-house as he completes his tasks or oversees the other workers. How different he seems outside these factory duties, how fond of games.

I choose a pebble and move closer to the shore, position my hand and focus on the point where I want the pebble to bounce. The water eddies darkly, our reflections silhouetted against it. Two figures skimming stones, the damson-skin hue of the river's rippling surface giving the impression we have been printed in hatching lines. Just like the tower wallpaper. Indeed, it feels as though, if I walked forwards, I would not find myself in water at all, but in a vignette, merging with Madame Justine until we became one figure.

I shiver, release the pebble too early. It breaks the water with a plop and then sinks.

'Pitiful!' Josef laughs.

I step away from the river, watching my reflection do the same. We skim more stones, but I cannot concentrate on the game. I know I'm being silly, letting that wallpaper and the woman in it haunt me when I should be enjoying the present. But I cannot seem to help it. The sky darkens, crowding with clouds.

'I think it will rain,' I say. 'Perhaps we should return to the cottage?'

'Let's go this way instead,' Josef answers and continues along the path.

Colin-Maillard

Lara

'Do you want to play a game?' he asks, when we reach the woodstore.

'We just played one,' I tease. 'Now you're seventeen you want to play more games than you did before.'

Josef shrugs. 'How about *Colin-Maillard*? Blind Man's Buff?'

'Can you play that with two people?'

'Let us try. If you want.' I mark how courteous he is, always asking if I want to do something before we do it. 'Fancy going first?'

'All right.'

'Close your eyes.'

'Do we not need a blindfold?' I say. 'It would feel like cheating otherwise. And I think the game's called Dead Man if you do not use one.'

He detaches a length of cotton from his cravat and offers it out. 'Will this do?'

I turn my back to him but he does not move. 'Come on, then,' I chivvy. 'Aren't you going to tie it?'

Finally, Josef reaches across my face and covers my eyes with the fabric. As he knots it behind my head, I feel his hands shudder. 'Not too tight?' he asks.

'No,' I reply. 'Now what?'

'Now I spin you around,' Josef says, and he does, once, so I am facing him.

'Don't you think you should spin me more than that?'

He takes my shoulders with his fingertips and turns me again.

'Ready,' he says vaguely, stepping away. 'Come and find me, if you can!'

I shuffle forwards, hands fumbling before me. I cannot hear Josef now, cannot hear him swerve around the woodstore to dodge my touch, cannot even hear him breathe. I wonder if he is holding his breath, begin to wonder if he has forgotten he is playing a game at all. I arc around the barn, toes stubbing logs, sensing my mouth spread and tense between amusement and concentration. Eventually, I come to a stop. I take one step, two, and the ends of my fingers graze his chest.

'Aha!' I exclaim.

Still Josef doesn't move. My palms pat softly against his front, feel their way upwards to his face. They come to rest at the sides of his cheeks, and I'm certain I feel them flushing instantly.

I perceive Josef's hands, reaching towards my own face to lift off the blindfold. The gesture is gentle, but slow and stiff. He is trying not to let his hands shake this time. As the blindfold comes free, so does my cap, fluttering to the floor like a large white moth.

'There you are,' I say.

He opens his mouth as if to speak but he does not, and is it my imagination, or are our faces inclining towards one another, tingling from the unfamiliar proximity? Our lips are but a whisper apart and then they are together, pressing thin skin onto skin. My racing pulse hammers hard against my bones.

I think of Guillaume and it feels like an age before I pull away. Josef stands there, immobile, looking neither lost nor found, my cap in his hand.

Wolf!

May, one month later

Sofi

Another Sunday, our one day of the week free from factory work. It is late afternoon, and Lara and I had planned to take our drawing things to the river, but after finishing our chores an hour ago, my sister took to our chamber with a headache instead. She is still plagued by them, ever since the accident. So, with Mama grudgingly granting me her permission, I leave the cottage by myself.

I decide to go to the river anyway, parchments and graphite in my apron pocket. Walking along the track, I see a figure I recognise in the distance, held in the palm of the forecourt.

'Sofi!'

I stop, smile. Give an enthusiastic wave.

'Off for a walk?' Josef asks, starting towards me.

'I am.'

'And where is your sister today?'

My smile dims a little. 'At home. With Mama.'

'Ah.' Josef runs a hand through the waves of hair on his crown. 'But it is nice to see you, anyhow.' He swivels, glancing at the chateau. 'I was just out for some air myself. The house can get a bit much at times. Mind if I join you?'

A dozen insects bump and quiver against the lining of my

stomach. 'No,' I answer, attempting to screw a lid on my delight at the question, 'not at all.'

We walk further than I expect, along the boundary of the chateau's gardens first, Josef going in front. As we pass that towering sycamore, a mark on its trunk catches my eye. Jagged lines, freshly cut. *J. O.* I briefly trace my fingers across Josef's initials, then continue to follow.

A breeze ruffles his shirt as he goes on ahead, carrying with it the smell of wild thyme. We are at the edge of the woods now, following a narrow meandering path, scarcely more than a bare line in the grass really.

'Old wolf track, so they say,' Josef remarks.

'Indeed?'

'Not scared of wolves, are you?'

'Of course not.'

He pauses, turning to face me. 'I am.' His expression is surprisingly grave, his voice solemn. 'My mother used to tell me a story when I was little. *Le Petit Chaperon Rouge. Little Red Riding Hood.* The wolf scared me witless but it was my favourite, as Mother would hold me extra tight when she told it. She knew how scared I was, you see.'

It is the second time he has raised the subject of his mother with me in almost as many months. I wonder if he does the same with Lara. 'Our father told us that story, too.'

'He did?'

'Well,' I reply, 'his version was a little different. The wolf in his story was starving, desperate. She ate Red Riding Hood because she had cubs to feed.'

Josef's brows hitch. 'A she-wolf.'

I nod. 'When the wolf saw Red Riding Hood, noticing the red of her cloak, the blue of her eyes, the whiteness of her skin, she bit off her head quite cleanly. To prevent her from suffering.'

'I see,' Josef says, continuing along the track. 'That *is* a different version.'

Eventually, he turns back to face the factory, choosing a spot just above the water. I have not known him to come here with Lara and the notion pleases me. The river is hidden from our vantage point, the view before us dominated by the vast expanse of sky above the meadow, a cut of pale cobalt cloth over green. The wind pushes the clouds across the open blue like a great parade, and Josef drops to the ground and points at them. 'What do you see?'

I go to where he is and sit down, too. 'Do you mean—?' I ask, not knowing what he means.

'In the clouds. What shapes do you see?'

My eyes dart from his face to the sky and back again many times while I wonder how to answer. 'I'm not sure,' I say at last. 'How about you?'

Josef searches the space above, left to right and back again. 'I can't see anything,' he replies, uprooting a handful of grass. 'That's just it.' There is a pause. 'It was another of the games my mother taught me, you know. She taught me lots.'

Once again, he mentions his mother. Once again, he mentions something he did with his mother that I also did with Pa.

'A long time ago,' he continues, smiling sadly. 'The game hasn't really been the same since. I don't see anything now.'

'My pa and I used to play something similar . . .' *Pa*. The word feels wrong in my mouth. It is the first time I have spoken it aloud to anyone other than Lara since the accident. I think, fleetingly, how strange it is that when someone dies our instinct is to shutter them away within our brains, to seal our lips and cease to speak of them aloud, as though any mention of that person might inflict some terrible injury on those left behind. It seems like the wrong way of living.

'. . . With marks, on parchment,' I go on. 'It was a drawing exercise. We had to find shapes within the marks, add our own to them and turn them into fully formed things.'

'Really?' he asks. He turns to me again, studies my face.

I want to tell him that it has not been the same for me either, not since Pa died, but I'm worried he will think I am just saying that because he has, just gushing it out to bring us closer in the moment. Yet it is true. My throat clenches.

'I'm sorry about your father,' he says. 'It can't be easy.'

'And I, about your mother.'

'Do you mind me asking what happened—'

I don't let him finish. The words spill out, unstoppable, like grain from a split sack. 'He was returning home one night when some ... men deliberately hurt his ponies. They were drunk, wouldn't get off the lane. The ponies bolted and Pa lost control of his wagon. It ... overturned.' My throat tightens with every syllable, until my voice grows so high I have to stop.

'Oh,' he says quietly.

It takes another minute of silence before I am able to talk again. 'I haven't spoken of it since.'

'I understand. I have not spoken of ... well, my mother, either.'

I look at him in disbelief. This is not how I thought the afternoon would go when I stumbled on him in the forecourt. I thought we would laugh together, as I have seen him do with Lara. Yet we came straight to this, two lakes undammed and sluicing forth the huge weight of their water. 'You have spoken of it with no one?'

Josef shakes his head. 'The worst thing was not being able to do anything. About any of it.'

I want to ask what he means exactly, what happened to his mother, as he asked about my father, but I don't want to risk spoiling what is between us at this precise second. Rather I should show him how mature I am, how I understand that if he wants to tell me, he will.

I picture that wallpaper in the tower. The scenes from his childhood forming the pattern, the vignettes of his laughing, light-haired mother. How free and how happy the both of them had looked, and it hits me then, with the force of thunder, how suddenly and shatteringly change can come, how we are powerless to stop it. How I no longer want to be powerless.

'I know exactly what you mean,' I say. 'I feel the same.'

I want to spurt more words at him then, explain how very glad I am that we met, that we are here now, in this moment. How lucky

I am, despite the misery of everything that has happened, to have found the very person in the world who understands me as well as I do him. How I began understanding him after studying those scenes in the tower wallpaper.

Josef lies back on the mossy grass as if suddenly exhausted and so do I. He adjusts his head a little to the right, causing his hair to brush against my cheekbone. His eyes close. I close mine also and there we lie, side by side like two effigies, faces blurred by the fast shadows of the scudding clouds above.

The Cupid-Seller

One week later

Sofi

As dawn seeps higher in the sky, I edge higher up the hill, keeping to the cover of the poplars, until, about twenty paces from the chateau, I suddenly stop. Josef is up ahead, right there near the doors of the building.

He has been busier with Monsieur Marchant of late, so I haven't seen him since that afternoon by the river, when we sat on the grass together and spoke about our parents, exchanged the most painful, intimate details of our lives. That is why I have come to the chateau this morning, in the hope of catching him, of asking whether we might walk to the wood above the river once more.

Josef is angled away from the approach, so I can only see him in a sort of half-view. He is pacing back and forth whilst smoothing his hair, which is flat and neatly powdered. His clothing is immaculate, too, unlike anything I have seen him wear before. He is dressed in a sea-green suit, culottes matching waistcoat matching jacket. There is lace at his neck, and his collar is set in a row of freshly pressed pleats. The clocks of his cream stockings are precisely aligned, one above each ankle. Despite the still-feeble light, I can even see the glint of his shoe buckles, the sheen of polished leather beneath.

The sight of him dressed this way makes me queasy. I have only ever seen him clad in plainer garments, which become him much better than these. He isn't the person such clothes make him seem, despite his father's wealth. Yet at the same time I cannot stop looking.

Josef withdraws something from one of the lower pockets of his waistcoat. It is not easy to tell what, even when I crane my neck to try to get a better view. He studies the object, and replaces it in the same pocket. Then he brings his heels together, draws himself up tall, and clears his throat.

In a low voice Josef speaks a sentence or two aloud, each with a different tone, before beginning the whole strange routine from the start. It is as if he is a player, about to perform some part upon the stage. I check myself. Why am I standing gawping when it is he I have come to see? But just as I am about to call out, he tugs his waistcoat straight a final time and goes inside.

I do not pause to consider what I should do, which is to heed my sister's warning and not be caught creeping about the chateau again. I simply follow him through the door and into the dim passageway regardless.

Josef comes to a halt at the far end of a long, polished floor. His back is to me, hand extending nervously upwards to the door in front of him. He sighs, curls his fingers, and knocks.

No response.

Josef knocks again, more agitated this time. 'Father?'

A very faint voice utters something from within, and at last he goes inside.

I wait a few seconds before stealing closer. The door has not been properly closed, but I dare not peek around it. Instead, glancing up and down the passageway to check there is no one else about, I step to the crack between the hinges and squint into the room.

From this position, I cannot see Josef at all. I can, however, see the Monsieur. And this room must be his study, the place in which he spends so many of his days, for he is seated behind a large bureau, set perpendicular to the door.

I remember what Aunt Berthé and Bernadette said about him being a recluse, not knowing how to interact with people since his wife's death. But I also remember our first day in the factory, how Josef's face shadowed when he spoke of his father. How I caught Monsieur Wilhelm staring through the office window so fixedly at my sister.

The Monsieur is planted in his chair, rigid as a board. Rather than looking at his son, he keeps his eyes firmly on his oxblood leather bureau-top, on the items ordered meticulously across it. Papers are clasped tidily together with silvered fastenings, globed glass paperweights polished clear as water drops. Sample-books are fastidiously stacked and quills line up with blotters that line up with ink pots.

'Father,' Josef begins, 'I trust you're well.'

Still Monsieur Wilhelm does not raise his eyes.

'I ...' Josef says uncertainly. 'I see the garden is looking well. Despite the inclement weather.'

The way he is speaking is so stiff and uneasy. His tone is strangled and my chest cramps for him. I want to step right into the room and take his hand.

Despite there being no reply, Josef continues. 'There is something I would speak to you about, Father.'

The Monsieur examines a small square of paper, printed with one of the factory's designs. 'Yes?' he answers crisply, not looking up.

'It is ... well, it is a delicate matter,' says Josef. 'It concerns a young lady.'

I press closer to the crack of the door and my forehead smacks against the wood. I pray they have not heard me, expecting the door to swing wide any moment and to be discovered, tingling and red-faced at what has just been said. But nobody moves. I run Josef's last five words over in my head.

'What I mean,' he goes on, 'is there is a young lady of whom I am very fond and ...' he pauses again, 'I believe she feels the same way ... and, well ... I wish to make her my wife.'

I cannot believe it. So this is why Josef is here, groomed and primped in these alien clothes. My hands start to shake.

'I have known the young lady in question for some months now, Father. It is my dearest wish that ...' Josef tries to slow himself. 'That you will permit me to ask for her hand in marriage.'

148

Some of his words have a familiar pattern to them, I recognise. They must have been amongst those sentences I heard him rehearsing outside. But his voice is much blander now, he is talking of the matter in the way a businessman would discuss a transaction. I wonder how he can possibly speak so of something that concerns the very wellspring of his happiness. Maybe it is all the language his father understands.

Monsieur Wilhelm gazes critically at the largest of his inkpots. 'It is my wish you make a good marriage,' he replies, at length.

I hear his voice properly for the first time, cold and colourless, a thick German accent sticking on the French and tripping over some of the words.

'Oh, thank—'

'However ...' His father steadies his elbows against the tabletop, fingers pressed into a spire. 'There is a family I have dealings with. A very old Versailles family who purchase often some of our best wallpapers. I am told they have a daughter, of marriage age.'

My stomach flips to my throat. The Monsieur already has a girl in mind for his son. And not only that, but a spoiled, pinched little thing from Versailles.

'I have not seen the young lady in flesh,' the Monsieur continues, in his broken French. 'But her portrait shows her very handsome. And her father wishes most dearly for her to be married. His staff have been making enquiries for a suitable match.'

Another pause.

'They are a very good family. Good blood. A good dowry—'

'With respect, Father,' Josef cuts in, 'the young lady I am referring to, she is also from a good family, a hard-working and honest one—'

'Is not that easy,' the Monsieur barks, resentful of the interruption. 'What you need understand is how difficult running a factory is nowadays, a large house. Is a costly business.' He pushes his chin indignantly to his chest, and the loose flesh of his neck bunches together.

If the man thinks running an extravagant house so difficult, he should try a day in the dye-house on half a crust of bread. He should try making ends meet on a worker's wage as the taxes rise, as the price of grain climbs ever higher. In devising this marriage for his son, he is thinking only of himself, of preserving his wealth. Does he not recall the events of the previous month? Jean-Baptiste Réveillon, the owner of his own wallpaper factory in Paris, had spoken at a debate, made a comment about workers' wages. Days later, a riot ensued. Dozens were left dead and Réveillon's factory razed to the ground.

'Pardon me, but have you forgotten what happened to Monsieur Réveillon, Father?' Josef exclaims. 'Surely our workers would prefer their new mistress *not* to be a member of the aristocracy?'

'From what I heard, Réveillon's remarks were misunderstood,' the Monsieur returns. 'There is no doubt, financially, that this marriage would be beneficent. Not just for now, but the future. *That* is my concern.'

'And that is my concern, too,' Josef urges. 'However, this young lady is from a family who has worked loyally here with us for many months . . .' His voice trails off as he evaluates whether to continue. 'The Thibaults.'

My own last name is deafening in the passageway's cool air. The blood rushes to my head, and I press a hand to the wall to steady myself.

Everything inside the room has fallen quiet. I will the Monsieur to respond, to say something to break the silence, to say anything to reveal what he thinks of his son's last words. But he merely sits, rigid again. I can guess full well what is ticking through his head. That even though our name is as old a family name as whatever these nobles are called, it has no country estates, no wealth to recommend it. That, to men like him, power and breeding and privilege will always prevail.

Moments pass.

'My intentions towards Mademoiselle Thibault are entirely honourable, Father,' Josef suddenly blurts.

Again, silence.

'*You* married for love, Father.' Josef's voice rings loud and desperate, the end of every word running into the next.

Monsieur Wilhelm squirms uncomfortably in his chair, as though trying to quash an unsought memory. At that precise moment, the still-rising sun falls into the room in a strip of pure golden light. As it does, the Monsieur looks properly at his son for the first time, and it is impossibly strange. His demeanour alters, his countenance overwhelmed by wonderment, as though he is gazing on the face of the Madonna herself. He shifts forwards, and it seems that he will rise from his chair or reach out to Josef at last.

'I only want the best, you know,' the Monsieur mutters. 'I always have.'

There is another long pulse of swollen silence, in which father looks at son and son at father. Then the sun goes in and the golden moment is gone.

The Monsieur moves his eyes to his papers once more. 'Well, that is all,' he says. 'Now you may go.'

I trip, groggy as a sleepwalker at the scene I've just witnessed, down the passageway and back outside. The clipped box borders of the chateau's gardens form sharp lines of green, bellflowers nodding above them like amethysts. Despite one of the harshest winters in living memory, and then one of the driest springs, these plants have flourished once more. Despite everything that has happened, I heard what Josef just said. My fingertips brush the green ribbon at my throat. After those hours we spent by the river, surely it must have been me he was speaking about to his father.

I hold the notion, precious as one of those amethysts, in my hand. I will never let it go.

The Royal Park

Versailles, one week later

Hortense

I am out on a carriage ride. With my father, of all people, and only my father, despite the fact I can count on one finger the number of times we have ever done anything together in the past. We are some distance from the Royal Park now, the two of us, locked inside this gilded box, moving along a nondescript lane somewhere outside the capital.

The particularly odious thing about travelling by carriage of late is the stinking beggars that converge at every roadside. There seems to be no escaping them. Whenever one peers from a window, there they are. Hollow eyes staring at the passing traffic, clavicles sticking from their fronts like mantels. Always complaining about their lack of bread, their inability to find work, the cost of living. Yet, as I've often heard said at Versailles, not one of them seems at all inspired to do anything about improving their situation. I fancy I can smell them through the glass. As if also repulsed by their stench, my sweet Pépin burrows his nose into my skirts until only his small auburn derriere is visible.

I catch my reflection in the carriage window. There isn't a woman amongst those vagrants who looks younger than seventy, yet I doubt they are very much older than I.

'Really, Papa, must we go much further?' I ask.

My father makes a noise in the back of his throat, as though a bone from last night's trout is lodged there.

'I do apologise, Papa, but I didn't hear you,' I say.

He flusters awhile before coming out with it. 'I'm afraid so, my dear. You see, there was something I had thought to speak to you about.'

I give no answer but fix my eyes upon him.

'It concerns your marriage, in fact. As your mother has no doubt informed you, since there are no suitable matches left at Versailles, my man has been making enquiries elsewhere.'

I curse myself then for not having been able to predict his machinations before we left the palace, for remaining ignorant of the true reason for this impromptu outing. After I have processed his words, I try to concentrate, make a mental list of the eligible young nobles whose family estates are further away from the palace. But the atmosphere in the carriage turns leaden, and I begin to sense that something is awry, that I am stumbling blindly down the wrong path altogether.

'Indeed, Papa,' I say, 'there are several families elsewhere in the country that Mama has high hopes of my marrying into.' I mention my mother again deliberately. I have no idea which dolt my father has lined up for me now, but I'm willing to wager my best diamond droppers that if the man is not a noble, my father will not yet have broached the subject with Mama.

'I do . . .' Papa continues, 'have a young man in mind already, in fact.'

So, the man is *young*. I should be grateful, at least, that Papa is not planning to bind me in holy matrimony to a man with liver spots and wilting buttocks.

'Indeed, Papa? And may I ask who this gentleman might be?' Better to gather some facts than to fly at him yet, I reason.

His face brightens, my response encouraging him to divulge more details. 'He is a handsome young man from what I can gather, with much to recommend him.'

'At which estate does his family live, Papa? Would I know of them?'

He hesitates. 'I doubt it, my dear. Though they reside just a short distance from Paris. To the south-west.'

'A short distance from the city, you say?' I bring the tip of my index finger to my chin, as though pondering this mysterious stranger's identity. 'I know, the de la Tours! Or the Marbot-Lavals?'

'Ah, no,' my father answers. 'The young man in question is called Josef—'

I search my mind for anyone I can recall by that name.

'Josef Oberst. Son of Wilhelm Oberst.'

My mind remains a blank parchment at first, but in that last word chimes some dreadful recognition. *Oberst. Wilhelm Oberst.* And then I remember with an almighty clang where it is I have heard the name before and recoil in disgust. The apartment refurbishments, the sheeted furniture. 'Surely you do not mean that German who supplies your wallpaper?'

My father sucks in his breath and gazes from the window.

'Papa!'

'My dear, do not dismiss the family so readily. Allow me to explain. Wilhelm Oberst is quite a rich man. He has a fine . . . ' he corrects himself, 'a *somewhat* fine house, a respectable income, has made many wise investments. All that will be his son's, you know.'

I slump back against the seat.

'Young Josef will soon be very wealthy. I hear his father has never been quite right since his wife died.' He circles a finger at his temple as he says this, as if to convey intellectual impediment. 'He might still be able to run his business, but I understand he scarcely leaves the place these days. His son will come into his fortune sooner rather than later. You mark my words.'

So, he *has* told Mama, for this is exactly the kind of point she would have raised. I am incredulous that she has managed to keep the matter a secret, let alone acquiesced to Papa's plans, agreed to have a mere tradesman as a son-in-law.

'Apart from the obvious difficulties in finding a suitable match for you closer to home,' my father prattles on, 'you are surely aware of the state of the country at present. The famines, the grain riots. How else do you explain . . . ' his gloved hand gestures at the window, 'such people. It is the common view that the likes of us are to blame for the country's debts, obscene as that sounds. That your mother's escaped pets, even – her finches and so on – are responsible for deci-mating the people's crops. We need to be seen to be willing, at least. To not be so entirely preoccupied by our own bubble.'

I offer no reply.

'And you, my dear,' Papa continues. 'It surely isn't news to you that you can be somewhat . . . *trying* on occasion. With the dowry I'm forced to offer as a result . . . well, this factory owner's son is far more likely to tolerate such behaviour than someone of your own standing.'

What certainly isn't news is that my father has no understanding of me at all. I think his speech ridiculous and again turn my face to the glass. There are even more beggars out there now, lingering along the thoroughfares. Scrappy, tanned things with far more of a resemblance to scarecrows than civilised humans. I think of that gaunt mob of chimpanzees in the Ménagerie Royale, setting upon the nobleman and tearing off his skin.

Suddenly, I'm bilious. The air is stifling, the atmosphere unyield-ing. I beat my fan at my face, loosen the window in the hope of fresh air. But the stink from outside wafts in, and I have no choice but to snap it shut again.

Scenes from Ancient Myth

Jouy-en-Jouvant, one week later

Lara

Josef has me working in a different part of the print-house today, at the printing tables on the lower floor. The air here is busy with noise, with workers calling instructions between them, the jangle of the chains from which the printing blocks are suspended, the tamping of wood into dye and the wet crinkle the paper gives when the blocks are lifted free of its surface. There is something hypnotic about the process. First one scene appears on the blank paper, then two, three, four. It is like watching the progression of a life, one moment at a time.

It is my task this morning to gather the waste cuts of paper for disposal. I pluck the curls of unwanted pattern from the tables and the floor, feed them into the sack I carry. I must start at the end of one table and work my way along it, proceed to the next and move along that one in the same way, until I have travelled up and down all four tables.

Four designs are being printed today, each at a different table. Scenes from ancient myth in varying colours. Pygmalion and Galatea in bronze, Apollo and Daphne in gold, Icarus in bold red madder. The Cupid and Psyche pattern in a deep and dusty indigo is my favourite. Every vignette is exquisitely composed, the full rose-heads of Psyche's garden bending gracefully from one scene to the next.

Like the chapters of a book, each section of the pattern shows a new part of the tale. Here is the beautiful Psyche being borne by Zephyrus. Here is Venus, Cupid's equally beautiful mother. And here is Cupid himself, a length of wool tied about his eyes.

I pluck up the discarded paper scraps, glance at them briefly, drop them into my sack. Pluck, glance, drop. The repetition is calming. Pluck, glance, drop. Pluck, glance—

I stare at the paper off-cut in my hand. Its bottom and left edges are razor-straight, the top and right ones torn in two fat curves, the whole thing almost forming the shape of a heart. But when I go to dip the piece into the sack I have to draw it out again. Motion stops, time collapses. The scene printed on it, I realise, is disconcertingly familiar.

This particular vignette should show a blindfolded Cupid, but it does not, for the picture has changed. There in the print, lips parted and fumbling hands extended in front of her, is a blindfolded woman. She is fair-haired, no longer clad in the drapes of antiquity, but wearing altogether more contemporary dress. And she is not alone. A young man is watching her intently, expression utterly rapt.

These figures are not Cupid and Psyche, I know. They are far too close, too familiar, the timber-walled structure they are in could almost pass for a woodstore, their strange interaction a game. *Blind Man's Buff*. It feels as though my mind has blown clear of my body like a seed from a stem, that I am watching the scene play out from afar, a scene I have already lived. My body starts to buzz with a vertiginous panic.

'Oi!' a man shouts. 'Get out of the way!'

His voice makes me start. I apologise and jerk forwards, the paper I am holding falling to the floor. I scramble to retrieve it, searching frantically through the off-cuts at my feet for that all-too-familiar scene. At first I am certain that I will not be able to find it, that even if I do locate the correct scrap, the image will have faded from it entirely, the woman dissolved to an indigo ghost. But then I do find it, and what I see now in its pattern is somehow even more alarming than before.

There on the paper the figure remains, in the exact same posture. But it is a woman no longer. It is Cupid, his lips parted, hands extended in front of him, a length of wool around his eyes. At his side is Psyche, watching entranced. And behind them both, the timber-walled structure isn't that at all, I see, merely the knotted, upright trunks of densely positioned trees.

I examine the paper's blank reverse before turning it over once again. Two cut edges and two torn ones forming the shape of a heart. I could have sworn that, not a minute ago, this off-cut showed a very different scene. How can this be?

Hastily stuffing the scraps into the sack I continue my task, taking care this time not to glance down at them. Pluck, drop. Pluck, drop. I cannot abide to look at those paper pieces again. I cannot trust what I might see there.

Once the sack is full, I align its mouth over the waste-basket exactly, so none of the papers inside can flutter to the floor. As I shake free the last of them, like the blindfolded Cupid, I make sure my eyes are closed.

Birds on a Flowering Tree

Versailles

Hortense

The morning the Obersts are due at Versailles, there is a succession of nervous tappings at my chamber door. First comes my lady's maid, Mireille, whom I ignore. Next arrives Adrien de Pise. I ignore him, too. I might have known he would be here today, the slithering wretch. I can picture him in the passageway, with his below-average looks and even slimmer intellect. He will be overly dressed for the occasion, no doubt, with the sole purpose of proving he is a worthier suitor than this Josef Oberst. Luckily for me, Papa wouldn't hear of a match with a fortuneless social grasper such as de Pise. He is useful to have around, however, like a well-placed chamber-pot. Useful, though usually full of shit.

Mama is next to arrive. '*Ma petite!* Won't you come out, my darling?'

'Go away!'

From my chamber windows, I see a coach approach, watch as a boy begins to disembark—

'Dar-ling!' my mother's voice coos again.

'*Laisse-moi tranquille!*' I spit and fling a hairbrush at the doors so I can be left alone to concentrate.

I determine from my position at the window that the boy is fair-haired, but can make out little more. The man who is with him strides silently to the entrance and the boy follows, as though edging towards the lair of a dangerous beast. It only then crosses my mind that he might have as many objections to this so-called match as I. A footman opens the door and they disappear inside.

I check myself in the looking-glass. I am still in my night attire, so this Josef Oberst, if he is to see me at all, may wait for me to properly dress. De Pise's voice slinks from further up the passageway.

'Good day, gentlemen,' he declares, a note of haughtiness about his voice. 'The Marquis du Pommier will join you in a few moments. Meanwhile, some refreshments?' I can see straight through him. He has only come here today to scrutinise my intended, for he has no need to hover like a minion, offering drinks to these Obersts as though he was a manservant.

I hear the men advance towards the second-best salon – Mama's salon – the one dominated by her hideous birdcage. She has most likely arranged this especially, assuming I shall take advantage of the proximity of the room to my chamber and oversee what is happening. She is, of course, correct.

Ensuring Pépin is still at rest on his cushion, I pull the door open a sliver, peering out to see two footmen following our guests, each bearing a golden tray. On one sits a gilded mocha pot, matching cups and spoons. On the other, two scallop-shaped dishes of petit fours, thick with cream and gold leaf. The salon door is left open and I observe the Obersts within, gaping at the birdcage, at its golden bars, inlaid jewels, potted vines and filigreed loveseat. At the lengths of mirror curving tightly around one half of its inside. At the quick, whirring creatures it contains.

'The Marquis Philippe-François du Pommier,' de Pise announces, performing a servant's task once more, and Papa enters.

'Ah, Monsieur Oberst!'

'Marquis, is an honour to meet you,' the other man replies, so stiffly it makes him shake. 'Please, allow me to introduce to you my son, Josef.' At this point in the proceedings, Wilhelm Oberst changes languages, adding laboriously in English, 'My son *and* my sun, the light of my life.'

Papa looks at the man with bewilderment, and I infer the remark must be a piece of spectacularly awful wordplay. My father takes a step to the side as though avoiding the pun, and I see Josef Oberst's face properly for the first time. He is handsome enough, but his demeanour is as awkward as his father's, though in a very different way. His countenance is traced with anguish, his cheeks colouring at his father's remark. His right hand, I notice, keeps dipping into the pocket of his waistcoat to fidget with something.

Papa, barely taking an interest in the man I am to marry, continues to converse only with Oberst Senior. 'I shall speak frankly, Monsieur,' he says, 'since, as you see, my daughter is not here to greet you. In recent years, her behaviour ... well, it has become ...' He pauses and runs the index and middle fingers of each hand across his forehead, as though soothing an ache. 'Rather unusual.'

The impudence, to purposefully broadcast such information. My lips tighten.

Josef Oberst shoots an exasperated, imploring look at his father, but Wilhelm Oberst's eyes remain planted on Papa.

My father lowers his voice conspiratorially and I strain my ear to the gap in the doors. 'I should not say this, but I'm afraid her mother hardly helps matters.'

Again Wilhelm Oberst says nothing, and I remember what my father told me in the carriage, that this man hasn't been all there since his wife died.

'Women,' Papa continues, realising no answer is forthcoming. 'Querulous creatures. They quite wear one down. Please, sit.'

Wilhelm Oberst rigidly lowers himself into an armchair, while his son selects a chaise. I see de Pise hovering near the window, continuously examining Josef Oberst through narrowed eyes. How obvious he is.

'My daughter, ah ...' Papa pauses, trying, it seems, to recall my name. 'Hortense, yes. Hortense is somewhat out of sorts currently, in fact.'

'Out of sorts how?'

This time it is Josef Oberst who speaks. He has an interesting voice, hollow and uncertain, yet there is a richness to it, a nap like velvet.

'After breakfast, Hortense became quite convinced that her pet dog had taken against chartreuse,' Papa says. 'She retreated to her rooms and has refused to leave them since.'

'Chartreuse?' Josef Oberst asks. 'Another dog?'

'Ah, no,' answers Papa, wearily massaging his brows again. 'Chartreuse. The colour.'

'Well, perhaps an hour in her room or thereabouts—' Wilhelm Oberst begins.

'No, Monsieur.' Papa looks at him as though he has not understood. 'The episode occurred after breakfast . . . one week ago.'

This had been my ruse once Papa told me I was to be married into trade. I took advantage of a tried and trusted tactic, inventing some excuse about Pépin being averse to the colour of the cushions, throwing a little fit and removing myself to my chambers. There, I decided, I would try to calm myself, to mull everything over and take steps to resolve the situation. However, when, in the week that followed, no other scheme presented itself, I knew there was no choice left to me but to let the interview with this Oberst boy happen and take matters from there. Perhaps I should also have told Papa that Pépin didn't like Germans.

At that moment Mama appears, as amply upholstered as the salon's bolster cushions, yet still dwarfed in the room's entrance.

'I hear you, François!' she announces in a false, insouciant tone.

'My dear, here we have Monsieur Wilhelm Oberst and his son Josef, the young Master Oberst,' Papa responds hurriedly. 'Gentlemen, this is my wife, the Marquise Jeanne-Madeleine du Pommier.'

At this, Mama sets about scrutinising Josef Oberst, waddling around him as though he is some stud at a horse sale. 'Not at all bad, I suppose,' she declares. 'Tall, handsome enough, clear eyes . . . a tolerable jaw.'

Papa tries to ignore this. 'My dear, might you ask Hortense to come and be introduced to these gentlemen, please?'

'That rather depends upon whether the dog has recovered,' Mama retorts, clicking her fan shut. 'You know how she dotes on him.'

'I did inform our daughter that her company would be desired this morning,' Papa says, his nerves fraying as another rejection flashes on the horizon.

'Oh, very well!' Mama flaps her arms, looking, in all her layers of white feathers and lace, like a corpulent snow goose attempting to take flight.

Closing the chamber door silently, I assume a position on the bed, as though I had been there all along.

Old Breeds

Hortense

Aware I must eventually surrender, I nevertheless steadfastly refuse to meet Josef Oberst for more than half an hour, during which time Mama's face flushes to the colour of an overripe strawberry.

I have a maid bring in a selection of the petit fours, while Mireille drags her bones into the chamber to dress me and arrange my hair. I watch the woman in the looking-glass, hooded eyes conducting a rheumy examination of every pin she affixes to my wig. Widowed young and childless, I believe she had once been nursemaid to the Marquis de Launay – Governor of the Bastille – and thought of him as her son, though I forget now the particulars. One of my father's less interesting anecdotes.

As I am pinned and preened, I hear Mama announce to the waiting parties, 'Gentlemen, you are honoured. My daughter will join us shortly. Go, go!'

This last command is directed at the maids she has taken into the salon with her. The girls have been instructed to see to it that anything containing the merest traces of green or yellow is removed from the room. *Chartreuse.* A nice touch on my part and the only morsel of control I am afforded. I rather think those Obersts are supposing the Queen herself is about to materialise.

When my reflection in the looking-glass pleases me, I dismiss Mireille and, scooping Pépin from his resting place, move into the passageway. The salon doors are closed now, with de Pise lurking

164

outside. I would not put it past him to have been watching me dress through the keyhole.

'Ravishing,' he murmurs, wetting his lips. 'As ever.'

I fire off a smile and he opens the salon doors, declaring, 'Mademoiselle Hortense du Pommier.'

'Our darling Hortense, here she is,' says Mama, ushering me in before her to prevent me from absconding. 'Come, your favourite seat is ready.'

I glide into the room, feeling the eyes of the Obersts upon me, and arrange myself on a chaise. With Pépin on my lap, I order my skirts, an ensemble of apricot and cream chiffon and my fullest petticoats.

When I glance up again, I see Wilhelm Oberst and his son gaping wide-eyed at my dog, prompting the little thing to start trembling and showing his teeth, and I cannot say I blame him. If propriety allowed, I should find myself doing the same. 'Look away!' I tell them and shush the creature. 'You're making him feel threatened.'

'Monsieur Oberst,' says Papa, 'shall we adjourn to the gallery?'

They file out of the salon and a long pause ensues. I do not believe it is I who should break this awkward silence, so say nothing, instead staring at the Oberst boy whilst running a hand across Pépin's soft fur. It is up to a young man to dazzle a lady with his charm and wit, is it not? And yet here is Josef Oberst, pressing his palms uncomfortably together, the faintest sheen of sweat across his brow.

At length, he speaks. 'Does your dog have a name?'

My pet, seeming to know he is being talked about, responds by flattening back his ears.

'If you really must know,' I reply, 'his name is Pépin.'

Another pause.

'What breed is he?'

Josef Oberst, I deduce, knows nothing about fashion. I look to the ceiling to warn him he is already in danger of boring me. 'Don't you know? He's a Pomeranian. A breed that originates in Germany. Like your father.'

The Oberst boy makes no reply.

'It's a very elegant breed, the envy of many other ladies,' I continue, and straighten the animal's cravat. 'I have his outfits coordinated to mine.'

Josef Oberst offers out the back of his hand for my pet to sniff, but Pépin is up on his haunches in an instant, growling and snapping his jaws together. 'Oh, shhh,' I whisper, amused, and lavish kisses on the creature's head. He quietens but continues to bare his teeth, giving the impression of a demented smile.

'You won't be able to control him, if that is what you seek,' I tell the Oberst boy. 'He's an old breed.'

The birds in the cage chitter behind us, flight feathers thrumming incessantly against the bars like gloved fingers.

Whiteness

Hortense

The rest of the interview is over quickly and passes without event. I retire to my chamber and cross to the window, sliding the lower pane upwards to sit below it, my ear to the glass.

The Obersts exit the building and proceed to the coach, their talk muffled nonsense at first, coalescing into sentences beneath my chamber window.

'That such a family would even consider a factory owner's son suitable for their daughter . . .' Wilhelm Oberst mutters, picking up his pace as though desperate to return to said factory.

'That is because no man of her own class would put up with her.'

My blood rises. I am surprised by how blunt Josef Oberst's words are.

'Her manner makes her one of the least attractive girls I've ever known,' he goes on. 'And her dog is equally as loathsome.'

They near the waiting vehicle. I hope it has a wheel loose.

'Yes, the little dog. Such a character,' says Wilhelm Oberst, an ominous edge to his voice that I had not detected earlier. 'You will have to learn how to deal with them both—'

The coach doors shut and I hear no more.

I steady my breath and hold the cold backs of my hands to my cheeks, my pulse leaping. I've not the faintest notion why their words have elicited such a reaction from me, I would not usually care two straws for the opinions of the likes of the Obersts.

As I look straight ahead and force my breath to slow, the

chamber's wallpaper catches my eye. The product of the Oberst factory. I usually do everything I can to avoid it, have never stopped to examine the scenes it comprises, a collection of supposed rural idylls populated by peasants. It is one of these vignettes that arrests me now, and I move towards the wall as Pépin scrambles free of my arms to scuttle beneath the bedstead.

Two boys stand in the centre of the scene, tattily dressed in rough, labourers' clothes. They are holding something between them, a smaller object, lifting it to the sky. At first glance one might think they were marvelling at the article, raising it in admiration as though rare and precious. But this is not what the vignette shows. I draw closer, my cheeks clammy, my flesh, in fact, cold all over.

The item the boys hold is a tiny songbird. Yet they are not holding it, they are tearing it, rending it between them and ripping it asunder. One of the creature's wings has already been plucked free. It flutters to the ground like a jewelled shred of vellum, impotent in the breeze.

I seize one of the petit fours from the dish and smear it across the wall, obliterating the scene to whiteness.

Chicks

Jouy-en-Jouvant, the following month

Lara

Down by the old stone bridge, the water is stiller than usual. The country is in the grip of yet another drought, which has turned river to brook, hardened its banks and made fired clay of the earth. Crops are struggling again and tension is growing. There is already little enough grain to go around.

I adjust my cap. I have misplaced the one I usually wear and this new garment is stiffer, itchier against my skin. It is a Sunday and Mama has kept Sofi back for a chore. I'd originally gone out intending to find a quiet place to sketch. Then Josef happened upon me and we're now sitting overlooking what is left of the water, watching the slow whirlpools below us, the lagging jetsam. Josef has hardly said a word since he got here. I wonder what he is thinking.

'You're quiet today,' I say, but he does not hear. 'Quieter than usual.' With Josef not at work in the print-house as much, it has been a while since we last spoke.

He cuts the end off a stick with his pocket-knife and throws it to the water.

'What is the matter?'

'It's my father . . .' he begins, but his voice falters.

'I am sorry to hear it. Is he unwell?'

Josef locks his gaze on the furthest bank of the river, where a moorhen is paddling along the trickle of water, trailed by four fuzzy chicks. 'He had me accompany him on a trip to Versailles.'

My eyes widen. 'That is good! It shows he trusts you to deal with his most important clients.'

'Important?' Josef snorts. 'Odious would be a better word.'

The force of his contempt throws me. 'But they're just clients?' I offer. 'It is all part of doing business, is it not?'

There is a pause. 'He means . . .' he starts, flounders, then blurts the words as one. 'He means to marry me to a girl there. Very soon.'

The moorhen has stopped swimming to entice her brood close to the drying reeds. They crowd around her, waving their tiny, un-formed wings, begging to be fed.

Josef nods towards them. 'Look pathetic, don't they?' he says. 'Those stupid little stubby wings. Utterly helpless without the adult bird.'

I frown. 'I think—' I begin, but he cuts me off, spinning to face me and taking my wrists in his hands.

'It is the last thing I want to do,' he says, his eyes even paler than usual. 'You must know that?'

I look down at his fingers, curled around my bones, and recall what happened between us in the woodstore on his birthday. A knot forms in my throat.

'Surely there are your father's wishes to consider, though,' I say. 'The business—'

Josef shrugs me off and leaps to his feet as though startled by gun-fire. 'My father's wishes, indeed!' he cries and turns abruptly from the riverbank.

After a few pained seconds, he brushes down his culottes and straightens his collar. 'I should be getting back now,' he says.

Calissons

Lara

On the way back to the cottage, I see Sofi, sitting at the edge of the meadow.

'I finished my chores already and tried to find you,' she says. 'Where have you been?'

I glance over my shoulder, still trying to make sense of my interaction with Josef. I debate whether to tell Sofi about it, decide not. 'Just sketching,' I reply, holding up my paper. 'Near the river.'

I expect her to press me more, to enquire if Josef had been there, too, but she doesn't. There has been a change in my sister recently, a distractedness dissipating her anger. I suppose it started in part not long after we came to the factory. But around a month ago, she became a little cheerier, softer. The sharp, unwieldy edges of her torment blunted. I do not know what prompted it, but I am happy for her.

'What a surprise, me, too!' Sofi beams, waving her parchment.

I go over and sit next to her, and she pushes a twist of hair behind her ear as she studies my paper. 'There's nothing there!'

'Yes,' I reply. 'Didn't get anything done, I'm afraid.'

'We've swapped places, in that case,' Sofi remarks. 'It used to be I who didn't practise.'

I consider her words for a moment, spot the embellished oval-shaped sketch on her parchment, the three figures nestled at its centre. I realise I haven't seen many of my sister's sketches for some time, though I have noticed her board folder fattening with new work. 'May I see?'

171

She seems reticent at first, before placing the paper on my lap.

'Goodness,' I smile. 'I remember that day!'

On the page before me is a single scene. A morning from our childhood in Marseilles, when Mama had been in a temper about something, and Pa had taken us out. We had ended up amongst the stalls at the market, and Pa had exchanged a coin for our favourite Provençal candies. *Calissons*, shaped like petals or smiles, the sweet almond centres sweeter still against their sharp, citrus toppings.

'I love it, Fi,' I tell her. 'What a lovely memory, you've captured us exactly. You are improving so much. Every day.'

'I must be, in that case,' she replies. 'For you're the second person to have told me so.'

I ask her what she means, but she simply utters, 'Oh, just Mama,' and wraps an arm around my shoulders. I nudge my head against hers, my eyes lingering on her sketch. A moment from our childhood, caught and held on the parchment. A moment we will never live again.

'Sofi—' I start, the words failing. I have the sudden desire to tell her what I've so far kept fast to myself. How when I look at the wallpaper my head hurts and my vision swims and I can no longer trust what I see. How it seems like I am reliving the paper's pattern, and there is nothing I can do to stop it.

'What?' Sofi asks.

I take in her expression, her earnest dark eyes, less troubled than they were. I do not wish to ruin this, do not want to worry her.

'Nothing,' I answer.

The Little Toper

—

Sofi

Something has brought me to the window of our chamber, and I peer through the glass. It is dark out tonight, despite the month, the moon reduced to a fingernail clipping. I squint up towards the Obersts' chateau, as I do every night, but I don't see any lights on.

Then suddenly a shape appears, careening out of the blackness, and though I know it is him instantly, his movements astound me. Josef falters, zigzagging along the track all the way to the cottage door. There he stops, swaying to the ground as though taking up a handful of stones. I snatch my jacket and, careful not to wake Lara, fumble for a candle and race down the stairs.

By the time I reach him, Josef is attempting to aim the first of the stones at our chamber window. Fresh scuffs stand out on the leather of his shoes and the unnatural pink of his cheeks is visible even in the dark.

'Josef!' I call quietly. 'What are you doing?'

He swivels unsteadily towards me and bows. 'Mademoiselle!'

I would laugh, but his manner prevents it.

'I'm here for ... for ... well ...' The words that escape his lips run into one indistinct sound. It makes little sense and carries with it the stench of alcohol.

'Oh, you have been drinking,' I say, more reproachfully than I intend. I cannot keep the disappointment from my voice, not least since his looks have changed with his manner. Josef's eyes are unfocused, unable to remain on my face and drifting all over. When he

173

is not speaking his mouth falls slack, and a lock of dark blond hair is plastered to his brow with sweat. I have never seen him like this before.

His gummed words and careless movements prompt a memory to stir, one I've managed to keep down for weeks. But it rises now, like pus to the surface of a wound. That night at the horse-pond, those lurching, leering men the worse for drink, stinking and swearing and striking at the ponies.

Josef opens his hand to select a stone and tries to align it with our chamber window once more. Not only is it ridiculously large for the task, but he has no need to summon me this way, since I am standing right in front of him. In his state all judgement has gone.

'No!' I hiss. 'You'll break the glass!' I unwrap his fingers with my own and angle his palm so the rest of the stones fall to the ground. For a second my hand remains folded over his, and I consider leading him inside the cottage, to sit him down and lay something cool upon his brow. Then he stumbles backwards and forces us apart.

As he does, an object drops to the ground from one of his pockets. It only gives the briefest movement as it falls, but that is enough to catch my eye. Before Josef even knows what has happened, I have reached down and picked it up.

The light from my candle reveals it to be a smallish piece of paper. For a moment I think it might even be a sample of wallpaper, but then I see what it is and recognition hits me like a punch to the gut. It is a drawing, *my* drawing. The one I gave to him that day in the cottage, the one of Lara and me. Yet now it is completely ruined, torn so that only the likeness of my sister remains.

I realise with a plunging, crashing heart how stupid I've been, how wrong. This past month I have been fooling myself, hoping against hope he meant me when he gave his speech in his father's study that day. But he meant Lara all along.

Josef snatches the paper from my grip and hastily shoves it back in his pocket. His action, crude and heavy-handed, accidentally knocks my candle away, extinguishing the flame.

'She doesn't love you, you know,' I tell him, eyes smarting. 'She has someone else.'

'Wha—' he begins, my words slowly sinking in. 'What do you mean?'

I say nothing, chin thrust out, lips taut.

'Sofi?' He steps towards me, and I have to hold my breath to avoid his. 'Please—'

His hip bone presses to mine and there is a pain in my throat, and I cannot help myself. 'There was a boy . . . a young man . . . back in Marseilles. He helped with our deliveries.'

Josef starts to laugh.

'Lara and he, they were—'

'No.' He makes this one small utterance like the matter is ended and before I can speak again he has turned back to the chamber window as though he has already forgotten it. 'Lara—!' he shouts, and I try to hush the sound.

My sister emerges from the house, a jacket fastened over her chemise. 'What is happening?' she whispers. 'You'll wake Mama!'

'Ah, here she is!' declares Josef. 'Mademoiselle Thibault!'

Lara doesn't look at me, but attempts to pull him into the darkest part of the track, further away from the cottage. 'Thank you, Fi. Go back inside now.'

I do not move. Although I am shaking, I'm not ready to be so easily dismissed, to be banished to bed like a child. 'I will stay,' I tell Lara. 'I will help.'

'No, Sofi. Go. Now.' Her voice is firm.

I hesitate, conflicted. Disgust at Josef's drunkenness fighting my desire to soothe him, the hurt of my discovery puddling like vinegar in my chest.

Finally, unable to bear watching the two of them any longer, I do as Lara says. I return to my chamber, thoughts whirring too selfishly to care whether I wake up Mama or not.

Lozenges

Lara

'What is it?' I ask Josef. 'Why have you come?' I do not tell him that he reeks of drink, that I've never seen him in such a state before. He flounders closer, and I shoot out my arms to steady him. 'Please, go home and lie down.'

My touch seems to untether him, somehow. 'Lara, please.' His words come as one. 'Please, my father ... this wedding I told you about. It's being arranged for next month. Next month! Oh God, I can't marry that Versailles bitch. Please, Lara, what can I do?' He gulps, a hard, dry sound I cannot bear to hear.

'Go home. Get some sleep,' I say gently and squeeze his arm. 'You will feel better in the morning, you'll be able to think more clearly.'

Josef wavers then, his face altering, becoming younger. 'Do you remember,' he says, 'that time we went to the market? I couldn't decide between the sugared almonds and the *pastilles au citron* and you said I must choose? So I chose the almonds, but when we got back and you handed me the basket, I saw you'd bought them both. You said it was impossible to have the sweet without the sour. Do you remember—?'

I don't remember and the words throw me. I recall the conversation with my sister earlier, about Pa taking us to market and buying us those sharp, sugary candies. I picture Sofi's drawing of us there, a scene from our childhood preserved in graphite.

Josef looks at me earnestly, as though awaiting a reply.

'Well ...' I begin, wanting to calm him but not really knowing how to answer. 'We can do that again, if you wish.'

He moves closer, like he wants nothing more than to be held but is too bashful to request it, and I remember the tower wallpaper, the vignette of Josef and his mother at the market. That wallpaper, again. My skull starts to hum.

It is at that exact moment I see her, through the night engulfing us both. A light-haired woman, lurching out of the pulpy blackness, one arm outstretched as if to touch Josef's hair, the other curled around a basket, her open mouth drawn in a silent scream. The tower wallpaper made flesh, guttering and flaring before me.

'No!' I cry, starting backwards.

A woman's laugh sounds from the dark. Josef recoils from me suddenly.

'No!' I say again, to him this time. 'I did not mean—'

I cannot see the woman now. I rub my eyes, open my mouth to call to her, close it again. She has vanished completely, yet she was so real.

'I'm awful sorry, Monsieur,' comes a voice I recognise. 'I'd no idea it was you. It's so dark out tonight, I can't see a thing.'

Josef moves precariously to face the words, and the woman who spoke them steps forward. Still holding my breath, I squint around him.

Of course. It is just Sid. Sidonie Belanger, from the *papeterie*. Bernadette and Pascal's friend. Though I have no idea why she should be out so very late. She bids us goodnight and melts into the darkness. But as she does, the scent from her basket reaches me. Sugary, like bonbons, cut through with something tart. I remember the *calissons*, the citrus and sugar, sour and sweet on my tongue.

I want to be away from that spot, out of the dark and back inside the cottage as soon as possible. I want to lie down, to stop the pounding in my head. 'Come,' I say. I take Josef's arm and guide him as quickly as I am able to the end of the track, apologise and tell him I really must be getting to bed. He nods sadly.

'Of course,' he says, his voice a little less slurred. 'I'm sorry too. I never usually drink, you see. It clearly doesn't agree with me. I'm sorry about . . . well. It was wrong of me.'

When I am almost at the cottage door, I look back. Sid has gone now and just one figure remains, barely visible against the span of the meadow. Josef. Still at the place where I left him on the track, aimless as an abandoned child.

Letters

Lara

All night and early the next morning, my mind plays over Josef's words. Over my headache, my muddled thoughts. Over the way I believed Sid, with her light hair and her basket, had stepped straight out of the tower wallpaper.

Sofi has not said a thing since we rose. Every time I have tried to speak to her I've been met with silence. I decide it is best to give her some space, to let her explain what is troubling her when she feels that she can. Though I fear I already know.

Once we have crossed the meadow on our way to the factory, Mama bids us farewell. She is wanted in the wash-house today and goes by a different path. A few steps later I realise Sofi is no longer with me either. I stop and look around, only to see her some distance behind, still as a statue and staring right back at me.

'Sofi?' I call. 'Come, we shall be late.'

'You're so selfish, you know,' she announces, quite without warning.

'What do you mean?' I ask, hastening to where she stands. 'Come. Please.' But she is not to be moved.

'You heard. You already had a sweetheart in Marseilles. Why did you need another here?'

I feel myself colour and glance anxiously about. 'Sofi, please, I do not know what you mean. Let us talk about this later.'

'No, now!' she insists, loud enough for the nearest workers to turn and observe. 'I want to talk about it now!'

More people start to surround us, muttering amongst themselves, their excitement heightening.

I draw even closer to Sofi, but she jerks away.

'Well, why?'

'Please, I beg you to let us discuss this later, in private. Not now. It is not the time.'

'It is the perfect time,' she continues, unperturbed. 'You knew how I felt about him, do not try to deny it. And you had Guillaume, so why—' She is about to say Josef's name but thinks better of it. 'Why *him*, too?'

'It's about a beau! They're fighting over a young cock!' a woman shrieks from the side. Another hushes her.

'Sofi,' I whisper, 'you do not know what you're talking about. I haven't heard from Guillaume since we left Marseilles. There is no reason why I should.' The mention of his name, of how long it has been, leaves me fighting to keep an even tone.

To my surprise, my sister just laughs. 'Not by his choosing!'

I am about to try and quiet her again when her words register. 'What do you mean?'

She stares at me, unyielding.

'What do you mean?' It is my turn to demand an answer now.

'You can be so slow, Lara,' she replies. 'Guillaume came to the house, the day before we left. He tried to find you, only to have Mama send him away. Presumably by telling him you never wanted to see him again.'

He tried to find you. Sofi cannot be correct. I pause, search her countenance for signs she might be exaggerating. 'I don't believe you.'

'Then more fool you! You say you haven't heard anything, but if he did have someone write to you, Mama would always get to his letters first.'

'She may have her faults, but Mama would never do such a thing.' I shake my head, try to shake the notion away. Could it really be true, could Mama really have intercepted Guillaume's letters?

'There is plenty our mother is hiding,' my sister continues, her voice increasing in volume with every syllable. 'You must be plain stupid if you cannot see!'

Sofi's anger bubbles and roils, breaking the crust that has been settling over it for months. 'And with Pa gone—' Her voice snaps.

'Sofi, please—' I reach out, try to put my arms around her.

She shakes me off, lowers her head and hurries in the direction of the dye-house.

The Marriage of Figaro

Versailles, one month later

Hortense

The morning of my marriage dawns overcast and continues in the same vein. It is an ungodly hour, perhaps as early as nine, when Mama has the servants flap into my chamber, with her not far behind.

'My dear, the day is here!' she crows. 'Surely you're not still abed? Come along, *ma petite* . . . up! Up!'

'I think I shall lie a while longer,' I murmur, feigning sleep. 'So I might be fresher for proceedings.' I have already reasoned that the day will only be bearable if I can take any opportunity afforded me to have events unfold on my terms.

Mama pauses to consider my words, before deciding against them. 'Nonsense, darling, it is time you were out of bed, the woman from the royal apartments is already waiting to dress your hair.'

Mireille lurks at her elbow like a spare part, neck bent as though emerging from a shell, something of the tortoise also in her expression.

Some interminable hours later, in a set of dressing-rooms near the Chapel Royal, I finally stand to regard myself in the largest of the looking-glasses and see, for the first time, the dizzying vision of it all. The wide and elaborate gown of expensive white crêpe it has taken two hours to stitch me into. The *aunes* of the finest Brussels lace layered like a millefeuille, embroidered with real gold thread and beaded with silver and pearls, ivory silk *barbes* quivering from its sleeves.

My face is porcelained with tinted lead and rosewater, my cheeks powdered and, like my lips, rouged a brilliant vermilion. Black silk *mouches* have been placed strategically over the two pimples that have materialised overnight. And there is my hair, straited with pins and invisible under the highest, most elaborate wig ever to grace my head, an enormous structure of the lightest pink, rendered lighter still by its lacquer of wheat powder and set through with silk flowers, feathered birds and glass butterflies. I am beguiled by what I see. An immaculate china figurine, pure and untouchable. On the surface, at least.

Mama's reflection totters up behind me. '*Ma petite*, you look exquisite! My precious bonbon!'

'I wonder it takes you by such surprise, Mama, since you have been here for every stage of my toilette. I do not think I have seen you move from the chaise for the past four hours!'

She ignores this and, at the exact moment she starts to fuss with my lace, I discern an additional reflection in the looking-glass. A young man, almost as still as I in his pale orange and silver ditto suit, hair powdered silver to match. He is gazing directly at me through one of the doors, his blank face reflected multiple times between the vast arrangement of mirrors. My soon-to-be-husband.

'If you are looking to relieve yourself, try the East Wing!' I shout at the glass.

'Hmm?' says Mama, not really listening.

I once heard Papa remark that, in his younger days, every unending corridor at Versailles stank thick with the piss of courtiers too desperate to wait until they reached an appropriate room before they urinated. Especially if it meant leaving the King's company.

Josef Oberst makes a face then, as though his culottes were already full, and the reflection vanishes as abruptly as it appeared. From somewhere beyond the doors to the dressing-room sounds de Pise's slippery voice.

'Come, Monsieur, with me. We will have you refreshed beforehand.'

I see de Pise's scheme at once. He is planning on plying my intended with drink in the hope he will disgrace himself in front of the guests. I cannot say I care.

Behind me, Mama has ceased fretting over my gown and is looking perplexed, frowning left and right as though she has no idea where the voice might be coming from, as though she doesn't understand how looking-glasses work. Absurd, given the number of hours she spends in front of them.

'They've gone, Mama,' I groan.

'Indeed?' She shuffles a few paces back in order to examine me fully again. 'You do look so lovely, my darling, but you'd be a lovelier jewel still if you smiled.'

I'm about to be tied to a man, I think, with the personality of a louse and nothing else to recommend him. If she believes I have any reason to smile, she is stupider than I thought.

'Mama, how can I?' I say instead. 'You just told me yourself that the lace on Pépin's cravat doesn't match this!' I tug at my sleeves, making sure she is watching.

'Careful, my darling, careful! You don't want to tear it!'

The panic that crosses her face gives me a little spike of pleasure. Pretending not to hear her entreaties, I continue to pull vigorously at the lacework.

'*Ma petite*, please!'

Soon bored, I lower myself into a nearby chair. As much as I approve of my current concealments, my spine is already aching, crushed by the weight of the wig.

'It would be better not to sit either, my dear,' Mama beseeches. 'You're likely to crumple.'

As I make my way down the chequerboard corridors to the Chapel Royal, my wedding garb weighing heavier still, I feel like some elaborate piece being moved upon a gaming board. Marble, glass and gold stretch out before me, bald-eyed statues and beady-eyed members of court lining the walls. I cannot see where any of them end.

For today is a momentous day in more ways than one, and in an effort to distract myself, I begin to count my steps. *Five, ten, twenty, thirty.* I count and I count, my expression fixed and impassive. *Thirty-six, forty-three. Maybe I am dreaming,* I muse as I go. *Or maybe this is some form of limbo or purgatory.* I can imagine the distinction will become clear enough once I am married. Yes, purgatory is the best word to describe such a coupling. And nobody to provide absolution except myself.

As I reach the chapel doors, a great swell of a trumpet fanfare rises up before me like a wall of water.

Inside the Sun

Hortense

The ceremony itself passes very like a play. It seems as though I am entirely removed from the occurrence, merely watching a farce being performed on the Royal Opera's stage. It is the same during the hour upon hour of subsequent rituals and breakfasting. So, when it is time for Mireille and a litany of other servants to escort me to the marriage chamber, it comes as something of a surprise.

My new husband is, of course, meant to be accompanying me, but nobody can seem to locate the fool. Someone ought to have checked the parterres. Given de Pise's interference, Josef Oberst could very well be out there spewing his guts into the ornamental yews. Not fit for purpose. Not that it matters. The activities of a wedding night lost something of their mystery to me exactly four years ago, an ironic coincidence and an anniversary I try to expunge from my consciousness year after year. My finger and thumb find a stray hair at my neck, and I pluck it out.

The vast chamber I am eventually shown into, through two high doors encrusted with ornamentation, is lit by hundreds of blazing tapers, their flames cutting blindingly off the mirrors and the gold. It is dominated by a lavish gilded and canopied four-poster bedstead standing high on its own staging, plumes of white ostrich feathers sprouting from each of the topmost corners.

Sitting next to this bed is its copy, constructed one-tenth of the size. This is where Pépin will be sleeping, one of my wedding presents from Mama. It will be a wrench not having my dog at my side tonight, since we have never been parted for more than a minute. As much as I am dreading the deeds to follow, it is this notion that makes me the gloomiest.

The gaggle of maidservants with me, led by that antiquity Mireille, remove my wedding attire, laying each piece of it aside as methodically as though conducting an autopsy. By the end of the whole procedure I am left unarmoured for the first time in years. My unpinned hair falls loosely to my shoulders and I wear nothing but a satin night-chemise more transparent than the waters of Versailles' Latona Fountain. I begin to shiver, remembering an anecdote I heard about the Queen, who was once left for hours without a stitch to her skin whilst her ladies quibbled about which of them had the right to dress her. The thought gives me comfort. That Antoinette herself isn't above such distress furnishes me with something of the fortitude to endure it, too.

The seconds lag, becoming minutes then hours, as the maids linger meekly by, taking great pains not to fall asleep. The exception is Mireille, whose efforts on that score failed some time ago.

I am just becoming hopeful that Josef Oberst will not turn up at all when I hear a noise against the door, a series of dull thuds. In fact, it sounds as though whomever is in the passageway might be thumping their head against the panelling. Could it be my new husband, weapon unsheathed and in hand, eager to enter and be about his business? I very much doubt it, I fancy I can hear him groaning out there already. And not with pleasure.

One of my maids scurries forward to answer the door, and Josef Oberst must indeed have been leaning against the thing, since the action of it being opened so swiftly causes him to lose his balance and fall. He lands heavily, just inside the threshold, in an unmanly heap.

Under any other circumstances, it would be a comical affair, and I effect a laugh of derision. 'Ah, husband!'

Husband. Josef Oberst balks at the word, getting to his feet and attempting to smooth himself down. He looks like he has been sleeping amongst the Ménagerie Royale for at least the last fortnight. His hair has sprung free of its powder and rests in unruly waves

187

across his forehead. His cravat is askew and half of his shirt has come untucked. His jacket is missing altogether and dubious light brown liquid spots both the silk of his open waistcoat and his culottes, the top buttons of which have also popped unfastened. He is, as is evident from the fumes that pour from him, as drunk as I supposed.

The maids scatter, leaving us alone, and I presume they have all departed when a noise like an anguished goat sounds from an armchair.

'Wakey-wakey!' I shout at the snoring Mireille, my voice shrill as a whistle.

The old woman stirs, apprehending the situation with a painful slowness. 'There is no rush,' I call. 'Would you rather I wake you in an hour or two?'

Mireille colours scarlet and creaks to her feet. 'Oh, I'm dreadfully sorry, Mademoiselle, forgive me.' She attempts a curtsy, but since she is still half-asleep it is little more than a stumble. The word 'mademoiselle' lingers in the air like a bad smell. She has forgotten I am a 'madame' now. Madame *Oberst*. How ugly the name sounds.

I do not think my husband has registered much of this pantomime. He stands ogling the bedchamber, infested as it is with cherubs and caked with gold. Even the rugs on the floor have stripes of gold woven into them. That is Versailles. One day it is like being trapped inside a sewer, the next like being trapped inside the sun.

Josef's eyes alight on the miniature four-poster. 'What . . . is *that*?'
'Pépin's bed, of course.'

My dog isn't yet using his purpose-made cot, but is instead curled, prawn-like, at my side. He is, however, no longer asleep. He opened his eyes and pulled back his ears as soon as Josef made his undignified entrance.

I notice with relief that at no point does my husband seem to have realised just how little I am wearing. I remove myself from the chaise, trying to disguise the tremble in my limbs as I cross to the marriage bed, Pépin in my arms. Josef follows, extinguishing as many of the tapers as possible.

When he is almost at the bed, Pépin springs up and down on his little paws, snarling in Josef's direction. The latter eyes my protector with irritation. 'Aren't you going to stop him?'

'I believe he is merely objecting to the lights being put out,' I reply. 'He prefers them to remain lit. Pépin is a great believer in being able to see in advance what horrors await.'

Josef tries to look angry, but since he is slowed by drink he rather gives the appearance of a man who has lately had a portion of his brain removed. My thoughts, I note, are following harsher and hotter on the heels of one another at present. As they usually do when I am under duress.

'Take him to another room, then,' Josef spits.

'I doubt that would be possible,' I counter, determined to keep my tone even. 'He does not like to be apart from me, you see. We usually sleep together.'

My pulse quickens. It is getting excessively late now, and I am torn between wanting to have this torture over with immediately and wanting to delay it for as long as is possible.

'He will have to move.' Stepping towards my pet in an attempt to get hold of him, my husband is met by energetically snapping jaws.

'He cannot get down from the bed without his stairs.' I cock my head to one side to indicate their position, but Josef simply looks vacantly on. 'Well, fetch them, then!'

At last he sees the set of wheeled golden steps to the side of the bed, and pushes them over impatiently. 'Make him move,' he mutters, his tone staccato.

I do move Pépin, but at my own speed and with the utmost care, as if he were possessed of an external skeleton crafted of the most delicate Venetian glass. I place him on the top step and, to his little head, I murmur, 'Go, now. For there is something your *maman* must do, my darling. She has no choice.'

My words make Josef blanch as much as they do me. Having put out as many tapers as he can, he now awkwardly removes every piece of his clothing with the exception of a long shirt, losing his balance no fewer than three times in the process. Then he hoists himself wearily upon the mattress, and I flinch at the thought of what is to come.

Only when Josef sits there, inert for many minutes more, do I realise that he does not know what to do, how to begin. That I, therefore, must know far more than he. I puzzle at the fact that his father has never employed a female to educate him in such matters. But then, Wilhelm Oberst probably knows little more about women than his *sun*.

'I can assure you this is much worse for the lady,' I remark, trying in vain to temper the dread behind my words.

He makes no comment but lies next to me, prone. Heart clamouring, I wait for him to move, to reach out and touch me in some clumsy way, likely by making a grab straight for a nipple, as a *duc*'s tame baboon once did to a serving girl, here in Versailles, but he lifts not a finger.

Following a further few minutes of inertia, Josef suddenly gets down from the bed and retrieves his waistcoat from the floor. I hope against hope that he might be preparing to leave but, keeping his back to me, he removes something from one of its pockets, a small object evidently, small enough to bend his head over and cradle in his hands.

'What are you doing?'

He ignores my question and, much to my utter dismay, after he has replaced the thing climbs back onto the bed with fresh intention. This time he positions himself squarely over my body, lying the length of me. Given his inebriation and previous inactivity, his stiffness now takes me by surprise. I can feel it pressing into the tops of my thighs, forcing me to elicit an uncontrollable gasp of alarm.

Josef appraises me through narrowed lids, touches my hair, breathes harder and causes several pillows to tumble to the floor. He closes his eyes, apparently in a world of his own, and reaches down towards the hem of my chemise, begins to lift it towards my stomach.

I want to screw closed my eyes, but I cannot move a muscle. There is something in his purpose, in the strangely determined set of his features – putrid stink of vomit and alcohol aside – that begins both to appal and intrigue me and, breath shallow, pulse flying, I brace

190

myself for what is to follow. But then, without warning he stops, and cranes his head around.

'*Rrrayip!*'

There is Pépin, standing on Josef's back, turning this way and that whilst yapping as triumphantly as if he had just reached a hitherto unexplored summit.

Every part of my husband's body, I notice, is now stiff save one. He extricates himself from me, and I can suppress neither my laughter nor my unbridled relief.

'Ooh now, come to *Maman!*' I say, puckering my lips to my dog's sweet nose. My little saviour, once again. 'Do not worry, *bébé*, you did not miss anything.'

I peek past Pépin to see what Josef will do next. He throws himself down on the edge of the mattress, facing away from me, having left as large a gap between us as possible. He does not move again.

I have gone past the point of sleep now, so lie awake, mulling things over in my mind. Somewhere in this building, more than a hundred wedding guests will still be carousing, toasting the occasion of our marriage. And yet, not two days ago, Versailles had been thick with the news. The King had installed troops of thirty-thousand in Paris. Thirty-thousand trained soldiers. And all to quell a few peasants with pikes. Either His Majesty is using a wheel to break a butterfly, or the pikes of those peasants are sharper than they seem.

After a while my thoughts become tedious, even to myself, so I resolve to put my mind to something else. I prop myself up on my elbows. There remain a handful of tapers lit, and my eyes are drawn to the disarray of Josef's clothing on the floor. Then I remember.

I climb softly from the bed and tiptoe around it. My husband appears to be asleep. I gently flap my hand before his face to check. He does not stir.

I make my way to the waistcoat he has been wearing all day, shed like an expensive skin, and pick it up. Feeling inside each pocket, it doesn't take long for my fingers to close around a small scrap of parchment. I glance over my shoulder to make sure my husband has not woken. Then I turn it over.

191

A face greets me on the other side, the face of a young woman with lightly waving hair, her profile bordered by decorative detail, half of the picture seemingly torn away. She has been sketched in graphite, crudely but competently, a fascinating, indefinable quality to her likeness.

As I run the tip of my index finger over the delicate features of her face, astonishment tingling my skin, I wonder who she is.

Deer and Wild Boar Hunt

Jouy-en-Jouvant

Sofi

I am at work in the factory, late in an unending day, like the three before it. It is a sultry evening, the sun having beaten down again relentlessly since dawn, and the dye-house is a bread oven. Another drought.

Ladle in hand, I am dumping salt from a sack to a pail, one scoop at a time, scattering much of it to the floor in the process. The muscles of my back are screaming, the skin of my knuckles tender and raw, aggravated by the salt. But I feel them less than I usually would, my thoughts fastened to the same few words. Josef is married. Josef married, three days ago.

Monsieur Wilhelm has had his way. Forced his son into marriage with the over-indulged daughter of a Versailles marquis for the sake of his coffers. But I am not the only one to disapprove of his actions, it seems. About a week before the ceremony, declamations of surprise had rippled between the buildings of the factory, deepening into rumblings of objection, in calls for higher pay. In calls for a meeting with the Monsieur.

There have been gatherings, clandestine, for the past few weeks. In the factory late at night, in the village during the smallest hours of the morning. Amidst the thickening dusk one evening, my sister and I ran into Sid, a basket tucked over her arm. Lara's face paled at the sight of her and Sid must have seen it, too.

'Sorry about scaring you, Lara,' she chuckled. 'I didn't mean to. Master Josef was in a right state, wasn't he?'

Sid laughed again and I realised she was referring to the night, about a month ago, when Josef came to the cottage reeking of drink. When I saw how my drawing had been torn, my own likeness discarded as rubbish. My sister and I had made up after our quarrel on the way to the factory, but my guilt at speaking to her so bluntly, at blaming Lara, remained. And I couldn't bring myself to explain this to her. Neither could I bring myself to stay angry at Josef, as much as I wanted to, that bright green ribbon still tied at my throat.

'I was coming back from Bernadette and Cal's that night,' Sid went on. 'Same as tonight, in fact. You two should come next time.' She dipped a hand under the cloth in her basket and withdrew a sheet of paper, a pattern of text printed across it. 'We've been discussing this factory business. Reckon the workers will press Monsieur Oberst for a fairer wage soon with grain prices up again, same as workers are doing all over the country. Especially with this new Madame arriving. Here—' She pressed the paper into my hand with a wink.

It was a pamphlet, like nothing I had read before. It called for employers to listen to their workers, to pay heed to their concerns. It called for reform. And, most of all, it called out the greed of the nobility, de Comtois' class, this Hortense du Pommier's class. Of how they could no longer drive the working people into the ground. The words swelled and shimmered, a mirage before me on the page.

And so the meeting with Monsieur Wilhelm is to take place tonight. Straight after work and outside the chateau, a chance for the staff to air their grievances. The notion gives me some comfort, dampens the pain of the rest of it. But only a little.

Many of those working in the dye-house stop what they're doing even before the late bell rings, rinsing their hands, cloths and pails, hanging cleaned tools on the pegs by the doors. There is a low thrill in the air, of anticipation, of excitement. Of change.

As soon as the bell sounds, Lara, Mama and I move amongst the throng to the forecourt. Nearing the far side of it our pace slows, as the workers bottle-neck their way between the two lines of poplars into the chateau's approach. There we come upon Bernadette, Pascal and Sid, Madame Colbert's arm looped through her daughter's. The seven of us edge towards the big house together, coming out a minute later onto the open sweep of gravel to hear a series of exasperated cries go up at the front. Lara throws me a look.

'Monsieur Oberst!'

'Where is he?'

'Li-ar!'

The chateau's entrance comes into view, twin stone staircases leading to the balconied area before the pair of front doors. Monsieur Wilhelm promised to be waiting for us on that balcony, promised to speak to us there. But it is empty. The lower rows of windows are shuttered, the doors closed. The place looks deserted.

'Might have known a man like him'd never keep his word,' Mama mutters.

Grumblings crackle and grow around us, that although Josef is still at Versailles, Monsieur Wilhelm returned two days ago. That there is no reason he should not be here. That he has broken his word. Then the doors start to open and everyone falls to a hush, but only one man emerges from the vestibule. And it isn't Monsieur Oberst.

'Monsieur Wilhelm is, alas, currently indisposed,' Monsieur Marchant announces, offering a conciliatory smile. His voice is firm, but his manner distinctly uncomfortable. 'He sends his profusest apologies.'

'Looks like he expected the Monsieur to be here as much as we did,' comments Pascal.

I squint at the chateau. He is in there all right, I think. Not indisposed at all, but sat in his study counting his money. Too self-interested to come out. The crowd may have had the same notion, since they begin to yell the Monsieur's name, louder and louder, to clap their hands and stamp their feet.

'Now, I'd be happy to convey your issues to Monsieur Oberst myself,' says Marchant, palms raised like a vicar attempting to placate an increasingly restless congregation. 'If you would just—'

'You could have done that days ago!' a man bellows.

A woman near him pipes up in agreement. 'We want to speak to the Monsieur directly, thought that was the whole point of this meeting!'

Shouts and applause again ring from the building, morphing steadily into a chant. *'Sor-tez! Sor-tez!'*

'Calm, please,' Marchant pleads, sensing the heat of the situation rising as the heat of the day dwindles. 'There is no need for—'

Suddenly, gravel pings from the iron railings Marchant is now gripping, fast as a musket ball. Another piece hits a shutter, another the wall at his back. It's impossible to see which of the workers is launching the missiles, but they leave Monsieur Marchant scrambling for the door.

'Very well, very well!' he cries, retreating into the building. 'I shall fetch the Monsieur!'

Minutes pass. The workers talk amongst themselves for a while, another chant demanding the Monsieur come out sparking in pockets and swelling across the whole assembly. Then there is movement at the doors and they open, wider this time, to reveal Monsieur Oberst himself, framed in the entranceway below the lunettes. It is an unlikely vignette, the man standing there awkwardly before stepping out onto the parapet, Marchant hovering, anxious, at his side.

Everybody falls silent, waiting for their employer to speak. The air is close, the ambience closer. There is not a breath of wind, not a breath from the workers.

I catch sight of Sid. She has broken off from our group to scale the nearest tree for a clearer view of the Monsieur. I do the same. I can see him much better from up here, mark the sweat on his face, the glistening backs of his hands. At first I think he might be drunk, appraising us disdainfully through a fog of liquor. Then I realise the peculiar warp of his face isn't the result of contempt or alcohol, but panic. It's the first time in years, according to Madame Colbert, that the man has faced his workers. Perhaps it is the thought of parting with his profits that has him so rattled. Or perhaps he has Réveillon in mind, as he stands and perspires before us.

Monsieur Oberst opens his mouth and closes it again, apparently rooted to the spot. A boar, cornered.

'I . . . understand you want—' he begins, voice barely audible.

'We want more pay!' someone interrupts.

'So we can afford proper grain!'

'Our wage barely covers our taxes!'

'And an extra half day off every Saturday—'

'An extra *day* off every Saturday!'

Monsieur Marchant raises his hands. 'Now please, please listen,' he declares. 'Monsieur Oberst is here today to announce that he is happy to meet your demands. Monsieur . . .'

Marchant signals for his superior to step forwards and take over, as bubbles of amazement burst through the crowd. But Monsieur Wilhelm does not move and Marchant is forced to go on.

'You will receive a rise in your pay from tomorrow,' he says. 'And an extra half day off every Saturday. Is that not right, Monsieur Oberst?'

The man nods, still not moving.

'See, you have Monsieur Oberst's word,' Marchant says. 'All that he asks is that, in two days' time—'

'In two days' time—' a voice cuts in and the workers' mouths drop open. Monsieur Oberst is addressing them at last. 'In two days' time my son's new wife will arrive here in Jouy. I ask you to make her welcome. Is of utmost importance.'

My insides tighten and simmer. He might be incapable of speaking about the welfare of his workers, but the man seems to have no problem talking about that du Pommier girl. I heard what he said to Josef in his study, that his son's marriage was being arranged for the sake of the factory purse.

The workers converse in feverish, animated surges.

'If you swear to what you have just told us, Monsieur,' shouts

197

a man near the front. 'About the hours and the pay ... then we agree!'

Others clamour their assent and a fresh wave of applause breaks through the crowd. It continues as Monsieur Wilhelm gives a stiff nod and turns back to the door.

'Well, at least we will have more coin in our pockets,' says Bernadette.

The Monsieur is only thinking of himself, I want to answer. Trying to get this du Pommier family and their money on his side. Trying to protect his own business. But he knows as well as I do. What happened today is just the beginning.

I grip the trunk of the poplar, swivelling to stretch down a toe, when my gaze hooks on a man, alone and apart from the rest of the crowd. I know that slender figure, that lurking posture. It is Emile Porcher, the rat-catcher, hunched into the collar of his jacket and stock-still. I wonder why on earth he has come. He isn't one of the factory workers, yet here he is all the same, watching Monsieur Oberst head back inside the chateau, glaring at him as if trying to bore into his brain. As if he hates the very bones of the man.

Without warning, Porcher turns on his heels and hurries away. I crane my neck to see where he is going. Not to the factory gates and into the village, but onto the path snaking down from chateau to churchyard.

Before Mama has the chance to notice, I jump from the tree. I slide into the mass of cheering, jostling workers and make in the direction of that path. I do not know exactly why I do it, only there is something about this man that I do not trust. Why was he at the window of the cottage last spring, starting away as though he had something to hide? Why was it him, of all people, who came upon Madame Justine's body, in the Monsieur's private garden, in the deadest part of night?

Emile Porcher lopes stealthily on, the rail-thin calves poking from his culottes keeping up a rapid pace, drab, greyish jacket merging with his hair into one oily pelt. Occasionally, he glances skittishly over his shoulder, and when he does I duck out of sight.

I presume that when Porcher reaches the church he will proceed to the lychgate, or maybe go inside, but instead he circles a section of the churchyard's outer wall, vaulting the stonework more nimbly than I would have imagined for a man of his age. He passes between the grave-markers, the angels, tombs and crosses, and then he comes to a halt. I move closer, put my foot to a nook in the wall and climb it, too, drop behind a nearby headstone and cautiously peer around.

There he is, crouching by a tomb of pale-grey limestone and fiddling with something. The thin laces of hair dangling to cover his face make it impossible to identify his expression. Neither can I discern exactly what it is he is doing, but he is passing his right hand in small, sweeping arches across the stone's surface, pausing at intervals to lean back on his haunches and examine his work. If it didn't seem so peculiar, I could almost believe he was drawing.

In the distance, the factory workers wind their way to the village, talking loudly. They are getting closer, and I think I really should be going, before Mama realises I have slipped away. But I cannot resist lingering a little longer, in the hope Porcher might soon slink into the dusk, and I can see what he has been doing to that stone.

At length, and with the noise of the crowd subsiding on the main street, Porcher gets to his feet, bows his head and leaps back over the cemetery wall. I wait in my hiding place a few moments more and, when I'm absolutely certain he has gone, I move towards the tombstone.

Although the stone is sizeable and finely carved, I assume it will belong to some family member of Porcher's, and therefore bear an unrecognisable name. But it does not. It bears a name I have come to know well. I frown, study the inscription once again to ensure that I am not mistaken.

JUSTINE EMILIA OBERST
DEPARTED THIS LIFE MARCH, 1783

Above this inscription is a small but exquisite piece of carved decoration. An oval, bordered by clusters of beading and foliage. An intaglio, a lozenge, a cameo. A likeness of Josef's mother, her expression open and serene, just as it appears on the wallpaper.

And then I see what Emile Porcher had been doing. On the flat area of stone beneath the date is an image, sketched onto its surface in charcoal. He *had* been drawing something.

A wolf.

Last Days at Versailles

Versailles

Hortense

The better part of a week after the ceremony and we are still at Versailles, having stayed in one of the apartments overlooking the stables. A very slight step up from the view from Papa's apartments, at least. This is the so-called honey-moon of our marriage and I should be grateful it does not drag on for a month, as the term implies. It is by no means sweet, however, more sour-gloom than honey-moon. I expected nothing less.

I knew from the moment Papa told me of the match, that day in the carriage, that Josef Oberst would make a tiresome spouse. He might be mannered enough, and doubtless his looks may turn many girls' heads, but there is an air of tragedy about him, a perpetual infantile melancholy that engulfs him like a thunder-cloud. He has not tried to climb on top of me again since the night of the wedding, however, and for that, at least, I am profoundly grateful.

This morning we are due to leave for his father's factory and last night I slept not a wink. Married off to a labourer, the son of a self-made wallpaper pedlar. And apparently I have the state of the country to thank for it. *Factory*. The mere word makes my skin crawl, dull as old tin.

I am only permitted to take one servant with me to my new dwelling, the sloth-like Mireille, and I had to plead my case even for this. I look now at the objects surrounding me, the things I must surrender to Versailles. My eyes move across the rich furnishings and elegant armoires, stuffed with my soon-to-be abandoned jackets and skirts, stomachers, petticoats, hats and other fine things, the silk, crêpe and damask layered one over the other like the centre of an extravagant cake.

I open the doors to an armoire and run my hands over my armaments once more, feeling a lance of alarm. I have been – I want to say *advised* but it is too paltry a word – I have been *instructed* to pare down my belongings, taking with me to this Jouy-en-Jouvant only what is deemed necessary. As a factory owner's wife, I am told, I should be seen from now on to be more soberly dressed, more sparingly adorned. I should avoid exhibiting my finery and good taste to the workers, to avoid rubbing their faces in it lest they become fractious, as the rest of their kind have of late. When I see the chests of beautiful objects and cosmetics, novelties and accessories to be left behind, my flesh turns to ice and I have to still my breathing until it is scarcely there at all. I scoop up Pépin and press him close. At least he is to be accompanying me. That was not subject to negotiation.

Dragging myself into the salon, I see my new father-in-law has arrived, returning here in his coach to convey my husband and me to the sticks in which he lives, and I experience a sudden rush of dread at where I am heading. Josef is in the salon with him, shrinking awkwardly into the cushions of the chaise.

'Ah, Hortense,' Papa declares. 'You have joined us at last.' He gestures to a footman. 'Fetch my wife, please.'

'Yes, where is dear Mama?' I ask. All morning long I have heard her, traipsing melodramatically between rooms, wailing of my departure like Melusine. The fascinating thing about my mother's histrionics is that they never seem to occur without an audience.

Right on cue, she flusters in, clutching at least two damp kerchiefs to her person and flanked by her maid, who is holding several more.

'Oh dear!' she announces from the doorway, rather to let us know she is there than to convey any genuine anguish. '*Ma petite*, my last and youngest child flying from us. However shall we do without you?'

She draws me into one of her smothering, bosomy embraces. Narrowly avoiding a fleshy demise, Pépin scampers to the rear of a cushion for safety. Mama's birds chitter at our backs, twitching restlessly amidst the foliage of the birdcage.

'Well then, I am ready,' I say, rising, more in an effort to shake her off than in any desire to leave. 'I trust you are ready, too, husband?' I pick up my dog and look to Josef, witnessing anew the discomfort the title causes him and resolving to use it more often.

We proceed, trailed by Mama and Papa, Wilhelm Oberst and various servants, downstairs, Mama indulging in more theatrics as we go, dabbing her cheeks and keening like a hired mourner at a funeral.

Outside, the palace and grounds are drenched in the peculiar light that follows a shower of rain. Everything is rich and vibrant, the building's walls shining like precious metal, the topiary brilliant as crystallised lime. How hateful my new home will be compared to this grand place, despite its many flaws. Speaking of which, the Oberst coach is waiting at the entrance, I see. A drab and boxy thing in a tasteless shade of brown, sitting on the paviers like a turd on an expensive carpet.

'Farewell, my dear—' Papa utters distantly.

'My darling, oh, how I shall miss you!' interrupts my mother, pawing at me and sobbing.

I ensure I am seated on the furthest side of the dingy vehicle from Mama, who begins the final act of her performance as the coach pulls away. When I do venture to look back at my parents, they seem astonishingly small and indistinguishable. Nothing more than minute limpets, clinging to the royal facade.

House Beside a River

Jouy-en-Jouvant

Hortense

The coach slows and two gates come into view, iron constructions in black and gold, with letters set into the metal. They look ridiculous, forming far too grandiose an entry for a village factory. The initials *W. O.* are picked out in gilding on the gate closest to me. The unmistakable insignia of a man with ideas above his station.

'How common—' I utter, loud enough for Josef to hear, but the wretched creaking of metal on metal as the gates are opened stops me short.

As we pass through this purported entrance, the men either side of it tip their hats to the coach, inducing Pépin to withdraw into my lap and produce a low rumbling in his throat. 'There, there,' I say, running a gloved finger over his scalp. I glance to the left and mark that there are corresponding letters on the other gate. *J. O.* My husband dips his head at the spectacle, humiliated by the indignity of having his initials emblazoned in such a vulgar fashion. And indeed, curiously, I catch sight of my father-in-law recoiling at his son's monogram, too, the only reaction forthcoming from him since we left Versailles. He has spent the rest of the journey silent and inert, gaze fixed through the window-glass.

We finally come to a stop in some sort of squared-off open area, surrounded by ugly working buildings. Beyond them, I can just

204

about discern the curve of a river. A track leads off this dispiriting square and up a hill bordered by tall trees, and there are people gathered either side of it, assembled for my arrival. Dog-eared lengths of greenery are pinned to their jackets, in what I assume to be some sort of rustic tradition.

'*Félicitations!*' someone calls dully.

I suppose that the coach has only been halted for a moment, to allow us to wave to the waiting hordes before we move on again. But then I see a man unlatching the door, allowing my husband to alight.

The opened door provides a clearer view of the hill beyond, at the top of which I see is a house. Little more than the upper floors are visible, but it is a miserable sight, a gloomy, unadorned building, facade blending with sky into one insipid mass of grey. And there is no harmonious architectural symmetry here. The single tower poking from the nearest end of the structure resembles an unsightly growth, the glass of its lone window glaring back at me like the eye of a Cyclops, the horrible dome to its roof making me shudder.

'That dreary, poky building,' I state to distract myself, pointing a finger past the crowd. 'Lord, I had a grander doll-house than that as a child. Please tell me it is not where I am expected to live.'

Only Wilhelm Oberst and his son register the remark, or at least the servant at the coach's door pretends not to. The crowd outside is too busy talking amongst themselves, craning at intervals towards the vehicle to judge any glimpse of me they can catch.

'*Bienvenue!*' they cry, somewhat unenthusiastically. '*Bienvenue,* Madame!'

'Come.' Josef disembarks and extends his hand, his face hardening when he sees I have not moved a hair. 'Come!' he repeats, less patiently. 'We will proceed to the house on foot from here, in order to greet the staff.'

As I shuffle my body reluctantly along the seat, the shouts from the track grow louder. I pause, assessing the situation.

'Come. *Please.*' Josef is speaking through clenched teeth this time, the faintest traces of crimson kindling his cheeks. 'All this was organised especially, these people have been waiting some time.'

Not only does the sky look as though it is threatening another shower, but I deduce it would take an age to traipse to the house from our present position. And I do not crave for a second the pleasure of having the walk take longer still as I stop to make conversation with every Tom, Dick and Henri along the way.

I shake my head and slide back along the seat. 'I think not,' I say. 'I'll go directly to the house by coach. I haven't the appropriate footwear for such a walk.' I rap at the wall of the vehicle to tell the driver to move off and, obeying the signal, the man gees the horses, my husband lurching clumsily forwards to stop him. A lull falls over the crowd, murmurs beginning to ripple along its lines.

Wilhelm Oberst leans towards me, bracing a large hand on mine, his gaze uncompromising. 'As my son said, the workers have gathered especially. They would not take being snubbed very kindly.'

I remain silent awhile, weighing his unsettling request, before deciding, on this occasion, to comply. Against my better judgement, I allow my husband to assist me from the coach.

The crowds come into view in earnest then, and for the minutest second I freeze. There are more people gathered along this trackway than I thought, their faces stiffened by disapproval. Pépin teeters nervously in my arms, his tiny body tense with the trepidation I am attempting to conceal. There is something of the mob about these people. I do not like it. A scene coalesces in my mind, those chimpanzees at Versailles, crowding the nobleman, lunging for him with their fists clenched and their teeth bared. Exhaling hard, I dismiss the thought. I refuse to let them intimidate me.

Wilhelm Oberst, his *sun* and I plod laboriously up the track, which I now realise is the approach to the Obersts' house. I flash quick, thinly appeasing smiles at the labourers as I go, not listening to what they have to say. More importantly I try to focus, to concentrate on taking in my surroundings. How dismal that house is, how like a cage the grilles of its windows. A bead of panic begins to form inside me, my head itching beneath my wig—

The sensation is interrupted by a squelching under my slipper, which forces me to peer down at my hems. They have been dirtied by the rough ground, the material ruined. I scowl with disgust and when I look up again I am somewhat unnerved to see a girl right in front of me, a tan-skinned peasant, staring directly into my face with an undisguised repulsion that surpasses even my own.

White Vapour, Black Powder

Sofi

I did not want to be here at all, it was Monsieur Marchant who rounded us up. We'd had our terms met, he said, so now it was best to have things start as they mean to go on with this new Madame, to make a good first impression. To show willing on both sides and avoid trouble later. A wide-eyed notion.

The woman isn't aware of me staring at her for some time. I watch closely from the moment the carriage door is opened, I notice everything. The way she belittles Josef, the blatant contempt. The way she flounces from the vehicle with a face full of scorn, as though everything about this place is beneath her. The way her eyes, set apart on her face at an acute and unlikely angle, are like gemstones, glittering coldly.

By the time she arrives we have already been congregated for more than an hour, yet she doesn't even care to acknowledge us. I get the measure of her instantly, interested in nothing past the hems of her fine satin skirts. No regard for how our own clothes have been darkened by drizzle as we have stood here and waited.

What she is wearing herself is ridiculous, as out-of-place as a powder puff in a granary. A white-blonde wig is plopped on her head and she is encased in copious amounts of cream chiffon and petticoats, done up like a rancid meringue. The ludicrous ginger animal balanced in the crook of her arm is the slither of bitter orange-rind on top.

I look more closely at it. A dog, little bigger than a rat, and covered all over with fluff. Around its small neck is a miniature cravat, frilled with the same lace as the woman's own gown. The animal is shaking, but at the same time showing its fangs in hostility. It looks like a scabbard fish I once saw at the harbour. I recall its spiked teeth and disproportionately bulbous eyes. How absurd breeding has become, I think, when a dog looks more like a fish than a dog.

The woman is moving closer now, making no effort whatsoever to speak to any of us, merely shooting off the odd smile, wholly absent of sincerity and with all the warmth of a claw. When I see her reaction at realising her skirts have a few meagre speckles of mud on them, I do not even try to hide my revulsion. At first she blinks back at me with disdain. But in the end it is she who looks away first.

As I start to make comment to my sister, a knot of sickness tightens inside me. Lara is gazing at the newly arrived party and Josef, I see, is gazing back. I have to look away, and when I do, I mark that the new Madame has also noted their wordless exchange. She blasts a final barbed stare at my sister and turns away, too. She must have decided she has had enough of rubbing elbows with the masses, and strides up the approach to the chateau. As she goes, her words reach me on the wind.

'When my things arrive with my lady's maid, they're to be brought to my rooms at once,' she declares. Her voice is glacial, precise. Engineered to demean. I've heard the like of it before. That night, outside the tavern.

'Well, she's started as she means to go on, just as her lot have always done,' Mama remarks.

The abruptness of the new Madame's exit leaves Josef fuddled and awkward. He shakes as many hands as he can, hastily thanking people for being there to welcome his wife. *His wife.* The words turn my empty stomach. Though better her than Lara, I reason. Better he be married to someone he doesn't care for. The unpleasantness of the thought takes me by surprise.

I catch sight of Monsieur Wilhelm, moving impassively along the chateau's approach. Then his eyes come to rest upon my sister and there they linger, fervidly, just as they did from the office in the print-house. He is the cause of all this, I think. This marriage. His preoccupation with wealth and status. His head still stuck in the past.

The workers are muttering to each other, their faces set in offended astonishment at the woman's slight. The sprigs of greenery pinned to their fronts, hours before in her honour, are wilting.

I look from one worker to the next, hear them talk of food, of not having eaten this morning, then waiting for hours in the drizzle. We may have more coin in our pocket now, but the droughts and the freezes have left less bread to buy. The loaves at yesterday's market were the worst yet – gritty and foul and black as scabs. I hear a woman behind me complaining hers was so hard it could only be cut with an axe.

Overhead the clouds have gathered again, deepening in colour and density. They seem to solidify before my eyes, shifting from white vapour to black powder. One spark and they will ignite, and set everything to change.

Ghosts

Hortense

A plumpish, plain woman attempts to intercept me on the front steps of the Obersts' dwelling, fussing like a mother duck when I continue into the vestibule so that I might familiarise myself with the depressing pile. The interior is as I expected, squat and unremarkable. Rather like this woman, in fact.

'Please, Madame,' she implores. 'Allow me to introduce myself and show you around the chateau.'

I turn to face her, at which she quietens, eyes coming to rest on my little dog as though she had never seen the like of him before.

'I am Berthé Charpentier.' She curtsies. 'Your housekeeper. Housekeeper for Monsieur Wilhelm for the past—'

'I presume I shall find my chamber up here?' I cross the vestibule and climb the stairs, pausing at the top and pondering whether to go left or right.

'If you please, Madame, your chamber is *this* way,' the housekeeper announces at my back, scurrying down the passage to the left. There is a heightened insistence to her tone and, as I allow her to show me into the room she is standing flapping towards, I wonder what is causing it.

My husband and I are to keep separate chambers here, and mine is a poky affair. Its walls are covered in more of the wretched paper the Obersts manufacture, and the space arranged with inharmonious furniture of a middling size and quality.

'This is it, is it?' I ask.

The housekeeper hesitates, unsure how to respond. 'We hope you will be very comfortable here, Madame, and happy in your new home.'

'Hmph.' A quick, derisive sound. *Comfortable. Happy.* This woman is a greater wit than I first thought. 'Speaking of which, I shall see the rest of the place now.'

'The rest, Madame? Now, Madame? Might you rather take some refreshments first?'

I circle an arm at her as Pépin regards his new quarters suspiciously from the other. 'No, I would not. I should like to see the rest.'

There is a slight panic about her ruddy cheeks and she glances over her shoulder as if in search of my father-in-law or husband. But they must still be outside with that mob.

'You need not fret about showing me the servants' floors, if that is your worry,' I tell her. 'We shall start with the bedchambers.'

When she comes to understand that I am not for moving, and neither is her master coming to save her, she finally relents.

In addition to mine, another chamber faces out to the back of the building, with four more at the front, one of which belongs to my husband and another to his father. However, the fun and games begin in earnest when I insist upon seeing the locked room leading off the central part of the landing. Judging not only by the space it occupies, but also by its set of grander double doors, it must be the largest of the chambers and should, therefore, have been mine.

'In here next,' I say to the housekeeper.

She purses her lips. 'That one's never used, Madame. Hasn't been for some years.'

'Indeed? There is no reason why I should not go inside, then, is there? Several of the chambers I've just seen are not used, yet you showed me those. I presume you have a key.'

My remark renders her mute. She either cannot devise a response, or is trying to calculate whether she should lie and tell me she does *not* have a key. Evidently she thinks better of the latter and withdraws a jangling collection of them from her skirts. 'Madame.'

I was quite right. The doors open to reveal a much larger chamber

212

than any of the others, with sizeable bay windows onto the grounds. But it is the objects within that disturb my mind the most.

Everything is sheeted in pale cotton, as though the chamber is about to be redecorated. When I slowly lift a corner of the covering closest to me, I see a walnut-inlaid toilette languishing beneath. Under another is a matching commode. Under the next, a fine four-poster bedstead. A painful spark of memory. That summer, four years earlier, when my parents' apartments were redecorated. That vast, round birdcage of Mama's under its protective tent of linen, enclosed like a wigwam. My skin prickles.

'As I say, Madame, this room isn't used,' the housekeeper ventures.

Pépin makes a noise in the back of his throat and smacks his jaws together, sensing my discomfort.

'I shall see downstairs next,' I tell the housekeeper, keeping my tone even so she cannot detect how keen I am to cross back to the landing.

On the lower floor I am shown into a succession of utterly tedious spaces, the largest of which are the dining and withdrawing rooms. A panelled door in the library, I'm told, leads to my father-in-law's study, a place I certainly have no desire to see. But the handful of other rooms – the parlour, the salons and the music room – are more peculiar, in that they hardly seem to be used at all. In the last of these, indentations show in the rug before the window, the ghost of something lingering still, as though a fortepiano had, at one point, stood there.

I am led back into the vestibule, where I pause, something niggling at me.

'Might I have some refreshments brought to your chamber now?' enquires the housekeeper.

I start to say that I shall have a carafe of cold, sweet wine when the realisation suddenly dawns. 'No, wait,' I tell her, 'I have not seen the tower. I noticed a window up there, so I presume there is a room—'

'There is, Madame, storage room only,' the woman answers, far too quickly.

'Then I take it you have a key?'

'Afraid not, Madame.'

I glare at her, awaiting further explanation, but she cannot meet my eye.

'I'll bring that wine up immediately,' the housekeeper says, disappearing along the corridor.

For a moment I think of demanding that she unlock that room in the tower at once, but then I recall the furniture of the master chamber, looming like great ghouls beneath those sheets, and realise I do not want to see it after all.

Ballooning

Hortense

Back in my chamber, I await the arrival of my things. I drift around the room, with little to do but have Pépin test the softness of the bed, idly open a commode drawer here, an armoire door there. Aside from a collection of lace *pochettes* filled with dried rose petals and *camomille*, the furniture is empty.

I move towards the last armoire and lift the latch. I expect it to be empty, too, but as I pull the door ajar a mass of fabric balloons out at me through the opening.

My immediate thought is that it must be an article of clothing left by my husband's dead mother, maybe something she wore in her confinement, as the garment is huge. It is also loud and garish, with a rough and unpleasing texture, cut from a coarse cotton weave. Then I examine it more closely and realise it is even more tasteless a thing than I first thought.

Hanging before me is a gown bearing the same pattern the Obersts use on their wallpapers, those peasant pastorals crowding every part of its surface. The print is purple on a cream ground, the vignettes clumping and spreading across the fabric like mould on a slice of Roquefort. In short, the thing is hideous.

'Your wine, Madame.' The housekeeper sets the tray down behind me. 'Ah, I see you've found it!' There is an irritating, childish glee to the woman's tone.

'What,' I pause, 'is ... *it*?'

The housekeeper moves towards me. 'Why, it is a gown, Madame.'

215

'Obviously. But what is it doing here?'

'It's a very unique garment.'

'Unique,' I say, 'yes. That certainly is one way of describing it.'

'Monsieur Wilhelm thought you would like it. He was very keen for me to have it ready for your arrival—'

'Well, you may inform Monsieur Wilhelm that he can take it away again,' I interrupt, finding myself increasingly unable to quench my annoyance. 'How he thought such an ugly thing a good idea in the first instance is quite beyond me.'

The ends of the housekeeper's mouth turn down. 'Oh, Madame, you do not mean that? Monsieur Wilhelm instructed his manager to have it made especially. An exercise in cotton printing.'

A flush of indignation. Surely the woman doesn't mean that my father-in-law actually had the gown made for *me*? It would fit a woman twice my heft. Wilhelm Oberst must have had my mother's build in mind when he designed it.

'What my father-in-law seems to forget,' I say, raising an eyebrow, 'is that I am the daughter of a marquis and, therefore, not accustomed to making myself a walking advertisement for a ... *factory*. In any case, it's far too large.' The woman's eyes flick between the gown and myself, her mouth open. 'So you may take it away, this instant. Find some other place to put the thing. The rubbish heap, preferably.'

The housekeeper seems lost for words, perhaps thrown by my surging candour, perhaps by my ability to see through her master's crude money-making schemes so astutely. Nevertheless, she makes no effort to remove the gown from the armoire. On the bed Pépin yaps, as though voicing his own displeasure.

The woman's inertia is the last straw. Impossible to censor my vexation any longer, I go to extract the gown myself but, as I do, I observe that the dots in the pattern I had assumed to be flower heads or blobs of decoration are not so nondescript. They are little birds, finches, hopping and flapping between the scenes. I can even discern that one of the creatures has a leash tied around its tiny leg, and is being jerked back to the earth by the peasant who holds the string. I snatch the remainder of the fabric into my arms and stride to the door.

'Take it away, I said!' I fling the words in the housekeeper's direction along with the gown, steering her out into the passageway.

The woman is still protesting as I close the chamber door and, in an effort not to slip my fingers beneath my wig, reach unsteadily for the wine.

Le Jour

14th July, two weeks later

Sofi

I am dreaming of a wagon, of weighted wheels lumbering along a track, a rumble like a distant storm. I tense, flesh hardening to granite as I anticipate the increase in the speed of that wagon, wait for it to career and thunder and crash.

I bolt awake and uncurl my fingers from Lara's. There are voices outside, lowered and careful in tone. I rub my eyes and cross to the window. They must be early, even earlier than they said they would be, for the sun is not yet up and there is only the faintest vein of light tracing the horizon.

The wagon, I see, has come to a halt on the track. Just as Bernadette promised. I unhook the window and open the glass. Pascal and two other men sit squashed up front, with a handful more workers perched on its open back, Bernadette and Sid included. Others headed in the same direction on foot have stopped to talk to them, and their words float up to me. Patchy at first but growing clearer, bolder.

'We're going there now ...'

'... us, too.'

'Today's the day!' It is Bernadette's voice and it is strident, exuberant as a trumpet. 'Today's the day they're storming the Bastille! Things are about to change!'

There has been talk of it for days, weeks. That the Bastille must fall, the nation's emblem of royal authority and all its rampant greed and injustice. But as soon I hear the fire in Bernadette's voice, that is when I know for sure. The people are about to put a light to the fuse and blast the old order away. Out on the track, the little party all cheers, fists to the sky, feet drumming the wagon's slatted floor.

I nudge Lara awake. 'We must dress!' I tell her. 'Quickly. They're here!'

My sister stirs sleepily, watches me pull skirt over petticoats over chemise. 'Sofi,' she croaks. 'What time is it?'

'Early,' I reply. 'But Pascal's wagon is down there already. We need to make haste.'

'Then it really is happening? And everyone's going?'

'Of course,' I reply, 'and so must we.' I pull on my jacket. 'Come, there's no time to lose!'

Lara gets out of bed and starts to dress, too. 'What about Mama?' she murmurs. 'Not that I think she should join us, it might be dangerous. But she won't know where we have gone. We cannot even leave her a note.'

'She will soon work it out,' I say. 'I'll wager hardly anyone will be left in the factory today ... look!'

We are in the open doorway of the cottage now, having quietly turned the key and lifted the latch. I point to Pascal's wagon. Even more workers have clustered around it in the minutes it has taken us to dress, a second vehicle further off towards the forecourt also laden with people.

'Lord, we thought you two'd never come down,' Sid calls to us, feigning a yawn.

Bernadette laughs. 'Ready, girls?' She extends her hand and pulls me up to join her, Pascal geeing the horses to rattle the wagon into motion.

'Lara, come!' I cry. 'Quickly!'

My sister glances back to the cottage, wavers for the briefest moment more, then, lips set in a thin line of determination, clambers onto the wagon.

219

Monuments of Paris

Paris

Sofi

Paris is not what I expected at all. It is teeming and filthy, more so the closer to the centre we go. It's as though the city is a giant midden of unrest, putrefying from the inside out under the hot July sun.

The roads are rammed, with horses and carts, with livestock and carriages and foot traffic. Many here are gaunt, bow-legged from lack of food. Their faces are warped with desperation or else void of expression altogether, as though they were already dead.

Little by little, the wagon slows in the crush of in-going traffic, until it comes to a complete standstill. A plume of smoke rises to our left, hazing the remains of the once-elegant building it has ravaged. The sight of it is captivating, smoke fuming from the empty eye-sockets of the windows, from the missing roof. The structure could almost pass for a scaled-down chateau, extinguished by the working people.

'They've been burning the toll booths,' the man next to Sid says, noticing me staring. 'Screw the taxes! Any chance we can get moving, Cal, eh?'

When it becomes clear that we will not be moving again, some of the workers start to yell for Pascal to turn, to take another route. But in this jam of people it is hopeless, so Bernadette suggests that we proceed on foot.

'You'd best follow us,' she says, leading the way.

As we push down the choking lanes I take my sister's hand, the city around us an expansive, unwieldy mass. Every bit of the capital is engulfed, not by smoke or by stench, though there is plenty of both, but by a constant, growing, bone-shaking rumble. At first I think it is the mere size of the crowds, but it is not. It is the size of their fervour, a separate entity in itself. The people are advancing to the Bastille like fractious drones to their queen.

I glance sideways at Lara, who is biting her lip. Perhaps she is thinking of the riots and marches, the turmoil that has erupted in the capital over the previous few days.

'We couldn't miss this, could we?' I say in her ear, gripping her hand more tightly. 'A chance to see Paris? You don't need to worry, it will be all right.'

'It will,' my sister replies, her tension softening. 'We will look out for each other.'

We have been trudging for what must be hours, but from the snatches of conversation around us I gather that the Bastille is close. My spirits lurch, the streets here are the worst I've seen in the city, shit-smeared and foul, with the buildings little more than teetering shacks of ramshackle parts, nearing collapse. Locals nurse bellies swollen with hunger, and there are more and more of them as we shove our way on, carrying children who haven't the strength to stand. That is what today is about, I tell myself. Justice. For everybody.

As the crowds grow denser, wilder still, jabbing metal glints from all around. The barrels of muskets and sharpened blades, I realise, brandished by the people. Sickles, knives, shanks—

'We're here,' Bernadette announces, 'if you couldn't tell. La Grande Bastille!'

I try to look in the direction she indicates, but it is impossible. Hordes of people, thousands strong, line every distinguishable road-way and alley.

An older man next to me gives a sudden, violent thrust of his fist.

'Toffs in there eat better than we do!' he exclaims, slapping his upper arm and spitting curses to the air.

I follow the direction of his gesture and, through the melee, I finally see. The Bastille, looming into view, eight-towered and inscrutable as a cliff-face. It reveals itself at last, that edifice of four centuries, the symbol of the people's oppression, of royal gluttony and the greed of their grasping, fawning minions. Even above the clamour, I hear de Comtois' words as though he was right next to me. *Prisons like the great Bastille are filling up with men unable to pay their way.* My heart pounds, the rhythm a drumstick at my chest. *Justice.*

'Come on, then,' Bernadette says, clutching the jacket of the man in front of her with one hand and Sid's sleeve with the other. 'So we don't get separated, crowds are thicker here.'

Sid does the same to me and I to Lara, and together we gradually advance to one of the high buildings opposite the prison's walls.

On reaching its door, Bernadette stops to greet someone. A woman of about thirty, her clothing startling. Her overall appearance, in fact, extraordinary. Instead of wearing her hair neatly pinned beneath a cap like ours, this woman's head is topped by a bright felt hat. Her brilliant red hair is completely loose, spilling out from under it and almost to her hips, on which the waistband of a pair of men's trousers sits, striped and snug. Suddenly conscious of staring, I draw my eyes away from her lower half and see the sprig of foliage pinned to her jacket. I glance around, notice others are also wearing scraps of green about them. Leaves, torn strips of linen, a few shining feathers.

'I see you, too, are wearing the colour of liberty,' the red-headed woman says to me. 'Of hope.'

I touch my hand to the velvet ribbon at my throat. The bright green of a chive leaf.

She signals for us to enter and in we go, climbing a sequence of staircases in procession, all the way to the building's attic. There, the others start to squeeze themselves through a dormer window and onto the roof.

'Careful, Sofi!' Lara warns, as I go to do the same.

I glance outside. Bernadette and Sid have made it across the tiles already, and are settling themselves on the ridge as though it was the highest row of seating in a playhouse.

'It's fine,' I tell her. 'Come on.'

We wedge ourselves through the attic window, picking our way like mountain goats across the sloping roof. Unable to remove our gaze from our feet as we go, we do not stop to take in our surroundings until we reach the others. When we do, the panorama that confronts us takes our breath away.

We can see everything, the rise and slope of every rooftop of every quarter, the huge grey sweep of the Seine. Drifting plumes of soot ring the city, the remains of the other toll booths burned. I watch as the smoke swells and merges, surrounding the entire capital like a tightening, smouldering girdle.

At the base of the Bastille, the people's forces throng. And they are equipped not with modern weapons, but old axes, pikes, some with muskets made a century ago. Ancient arms to topple the *ancien regime*.

'Citizens' Militia,' says the red-headed woman, who has also made her way onto the roof. Her voice is husky, as if cured by the city's smoke. 'Seized that old haul of arms not an hour ago.'

'But can they really do anything with antiques like those?' my sister whispers, nodding to the prison, to the opponents of the people. Its walls bristle with the barrels of cannons and blue-jacketed guards.

We crouch on the rooftop and wait. The atmosphere builds, the tension on the streets ebbing and flowing. Every time I think it will crest into action, it settles again. Hours pass. Delegations of men are admitted into the Bastille and let out of the Bastille. Nothing is happening and yet everything is happening.

'This is pointless!' a man on a neighbouring rooftop shouts. 'Can't be more than seven of the King's prisoners in there to liberate anyhow!'

He is dug in the ribs by another, told to shut up.

'It's what the place symbolises, them and us!' I hear a voice rising, fervid and hard-edged. Only after some seconds do I recognise it as my own. 'It cannot go on!' The words are a geyser in my throat.

My sister looks at me worriedly and the red-headed woman must notice this, too. 'Hear, hear!' she shouts, casting the faintest echo of a glare in Lara's direction, before tossing me a smile as vivid as her locks.

'And our troops need the Bastille's gunpowder!' someone calls.

'The gunpowder will be liberated, and so will we!' the red-headed woman calls back, cheers echoing all around, not least from Bernadette, who seizes my arm and points. 'Look, there!'

Ladders have been flung, not only against the sides of the Bastille, but against the buildings next to it, and men are scrambling up the rungs like swarming ants. Some have made it onto the roof of the perfumier's next door, to throw themselves into the courtyard of the prison and attempt to lower the outer drawbridge.

A cry goes up. 'Back! Back! *Vite!*'

The crowds nearest the Bastille try in vain to rush away from the structure, but it is too late. The drawbridge lands with a deafening bang, crushing a man beneath it.

Cannons are pushed closer to the prison by the Citizens' Militia, scores of people piling over each other behind every one. A fearful whoosh, a blast so loud it shocks the air, reverberates like a quake along the streets.

A round of musket fire next, so many shots together they are as loud as the cannons. *Crack crack crack.* Instinctively I cover my head and Lara pulls me close.

Below, frenzied shouts start cutting through the cannons and the muskets and the crowds. 'The guards are firing on the Governor's orders! On de Launay's orders!'

The muskets were not fired from the streets then, but from the Bastille itself.

'That bastard's trying to kill us!'

'Treachery!' the red-headed woman screams. Three syllables in repeat, her cry so loud it rips the air from her lungs. For the slightest second it gives the sensation of eclipsing everything, as though the people in the streets, the Militia and the spectators have all paused, tuning their minds to the true meaning of the word. 'Trea-che-ry!'

This last scream seems to spur the people on, and they flood over the drawbridge and into the prison's courtyard, as those left on the streets work together to push a series of pale, wheeled domes towards the ramparts. They are carts, I observe, their backs piled high with straw. Torches are put to this cargo and it lights with a terrific roar, burning fast as wildfire. So many mountains of flaming straw create a smokescreen, a chaos, blurring the guards' view of the streets and allowing the Militia to advance inside. Just as they intended.

But their plan is almost too good. There is so much smoke it begins to obliterate everything, billowing high and solid as the prison's eight towers.

'Dear Lord,' murmurs Lara.

Without thinking, I let go of my sister's hand and step closer to the edge of the roof, engrossed in what might happen next. The coughing of the crowds rises and thickens as fast as that dark-grey annihilation of smoke.

Surging upwards by the half-second, the pall swallows the lower part of our building and comes up fast to meet us. For a moment it is mesmerising, like gazing down on a roiling cloud from the heavens, a cloud of powder, the blackest, most impenetrable grey.

More shouts go up and, in fitful glimpses through the smoke, I see a cannon has been hauled by the crowds towards the fallen drawbridge, and it is the largest one yet. A blaze of orange as the torch is brought to the breech—

It is only then that I realise I can no longer see my sister. The force of cannon fire knocks me off my feet.

Butcher, Baker

Lara

The sound is an earthquake and the surface I am standing upon ceases to be solid. It shudders and resounds beneath my feet, the convulsions tearing upwards to my head. The skull-splitting roar of that enormous cannon. That billowing smoke, those thundering wagons—

I take my head in my hands, willing the sound to stop, the shuddering to stop. But if my head is in my hands then my hand is not in Sofi's. Where is she? She was right next to me, only moments ago.

'Sofi!' I yell. 'So-fi!'

My insides rinse with dread, she could well have been knocked clean off the building. I teeter through the smoke, across the roof tiles to the place where I last saw her.

'Sofi!'

My hands go before me, frantically grasping the air. But I am blinded by curtain upon curtain of smoke, and my throat heaves. Coughing, I draw my apron over my nose.

'So-fi?'

My feet stumble into something, and I crouch to meet it. Through the churning, turbid grey, my sister's head at last comes into view.

'Sofi! Thank heavens.'

I help her up and as we right ourselves, there are mumblings in the distance, words starting low before rising higher above the commotion. The smoke begins, by degrees, to subside a little, and the

226

Bastille hones fitfully into view. A pure white flag is showing from its ramparts.

'The Governor's surrendered!' someone calls.

'But that means we have—' my sister begins and I know she intends to say *won*, but her sentence stops short.

Down below men are emerging from the prison courtyard, a teeming mass of bodies coursing across the drawbridge. 'Goodness, they have someone,' I say.

'It's the Governor! They've got de Launay!' the woman near us screeches with unbridled excitement. She is smiling as though infatuated by the scene, her skin having flushed the shade of her hair, all the way to the tips of her ears.

'Please . . . just let me die!'

The five words ring out eerily, both plaintive and primal, and the gathering of men in the street suddenly parts as if backing away from the cry, fearful it might contaminate them. I realise that the woman up here on the roof with us was right, it *is* the Governor of the Bastille they have.

Held fast by both arms, the Governor lashes out a foot. It is impossible to tell whether the deed is deliberate or just an accident of the struggle. It is hard to be sure of anything in this fevered unravelling of events, even without our distance.

De Launay's kick catches another man between the legs, causing him to double over, and a frenzy ensues. The Governor is submerged by waves of men, breaking one on the other, fast-moving metal flashing behind the pistol smoke. When the men part, a body is revealed, a mess against the ground. Lifeless. It is de Launay.

'Dead from a kick to the balls!' a man cries.

'It's done, Fi,' I say to my sister, noticing her still watching. 'The Bastille is taken.'

I spoke too soon. The words have barely passed my lips when the man on the receiving end of de Launay's kick is pushed forwards. Still clutching his groin he staggers towards the corpse, encouraged by those around him. It is just possible to see that he is carrying something. He puts the object to the Governor's throat and his hand begins to move, back and forth, back and forth, a relentless, see-sawing motion. For that is exactly what the man is doing. Sawing. My stomach turns. The exertion of the undertaking makes him pant and pause, de Launay's blood dyeing his clothes, his skin, his hair, like red madder.

'Is that Desnot, the baker?' I hear. 'I think that's Desnot! Keep going, Desnot, you'll get there!'

That man, I think, is more butcher than baker. As he pauses again to rock back on his heels, someone passes him a flask. He gulps the liquid down, gasps, smacks his lips. Whatever it was has re-lit the fire in his gut. The man grips the pocket-knife tighter still, ready to finish the job.

My mouth floods with saliva as a wave of nausea overtakes me and I have to stoop and retch. When I right myself again I see the expression on my sister's face, the horror.

'Look away,' I tell her, 'please. There is no need to watch this.'

But Sofi fixes her eyes on me, large and dark as I have ever seen them. 'We owe this man's life a witness,' she murmurs. Her voice is shaking.

The woman with red hair watches, too. She watches it all, nostrils flaring, teeth bared like a hound scenting flesh.

I only look back to the street when I hear the crowds begin to cheer and I know the deed is finally done. Into the neck of the Governor, the end of a pike has been thrust, blood streaming down its handle to glove the man holding it. Up and down it goes, marched along the street for the people to see. Up and down like a puppet.

My nose is thick with smoke once more, with gunpowder from the celebratory musket rounds, with dust from the stones that are already beginning to loose and tumble from the fortress.

When we go to leave with the others, the red-headed woman pushes something into my hands. It is a badge. A *cocarde*. Red, white and blue paper ruffled around a flat centre, where words are printed in black ink.

Liberté. Égalité. Fraternité.

Sofi fixes it to my front, covering the gap on my jacket left by a missing button. Back on the streets, the shouts are deafening.
'VIVE LA RÉVOLUTION! VIVE LA FRANCE!'

Private Chambers

Jouy-en-Jouvant

Hortense

Word reaches me at supper and at first I cannot help but laugh. Mama's missive is untidily folded and the seal an outright mess. The du Pommier crest is nothing but a blur, the dark red wax dripped across the parchment like spilled blood. Nevertheless, I do not, initially, presume anything to be awry. Mama will often misalign her seal and slosh her wax about in order to prove a point, to arouse in her recipient the reaction she desires.

My mother's correspondence, resting on a silver-edged platter, is placed upon the table by the housekeeper. I pick the letter up and use my dessert knife to slice it open. I expect to be faced with a long and tedious summary of my father's faults, the least interesting comings-and-goings of the court, and how many times that hanger-on de Pise has imposed upon Mama over the last week. The content that confronts me, then, is most unexpected.

Never previously known for her brevity, Mama has scrawled only one sentence haphazardly across the parchment. I read the three words she has written multiple times, as though the repetition of the action might change their meaning.

Bastille is fallen!

A great flood of feverish sensation rushes over me, and the heavy-handled knife I am holding falls to my plate with a crash. July is the month for disaster, I think. For cataclysm. When I look down, I see the knife has cracked the china. A jagged line cuts from one side of the plate to the other, right across the necks of the glazed figures that adorn it, *jus* pooling crimson on the stark white tablecloth.

It is fortunate that I am dining alone, with only a couple of servants to bear witness to my discomposure, as it takes some effort to regain my equanimity. My appetite, however, is lost. I cannot eat another bite. One of the maids frets over the stain on the tablecloth and I push my chair back to leave, almost sending her reeling.

I do not consider formulating a reply to Mama. I do not see what there is to say on the matter and am, in any case, certain my mother will have no sensible thoughts to offer on the subject. I go straight from the dining-room to my chamber instead, questions whirling in my mind. Did we not all believe the Bastille was impenetrable, a royal stronghold, an untouchable symbol of monarchical rule? Were we not informed that the King had stationed extra troops in the capital?

Despite the warmth of the month, my chamber is chilled. It is a dreary room at the best of times and, poky though its proportions are, the belongings I've been permitted to bring here have barely filled a quarter of it. Yet tonight, something more seems to be missing. It puts me on edge and, after Mama's letter, I am on edge enough as it is.

To quiet my thoughts, I cross to the commode for a glass of the sweet muscat my lady's maid usually prepares for me. But the cooler, I see, is empty and the glass that accompanies it still upside-down on the salver. Then I realise. My lady's maid. The wine is absent, the glass unprepared and the old woman nowhere to be seen.

I jerk impatiently at the bell pull, my ire rising. How dare she disappear, tonight, of all nights. Moments later, when there is a hesitant knock at the door, I expect the woman's shrivelled countenance to appear around it, bleating some apology over neglecting her duties, most likely as a result of having fallen asleep. But it isn't Mireille at all, only the housekeeper who comes.

'Where is my lady's maid?' I demand. 'Please fetch her this instant.'

Discomfort clouds the woman's face. 'I am sorry, Madame, but I'm afraid I cannot.'

A burst of scorn instinctively departs my lips. 'I beg your pardon?'

'I'm ever so sorry to inform you, Madame, but she isn't here.'

'Isn't here? What do you mean she isn't here?'

'She isn't in the house, Madame. Hasn't been seen since you started your supper.'

I believe I am too wrong-footed to reply. This is most unlike my maid, who has been impossible to shake off for nigh on the past five years.

'I'll have one of the girls come up directly, Madame,' the house-keeper continues. 'She may take over some of the duties until your lady's maid is located.'

I flick my hand at her, indicating she should leave. For a single, misguided second the thought occurs to me that it is the events at the Bastille that have prompted my maid's vanishing. Did my father not mention that she was once nursemaid to the Governor de Launay, and thought of him as her own son? But I cannot believe it. That would have been so many decades ago now I do not see how a woman with her various deficiencies of memory could recollect much about it at all.

Throughout the long, uncertain evening I fancy Mireille will, at any moment, materialise at the door. The notion returns to me endlessly, like an image on one of my childhood spinning-tops. But when the clock passes midnight and still she has not come, it is one of the other serving girls who must prepare me for bed.

That night, the dark, it seems, has talons. I catch sight of them in the chamber's gloomy half-light, there in the wallpaper. The way those scenes cluster together, the way the vines and curlicues slink into the areas surrounding them. More than once I open my eyes and I do not see the pattern of the wallpaper at all, but rather only the negative spaces between it, merging to form the claws of a large and monstrous eagle.

I reach for Pépin, bring his warm form closer to my middle. He has always comforted me in the past, through such dark and sleepless stretches of haunted nights. But not this time. This time, the dark is emptier and more menacing than ever. The blood and tumult in Paris, the overthrown Bastille, my absentee maid. This dismal coop I now find myself in. And that other cage, incessantly breaking the surface of my thoughts, try as I might to cudgel it down.

In the earliest hours of the morning I give up on sleep altogether, leaving my little pet where he is on the counterpane. I light a taper, not being able to remember the last time I did so myself. I have only the faintest notion of where it is I am going, still in my night-chemise and with no cover or robe about me. I move into the passage and, on bare and silent feet, I steal all the way along it.

Outside the chamber door, I pause to listen. There is no noise from within. I tap, softly. Nothing. I tap again and when still there is no answer I try the handle. Only as the door starts to open do I become conscious of the fact that I have never before set foot inside this room, that it is one of the family's few spaces I am still yet to see. I tiptoe inside, my breath imperceptible as I close the door noiselessly behind me.

I am barely across the threshold of the chamber when a startling gust of wind assaults my taper, almost extinguishing it completely. When the flame steadies I look around, observing the peculiar details of the space. I see that not only is the window wide open, but the drapes and shutters are, too.

This chamber is like none of the other rooms in the house. Instead of being covered in the same oppressive factory wallpaper, the walls here are totally bare, a whitewashed plaster devoid of any colour or hangings, as if it has lately been stripped. There is no luxury, no comfort. Indeed, I believe it is the most comfortless room I have ever seen in my life.

Furniture, too, is sparse. Armoire, chest, a single chair, a nightstand on which sits a decorative rosewood box. With its mother-of-pearl inlay and embellished silver escutcheon, this box is the finest thing in the entire room.

The bed takes its place in the middle of this spartan cube, a four-poster missing the drapes, the structure rising from the dark like a rib cage. And then I see him, my husband, lying inert on the mattress, his top half bare, lower half obscured by the counterpane. I stand and regard it all, taking in the sight of him. Pondering what might have brought me to his chamber.

It does not take me long. If I am honest, I know exactly why I have come. To outrun the awful, unrelenting cavalcade of my thoughts, to attempt to take back control. To eradicate a memory once and for all as if extracting a festering splinter. To treat a pox with a pox and have both of them cancelled forever.

Another gust comes then, rattling the casement. I shelter the taper with my hand this time, but the wind billows my night-chemise about me, the whipping ends of my thin hair fanning back, catching the edges of my vision and looking quite white in the taper's light.

My husband sits up without warning, as though seized by a fit. 'Is it you?' he says. The tone of his voice, imploring and erratic, carries with it both a fear and a longing.

'Yes, it is,' I call, already knowing I shall not divulge why I have come. 'Did I wake you?'

The wind calms again and there is absolute silence. My husband watches incredulously as I move to the bed, and it is only when I come to rest upon the counterpane that he seems to see me properly, and for the first time. Staring at me, recognition dawning, he runs one hand down his face. 'Oh,' he says, dazed. 'It is you. I must have been dreaming.'

Whatever sensibility had just befallen Josef seems now to hold me, too, for I feel caught and suspended by the glow of the taper which falls across his body, illuminating bare skin to the bones of his pelvis. Fighting back the fear rising instinctively in my throat, I force myself to study him dispassionately. I have never seen so much of him before.

Aware of my gaze wandering across his nakedness, he grabs a handful of the counterpane and pulls it higher, like a bashful bride. I reach towards him slowly, and gently place my hand on his. 'There is no need,' I murmur, tempering my voice to the drawl I presume always precedes such encounters. A co-mingling of sordidness and seduction. 'We are married, are we not?'

I move Josef's fingers to lower the counterpane again, and my hand comes to rest on his thigh. He looks at me with huge-eyed amazement, too stunned to move, the muscles of his torso tightening. A bead of perverse satisfaction at his frozen state buzzes inside of me.

I shift myself closer to him then, feeling the warmth emanating from his skin. At this unfamiliar proximity, I can smell traces of sandalwood, drink and sweat upon him, mingling with a fourth scent, which, had he been a woman, I would have sworn was lavender.

There is now scarce a foot's width of space between us. I lean towards him and put my lips to his. They tense slightly, but he does not pull away, and to my surprise, I find that I can bear it. I kiss him harder, place the taper down next to the box on the nightstand by feel alone, all the time pushing ever closer, sensing the press of his body against me. The hand of mine that was resting on his thigh edges upwards, fingers searching beneath the counterpane. That is when he jerks himself away and out of my touch.

'What are you doing?' His aghastness is tinged with dismay, shame almost, as though we were not man and wife at all, but rather he a serving girl and me his lecherous master.

'I—' I whisper and go to shuffle closer again.

'No,' he says firmly and pushes me from him. Since I am close to the brink of the mattress, the act near topples me altogether. 'Go to bed, for God's sake.' He draws the counterpane decisively to his chin and turns away.

For a good many moments I am too shocked to respond. I have not known or heard of such a reaction from a man to a woman's touch in all my life. I pick up my taper and with a voice like a blade, thin with a sharp edge, I say, 'As you wish, *husband*.' My cheeks smart, my body shaking at the ignominy of what has just occurred between us.

Back in my chamber, I reach up to my head. With trembling fingers I pluck out one hair and then another, concentrating on every little prick of hot pain as each strand comes free.

The Crowning of the Rose Maiden

Lara

Though I have been told by Monsieur Marchant that Josef is waiting for me outside, I do not see him at first. I only really notice him at all as he is at such an odd angle to everybody else, on the far side of the crowd, and there is a moment when I think I must be imagining him. We have not spoken since before he was married, weeks ago now.

'Hello,' I say, approaching. 'I nearly missed you.'

His eyes shine at my words, as though spectacled by the sun. 'And I you,' he replies, and I wonder if he may have misheard me.

In the pause that follows, Josef smiles and holds my gaze. Then he peers uneasily around, as though fearful of being observed, and attempts to settle his smile into a more neutral expression.

'The reason I wanted to speak with you is that the lady's maid of my wife ... Well, she has left Hortense's employment. Quite unexpectedly, as it happens ...'

As Josef's words fade, I try to guess what they have to do with me. He marks two women exiting one of the other workshops. They are looking towards us, one muttering something to the other. He takes a step from me, as though we were doing something wrong.

'What I mean is that Hortense is in need of a new lady's maid,' he says. 'And I wondered whether *you* might consider the position?'

The question instantly catches me off-guard, it is the last thing I could possibly have expected. I open my mouth to respond, but Josef continues.

'I must tell you that Hortense isn't the easiest woman to deal with, but I'm sure you are aware of that already. I can well imagine what people have been saying since she got here.'

'Oh . . . it's not that,' I say.

His eyebrows twitch, hopeful and questioning.

'Sorry, what I mean is . . . I've no experience of the work. Are there not dozens of women in the capital who would be better suited?'

'It would not be wise to bring a woman from the capital,' Josef replies. 'Versailles neither. Not given the way things are. It would reflect badly on us all.'

'But the Monsieur, your father. He would not object?'

'I do not see how he possibly could, all things considered.'

I catch myself biting my lip at the ambiguity of the remark.

'The work isn't difficult,' Josef goes on. 'Merely sorting her things, dressing her, drawing her bath and so forth. And I don't mean to imply that you would not be paid well. You would earn more than you do in the factory. Quite a bit more.'

His words disorient me a moment and I have no idea how to re-spond. 'I do not know. How would it seem—' I wonder that Josef is so keen to have me in his house, when he appears so uncomfortable conversing with me in front of the other workers.

'I shall see you are taken care of,' he interrupts. 'I hope you know that. And, in addition to the increased wage, you would have a chamber of your own.' He seems annoyed with himself. 'I should have mentioned that sooner.'

I had not contemplated this, but suppose ladies' maids must always sleep within reach of their mistresses. 'But Sofi—' If I was to accept such a post, it would be the first time we will ever have lived apart. How will she cope with Mama alone? Mama, whose sourness never seems to sweeten. I thought it would, after we left Marseilles. But she is as chiding and strict as before. A question arrests me then. Could her problem be *me*? Might Mama be different if I was gone from the cottage, easier for Sofi to bear—?

'Your chamber would not be in the attics with the other domestic staff,' Josef says, interrupting the thought. 'And I would see to it myself that the room is comfortably furnished.'

'Is it usual for a servant to have such a room? I would not want to be the cause of any ill-feeling.'

'It is normal for a lady's maid, yes. My wife's last woman should have had it, in fact, but for the stairs.' He smiles. 'The chamber is spacious, private . . .'

A shimmering blue butterfly flits behind Josef's shoulder, fragile and finite as a cut petal.

'And it has the best view.' His pale eyes again fix themselves appealingly on mine.

'But I am content in the print-house—' I contemplate the job I would be leaving behind. Not interesting or easy at present but, in time, if I am diligent, I might be able to work my way up, have my own design table in a year or two. Perhaps I could even see some of my drawings form the factory's newest patterns, my designs turned into something finished and enduring, just as my sister and I always wanted when we hoped we would work for Pa. But then, I consider, my headaches have been getting worse, my vision, too, disfiguring the patterns of the wallpaper. Perhaps some time away from it would give me a break, a chance to recover.

Mama is not getting any younger, either. Hers is a more physical labour, and one day she will be forced to give it up. With no husband to support her, any extra money I save could help her live more comfortably when that time comes. In a year or two, say, or when there is enough put by and my head is restored, perhaps I could go back to my designs, return to the print-house.

'I believe you would like it in the chateau. With your aunt and more comfortable quarters. If you did wish to work for Hortense, that is. And I hope you might consider it, at least. I hope that very much.' Josef is looking at his shoes now, scared of what my answer will be.

'I . . .' I start, considering once more everything that has whorled through my head since he started to speak. My words are not easy to get out. 'Thank you. I would be happy to accept.'

The breath gushes out of him and it seems as though he will draw me into his arms. 'You may start tomorrow.'

Mirrors and Opposites

Lara

For the rest of the day I feel my decision lingering over me, weighted like a blade. When my sister and I retire to our chamber for the evening, I know I can put it off no longer. I must tell her.

I hear Sofi at the bed, assembling her papers whilst chattering about one of the workers, about someone of note in the capital. It suddenly strikes me that this will be the last night I spend with her here, and I find I must move to the window so she cannot see my face.

'Fi?' I say. How to even begin to explain my new position to her? In my head it seemed reasonable, the right thing to do for us all. But I fear my sister won't see it that way. I fear my working for a woman like the Madame will be the last thing Sofi would want.

'What?'

I waver, searching once more for the right place to start. The view through the window quivers and clusters in dark shapes, my reflection hovering palely against the pattern.

'What, Lara?'

'I have to tell you something.'

Sofi pauses, turns towards me. But again I hesitate, an absence of words on my tongue. I know well my sister's opinion of Madame Hortense, her feelings towards Josef, her state of mind since Pa ... I try to push down the certainty that whatever I say will crush her, however I say it.

'Have you forgotten?' she asks.

'No . . .'

'Well, I daresay it can't be important. Anyhow, did you hear what I said? About Bernadette and Roux?' I must look utterly blank, as she adds eagerly, 'You know, that red-headed woman, from Paris.'

My mind focuses and I realise who she's been referring to, remember how that woman hadn't just watched the horrors unfold at the Bastille, but revelled in them. I do not understand how Sofi hadn't seen it, too.

My sister is on her belly now, groping beneath the bedstead. 'There it is!' she exclaims, waving a stick of graphite in the air.

I go to her and sit down. 'I do not think that woman a good person to know, Sofi.'

'Who, Roux? But she is a revolutionary, she wants change, progress. What's bad about that?'

'Her views are extreme, Fi, and she's on the lookout for people she can talk into sharing them. She is an agitator.'

'She is a reformer!' Sofi declares and looks at me agape. 'Lara, you know how important it is to me that those to blame are held to account . . . the aristocracy . . . for Pa . . . ' Her voice sputters and halts.

I take in her torment and fall silent. I wanted to warn my sister, to explain to her that some of these people are not revolutionaries but radicals. Like wolves they catch scent of the weak, identify the insecure and the vulnerable and do not give up. 'I'm just . . . worried, that's all,' I say instead. 'I wouldn't want such things to come between us.'

'Come between us?' Sofi exclaims. 'Never! Why should progress come between us? We are blood, we are sisters, are we not?'

She climbs onto the bed next to me and I swallow hard. 'Anger is like a disease, Sofi,' I say. 'It eats away at you if you let it.' I think of Mama. 'Please remember that.'

My sister brings her hands to her body. They are tensed, curling in on themselves tightly. 'I do not want to argue,' she sighs, 'not tonight,' and touches her forehead to mine. 'Now,' she adds, straightening, 'may I draw your likeness before bed, for I've an idea for a drawing of us both and . . . ' Hurt gauzes her expression. 'Well, I must have misplaced the last good one I did.'

Sofi passes me the candle. 'Here,' she says, raising my hand. 'Hold it like this.' She re-positions a pillow behind her, tilting our little square of looking-glass so she might see her own reflection, then drops her board folder decisively on her lap.

After a few minutes, the rhythmic scratching of her graphite becomes calming to us both, just as it had in Pa's workshop. With my sister absorbed by a tranquil concentration, my own mind starts to unspool.

'Do you remember what Pa used to say?' I ask. 'That we were mirrors—'

'Mirrors and opposites,' she finishes, fixing her eyes on mine.

'Yes.' She gives the briefest smile. 'We reflect each other's differences is what he meant, I think. Show up each other's flaws.'

'Though Pa was too kind to admit we had any.'

Sofi's countenance clouds sorrowfully, and she lowers her face to the drawing as though grappling with a troublesome part of it. 'I suppose it's like the printing. I'm the block and you're the paper. The same but mirrored. Different.'

She continues to work as we exchange memories of Marseilles, the moments between lapsing into peace and silence.

'There!' Sofi announces, after an hour has passed. She hands me her sketch.

I do not know what to say. She has indeed drawn us both, here together in the chamber, the spherical glow of the candle lighting our faces whilst casting the rest of the image into an elliptical darkness. These darker areas are shaded heavily, with energetic, densely packed strokes. Yet against this blackness, Sofi has captured our faces more delicately than I have ever seen her work before.

'You do not like it?'

'No, I do, Fi. So much. It's beautiful.'

But something dreadfully familiar in the likeness arrests my gaze. *We are blood, we are sisters, are we not?* And that is when it happens. That is when realisation hurtles through me, an intense, brutal sweep of it. My face falls.

Sofi ponders a moment, gauging my altered expression. She can see her sketch has moved me. If only she could recognise how. 'Keep it,' she says and places her hand over mine.

I draw her to me and when we part she asks, 'Have you remembered yet what you wanted to tell me?'

'I—' I begin, stopping again just as quickly. 'No. You were right. It can't have been important.'

Though it is too warm for the coverlet, my sister and I sleep with our limbs entwined, as always. I wonder if we will ever do so again.

Objets

Sofi

'I do not believe it,' I exclaim, barely able to conceal my disgust. 'You ... going to lady's maid for that ... that *woman*? Why didn't you tell me?'

I knew my sister was hiding something last night. Yet only now has she summoned the courage to confess exactly what, making the pain of her secret even sharper.

I watch, incredulous, as she gathers her possessions into a crate. Her clothing, her pen, the drawing I made of us before we slept. There isn't much to pack, her sketches forming the bulk of it. When she takes up that little *fiole* of fragrance, she tries to conceal it from me. I came upon the thing several weeks ago and guessed at once who it was from, knowing we couldn't afford scent at all, let alone any that fine. Eventually, Lara admitted it was a gift from Josef, and I wondered how I could ever have been so stupid.

My sister pulls a face and looks around. 'Where is my comb? Sofi, have you taken it?'

'You haven't answered my question!'

Lara sighs. 'Please calm down,' she says softly. 'Is it any wonder I did not tell you last night?'

Hot tines of anger are stabbing at my cheeks. 'How can you have agreed to it ... to be at the beck and call of ... of *her*. I cannot believe you would ever do such a thing.'

She quietly lays the last few items in the crate.

'Well, say something,' I protest. 'Lara, you cannot do this!'

Her expression darkens. 'Remember what I said last night, Fi. I'm worried about you. No good ever came from such hatred.' My sister runs her fingers over the objects she has assembled. 'And please lower your voice,' she adds, lowering hers. 'You will upset Mama.'

I snort. 'I hope she does hear, hope she realises what a grave mistake you are making and stops . . .' I pause, feel my shoulders stiffen like two tightening spindles of thread. Lara told Mama earlier this morning. Mama, who is always so sharp and censorious of her. The fact is like a knife to my back. '. . . stops you before you make a total fool of yourself. And us!'

Lara stills then and sits, looking me directly in the eyes. 'Of course she won't, Sofi. The money is twice what I earn in the print-house. Can you not see?'

'Yes, I can see, I'm not—' I stop, seething as I realise the truth in her words. Of course I understand about the money. It is just that I cannot bear the thought of my own sister serving one of *them*. A blue-blooded noble, as bad as all the rest. I cannot tolerate the notion of her working in that house with Josef, lodging there, having a room of her own whilst I stay here with Mama and toil day after day in the factory. And I know that is selfish of me, but really it is nothing compared to the part of all this that hurts me the most. The thought that if Lara leaves for the chateau, there will be just two of us left instead of four, the people I love most slipping away before my eyes. For if she really does take this new job, how often will my sister and I get to see each other? How often will we draw together, share our work and talk of the future? Once a week, perhaps, if we are lucky. Though I'm sure the Madame will have other ideas.

'I must leave now,' my sister says. 'And so should you. Or you will be late for work.'

With a look of resignation she picks up her small crate and carries it downstairs, where Mama is sweeping the hearth. 'Goodbye,' Lara calls.

Mama does not stop what she is doing, does not rise or turn at the word. 'Goodbye, Lara,' she says flatly. She offers nothing more.

Raising her eyebrows, very slightly, my sister continues outside.

I fumble desperately for something else to say, a last plea or truth that will make my sister see what an error this is and make her stay. 'Lara!' I cry, as she heads onto the track. 'Lara!' But no other words come.

She turns, smiles and walks on, crossing the forecourt and starting the climb up the long, tree-lined approach to the chateau.

I stand there for some minutes in mute stupefaction, half-furious, half wanting to cry, until a noise breaks my thoughts. Mama's voice. Her words are hoarse but quiet, forming a comment muttered only to herself. She must assume that I'm further outside than I am and cannot hear her.

'More in common with her new mistress than she supposes.'

The phrase leaves an odd, discordant quality in the air. I think my mother must finally be taking leave of her senses.

As the factory bell starts up, I rush in, grab my apron and make off towards the dye-house.

Garments

Lara

I am standing on the threshold of that strange room again. The morning sun renders both the pattern of the wallpaper and the violet of its print more intense, making the circularity of the wall and the overwhelming, teeming scenes that crowd it the only things one really sees. It is almost frightening, how that paper envelops both the room and anyone in it entirely.

The ache returns to my skull, and the pattern before me begins to liquefy and shiver. By working for Madame Hortense, I presumed I would escape the wallpaper. Yet now I find myself enclosed within it. I blink hard, turn quickly away.

'You like your new chamber?' Josef asks at my back, his voice eager, faintly pleading. He wants me to be happy here. 'I hope you do, with the view and . . . everything.'

I attempt to look past the wallpaper to where Josef gestures. There is furniture up here now, the room isn't empty like it was previously. A bed dressed with pristine white linen juts from the wall, together with a deep red wood commode and nightstand to match the armoire Sofi concealed herself inside, months ago. I cringe when I remember that night, shuddering at what our aunt told us of this wallpaper and the story behind it. A small, dark shape at the bottom of one of the armoire's doors catches my attention. A hole, its edges rough as though gnawed by some sort of rodent.

I drag my eyes to the stone fireplace set into the wall, the high window rising from the floor. It looks out across the chateau's approach all the way to the buildings of the factory, to the river and woods beyond. And there, at the very corner of the view, I see the huge old sycamore, rising up at the boundary of the gardens.

There is a table positioned in front of this window, and it is arranged with objects. A bowl and jug, parchments, graphite and ink. Set up to function as both toilette and drawing desk.

Disconcerting though I find the space, I'm touched by the effort Josef has gone to in making it comfortable. 'Thank you,' I say to him, 'very much. It is lovely.'

'I am glad you think so. I thought you might still want a place to sketch. Here, let me.' He lifts the crate from my arms, glances inside and sets it down carefully on the bed.

'Beg your pardon, Monsieur,' comes Aunt Berthé's voice from the landing, 'but as soon as you are finished I must go through the new garments with Mademoiselle Lara.'

'Oh, yes, of course,' Josef answers, removing a hand from his pocket. 'You may do so now.' He smiles at me proudly, as though anticipating my reaction to a gift.

Aunt Berthé looks between us.

'Please, do not mind me,' Josef ventures.

'Very well, Monsieur,' replies my aunt, with the slightest trace of surprise. She leads me to the armoire, opening it to reveal more garments on its shelves than I've ever seen together in my life. Piles of jackets, caps, stomachers and skirts edged with lace, all new and in muted shades from green to pink to blue. They are much finer than the clothes of the other servants, and certainly finer than anything I have ever worn before. I did not presume my new wardrobe would be so extravagant.

'There are several more things on their way from the *couturière* also, are there not, Madame Charpentier?' Josef says.

'Oh, yes, Monsieur. They'll be here later, I believe.' She turns back to me. 'But try these first. To see if they fit.'

My aunt goes through the articles one by one, telling me which of them I should wear and when. Once she has finished with the stacks of outer garments, there is only one shelf of clothing remaining.

Bundled together here are the more personal items, the chemises, the stockings and the stays. Aunt Berthé glances at Josef and I wonder if she might be waiting for him to leave. He smiles politely, seemingly oblivious of the fact, so my aunt moves sideways a little, discreetly positioning herself between Josef and the shelves.

I try to hide a smile which Josef must notice, as realisation dawns across his face and he clears his throat awkwardly. 'Oh, I'm terribly sorry,' he exclaims. 'I did not think. Please, forgive me.' Cheeks flushing, he hurries from the room.

'Goodness,' Aunt Berthé whispers. 'I thought Monsieur Josef would never take the hint!'

After going through the clothing, my aunt hands me the key to the tower chamber and instructs me to keep it safe, since it is the only copy, aside from the one she always keeps on her person. She then tells me when I will be needed to attend upon Madame, what to expect, how to address her, and passes me the lists of duties I must complete. I am to change my clothes immediately and go directly to her chamber, she says, moving to the door and bidding me good luck. Madame will have finished taking her breakfast soon. Far off downstairs, a clock begins to chime.

I stand unmoving in this unfamiliar room, anxious at the brink of the new precipice on which I find myself. My heart starts to tick fast, my palms sweat. I am quite alone, except for the countless, churning vignettes within the wallpaper and the woman who inhabits them. But as much as I know those strange, unsettling scenes are just a deception of eye and mind, I dare not check whether the woman in that purple print is indeed Madame Justine.

I dare not check in case she is me.

The Morning Toilette

Hortense

Breakfast is becoming a more paltry affair of late. Of course, I expected a decline in culinary standards after leaving Versailles, an insistence to be seen embracing a humbler way of living following the atrocities of the Bastille, but meals are growing more meagre by the day. There are no dainty sugared patisseries, petit fours or gilded tartlets here. This morning's offering is warmed milk and coffee, hot rolls with preserve, and a pitiful platter of fruit topped with a mean slice of Gruyere.

It is a ridiculous hour of the day to be up at all, and I have made my way down to the dining-room in my night-robe, plainer wig and chaster jewels, since I was not of a mind to have a serving girl disturb me earlier to see me properly dressed. My husband, however, who comes to breakfast late, does not seem to have noticed.

I pluck a red grape from the bunch on the platter and roll it around on my tongue, eyeing Josef at the other end of the table. At least we must not suffer the presence of his father. Heaven knows where Oberst Senior is, except that he seems to spend most of his time indisposed, shuttered inside one room of the house or another with only his papers for company. In the three weeks I have been here, I've sensed murmurings of discontent on this state of affairs from the workers. From what I can gather, my esteemed father-in-law has withdrawn ever more from them in recent years, and now has to be dragged out practically kicking and screaming in order to interact with anyone at all.

'My new woman starts shortly, I believe,' I say to my husband, bursting the grape between my teeth.

'Indeed,' Josef replies noncommittally, or so he thinks, but I detect the vestige of a smile playing on his lips.

Josef informed me that selecting one of his current employees to take over as my lady's maid was the only option available. That it was imperative for me *not* to be seen employing a more experienced, more expensive woman from Paris or Versailles. That it was a girl from the factory or no lady's maid at all. But, I conjecture, there is something else at work here. Something more.

I am well aware that my husband has taken it entirely upon himself to arrange this particular appointment. He must think me a simpleton if he suspects I have not recognised this intriguing fact. And he has not only selected and interviewed the woman, but had a room specifically prepared for her, filled with new garments and freshly furnished to boot.

Uninspiring repast consumed I return to my own chamber, where I await the thrilling arrival of the new woman, and not two minutes pass before she appears at the door. I've scarce had time to adopt an appropriate position at my toilette, perched upon the chair in an attitude of gathering boredom. Her punctuality vexes me somewhat but, curious to learn more about this creature my husband has found for me, I bid her enter and, as she does, I realise I have seen her somewhere before.

'Good morning, Madame,' she says brightly. The fact she is trying hard to appease is painfully obvious. Her voice is mellow and of an annoyingly pleasing pitch, with a mild trace of the south and a buttery timbre. She is about my own age, which I suppose does have its advantages, since she will at least be able to complete her tasks quicker than that shuffler Mireille. She is fair-haired, with skin only a little darker than mine, and pale, oyster-coloured eyes. But most displeasing to me of all is her countenance, which is not only handsome, ending in a delicately pointed chin, but has that uncomplaining, gentle sort of innocent openness to it, rather like that of a tender young deer.

I appraise her for a beat more and point at the wig on the stand next to me. 'Come, I must have my hair done. I trust you are experienced in dressing wigs, *coiffure à la Belle Poule?*' I smirk at the words. Of course she is not. She hasn't an inkling what I am talking about.

She comes closer to me then, reaching for the false hair and dish of pins with shaking hands. I begin to laugh out loud, for suddenly I know exactly where it is I have seen her. She was in that rabble of a welcoming party, the day I arrived in this God-forsaken place. She was the young woman, albeit more shabbily dressed then, at whom my husband stared for far too long, in front of his new wife, no less, in what was a distinct show of disrespect.

The girl removes the plainer wig I wore for breakfast and I stop laughing as suddenly as I started. In the looking-glass I see her pause briefly, to gawp at the small archipelagos of scalp showing on my head.

'Well, come along, then!' I say sharply and she jumps to it.

I watch the girl's reflection as she flounders with the task of preparing my wig. Then it strikes me. That crowd of peasants was not the only place I have seen her before. This girl bears a fascinating resemblance to the young woman from that scrap of a drawing my husband carries around in his waistcoat pocket, his little groin-tingler. Indeed, it *is* her.

'Well, this is a very interesting turn of events, Mademoiselle,' I say. 'Is it not?'

Ordered Stars

Sofi

I peer from the casement of my chamber, studying the chateau and its shimmering rows of windows. Stars plucked from the ebony sky and ordered into lines.

I sit on the ledge of this window most nights before bed, imagining which of the rooms in that huge building Josef might be in, what he might be doing. But now my mind turns to Lara. Which of those rooms *she* might be in, what *she* might be doing.

Saddened by the thought, I cast my eyes from the chateau, jumping as I catch sight of something below the window, faintly lit by the waning moon's light. There the darkness melts, shifts. Coheres into a human form that moves towards the cottage door. Someone is down there. Then I recognise who that someone is.

With Mama already in bed, I steal downstairs through the thick dark alone. To light a candle would be to risk having him notice me coming to the door, and as hard as my pulse is throbbing, I want to take him unaware. I draw a quick, deep breath, convert alarm to anger. That he thinks he has the right to prowl around the cottage at this time of the night. Or any time, for that matter.

Although I do not get too close to the glass, I can see him through the front window, skulking by the door. I move softly to the threshold, turning the key and lifting the latch as quietly as I can, before throwing the door inwards, taking him completely by surprise.

Emile Porcher's face erupts into shock and he jumps back a step. I have not seen the man since I followed him to the churchyard and watched him etch that wolf on Madame Justine's tombstone. His clothes are dark, collar high and head bare as always, thinning hair flat to his scalp. His legs are slightly bent, arms tucked to body as though tensed for a sudden retreat.

'How dare you come creeping about here in the dark!' I exclaim, emboldened by his skittish posture, but still desperate to disguise the fear behind my words.

He lowers his chin, his amber eyes remaining upon me, slim ebony lips parting and closing. Finally, in a voice strange and high as a whelp, he speaks. 'Your sister . . .'

A dart of heat passes through me, an indignation. What could he want with Lara? I recall the afternoon when I was here alone drawing, Porcher's silhouette slinking past the window. Was he looking for Lara then, too?

'My sister?' I reply. 'What about her?'

He says nothing, lips still parted a little as though panting shallowly.

My body is as tensed as his, but I'm determined to stand my ground. My thoughts fly back to the disturbing details shared by Bernadette. Madame Justine, naked from the waist down, the lines discovered around her neck when her hems were lowered. All of which this man knows. All of which this man saw.

'I know what kind of man you are,' I say, my pulse kicking through my neck. 'You leave my sister alone.'

His small, deep-set eyes stare directly at me a moment, then, to my surprise, he bows his head and walks away.

'I know all about you!' I call, exasperated, to the darkness, to his back. 'I know you had something to do with Madame Justine's death!'

He wavers, teetering on the track for the tiniest fraction of a second, before picking up his pace and loping into the night.

Eternity

Lara

Madame is taking a late supper when Aunt Berthé finds me. The rest of my new garments have arrived, she says. I must go and try them on before Madame finishes dining.

'The Monsieur says the *couturière* will be back first thing tomorrow and wants to know if there's anything that needs altering,' my aunt tells me. 'Try everything, he said.'

On reaching the tower chamber, I turn the key in the lock behind me and light an extra candle. The new articles have been laid neatly across the bed, I notice, and they are even finer and more exquisitely finished than before. Full skirts of satin in pale and dusty hues are trimmed with braid and beads, with pinked-edge pleats of taffeta. Tulle fichus stretch flimsy as gossamer, lace petticoats clustering like sprays of blossom. All are neatly assembled in stacks, indicating which garments should be worn together.

I select an elegant satin jacket to try first, the colour of sun-bleached wheat, taking up the skirt, stomacher and petticoat that accompany it. I step out of my clothes and into the new, moving closer to the oval looking-glass on the wall to remove my cap. The one I swap it for, delicate with cut-work, is smaller, and so I have to arrange my hair slightly differently to fit beneath it, pinning looser waves at my temples.

When I have finished, I back away from the looking-glass for a wider view and am startled by what I see. The woman in the mirror, whose gaze now holds my own, looks so different from me I cannot process the sight of her. She is only slightly familiar, glimpsed from somewhere outside myself that I cannot altogether place.

I take a breath and shake the wrinkles from my unfamiliar skirts, conscious I have several more outfits to try before Madame finishes her meal. But as I turn away from the looking-glass, the wallpaper suddenly stops me.

I thought I knew the design of this paper well, had examined each vignette with Sofi. But the scene that now confronts me is not one I have looked on before, and I begin to think I do not know this paper at all.

This particular vignette jars discordantly among the rest, Madame Justine seemingly nowhere to be seen. I step closer to the wall, my flesh bristling, and when I recognise what the scene actually shows, I find I cannot breathe.

There, in the pattern, is a picture of a chamber. A chamber containing a table set before a window, a dark armoire, a bed bearing several ordered heaps of clothes. A chamber decorated with hectic wallpaper, clustered with pattern, the hatching of the print suggesting the room was completely round.

But that is not all, for a woman is standing inside of that chamber, held captive by its pattern, staring, in turn, at wallpaper of her own. As her back is to the viewer, her face is invisible but, even so, I can see, with a heightening sense of creeping dread, that she is wearing exactly the same clothes as I. The same skirt, the same jacket, the same cap. The same light hair arranged in loose waves at the sides of her head. I can see it all so very clearly. For once this wallpaper is crisp, the print neither morphing nor stippling. And any moment, I think, the blood rattling in my throat, that woman will turn to face me. Her skirts begin to shift, her head and shoulders slowly swivel—

I spin around before she can, tear my line of sight from the vignette and try to calm myself. I am being watched, I could swear it, just as I could when my sister was hiding in that armoire. I am not alone. Someone else is up here, too. I cast desperately about, vision darting across the curving wall that envelops me, around and around.

It is her, the woman in the wallpaper. It is she who is watching me, from every scene on that violet print, her eyes forever fixed upon mine. She is everywhere and there is no escaping her.

PART IV

Cadeaux

January 1793, three years later

Hortense

Over three years since my wedding day and where to begin in outlining the doom, gloom and tedium that have occurred during that time? The inordinate lack of diversions. The extraordinary drabness of this nothing house in this nowhere village amongst the drone and plod of manufacture. And there is the issue of my father-in-law, too. Over the past months his health seems to have taken a plunge. Each time I see him, his pallor is a little sicklier than the last, his breathing heavier. His manner has altered as well. In place of his usual inscrutable dourness is a new insensibility, an almost imbecilic detachment. Yet still he finds strength to have his son constantly check and censor me about my clothes, my accoutrements, my spending.

It is an outrage that I should, with each year that passes, increasingly have to pretend to be something I'm not. An adult foot forced into a child's shoe. The fact that I am expected to spurn all the fine things I have not only become accustomed to over the years, but need as much as the air in my lungs. And all whilst the situation in France continues, even now, to worsen, corrupting the country like a cancer. The agonising years I've spent caged here among these workers, who grow more audacious by the day, are like the declination of a spiral. Each hour that passes, the smaller the spiral becomes. The tighter it holds me.

261

That is why, about a week ago, I decided there was nothing for it but to plan a little celebration. I had the cook forewarned, and sent some of the serving women out shopping in advance, including my lady's maid, the one my husband continues to skip and fawn after like a lost lamb. So I awake this morning with something of a re-newed sense of *joie de vivre*, for the day of the festivities has dawned.

My improved mood, however, does not last long, since no sooner have the morning's amusements begun than they are rudely inter-rupted by a knocking at my chamber door. The suddenness of the noise causes Pépin to near teeter from his chartreuse silk cushion. It might have taken several years, but he has decided he finds the colour agreeable again.

'Yes?' I shout.

Josef enters, nodding like a halfwit at my lady's maid and gaping even more witlessly when he sees the silver trinkets and other effects I have spread about the floor, the discarded bows and wrappings.

'What is all this?' he asks testily.

His tone annoys me, as does the sight of my maid looking meekly away. I have been keeping a close eye on proceedings between the two of them since she arrived at the chateau, but have so far noticed nothing improprietous.

'A good day to you, too, husband,' I reply, flapping my hand so the object of his affection might pass me the next beribboned item. 'It is a special occasion.'

Josef says nothing, waiting, clearly, for an explanation.

'It is Pépin's birthday!'

'So?'

Just like my husband to pose such an impertinent question. I show my displeasure by fixing him with a look sharp enough to slice bone. '*So* . . . we are celebrating, as you see.'

He raises his eyebrows.

'Pépin is presently engaged in unwrapping his gifts. And the festivities are to continue at supper this evening. The servants have already been informed, and the cook instructed to prepare a selec-tion of Pépin's favourite dishes.'

I am looking forward to this. Ever since I came to this place I have endured night after night of either dining alone or tolerating the tiresome silence of Josef's company. But tonight will be different. Tonight will be fun.

Quelle surprise, Josef has other ideas. 'In that case, they will have to be uninformed,' he says. 'For I came to tell you that several of the factory's associates and their wives will be dining with us tonight. It is already arranged. In any case, do you really think arranging a party for a dog is a good idea, given what is happening in the country?'

He spoils everything and I trust, for his own sake, that now he has said his piece he will leave. But I am wrong.

'And wear something simpler to supper, too,' he goes on, gesticulating at my gown. 'Something without all that usual froth.'

I have had enough of the sound of his voice and want him out. I hurl down the object I am holding, an exquisite cut-crystal bowl. It shatters on the floor, spraying diamonds of glass in all directions. My maid, who has thus far been pretending to be invisible, shields her eyes.

I look around for something else to throw, but Josef has already gone.

The Miller, his Son and the Ass

Hortense

The guests congregate for aperitifs in the salon, their voices gradually drifting upstairs. They are talking of a vote on the future of the King.

'He will not keep his head now!' a man barks. 'The country has spoken, has aired its grievances. He is a traitor and will die. Louis himself knows that.'

'But there is still time to do as the English have done, and form a parliament,' offers another. 'I don't see why not.'

'No, no, no!' the first man counters. 'It is too late for that, the monarchy has already been abolished. The King will go to the scaffold, and that will be what I call progress!'

There is a wave of laughter and my flesh chills. Businessmen. Commoners. What do they know?

While they speak, I make my way quietly down the stairs. I approach the entrance to the salon and declare felicitously, 'Gentlemen, ladies, what a pleasure to see you all.'

My father-in-law is lurking in the corner, about as far from the centre of the gathering as it is possible to get. He looks sicklier than ever tonight, his face unpleasantly bloated, like the risen skin on a heated custard. Perhaps all these years he has been locking himself away in his study, he has not been alone at all. Perhaps he has had several dozen bottles of spirits for company. It would certainly explain his complexion.

My husband gapes for the second time today and I know it is

because, deep down, he hadn't expected me to attend this supper at all. All light and sweetness, I am dressed in a modish gown – modish being what people call downright plain and ugly these days – and with little Pépin nowhere to be seen.

I can tell my husband wants to remark upon my appearance, but he is quickly intercepted by the businessmen and their women who, despite their perfidious talk of regicide, cannot refrain from showering me with compliments. It is an enjoyable appetiser to the evening, but the real entertainment is yet to begin.

When the drinks and small-talk are done, we remove ourselves to the dining-room. Here, I select my moment carefully, striking when they least expect it. Without warning, I stand and tap at my wine glass with the handle of a knife. The pockets of conversation around the table diminish.

'Ladies and gentlemen. Tonight we have gathered to mark a very special occasion. The birthday of my dearest companion!' I try to initiate a round of applause, but only one or two of the less dreary diners join me. 'So let us welcome our honoured guest for the evening.' I raise my voice and call, 'Bring him in!'

As instructed, the servants are outside awaiting their cue, and the doors open to reveal two footmen carrying aloft between them, on engraved metal rods, a velvet pad bearing Pépin. The footmen are walking steadily, but my dog is shaking as though he is being borne to the table for sacrifice rather than celebration. A chair is withdrawn and the rods balanced across its arms, allowing Pépin to sit level with the tabletop. I give my husband a look of intense satisfaction, but, hand gripping the stem of his wine glass, he is watching his father stare at my dog.

'The cook has prepared a special menu accordingly,' I declare. 'Nine delicious courses, but first ... the *entrée*!' I beckon to the footmen, who proceed to bring out and set down upon the table twenty-one bowls of a light-coloured soup. '*Crème de partridge*! I trust you will not mind if we wait for our guest of honour to eat first.'

I murmur encouragement at my pet, who begins to lick the

contents of the bowl. The cook must have made the soup too hot, however, as he does so with his mouth open, flicking globules of liquid hither and thither from his jaws.

It is just as I expected. The guests are fools. They could have started to eat at any time during this performance and yet they did not, choosing instead to follow my instructions. They say they have made progress when really they have learned nothing. In front of each of them is a dish of freshly prepared soup, slowly growing cold while my dog finishes his own serving. They sit there looking at it, pretending they care there are peasants starving, glancing occasionally to their neighbours like a flock of faltering sheep.

Pépin takes an age to finish the soup in his bowl, after which I tell them, 'Now you may eat. For the next course will soon be with us and it is one of Pépin's favourites. Stewed woodcock. *Bon appétit!*'

I do not know how I manage to keep a straight face. I smile triumphantly at my husband, but he is once more watching his father. At that second, Pépin starts heaving upon his cushion, sides distending like bellows before sending out a jet of warm, gamey-smelling liquid from his mouth. The sight of it induces several of the ladies at table to gasp and retch, to cover their mouths with the backs of their hands.

'Madame, it seems the soup has not agreed with your dog,' my husband says and drains his glass. 'Please remove him to a place where he can recover.'

Everyone at the table has stopped eating now. Spoons lie submerged in bowls or are else suspended in mid-air, somewhere between table and lips.

The fact that Josef has sought fit to take charge rankles. Though I cannot deny Pépin is looking off. I shall have some strong words for the cook in the morning.

'Of course, husband.' I stand and flash the table one of my brightest smiles. 'Do excuse me.'

Back in my chamber, Pépin retreats to his cushion, curls up and falls asleep. I mean to wait a while before going back down, to rejoin the guests at some point, but cannot face it. I find myself fiddling with the new things I unwrapped earlier, losing track of the time.

I suppose I should fear the consequences of my actions tonight, but I am the humble wife of a factory owner's son now. The people are too preoccupied with their political rivals or the bigger fish of *la noblesse* to worry about me. Nevertheless, the conversation I overheard earlier – of the King and the nobles – floats perniciously in the back of my mind.

Eventually, I grow restless. Deciding to rejoin the party after all, I quit my chamber and move towards the stairs, and am almost at the centre of the landing when I see him. Josef is at the foot of the staircase, hovering peculiarly, his head raised. I lean forwards, presuming he must have seen me, and open my mouth to call something disparaging to him. Then I stop. He is not moving a muscle, I observe, and his gaze is fixed to the upper part of the baluster. He stares at it, implacably, as though cast into a trance. As though he has seen a ghost. There is movement behind him, the footsteps of a second man joining him in the vestibule. The stranger places his hand on Josef's shoulder and I swear my husband's feet nearly leave the floor in shock.

He turns. 'Fa ... Father?'

From here, my father-in-law's face can be seen quite clearly, illuminated in the light from the vestibule chandelier. And there is something entirely different about it. Although he still does not look well, the older man's recent air of febrile imbecility is altogether missing. Gone, too, is his stiffness and glower. It is like a covering has slipped. In fact, the expression on my father-in-law's face is altogether unplaceable, not quite sadness yet not affection. Neither pride, nor regret. Rather it is all of these, mingling together in one countenance.

'Josef, I ...' Wilhelm Oberst places both of his hands on my husband's shoulders, spewing the words as though trying to rid himself of an ulcer, years in the festering.

'Father, what is it?'

A hair of a pause.

'Your marriage. I only thought . . . that it was for the best.'

'For the best?' Josef's voice is desperate. 'What do you mean? Papa?' I have never known him to address his father this way before. *Papa.*

'Yet it has been . . . that is to say . . . ' Wilhelm Oberst's grip tightens on his son, his large hands vices on Josef's shoulders. 'I see how she affects you. So you must remove her from the house if necessary. You *must.*'

Remove me from the house, indeed. I narrow my eyes.

The old man takes a long and laboured breath, as though his extraordinary little speech had expended every last drop of his energy. There is a single beat more then, no wider than an earring wire, before the covering moves back into place and Wilhelm Oberst sniffs insipidly. He lifts his hands from his son's shoulders, and drags himself upstairs.

Leaving my husband still hovering in the vestibule, I return to my chamber, where I weigh the peculiar interaction I've just witnessed.

Le Coucher

Hortense

It is late the next morning and I have not yet bothered to have myself dressed, so remain in my night-chemise when a great furore begins and voices can be heard calling hysterically for my husband to be summoned from the factory.

'What on earth is the cause of this uproar?' I ask my lady's maid when she appears in my chamber.

'It's Monsieur Wilhelm, Madame.' She curtsies. 'He's gone missing!'

'Missing?'

'Yes, Madame, apparently he's been gone since last night. He'd normally be in his study by this hour, my aunt always takes him his breakfast, but nobody's seen him all morning.'

I bring to mind the exchange I observed between my husband and father-in-law late the previous evening. 'Hmm,' I reply thoughtfully. 'Get me dressed.'

She duly obeys, and as the last pin is secured to my wig, I hear my husband's voice downstairs and exit my chamber.

'What is all this?' he says with alarm, seeing the servants rushing around the vestibule.

'Your father has done a vanishing trick,' I call from the landing. 'You'd better find out what has happened, before your staff flap themselves into an early grave.'

No sooner are my words out than a cry goes up from further along the landing. It is the housekeeper, screeching like a fish-wife from the largest of the bedchambers, the one with the bay windows and the best views of the so-called garden. It is the room that has sat unused since I came here, with its frightful sheeted furniture, the room my father-in-law usually keeps locked.

I am behind my husband as he edges closer to the threshold, exceedingly slowly and cautiously, as though the room was on fire. As he pushes the doors wider, the scene is revealed. The housekeeper is kneeling before the window-seat, flapping her kerchief like a fan. Next to her Wilhelm Oberst is slumped, wearing the clothes of last night. His wig is awry, face contorted and morbidly puffed, red as a kidney bean. His right hand is at his chest, invisible inside his waistcoat.

'Monsieur, quickly,' the housekeeper implores. 'Have someone fetch *le médecin*, he is still breathing!'

The footmen convey my father-in-law to his room, where they try to relieve the man of his shoes and outer clothes and lie him under the counterpane. Since I have nothing better to do, I watch it all unfold, perceiving the sense of panic amongst the servants rising with every hour.

It is afternoon before the doctor arrives, by which time my father-in-law's breathing has grown less shallow and more laboured. With each inhale there can be heard a clackering in his chest. And already William Oberst's face has something of a corpse's sheen about it, bloated as it is and an unnatural, garish puce, greying at the edges.

'It is his heart,' the doctor announces. 'There is little to be done now, save keeping him comfortable.'

My husband must have known from the sight of him that the old man's condition was serious. Yet he looks, in the instant after the doctor has spoken, like he has no idea what he is doing at his father's bedside at all.

'As an Englishman would say,' quips the doctor, exchanging French for English, 'he's gone from dyeing to dying.'

Even I am taken aback by the crassness of the remark. I wait for my husband's reaction. A few seconds pass.

'You speak English?' Josef asks. Then, inexplicably, he starts to laugh, so loud and so hard he doubles over with the effort of it, hand to his middle. I am dumbfounded. I believe it's the first time I have heard him laugh properly in all the interminable years I have known him. It is not the reaction I would have expected in such hopeless circumstances, especially given what transpired last night. Yet tragedy makes performers of us all, I suppose. I know that as well as anyone.

'Excuse me,' my husband says, when he manages to regain something of his composure. 'My father was very fond of the English language.'

I note that he is referring to Oberst Senior in the past tense, as though he was already dead, despite the fact the man still lies wheezing before us. There is a creak on the landing. My maid, I see, is lingering in the doorway, awaiting her next instruction.

The doctor answers with a nod. 'Well, they say that hearing is the last thing to go.' He picks up his bag and my husband moves to the door to see him out.

At that moment something remarkable occurs. I edge closer to the bed, a sound escaping my mouth, for my father-in-law's eyes have creaked themselves open, to turn directly on my lady's maid in an intense, penetrating gaze. The corners of his lips twitch. How incredibly strange.

'What is it?' Josef asks.

The old man's eyes close and his face falls limp once more.

'Oh, nothing,' I say.

I'm aware that I am dreaming, that the sensations causing my flesh to grow taut as the strings of a fortepiano are not real. Yet my whole body seizes all the same. That groan of metal, that absolute and unrelenting circle. Me powerless within it.

I wake with a terrific start, my hands flying to my head. I pull several hairs out at once this time, concentrating on the sharpness of the sting the action produces, which works in settling me as instantly as a strong tonic or a shot to the arm.

When I turn my head, I am amazed to see my husband lying to

271

my left. If he witnessed me being jolted from sleep, he makes no comment on it. He is on top of the counterpane and fully clothed, that wave of biscuit-coloured hair kinking over his forehead, eyelashes silhouetted by the window. He turns towards me, bringing his knees to his chest.

'Can you hold me?' he murmurs, his voice small as a grain of wig powder. 'Can you? It's been so long.'

I stare at him, bewildered. Balled on his side like that he looks like a child willing me to read him a story, and I could almost feel sorry for him. Then the dream I have just had swells again like the after-effects of a platter of bad oysters and I narrow my eyes. I am his wife, not his mother, and I remember well what happened after the mob destroyed the Bastille, how when I sought my own perverse comforts he pushed me aside as though I were nothing.

'Certainly not,' I say. 'I wonder you do not ask my lady's maid the same question.' He gives no reply to this and I turn away, leaving him to wallow in his own misery.

I lie and listen to his breathing awhile, coming as it does in fits and starts. Sometime later I manage to slip into a doze, during which Josef's feeble words and my insidious dream make more unpleasant bedfellows than my husband himself. In the end, my neck grows stiff and, when I stir again, I discover that Josef has, at some point, left.

I hear a noise out in the passageway and have a mind to see what is happening at the sick-bed, so I get into my embellished night-robe and, adjusting my sleeping wig, move stealthily to my father-in-law's chamber.

It is there that I find my husband. The door to the room is open, and he is leaning over the bed like a ghoul. Despite my noiseless approach, Josef seems to know that I am hovering behind him all the same and speaks to me without looking up.

'There was no need to close his eyes.'

I had expected him to berate me, to unburden his humiliation at my spurning his request to be held, so I find myself a little stunned by the oddness of the comment. 'Indeed?'

'They were already closed.'

I move forwards to get a better look at my husband's face, but it is as expressionless as his father's.

Josef goes to the window and opens the drapes and shutters. The crown of the sun is just showing at the horizon, glowing red as an ember. He mutters something which I miss. 'It could be rising or setting,' I assume is what he says.

'What was that?'

'Eh?'

'I just asked you what you said.'

He does not respond. The same stilted discourse as usual. After all these years, Josef and I still haven't engaged in a proper conversation.

'Well, he's gone then, has he?' I sigh, referring to my father-in-law. 'Then we will no longer have to tolerate his glowering presence. Or his insufferable puns, thank the heavens.'

Barb launched, I turn on my heels to go back to my bed. But then Josef speaks again, and his next words I do not miss as, for a moment, they slow my steps. His voice is icier than I have ever heard it, his tone pointed even more lethally than mine.

'You're right. He is dead. And from now on we will be doing things *my* way.'

Tricolore: Red

The following month

Sofi

I peer down at the crimson liquid near my feet. It is thick and dark, a sheen skinning its surface like the glaze on majolica. Gobs of the stuff have spattered one side of my slippers. I cast my mind back to three weeks earlier, recall the falling blade, the blood sheeting from the front of the appliance to flood the scaffold—

'Mademoiselle?'

The girl standing next to me is peering into my face with concern. She looks so young, I think, maybe fifteen. The same age I was when I first came to Jouy. I am twenty now.

'You all right, Mademoiselle? The mix all right?'

'Ah *oui, merci*,' I reply, snapping my attention to the present. 'It is ready. You may take it across to the print-house.'

The girl nods and I follow her outside to get some air. I travelled to the capital for the King's execution three weeks ago with Bernadette, Pascal and Sid, since Mama was too tired to accompany us and Lara too confined by the odious Madame. In Paris I joined a crowd a hundred thousand strong, saw the King's hands tied, his hair shorn, listened as the last of his speech was snatched by the sound of the drums. I also witnessed, even from my far-off position in the square, the guillotine's blade cut not the King's neck, but his jaw and his skull. As his mutilated head was presented to the crowd, I prepared to join in the chants.

'*VIVE LA FRANCE! VIVE LA FRANCE!*'

But as I watched the others, chins tipped to the sky and mouths straining wide, it was as though my own voice had also been snatched by the stuttering rattle of those drums. I thought I would feel gratified as I watched the King executed for his crimes. I thought I would feel like justice had been done. But I did not.

I ask myself what has changed in the years since the Bastille fell. I may have gained a slightly better position in the dye-house and some extra coin as a result, but Mama and I are still steeping leaves and grinding pigments, my sister still waiting on that woman. I see Lara as often as I can, but that is not often at all. And it renders each of the few Sunday hours we spend together sadder, the thought of what might have been in Marseilles thickening and weighing my chest. Pa is still gone, too. That has not changed, will never change. The outrage that he is dead whilst de Comtois and plenty of his kind are still here to saunter and swagger and do what they please consumes me.

As for Madame Hortense, she, too, carries on like nothing has happened, like nothing *is* happening. She broadcasts, with every haughty twitch of her person, that the Revolution is beneath her and that she and her ilk have no reason to be held to account. How very wrong she continues to be—

'Mademoiselle Sofi?' A voice to my left.

I turn to see Monsieur Marchant. 'Monsieur?' I reply, hastening to my feet.

'Mademoiselle, perhaps you could spread the word in the dye-house for me? Monsieur Oberst would like everyone to gather, up at the chateau, straight after shift. He has an announcement to make. One to the workers' benefit.'

Monsieur Oberst. In the weeks that Josef has been in charge at the factory he has been a good master. He is fair to his workers, keeps their rents low and has even started to provide each of us with a stipend for bread. He is also in the factory nearly every day, unlike his father, and is a more popular master as a result. But it has still been impossible not to notice the change in him since Monsieur

Wilhelm's death. His manner has become a fraction unsteadier, his complexion a hint ruddier, his eyes marginally less clear.

I do what was asked of me, spread word amongst the workers about the meeting at the chateau. And, as Mama and I make our way across the forecourt after the late bell rings, I think of the last time everyone assembled on the great gravel sweep, when Josef's father sullenly met our demands for better pay. It had been the same evening I followed that strange man, Emile Porcher, to the church-yard, and watched as he defaced Madame Justine's headstone. Just days after he came to the cottage asking for my sister, I heard his mother had died and that Porcher had left Jouy for good. I sighed with relief then. I had no need to warn Lara about him, after all.

The workers' talk heightens at our backs, speculation growing about what this announcement might be. At first it only half-registers, but as the chateau's facade draws into view, bookended by the two rows of poplars, fragments begin to catch in my ears.

'Could it be . . .'

'. . . *Bal* . . .'

'. . . *Printemps*.'

Bal de Printemps. The words immediately take me back to that wallpaper in the tower, to the scene of Josef and his mother dancing blissfully together. And then I remember the date on her headstone. *March, 1783*. Ten years ago, almost exactly.

I squint up at the chateau. A shaft of pale lemon sunlight slices off the glass of one of the lunettes above the doors. I bring a hand to my middle, feel my pulse beneath my stays, pounding with antici-pation, even after all these years. There have been other boys at the factory who have sought out my company, asked to walk with me and even attempted to press their lips to mine. But, try as I might, I have never been able to shake Josef from my head, nor the feelings that lift and hold me whenever we are together from my heart. I slip my fingers into the green ribbon at my throat. The flesh beneath it is slickened and hot, wet with sweat from the dye-house.

The chateau doors open.

Tricolore: White

Hortense

It is a dismal afternoon in early February, and there is a hum of noise outside the front of the chateau. I am only partly aware of it at first as, with nothing else to occupy myself, I have resolved to try something new with my little dog's light russet fur. Several days ago, I sent to Mama for my silver shaker, and now fill it to the brim with fine green powder. I tap the powder carefully over Pépin's small back before combing it through, smiling at how becoming his coat looks as it changes from auburn to peppermint. I have yellow and purple powders to try next.

As I work, I become more conscious of the noise outside, and soon the volume is such that it cannot be ignored. I remove myself to the landing and peer through the casement.

Down on the gravel, a large group of workers has converged. My first instinct is to flinch from the window-glass, as I did in the shabby coach that first conveyed me to this place, recalling those menagerie chimps. But I tell myself I am being silly. These people are not armed and look rather benign. I wonder why they are there.

'Do you know what is going on?' I call to my lady's maid.

'Madame?'

'There are workers outside—'

At that moment, my husband appears. 'Hortense, please be so good as to join me downstairs,' he says, adding indisputably more tenderly, 'You too, Mademoiselle.'

I leave Pépin safely in my chamber. In the vestibule, Josef gestures for me to join him at the front door.

'Must we continue this game of guessing much longer, husband?' I ask. 'What is it you want?'

'Follow me,' is all he replies, as my maid lingers at our backs.

Josef swings open the two front doors and advances out onto the *perron*. 'Ladies and gentlemen,' he proclaims, in the most authoritative tone he can muster. 'We are gathered here today—'

'Lord, it isn't a wedding,' I mutter, loud enough for him to hear.

My remark succeeds in throwing him, as Josef continues through gritted teeth, 'I have asked you here this afternoon so I might make a very special announcement. My wife and I are to be holding a spring ball, a *Bal de Printemps*. At this very factory, the first in a decade. And you, your families and friends are all invited.'

The rabble below cheers immediately.

'Madame Hortense and I want to offer thanks for your loyalty over the years, and what better way than with a night of food, music and dancing for all?'

I narrow my eyes as the crowd cheers again, babbling amongst each other like over-excited children. Since he took over the running of this place, my husband has constantly been inventing such stratagems. Trawling about the factory on a daily basis, begging his workers to like him. Wasting money on supplementing their food when they are quite capable of buying it themselves, with their own not inconsiderable wage. Coddling and appeasing them lest they take it into their heads to bring an uprising to his door.

My husband turns briefly to my maid. 'And I hope you will join us at the ball, too,' he murmurs, a syrupy look on his face. 'You will be relieved from all duties for the night, of course.'

The cheers from below subside and, buzzing at the idea of a free jolly, the labourers begin to amble back to their work.

'Tell the truth, husband,' I needle as we proceed inside, rankled by Josef's presumption. 'Why is this evening of fun *really* being arranged?'

'Why?' he scowls. 'Are you unaware how the servants are talking?

You think it appropriate to constantly be sending them out on fools' errands? Sourcing fripperies for your dog? If you ceased your flouncing, we would not need to go to such expense on a ball.'

'Those "fools' errands" are conducted more discreetly than you might think,' I retort. 'Unlike your own.'

'What are you talking about this time?' he snarls.

I look past him and see Pépin. He must have escaped my chamber, as he is now poised on the floor tiles of the vestibule, yapping amusingly. I laugh.

'That whilst I am having garments made for *my* pet, you are having garments made for *yours*.' I dart an incisive glance at my maid, who stands some paces away from us, her head lowered.

He comes at me then and, for a second, I think he might shake me. Over the past weeks, there has been an alteration in my husband. His behaviour has changed, his temper warmed and quickened, fuelled by the fumes of drink. I can't be the only one to have noticed.

'That dog,' he spits, pointing at Pépin, 'will keep to your room. I do not want him showing up at proceedings like last time. Are you listening? I shall lock him in on the night of the ball if I have to.'

'You will do no such thing.'

'You had better—' he goes on, wagging a finger.

'Oh, for heaven's sake.' I make for the stairs but hear him clumping up behind me, cutting me off and leaving me trapped before the iron railings of the balustrade. 'Very well, very well, he shall be left in my chamber. As if I would want him anywhere near those workers, anyhow.'

Josef seems content at this and leaves me alone, his footsteps fading down the passageway. I raise my hands to pull at my head and, when I lower them again, a cascade of hairs drifts to the floor.

Tricolore: Blue

Lara

Madame hastens up the staircase, clutching her dog to her chest. A few seconds later, I hear her chamber door slam. This is a signal to me that she is not to be disturbed, one of the many lessons I have learned the hard way over the years. I flitter at the bottom of the stairs, deliberating whether to proceed to my own chamber to finish the stack of sewing awaiting me there, then realising I have no desire to do so. On the dusky blue hems of my skirts, I see, have caught several strands of Madame's hair, so pale they are almost white.

I hear footsteps approaching and assume it is one of the servants, but when I turn there is Josef, hovering apologetically behind me.

'I do hope you didn't hear any of that,' he says softly. 'And if you did, I apologise. Please ignore her.'

I heard it all. Heard how Madame referred to me as Josef's *pet*. Like a lot of what she says, it contained just enough of a grain of truth to sting. For Josef does organise my clothes from the *couturière*. But only, as my aunt told me, because Madame is too extravagant to be trusted with the purse strings. Aunt Berthé knows as well as Josef, as well as the rest of the servants, how unkind a mistress she can be.

'That is all right,' I answer vaguely. 'I think people like Madame Hortense are usually just afraid. Unhappy, too. And being difficult is their way of coping and so it repeats. They make others suffer because they fear they will be made to suffer. It's their form of protection. Like those caddisflies, at the river.' I think of Sofi's anger,

280

of Mama's. Then I register how many words have just tumbled from my mouth without my realising.

Josef looks dazed before saying softly, 'And I meant what I said, too. You have no obligation to attend the ball, of course, but I do hope you might. It's been ... well ... it's been nice having you around these past years. It has made everything easier.'

I smile and thank him, watch as he hovers a moment, his eyelids twitching faintly as though he were thinking, as though he wanted something more. I cannot deny his kindnesses since I came to work for Madame. When she is cruel or cutting, it is good to have another friend in the chateau, an ally of sorts, as well as my aunt.

'I should get on,' Josef says, holding my gaze a second more before retreating in the direction of the study. Once his father's, Josef's now.

Knowing I have nothing to keep me in the vestibule and nowhere else to go, I head to the tower, starting up the stairs and along the landings. I think of what I just said to Josef and remember Sofi stealing her way up here all those years ago. As little as I see my sister now, I can still sense her turmoil, flaring and bubbling inside her, never far from the surface. I worry that one day it will bubble over completely, and that is when she will do something else impetuous, something that this time cannot be undone.

I begin climbing the spiralling staircase, my pace wearying a little with each tread. I have worked all these years for Madame uncomplainingly, doing everything that has been asked of me. I have saved my wages carefully. There is enough put by, I think, to provide Mama with a nest-egg for the future. So I will do what I've thought about doing for months. I will speak to Josef, ask whether, if I promise to serve the notice Madame requires, it would be possible for me to return to my work in the print-house. I will ask him next week. I do not see how, if I give enough time for a replacement to be found, anyone would mind.

Inside my chamber I turn the key, making sure the door is locked. I cross to the table at the window, where the sewing is stacked, my eyes fixed ahead of me to ensure my gaze is not in danger of falling on the wallpaper. Over the years, I have perfected this art. But still, there are times when that teeming violet print is unavoidable, and those are also the times that Madame Justine will have disappeared from the pattern altogether and I will have taken her place. My flesh still creeps on such occasions, my pulse quickening, for, although my head is better, I have come to accept the strange things I see in this wallpaper must still be the result of that blow I suffered jumping clear of Pa's wagon. Perhaps, frightening a thought though it is, it will always be so. I will always see things differently.

I sit at the table and examine the first garment on the pile. But I am just about to take up the threads for its mending when my breathing increases, the fine hairs along the top of my spine lifting in rapid succession. That sensation, once again, that comes to me at least once every day. I am being watched, I know it. I spin around, check the door. Still locked, as I left it. And mine the only key apart from the one Aunt Berthé permanently keeps on her person.

My back pressed against the door and my heart furious, I face the room. There is nobody else up here, there never is. And yet, it is the eeriest thing. One at a time, starting at the opposite wall and proceeding in a straight line, I hear the floorboards creak, see them shift, one after the next after the next. It is as though someone else in the room, unseen and unfathomable, is making their way directly towards me.

The Bal de Printemps

March, one month later

Sofi

I am standing amongst the crowd in the print-house, several hundred strong. The space looks completely different tonight, bright and joyful. The tables have been cleared from its vast floor and swags of spring foliage now wind up its walls, threaded with ribbons and blooms.

I have left my mother and pushed right the way to the front, so I might watch Josef stand on the polished wood platform, built to serve as a stage for the musicians, and address the gathering.

Suddenly, he stops what he is saying. His eyes have caught on someone, and I know right away it must be my sister. My chest constricts. Even amidst a mass of hundreds he can pick her out. I have not seen Lara tonight, she was not here when Mama and I arrived, and although I want to follow Josef's eyes and go to her, the crowds are dense and close at my back, so I stay put.

As though aware that she is watching, Josef launches into an energetic toast, raising the stem of his glass high. 'We are here tonight to enjoy ourselves, so eat, dance—'

'Drink!' someone shouts.

'Yes,' he says. 'Drink! *Santé!*'

He drains the contents of his glass quickly to cheers and whistles, before men's arms are cast around the waists of women, and the musicians play the opening notes of a reel.

Josef steps down from the staging and heads in the direction he was gazing as he made his speech. He means to find Lara, to dance with her. I weave through the now-moving revellers at speed, reaching him swiftly, and, feeling brazen, catch my hand through his.

As he turns, the press of other bodies sends us closer together and I see how well the smoke-grey satin of his jacket suits him. His face is clearer tonight than it has been in weeks. Focused, honed to purpose. The proportions of it, the exact ratio of cheek to lips to chin, the tone of his skin against his hair, against his rime-blue eyes, make my head swim.

My boldness has surprised him, but he has not shaken free of my touch. 'Sorry,' I say. 'I would not do this usually. But tonight . . . '

My words dwindle. All I can think about is how my hand is still in his, in this swarm of hundreds, how my heart pounds to the *contredanse*.

'Come, dance with me,' I say, emboldened anew by our linking fingers. I tug Josef's arm towards the music but, although he does not let go, he resists.

'I do not care to dance,' he replies. 'I never have.'

That scene from the tower wallpaper, of Josef dancing so deliriously with his mother at the *Bal de Printemps* a decade ago, passes fleetingly through my mind. I wonder at him organising this ball tonight, exactly ten years since his mother's death, a painful anniversary to commemorate. Unlike his father, he must be thinking only of his workers, I decide, of thanking them for their service. 'Come on!' I add. 'You may find you enjoy it.'

Josef scans the far end of the room and frowns. He must have lost sight of my sister.

'No,' I say, determined not to stop now, 'you are right to hesitate, I have not formally requested it.'

That is when he looks at me properly, fixing his countenance on mine. 'Whatever do you mean?'

I will amuse him, make him forget my sister, make him want to stay. I back away a little, step one leg straight in front of me and bow deeply. Then I near him once more, legs shoulder-width apart this time, slippers fanning out. I imagine myself to be some male water bird Lara might once have drawn, strutting out a display of court-ship. 'There. Is that not how the gentlemen do it?'

He laughs then. 'You are strange.'

I feel a great gush of ecstasy that I have managed to elicit such a reaction from him. How different his whole demeanour appears when he is laughing, how alive. It is a funny thing that, in all the years I've known him, I have seen him laugh so seldom. And then, to my amazement, Josef allows me to slip my arm through his.

As I turn in the direction of the dancing, I see Lara for the first time tonight. She is standing near Aunt Berthé and dressed finer than I have ever known her, pearl-blue stomacher and skirts hazed like a summer sky against her blonde hair, sprigs of early blooms pinned amongst it. In a way, I mark, she does not look like my sister at all. Or rather she looks like Lara, but from another existence.

We haven't progressed more than ten paces through the throng when a cluster of people in front of us parts and I am stunned to a standstill, forcing Josef to stop abruptly, too. Right there in front of me is a face I recognise, and it is as astonishing as a sunflower in winter.

'Well … after all this time!' I exclaim. I fear that if I let go of Josef's arm he might vanish in pursuit of my sister, but cannot help it. I pull Guillaume close and squeeze him tight, smiling as he squeezes me back. He looks well, and with that same inherent gen-tleness of expression he always had.

'Sofi!' Guillaume says. 'It is very good to see you again.' His eyes crinkle, mouth widening to a broad smile, revealing that tiny gap between his front teeth.

'Monsieur.'

He acknowledges Josef, who I'm relieved to see is still at my side, and I quickly take hold of him again before he has the chance to change his mind. 'We are going to dance,' I tell Guillaume, then lean in and murmur, 'If you're looking for Lara you will find her near the smaller pair of doors. At the back.'

I do not want Josef to hear my words, do not want him to know

Guillaume is here to see my sister, as I am certain that if he did he would leave me and go to her instead.

'Who was that?' Josef asks, as we continue towards the dancers.

'Oh,' I reply, 'that's just Guillaume.'

Josef looks back to Guillaume, who is hovering where we left him. And I do not think I am imagining it, but I swear I detect the glint of jealousy in his eyes.

Mingling

Hortense

Well, here I am at the peasants' party and, Lord, it's a tawdry affair. The print-house, which I have only set foot in once before, is decked out like a cowshed for an orgy. Using the word *ball* to describe this event was rather grandiose of my husband. A rickety staging has been cobbled together with what looks like firewood and, on top of it, a riffraff of musicians is playing a reel. The table of refreshments is as rough as the rest of it. Wine, ale and tarts, the latter there to serve the beverages.

The evening, not even that much advanced, is already interminable. To make matters worse, it feels as though I have been listening to that bore de Pise drone on for hours, though it cannot have been more than fifteen minutes since he turned up, dressed in a vivid mustard ditto suit, like a black sheep amongst white, or a white one amongst black, I cannot decide. He must have gotten wind of the event from Mama. His presence, so primped and conspicuous, is, I know, exactly the kind of thing my husband sought to avoid during this evening of lower-class revelry. Oh well, raising Josef's hackles will at least provide some form of entertainment tonight. Heaven knows it won't be forthcoming from anywhere else.

De Pise is, of course, hoping for a dance, but despite all that has happened I still have some dignity left. Nevertheless, I've resolved to tolerate his company, to keep him sweet. He might come in handy sooner rather than later, all things considered.

In order to avoid listening to his unctuous waffle, I have been occupying myself by watching my husband with that factory girl, the young, feral-looking one, the sister of my lady's maid. It is blatantly obvious what the girl feels for him, what a clod Josef is not to see it for himself.

'And where is your furry *gentilhomme* this evening?' de Pise asks, leaning closer.

Mind still on the dancing, it takes me a few seconds to realise he is talking about Pépin. 'Confined to quarters. By decree of my husband.'

'A shame.' De Pise attempts to stroke the back of my hand but I move it out of reach.

'Indeed. Lest one of these labourers decides he is leading a life of greater luxury than they. Ridiculous.'

'Quite ridiculous. The mingling of the classes. It leads to nothing but the fall of empires.' De Pise looks around. 'You know, if all the peasant girls here had died of starvation and left only the men, there might have been enough bread. And, consequently, fewer infants produced to be left wanting for it.'

'Hmm.' I have stopped listening altogether. A man, I've noted, has appeared at the side of that tan-skinned factory girl. Most probably a labourer too. Yet now they are embracing, as my husband stands mutely by. The girl whispers something to the stranger and, once he has finished peering gormlessly after her, he eventually moves, with an increasing sense of purpose, towards my lady's maid. So, it must be *her* he is here to see, I muse. My husband has a rival to his affections. Interesting. My lips quirk into a smile.

'Excuse me, Monsieur,' I say to de Pise, rising. 'I trust you don't mind, but there is something I must do.'

Tableaux

Lara

The noise of the gathering is intense, the place dense with bodies and feverish, drink-soaked laughter. I have positioned myself right at the fringes of the room, close to the print-house doors. I've never liked crowds. But that is not the only reason.

After seeing Madame dressed hours before, one of the serving girls gave me a message from my aunt, informing me that a set of garments had been left in my chamber for me to wear tonight. When I returned to my room there they were, hanging lifelessly from the pegs on the door, as though waiting to be re-animated, re-inhabited.

The garments themselves were, on the surface, exquisite. Cut from the palest blue silk so weightless it rippled constantly, like wind on water. I recognised that colour. Then I put the clothes on and, though they fitted well enough, there was something wrong about them, nonetheless. The way the silk ruched at the back ... the way the cuffs floated below the elbows ... the shape and thickness of the fichu, larger and with less trim. These were styles that hadn't been seen for years.

They make me uncomfortable, in more ways than one, incongruous amongst everyone else. So I am keeping out of the melee of the ball, my back to the wall. I am less noticeable like this.

I gaze self-consciously across the throng, consider my plan to ask Josef if I might leave Madame Hortense's service. In a few days' time I will do it. I meant to the week after the ball announcement was made, but everyone seemed so preoccupied with the preparations that I thought it best to wait—

Through the confusion of bodies, I see a man coming towards me, and before I so much as catch a proper sight of his face, I know him instantly.

'Guillaume!' I exclaim. 'I . . . I . . .'

A volley of questions rattles through my head. I cannot think where to begin. His hair has grown longer, brushed down smooth and reaching to his collar, his beard a little fuller, too.

'Mademoiselle Thibault,' he replies, bowing. He is smiling, an expression that colours his entire face with a bright affability. Just as I remember him.

I move away from the wall to embrace him, but immediately begin to feel the eyes of the workers upon me, sensing their murmurings as I did when I first came to this place. I rest a hand on Guillaume's arm instead. His chin dips at the gesture, eyes cast down.

'What—' I attempt to begin once more. 'How on earth do you come to be here, Guillaume? I thought—' I stop. *I thought I would never see you again*, is what I want to say.

He looks uncomfortable, shifts his weight from one foot to the other. 'I am sorry,' he begins. 'Truly sorry it has been so long. Lord knows I have tried.' He pauses. 'My brother-in-law lately found me a position in the north of the capital. He clerks for the owner of several smithies in the area, one of which makes ironwork for this factory. That is how I came to be here tonight. Please believe me when I say I would have come to see you all sooner if I could, but it was impossible.'

I take a breath and withdraw my hand, the linen of his shirt leaving the echo of a shiver on my skin. 'Of course.'

'Your sister—' he mumbles and nods at the people where, between the moiling, leaping dancers, come glimpses of Sofi, whirling blissfully. From where I stand I am not able to see her partner, though by the look on her face I think I can guess with whom she has taken to the floor.

'Ah, yes.'

Guillaume seems lost for words.

'Come,' I say. 'Let us get you something to eat and we can talk properly.' He smiles gratefully and, trying to ignore the gazes of the factory workers, we pass along the edge of the crowd to the long workshop table topped with wine and pastries.

We have almost reached it when a strange sensation assaults me. I become aware that a space has opened up, not far from us. A number of workers fill the space, separating themselves out into ones or twos or threes. I don't really think anything of it then, nor when I see the first pair, a woman and a boy, start to dance. Yet they do not so much dance as assume positions as though they are dancing, then freeze. Their arms are stuck, thrown into the air, their wide smiles mirrored, captured in time.

As this first couple stops moving the next pair starts, the man removing his jacket and falling to his knees, the woman doing the same. He draws a ring from his pocket and holds it out to her and the woman laughs, presses one hand to her chest, reaches towards him with the other. Then they freeze, too.

Next to them, a lone woman removes one of her boots, swaddles the object in her shawl and rocks it in her arms as though it was a real infant. She mimes words to the bundle and, though no sound escapes her lips, I think I hear them clearly.

'*This I must say, dilly dilly, and it is true. You must love me, dilly dilly, 'cause I love you.*'

A moment later, this woman is as static as the rest.

At her side, a man goes down on all fours and another balls himself on the floor before the first, coiled as a hedgehog. And then, to my utter astonishment, a woman sits down upon the curled-up man and begins to play the back of the other like the keys of a fortepiano.

The last is perhaps the strangest mime of them all. A very tall man extends one leg out in front of him, and a woman hitches up her skirts, swinging her foot over the man's leg as though sliding down a baluster. Next to them, a boy claps a hand to his mouth in surprise.

I stare at the five peculiar tableaux in front me, at the eleven factory workers all now perfectly still. I cannot pare my eyes from them. There is something grotesque about the scenes, the way the poses are held, the workers' expressions overly exaggerated, almost pained. There is also something stiflingly familiar.

The floor of the print-house starts to pitch, the strains of the music warp and dissolve. What I see before me is no party game and neither is it a trick of my vision. These are the scenes from the paper in my chamber, no longer confined to the wall of that tower, but capable of following me out of it, moving towards me across those shifting floorboards like a host of trailing spectres.

I look down at what I'm wearing. I had not really seen it in the moments after I dressed, but I see it now, as my eyes come to rest on the first tableau. The woman and boy have frozen in the exact same position Madame Justine and Josef hold in the print of the wallpaper. The *Bal de Printemps*. Their postures take my mind right back to that scene, to what Madame Justine was wearing. The same garments as I.

The very tall man slowly turns his head and looks directly at me. His lips peel into a smile. He raises one long, large-knuckled finger, and beckons.

The Allemande

Sofi

As soon as the *contredanse* ends, a voice calls for the *allemande* to be played. It is an old dance for pairs and I grasp Josef harder, not letting go.

I knew all along that he would make a wonderful partner. He is rhythmic and considerate, not stiff or lecherous as other men are. We spin and we circle one another, as the dance dictates, his hands taking my waist to pull me to him, and I find I am quite unable to stop every part of my body from tingling with joy.

I hope furiously that the band will play this dance over and over until we can dance it no more, but the closing notes of the *allemande* fade too soon and Josef releases his hold.

'I must go now,' he says.

'Stay, just a little longer—'

'There are others I ought to speak to.'

'Please, just one more—'

'No, Sofi.' His words are sharp and I feel their swipe.

'Your wife will not mind, if that is your worry. She seems to be otherwise engaged.'

Despite the rapture of being with him, of his touch on mine, I've made sure to note what the Madame is up to this evening. She is sitting with a man in a ludicrous yellow suit. I don't know who he is, but he leans towards the Madame constantly, his lips very close to her face whilst she stifles a yawn, eyes flicking continuously around the room, lizard-like. I go to wave across to them now, in order to illustrate my point to Josef, but am confused to see that they are no longer there.

'My lady's maid seems to be otherwise engaged, too, husband.' A voice, like frostbite, from right next to us.

I balk. It is the Madame and she has clearly heard what I just said. My cheeks flush scarlet, but I push the redness away with my palms and turn to face her. She will not intimidate me.

Several paces behind the Madame hangs that foppish man in the sickly coloured suit. Josef stares at him as though affronted by his presence, and so it takes him a moment to register her words. 'What?' he snaps, craning his head over the crowds. The other man grins.

'There is a challenger to the hand of your fair maiden,' the Madame declares and laughs, a thin, spiky noise like a rain of arrows.

Anger rises in my chest at the way she is talking, not only about my sister and Josef, but Guillaume, too. Several people close by look over.

'Keep your voice down,' spits Josef, growing as angry as I.

The man with the Madame steps forwards as though to rebuke Josef for using such a tone, but she lifts a hand to his chest to prevent it. 'De Pise.'

'Where is your sister?' Josef spins to look at me, his expression a world away from the easy joy that had infused it when we were dancing.

'How should I know?' I reply, simmering.

His eyes finally lock on the pair of them, as a swathe of people suddenly parts, revealing the scene. They are near the table of food, where a group of workers is playing a party game, miming out scenes from the factory's wallpaper designs. As Lara and Guillaume look on, his hand cups her elbow.

Leaving me standing there with his loathsome wife and her obnoxious peacock, Josef makes directly for them, his face a storm-cloud.

Hunting at Jouy

Hortense

The look on my husband's face as he takes off like a rat from a trap is the best thing I have witnessed in some months. The look on the face of that factory girl isn't far behind. Closely resembling a petulant child, her hands are fists at her sides, her expression like a slapped derrière. Then she departs through the melee as abruptly as my husband.

'I am glad I came, my dear,' de Pise drawls. 'A most diverting evening.'

In truth, I'd quite forgotten he was here. I dash him a smile and move in the same direction as Josef, for a better view of the proceedings.

By the time I have made my way through the hordes, with their stink of sweat and cheap drink, my husband has already downed a glass of wine with surprising speed. My lady's maid is staring at a nearby group of workers engaged in some kind of boorish activity, looking like she hasn't a clue what is happening. She is wearing an intriguing set of articles, the silk of them expensive but the cut embarrassingly dated. Her new companion is standing agape also, watching Josef stew.

Clearly, my husband hasn't been courteous enough to introduce himself properly. What a fool he is, charging in like a cock squaring up to a rival and all for a bland little hen like that. The factory girl is standing beside them, scowling like a madwoman, her hair frizzing from its pins like roughened springs.

'And you are?' Josef growls at the new man, who hardly looks worth the effort, with his scruffy attire, untidy black beard and benign expression.

'We met a little earlier, Monsieur,' the man says. 'My name is Guillaume Errard.' His eyes find the factory girl briefly before settling back on my husband.

'Ah yes, Guillaume Errard,' sneers Josef, swigging from his second glass of wine in less than as many minutes. 'You seem to know Mademoiselle Thibault from somewhere?' He slams his glass down on the tabletop, misjudging the action and causing it to shatter, the resulting puddle of dark wine twinkling with fragments like a night sky.

'Now, husband,' I say, unable to resist joining in. 'Have you forgotten why we are here? Tonight has been arranged especially for our workers.'

All around our odd and ill-tempered group, the labourers have ceased their merrymaking to gawp at what is happening between Josef and Black Beard.

'Monsieur, I . . .' the other man stammers, this Guillaume Errard, not realising what he has done wrong.

Josef moves towards him, until he is so close to his supposed challenger their noses are near touching. It is curious since, although my husband's temper has been quickening over the past months, I do not believe I have ever seen him behave in so unrestrained a manner before. It is also a truly farcical sight, that the owner and master of this place should now be conducting himself with such a lack of decorum, showing the true baseness of his class.

I step towards my husband at the same time as the factory girl, not so much to prevent him from taking a swipe at Black Beard, rather being unable to refuse the temptation to hector Josef further.

'Husband, please,' I say, innocently. 'There is no need to kiss the man, attractive though you may find him. You do realise we took a vow.'

At this, he twirls around. 'You—' he spits, looming over me, his face bearing down on mine, anger pitching to such a level that it stops his words. '*You—*'

For the tiniest fraction of a second, disoriented by his unfamiliar fury, I imagine I might almost be afraid of him. But then I begin to laugh. I laugh and I laugh at all of them, until one by one they turn away. I think they are finally doing so in embarrassment at their absurd behaviour. Then I realise it is something else that has caught their attention.

'Oh no,' my lady's maid moans.

A great roar goes up at the doors, abating to jeers and shouts. I forget my amusement instantly, recognising the manner of such cries, the inherent cruelty of them. They are bestial, the clamour of a mob having spotted its quarry. The scene from the wallpaper in Versailles, the ugly, twisted faces of the songbird's tormentors, flashes before me.

'We've got the little shit!' a man calls drunkenly and others join in, coarse with laughter. 'It's come to join our party!'

Every part of me floods glacier-cold. For, above the heads of the workers, something is being thrown. Up and down it goes, tossed as though it were of little more value or consequence than a dirty rag. I see, then, what it is. A small and helpless animal with pale auburn fur, yelping in shock and in panic as it flies through the air.

'Pépin!' I scream, the shrillness of the name piercing even my own eardrums. I shove the others out of my way and race towards him.

Let Them Eat

Sofi

My sister moves more quickly than anyone else. It takes her less than an instant to dart all the way up to the group of drunkards and slip into their midst. She shows no hesitation or fear at what she is doing, and does not think twice about it.

'Stop it!' she cries. 'Stop, at once!'

They continue flinging the frightened creature between them, ignoring her pleas. 'What's that? Your mistress sent you to retrieve her plaything, has she?'

The man speaking catches the toy-dog roughly but, as he goes to continue the game and throw it to his neighbour, Lara intercepts him, cradling the trembling animal in her arms and ducking out of danger.

The Madame is hot on my sister's tail, shrieking like a demon, screaming the dog's name again and again. She snatches the animal out of Lara's arms just as my sister is attempting to soothe it, whispering words of calm to the dog's tiny head, smoothing its coat.

'He is mine! How dare you! Give him to me! He is mine!'

These last events have unhinged her. In the short time it has taken her to realise the workers have hold of her animal, she has gone from taunting and purring to deranged and wild-eyed. It is as though something deep inside of her, a string long since pulled taut, has suddenly snapped.

'How the hell did that animal get out?' Josef demands, having turned his attention away from Guillaume, at last.

I expect the Madame to shoot off some derisive comment and

leave. But instead, she clutches her dog to her breast and rounds on Josef. 'How should I know how he got out?' Her voice is steeped in venom, thick with unbridled fury. 'I've been here the whole time, have I not? As you requested.'

Someone splutters a laugh. I see it is Sid, standing close by with Bernadette and Pascal.

'You would do well to keep your counsel, Madame,' warns Josef.

The Madame pays no heed. 'He probably got out since he couldn't stand it in that place!' she shouts, so everyone can hear. 'How could anything in its right mind live there!'

'You're mad,' returns Josef, turning away in an attempt to bring an end to the scene, perhaps sensing the Madame is far from finished.

'Oh, am I, husband?' Her voice grows more vengeful by the second. '*Husband!* What a travesty that word is. Travesty!' She proclaims this as though delivering the climactic line of a play. 'Some husband, who is unable to fuck his own wife!'

A number of the workers, Bernadette and Sid included, gasp at the Madame's sudden crudeness, shocked mute by the curse that so unexpectedly spews from her lips. Others, like Pascal, give low, uncertain laughs which stutter awkwardly through the silence. The mouth of the man in the yellow suit drops open like a flounder's.

'Oh yes,' she continues, her words surging as though in full tide. 'Three years in and our marriage still isn't consummated. Surely that means you aren't even my husband, *husband!*'

I look at Josef, unable to believe what I'm hearing, the manner in which I am hearing it. I do not know whether I am pleased or mortified, and have the urge to hold him and shield his ears from her spite. Livid colour mottles his cheeks. If there was a clearer path to the door he would have long since used it.

'And why would the state of our affairs be thus, you might well ask?' the Madame goes on. 'Well, allow me to enlighten you. Because *he* only has eyes for *her*—' she says, jabbing a pale finger in my sister's direction, 'while *she*—' this time it is me at whom she points, 'cannot help but throw herself at *him*—' she declares, gesticulating violently at Josef once more.

An insurmountable surge of indignity consumes me and I stride towards her. I don't stop to think what I might do, push her, slap her face, force shut her mouth. But I have not gone far when I feel myself stopped, feel gentle hands staying me from going any further.

'Do not,' Guillaume murmurs in my ear. 'You are better than this.' The tenderness of his voice stills me. If Lara wasn't some distance away, I know he would be at her side rather than mine, calming her instead.

The workers have surrounded the Madame now, and they are laughing. The woman opens her mouth to rant out something more, but before she has the chance, a man from the dye-house takes a single bound forwards and upends his glass, covering the Madame's creamy-white skirts in inky-red wine. She lets out a scream that seems to come from deep within the buried core of her, a scream of impotence and rage.

'Always griping about the lack of bread,' she blares, voice breaking. 'So, here! *Voilà!*' With her free hand she seizes a fistful of tartlets from the table and then another, and hurls them in rapid succession at her spectators. '*Voilà!* Eat these instead!'

The workers dodge the missiles as chunks of curd, egg and jam splatter to the floor. Nobody says a word or moves a muscle and I think this will anger her more, but when she speaks again her voice is quieter, raw from screaming. 'You think you have your progress now the King is dead,' she says. 'You have nothing.'

She is wrong. These are the ravings of a brat whose toys have been taken away. Several moments of absolute silence follow, before voices sound near the stage.

'Play a jig!'

'Yes, we want a jig!'

The musicians start up once more, as though nothing has happened, and partners link arms and take to the floor. I give a fleeting glance their way and at the far end of the long refreshments table I see my mother. I can tell from the look on her face that she has heard everything.

The Madame moves to a position right in front of me then,

blocking my view of Mama. The woman's face is seaming with hate, wine seeping from the front of her skirts and patting to the floorboards. For a second I think of mocking her further, of asking her to dance, but then she draws her toy-dog closer to her chest and flounces from the room.

My gaze follows, as the crowd of workers unwillingly parts to let the Madame through. And amongst them, a figure I recognise. My stomach clenches. Surely it isn't him, not after all this time. Emile Porcher. He is staring directly at my sister, small amber eyes taking in the entire span of her body – her waving locks of hair, her fine gown and fichu.

A shudder advances across my flesh before the crowds mass to-gether again and he is gone.

Revelations

Sofi

I do not remain at the ball for long, leaving a large crowd of workers still at their revelry. It was impossible to stay after the Madame's outburst. Her venom tainted the evening, her horrible declarations making my cheeks smart and embarrassment swallow me whole. Shortly after the woman strode into the darkness clutching her toy-dog close, Josef stalked away too. Not that I blame him. The way the Madame spoke to him, tonight of all nights, and in front of everyone. It was an outrage.

I wish that Lara and I could have chatted this evening, could have danced and spent time together, enjoyed ourselves as we were meant to, but it didn't seem possible after what happened. My sister was still there, lingering against the walls of the print-house when I left, as the party went on around her. I don't know why she stayed, when she looked so uncomfortable. Maybe she wanted to delay returning to the chateau, to that woman, for as long as she could.

I am not sure where Guillaume went. When he released his hands from me he seemed to melt into the crowds and I slipped from the building without even saying goodbye. The realisation saddens me now.

As for Emile Porcher, I didn't glimpse him again. I must have been mistaken in thinking he was there at all. In the years since he left the village I have never once seen the man, so I do not understand why he should have appeared again tonight. I remember the words he uttered from the darkness, all those years ago. *Your sister.* I hope my eyes did deceive me and he has not returned, for Lara's sake.

302

When I reach the cottage, the place is in darkness and I presume that my mother is abed. I was so embarrassed by the Madame's scene, so preoccupied by my embarrassment, that I could think of nothing else. Consequently, I've no idea what happened to Mama either, after I saw her evaluating events from the end of the table. Though she has never been one for a celebration.

I go inside and lock the door behind me, but as I cross to the staircase a voice sounds from the hearth.

'Quite a scene.'

It is Mama, still up and lurking in the blackness like a wraith.

I stop short, squinting at her. 'What are you doing, Mama, sitting about in the dark?'

I suddenly realise she must still be angry with me after the Madame's revelations and feel a further flush of humiliation, for I cannot deny the truth in that disgusting woman's words. Though I have no wish to discuss it now. And certainly not with my mother.

'The Madame was talking nonsense, Mama. She knows nothing. You oughtn't to listen to people like her.'

She gives a hollow utterance of amusement, which I suppose is meant to be a laugh. 'People like her . . . like Lara.'

There is a pause.

'She isn't your sister, surely you know that now.'

This last is a statement rather than a question and my entire body bristles at the words. I turn to face her, the darkness between us a shroud, and Mama veiled behind it.

'What do you mean?' My voice rises as I step towards her. I wonder how much she drank at the ball, except I have never really seen her take any drink before and her voice is crisp, even, sober.

'Tonight put me in mind of it. What Lara was wearing . . . done up like a lady and in his colours, too.' She sniffs, her voice lowering stiffly. 'It wasn't easy seeing it. I really am surprised you didn't notice the resemblance.' Mama raises her eyes to mine with this last sentence. Questioning, bewildered.

My temper flashes. 'Why wouldn't Lara be my sister? We share the same parents, do we not?'

Mama's sigh carries with it the slightest hint of irritation, as though she had forgotten to buy something at market. 'It happened just before I met Luqman. The . . . *liaisons* with her father.'

I almost miss the unnatural, strangled emphasis she puts on this last word, thrown as I am by hearing her say Pa's name aloud.

'Did . . . ' I try to steady my speech. 'Did Pa know?'

'Oh, Sofia, of course he knew she wasn't his. How could he not? You can be so naive about these things.'

The true shock of her words starts to reach me, and my hands begin to shake.

'He was a good man.' My mother's voice shrinks, and at first I think she means the man who fathered my sister. 'Luc married me because of it, to support us. He was a good man.'

My throat constricts painfully. 'And . . . Lara? Does Lara know?'

For a moment Mama appears not to hear. Then she gets to her feet, shrugging and shaking out her skirts with the indifference of a woman who has lately remarked upon the weather. 'She's never asked.'

'So you think it a good idea to be telling me and not her? You think—'

Mama brushes past me and onto the stairs. 'I only told you, Sofia, since I thought you would have seen it for yourself tonight. Perhaps I shouldn't have raised the matter.'

I consider grabbing her, to scream a question into her face and make her answer. There are a multitude of them, spinning feverishly in my brain, but a fire flares inside of me and, as I hear my mother ascend the stairs to her chamber, I know I cannot stand it there a second longer.

I step out into the night, the door crashing closed at my back.

Après la Bal

Lara

I dawdle at the ball far longer than I intend, though really I want nothing more than to be away from the crowds and out of my unfamiliar clothes. I cannot face the chateau, I think, that is what keeps me here. I cannot face that tower wallpaper wearing the garments I currently wear, cannot bear to see such an exact reflection of myself within it, as though I am standing before a mirror.

I ignored that man beckoning me at the dance, tried to ignore the tableaux altogether, to dismiss them as some strange game of the workers' invention. But those vignettes, living and breathing in front of me as though they had pared themselves from the wallpaper, were too close for that, too suffocatingly familiar. And I cannot help but think that they are following me now, those scenes, making me a part of them wherever I go. That if I thought there was no escape from them before, I am utterly trapped by them now, living inside the print of that pattern as it repeats with every new day.

Feeling suddenly stifled and short of breath, I turn and finally exit the print-house, the music behind me contorting and fading as I sway uncertainly along the track. I briefly imagine going to the cottage, leaving everything at the chateau behind and returning to Sofi and Mama for good. I saw the way my sister, swamped by shame at Madame's accusations, hurried away from the party and I want to go to her. But I cannot abandon the chateau so irresponsibly, and there is nothing else for me to do this moment but return to it.

As I go, my pace dragging, I think of Madame's earlier outburst.

There are no excuses for her conduct, but perhaps there are explanations. I saw the look on that tiny dog's face when the drunkards had hold of the poor thing. I saw the look on Madame's. It wasn't rage, but undiluted fear. I do not condone her behaviour tonight but, at the same time, neither do I blame her for it.

I recall Josef's steepening anger also, the way Madame flinched from him, almost imperceptibly. I recall the pity in Sofi's expression. I have never seen Josef behave that way before, wonder if the drink loosed something inside of him this night, in particular. The eve of the tenth anniversary of his mother's death.

And then my thoughts turn to Guillaume, appearing at the ball so unexpectedly, and I experience again the skip of my pulse when I saw him, how a wave of happiness overcame me. I wonder where he went, my heart heavy at the fact that there was no time for him to even share the address of his lodgings near the capital—

I am some way up the chateau's approach when I hear a noise beyond the poplars to my right. I stop, turn my head. A man's silhouette, a thing of pure blackness, is shifting out of the dark, hastening right towards me.

Night Owls

Sofi

I do not go far. I halt in the darkness at the side of the cottage and slide to the ground with the cold stone at my back. It is the early hours now and the night's chill has teeth.

I've no idea how much time passes as I sit there, the exchange with my mother breaking and boiling in my skull. Could it really be true? I think of Lara's skin, how pale it is against my own. How blonde and smooth her hair hangs, whilst mine spirals in coarse umber coils. Did I really not question why my sister and I look so very different?

Mama mentioned Lara's clothes, commented pointedly on how fine she'd looked at the ball. A stupid remark to make, since she knows full well that Lara's wardrobe is chosen for her, to please the Madame. I told Mama not to listen to people like that woman. *People like her ... like Lara.* That is what she replied. Surely she did not mean, could not mean—

The very notion is preposterous, insufferable. That Lara, my sister, is one of *them*? That her father was an aristocrat? The thought makes me sick, that the same blood might run through my sister's veins as the Madame's, it is unbearable, I cannot countenance it. If it really is true, it would change everything.

I squeeze my hands together in my lap until I hear the bones crack and try to bring my thoughts back to Lara. *It isn't her fault,* I say to myself, *it isn't her fault, she is still the same person.* I repeat the words, many times over, so I do not have the chance to doubt them. Then I know what I must do. I must speak to my sister at once.

Seat numbed by the cold, I rise to go in search of her. If she is back at the chateau I will never be able to get in, but perhaps I may find her still lingering at the print-house instead.

The last dregs of wine are being drained as I approach the building, and when I do not mark my sister amongst the remaining revellers, I proceed back along the track. I have just reached the edge of the forecourt when I detect a figure moving up the approach to the chateau. I squint. The peculiar, outmoded form of this person renders them unrecognisable suddenly, even after all the years we have spent together, though I know very well it is my sister.

'Lara!' I hiss as I follow, not calling louder for fear of arousing someone's attention. She doesn't hear me, but by the time she arrives at the servants' door I will have caught up to her, and then we can speak inside together, just the two of us.

The front of the chateau comes into view, large and moon-bleached, and, as it does, a light in one of its upper rooms is extinguished. An owl hoots overhead. I only notice it at all because Lara jumps, stopping to listen almost at the point where the approach opens into the great sweep of gravel before the house. Out of instinct, I pause, too, expecting her to continue on again after a few seconds, but she does not. It isn't an owl she is listening for, after all.

My sister starts to speak, very quietly. And whomever she is speaking to remains unseen, mantled by the dark, so it is as though Lara is conversing with nothing but the air.

I step towards the cover of the poplars and tiptoe forwards. As my sister angles into view, I see a man is with her. His black hair is slicked into the night and his beard blots the lower half of his face to obscurity, but there is the hint of an amiable glimmer in his eyes, even in the dark, and I know it is Guillaume.

I cannot hear anything of what they say, as down by the gates a party of straggling revellers must be leaving. They are slurring the words to an old folk song and laughing, the metal creak of the gates' hinges a grating accompaniment. But I can see that Guillaume and my sister are standing very close together indeed. So close, they are almost touching.

They continue up the approach then, my sister tugging at his arm, encouraging him to make haste. What could be so important it required such urgent discussion? Surely nothing could be more important than the information I have to share with Lara.

When they are almost upon the servants' entrance, they disappear into a deeper pool of shadow cast by the house. All the chateau's rooms are in darkness now, the window-glass squares of nothing but unblinking night. Then, as I glance up, I imagine I see movement behind the same window of the room in which the light was put out before the owl called. I rub my eyes. It is nothing, just the branches of the nearest poplar, its reflection spreading like a besom across the glass as though trying to sweep it clean.

I look back to the servants' door, but my sister and Guillaume are no longer there and I hear the door close. They must have gone inside. I rush forwards, extend my hand and grip the handle.

I am too late. The door has been locked.

Spoiled Silk

Hortense

I sit in the armchair, a single taper lit, and watch over my little Pépin. He is tightly curled against the bolsters on the counterpane, his soft belly rising and falling in sleep. When I consider what might have happened to him if those workers hadn't been stopped, I am paralysed by fear.

I pass several hours this way, the taper smoking lower on the nightstand. When I go to move, I become aware that my hands are sticky and, glancing down, I almost leave my seat in shock. My palms are covered in a dark film of crimson, the same shade that has eaten across the whiteness of my skirts, like blood on snow.

I churn my hands in the bowl of toilette water to rinse the dried wine from them and go to summon a maid. It is only then I remember that my husband has relieved every servant in this place from their duties tonight, rendering the entire household adrift.

A swirl of rage suddenly consumes me, my skirts utterly despoiled. That one of the factory workers should have the temerity to fling wine at his mistress, it beggars belief. I should insist that my husband dismiss him, recognising with a bitter certainty he never would.

The water in the bowl is dirtied now, so I make for the door to find some elsewhere, recalling a servant at Versailles pouring white wine on a spill of red once, in order to remove it. I exit my room and head for the cupboard on the landing, the one in which my maid keeps a supply of items for my chamber, several bottles of my

310

muscat included. The wretched cupboard, however, when I reach it, is locked.

At that moment, my gaze is caught by the faintest glow at the farthest end of the passageway, seeping from under the door of my husband's chamber before vanishing. Josef must just have extinguished his light and surrendered to bed, soused with drink, no doubt. I'm surprised he lasted this long.

It is when I move away from my husband's room that I see a figure through the window. A woman, scurrying along the chateau's approach, a second person following. I edge closer to the casement and peer around the shutters. I know that woman. It is my lady's maid, hurrying towards the servants' door. And the second figure, a man, is none other than that Black Beard from the ball. So he is here, still, even at this advanced hour, talking and walking so intimately with his sweetheart their lips might be touching, whilst my maid grasps his hand and pulls him close.

Almost pressed against the glass, I follow their progress to the door. There they disappear, leaving everything still and silent, save the distant sound of the latch clanking below.

So that is what my maid is about tonight, I think, turning directly away. *Seeking the pleasures of the flesh.*

That dark, blood-like stain on my skirts floods my vision, and I fly to my chamber to rip it from my body.

Romantic Scenes

Lara

A clock chimes downstairs, clear as a bell. It is two in the morning.

I am still in my ball-clothes, wearing the only cologne that I own, the forget-me-nots pinned in my hair. I feel their delicate heads quiver as he appears silently behind me, expression steeped with trepidation and nervousness. I put down my candle, turning from the oval looking-glass to move towards him.

We come to a halt in the very centre of the tower room, the focus of the circle, and face each other for many moments, not speaking. Then, suddenly, we are no more than a hand's span apart.

It is the most bizarre sensation I have known, the air of the chamber animated by a kind of a charge, an atmosphere laced with some precarious, unknown quality. It is as though the pair of us are balanced high and alone, teetering at the crest of a landmass. The smallest of movements might send us tumbling, set us to a momentum neither he nor I would have the power to stop.

He reaches a hand to my cheek and tilts my head to his, his breath so shallow it is barely there. Our lips meet, tentatively, then deeper, harder as he presses himself into me and I feel him properly, the length of him, for the first time.

The next thing I know, I am standing before him as he sits upon the bed, holding my wrists. I speak to him then and he replies, quietly, gently, 'Apprehensive? I think we both are.'

His free hand runs over the bodice and neckline of my stays, over the swell of my chest, and my hair loosens, spilling past my shoulders. It falls to drape either side of his head, forming the curtains of a private world. 'Like a tent,' he says, breathlessly and as though in wonder, in the briefest moment when his lips leave mine. His hands find my thighs.

Our positions are swapped hastily, me falling flat against the mattress, and my fichu loosens. It slips from my shoulders and comes to rest at my back, and even though it is no thicker than a kerchief, I can feel it beneath me, pressed against the coverlet like butterfly wings.

Reflections

The following month

Lara

I am carrying Madame's pot of tisane to her chamber on a silver tray. Sunlight floods through the large landing windows, and the glint of the tray's metal and the polished brass of the door handle sing garishly together. The dazzle of them dizzies me, and I must lean against the frame of the door awhile until the sensation passes. I have not felt myself recently. And I still haven't done anything about requesting to leave my position. So much has happened it has been impossible.

Just as I'm about to enter the room, a maid interrupts. 'Pardon me, Mademoiselle, but your sister's outside, says she wants a word.'

I feel my brow crease. Sofi has never asked for me downstairs before when she knows I am working. There must be an emergency.

Thinking Mama might have fallen ill, I take the tisane in to Madame and set down the tray. I remove the pot, cup and saucer, pour out the steaming liquid whilst trying to keep my hands steady and my mind upon the task. I place at their side the *bonbonnière*.

'Madame.' I curtsy, but as I lift the tray into my arms again, I shudder. The shape and lustre of it are exactly like the looking-glass in my chamber, that shining oval marooned in its purple tempest of wallpaper. Only now it is not just my reflection it holds. A man is there, too, peering over my shoulder, his face indistinguishable in the undulating bossing of the metal—

I drop the tray. As it falls it catches the saucer, knocking Madame's cup of tisane onto the rug. The spill spreads outwards, swelling and darkening the pile.

'Sorry, Madame, Monsieur—' I stammer, but when I look around I see that only Madame and I are in the room. There was no man, it must have been my dizziness, my mind playing tricks. A bead of sweat prickles down my breastbone.

Madame looks up and tuts. 'Summon one of the serving girls, then, instead of merely gawping at it.'

Apologising once more I hurry downstairs, finding a maid to mop the spill.

I am still shaken when I reach the servants' door, where I find Sofi, fizzing with impatience. The *cocarde* she was given the day the Bastille fell is pinned to her cloak.

'There isn't much time,' she starts, at breakneck speed. 'There's a meeting tonight, a political meeting for the women of the Revolution, I'm going with Bernadette and—'

'In the factory?' I ask, realising *this* is the reason she has asked for me, that there is no emergency.

She sighs and digs into the front of her stays, drawing out a roll of paper. 'No, not in the factory, in Paris. Here.'

I unfurl the paper and read the words printed across it.

Women of the Revolution!
Unite with us at the
Maison de la Lionne
8 heures du soir

'As I say, Bernadette, Sid and a couple of others are going. Cal's taking us. We're meeting shortly outside the factory gates.'

'Where did you get this?'

'Roux sent it to Bernadette,' Sofi replies, avoiding my eyes. 'So, are you coming or not? We must make haste, the others will be with the wagon in a few minutes. If you hadn't just kept me waiting so long—'

Such a comment from my sister would not usually find its mark so keenly, but today her words needle. 'I am at work, Sofi,' I return. 'As should you be.'

My sister taps her foot in irritation. 'So you don't want things to be any better for us, then?'

I might have known there would be no talking to her, not when she is in such full fervour. 'Of course I do. But I told you, that girl from the Bastille is a radical. People like her, they see what they want to see. They don't want change, only blood.'

Sofi gives a laugh, ridged with contempt. 'Well, *I* want change. Unlike you, I don't want to be at the beck and call of the likes of the Madame any longer.'

'And you think I do?' I have seen my sister so infrequently of late that I haven't told her of my plan to ask whether I might leave Madame Hortense's employment. And so her words, her careless assumptions, prompt my anger to rise, against my better judgement.

'*I* want progress, Lara.'

'Progress or vengeance?' I return. 'You're letting what happened to Pa eat you up, Sofi, year after year. You have to let go, make peace—'

'Peace?' she sputters. 'There will be no peace in this country until the aristocracy are gone. And yes, you might call that vengeance, but I call it progress.'

'Oh, Sofi,' I murmur. 'Don't you think there is enough suffering in the world already? Enough people forcing their inclinations on others?' I have to pause, to look away a moment. 'You must see that the way forwards isn't through riling others up until they are hell-bent on slaughter. People like Roux, they claim someone is standing in the way of the greater good, so that person is killed. Then they claim another must die for the same cause, and then another. Soon there are just as many lives lost as lives improved. Where does it end? It is not progress.'

A narrow silence.

'You would say that.' Her voice has lowered, her tone thick and molten.

If I wasn't so vexed I would leave it there, bid her farewell and tell her I must return to my work. But today I cannot. 'What do you mean?'

She turns to leave, then suddenly whips back around, hands coming to her hips. 'You're one of *them*.'

'What are you talking about?'

'You are not my sister!' she exclaims, eyes two blazing discs of chestnut.

My vision swims. This day was always going to come. It was inevitable.

'Your father ... your real father, I mean ...' My sister's voice cracks. 'Turns out he was an aristo who Mama took it into her head to, as she put it, *liaise* with.'

She waits for me to speak, to defend Mama, to counter her words or ask for more proof, but I do not. I recognise with a surge of sickness that the night of the ball had been a terrible hinge, a tipping point in more ways than one. That colour, on my body. Like Sofi's drawing it had confirmed what I suspected but never dared to admit.

Staring at Sofi's portrait that last evening in the cottage had been to hear the answer to a question asked many years before. The more I looked at it, the more certain I'd become, and I thought of Mama, not with resentment or pity but a new understanding. For I hadn't just seen my own face reflected in that likeness, I had also seen *his*.

Likenesses

Sofi

As soon as the words are out I want to gulp them from the air and swallow them back down. I did not mean to tell Lara like this. My stupid voice reverberates off the chateau's walls, as though I have shouted to my sister at the top of my lungs, and I am instantly reddened by guilt.

The few times I've seen Lara since the *Bal de Printemps* I have ducked away from her, made some excuse to leave her company early, shame heavy in my bones. I desperately wanted to talk to her about what Mama said, ask why she'd been conversing with Guillaume so intimately after the ball. But now, having blurted half the matter out so impulsively, I wish I hadn't spoken at all.

'Lara, I—' I reach towards her but she recoils from me.

'You're so quick to accuse, Sofi, without even so much as pausing to draw breath.' She sighs wearily. 'I already knew. About my father. I worked it out. You never stopped to think that might be the case, did you?'

I almost want to splutter out a laugh. 'You knew? But ... how?'

My sister gives a strange, resigned half-smile. 'It was your drawing. The one you did the night before I started working for Madame.'

'My drawing? ... What do you mean?'

'Don't you see? How very like him I look in it?'

I feel myself gaping at her, flesh shrinking as though pre-empting a shock of pain.

'Like *de Comtois*, Sofi.' An awful pause. 'My father is de Comtois.'

This time I do laugh, the action an agony in my chest.

'And before you imagine you are hurt or outraged, ask yourself how I might feel.'

Her words silence me. I reach towards her once more, open my mouth to object, to insist how wrong she is, about all of this, but again Lara moves away.

'I really hoped this day would never come,' she utters. 'Truly I did. I hoped all this would never come between us. The aristocracy, the Revolution. But I fear that it has.'

'What—?' I return. 'No, Lara, wait, I—'

'Just—' she says. 'Just leave. I have work to do.' And with that she shuts the door.

I start towards the factory gates, my legs shaking, mind reeling. I do not want to believe Lara. I could simply have put that vile man's likeness into my drawing unconsciously. But I cannot bear to unpick it, not now. In any case, I tell myself, I do not have the time.

Flowers and Rosettes

Paris

Sofi

It is dark when we arrive in Paris. During the hour or so it takes to reach the capital, I try fiercely to keep my mind from what just occurred between Lara and me, concentrating on the burbling conversation within the wagon, the peasants huddled along the roadsides. The same people de Comtois' class drive into the ground. De Comtois, Lara's father. The thought catches me before I can censor it, a pain like a thorn—

'No, it's definitely that way,' says Bernadette, as Pascal makes another wrong turn.

When we find the place, we see that the Maison de la Lionne is not a house at all, but a room under a café, halfway down a murky backstreet. Cal drops us at the end of it and we follow Bernadette to the café's side door, where she greets a woman. They exchange a few hushed words before Bernadette and Sid slip inside.

I step forwards. The woman eyes me and my *cocarde* approvingly, my fingers lifting to the round ruffle of paper at its centre.

'*Bonsoir*, Madame,' I say, offering a handshake. I don't know why I do it, except that my stomach is tingling, thrilling with excitement and nerves cut through with something else. Despair and regret, I realise, as the conversation with Lara once more swims, unwelcome, through my mind. I wish she was here.

Not taking my hand, the woman on the door issues a throaty laugh and directs me down the stairs. I find myself in a room fogged with smoke, with the smells of strong tobacco, wine, the closeness of bodies. The venue for tonight's gathering is small and, since it is below the level of the street, it has the feel of a den about it. The House of the Lioness.

Packed into this space are about sixty women of all ages. Some are rocking back on their chairs, others drumming palms, fists, or the bases of their glasses onto tabletops to agree or disagree with whatever is being said. It is vibrant, totally unlike anywhere I have ever been before. My despair subsides a little and I begin to feel glad that I came.

Because the room is so full by the time we arrive, we have to pack in, elbow-to-elbow, near the back. Several old crates against the opposite wall act as a podium and a woman is standing on top of them, pouring a speech out with gusto. It is Roux, flaming torrent of hair haloing her torso. She is gesturing passionately, punching the air.

'We are able to handle a sword just as well as a needle!' she cries. 'Not that our brothers believe so!'

Feet are stamped, walls and floor pounded in agreement.

Roux laughs. 'You know what the men say? That we are a *nation* of brothers! *Liberté. Égalité. Fraternité.* Huh! What about the sisters? They're forgetting over half the population. And those who produce it—'

Sisters. I think again of Lara, as a woman passing before me pushes a cup of wine into my hand. I have never liked the stuff before, never really wanted to touch it. Yet I force down the memories of the tavern in Marseilles, and I begin to sip.

I sip the whole time I listen to Roux's speech and it is only when I go to take another mouthful that I realise the cup is already empty. My head and heart buzz as I take in Roux's words, my anguish numbing. Lara was wrong today, this *is* progress. A meeting of this kind, of women delivering such opinions, it would never have been possible before the Bastille fell.

Roux concludes to rapturous cheers and the next woman begins to speak. By the time the third is on the podium, I have finished several cups of the fruity, intoxicating liquid that has been passed to me, and I feel untethered, emboldened. More impassioned, even, than I did before. My blurring gaze follows Roux as she winds her way through the assembly, greeting the other women. And then, before I know it, she is right in front of me.

'Bonsoir, ma sœur,' she says. 'I have seen you somewhere before, non?'

'Yes.' I nod, swallow another mouthful of wine. 'At the Bastille.' There is something about her that sets her quite apart from anyone else I have met. The flecked olive of her eyes, pupils ringed with burning gold, penetrates me to my core, makes me want to spill my secrets and everybody else's besides. Even though I do not know her, I feel as if I do. In this moment, I feel like I can trust her.

Roux takes in my wine-warmed cheeks, my revolutionary rapture. 'You have enjoyed the evening, I think?' She laughs again then stops abruptly, narrowing her eyes. 'But tell me, ma sœur, what really brings you here?'

My stomach plummets, my lips dry. I don't know what to say, where to begin. I open my mouth and close it several times as Roux continues to look serenely on.

'I hate them,' I spit finally, the syllables running into one bitter jet. The notion this statement might include my own sister suddenly occurs to me, sour as the coating of wine on my tongue.

For a second Roux gives no reply and, even when she does, she remains calm, expressionless. She does not judge what I have said, nor is she shocked by it. 'And by them you mean . . . ?'

I lean into her. 'The aristocracy. I hate them. They murdered my father.' The concentration I need to get these words out is immense, the first vowel of 'father' erupting in a painful hiccup. My voice slides into one unstable stream and I'm embarrassed to see spots of red wine escape my mouth with it, to fly in Roux's direction. I wipe the wine from my chin with my sleeve and feel it wobbling.

'I see.' Although she doesn't mention my state, her extraordinary eyes take in every part of me. She glances around, inclines her head closer. 'You know, if there is anyone in particular, there are ways. I know a man with a list, he is always interested to learn of enemies of the Republic.' The lower part of her face lifts, a smile which does not reach her eyes.

I note, fuzzily, that despite this gathering it is a man she knows with a list and not a woman. Starting to comprehend the true meaning of what she is saying, I find I cannot reply. It is as though my last sentences have taken every last drop of me with them.

'Consider this information a gesture of solidarity,' Roux goes on. 'Always room for one more at the Conciergerie. And to be tried from there ... well, nothing more than a formality.' She takes a sip from her own cup and touches it to mine. '*À la tienne, ma sœur.*'

I cannot remember what the Conciergerie is, but attempt a smile. She fixes her strange eyes on me a final time and moves on to my neighbour.

An hour later, when I climb the stairs and head back onto the street with the others, I notice how much lighter I feel, unburdened of discomfort, an abscess squeezed. I have, for the first time in longer than I can recall, the sense that everything is going to be all right.

The evening air, cooler now, numbs my face, but I do not feel its chill. And it is not just the wine. The fire inside of me, smouldering for years, is raging to inferno.

Good Herbs

Jouy-en-Jouvant, May, the following month

Lara

I am seated at the table in the tower, the night framed in the casement before me, the light from my candle showing the smudge of its twin in the glass. Outside, silhouettes break the horizon. The old sycamore at the border of the gardens seems much larger than the rest of them tonight.

I sat here a week earlier, the smell of the capon Madame had eaten at dinner still turning my stomach, head between my knees and counting to ten until the nausea passed. I sat here again a day after that, when I missed the chamber-pot and had to sponge the spots of sickness from my skirts. And finally two days ago, when, hands shaking, I upturned my mind to recall when my bloods should have started.

I stare at the parchment in front of me, at its words written in graphite. I'd heard the recipe days before, was desperate to record it before I forgot. But I hadn't been able to find my pen, could almost swear there have been days when I've returned here after waiting upon Madame only to discover my things not quite where I left them, the floor of the armoire disturbed. I drove such thoughts away at first, presumed I was seeing something where there was nothing, presumed it was a rat. Nevertheless, I will make sure to lock the door when I am out of this room in the future. I only wish I was out of here altogether, out of the chateau for good. But I know full well that the time for asking has passed, that I will never be able to raise the subject of my returning to the print-house now.

Take a quart of lavender flowers & put them into a quart of white wine. Take three fresh roots of rue, about the size of a finger, & slice them up.

I consider Mama, working at the soap factory in Marseilles, tipping the dried heads of lavender into the mix. Had she heard of this tonic? Would she have wanted to use it for the same purpose as me? It has been a while since I've spoken to her at any length, and neither have I seen my sister, not since she showed up here that afternoon last month and spat out her secret.

The letters on the page before me are clumsy, erratic as clustering flies. It feels strange enough to hold graphite for drawing, let alone writing. I think of the box beneath my bed, full of the pages of my work. I might have sketched these ingredients, too, once, the pretty stems of rue and lavender, ignorant of their hidden purpose.

Add the slic'd rue to the white wine mix, & add also four sprigs of savin, & a dozen drops of oil of pennyroyal.

I did not expect it to be so easy to come by such things. I needed worm fern as well, the only ingredient I could not find at first. Then, several villages away, a woman sold me four dried roots of the stuff, passed the parcel over the sill of her window as though it were a druggist's counter. I insisted the worm fern was for my mistress, but the woman knew.

I determined as soon as I realised what had happened that I would not tell him. I will keep the matter to myself and resolve it my way.

I fold the sheet twice and push it under the stack of unsoiled parchments on the tabletop.

La Baignoire

One month later

Hortense

Something is amiss with my lady's maid. There is an absent-minded distance to her that I cannot help but notice. More fascinating still is the uncharacteristic fullness to her cheeks, the increased plumpness about her figure. The girl is being too well-fed, doubtless the result of my husband's crotch-driven generosity. Or perhaps it is something else.

So, I ponder, as she mishears my instruction for the hundredth time this morning, I could either lie against my pillows and continue to twiddle my thumbs, or I could make it my business to find out what is going on. I daresay that, when uncovered, the matter will hold as much intrigue for me as the lint in de Pise's navel but, nevertheless, I concoct a plan.

I would not call it a trap, as such. I have my suspicions, so merely take the liberty of laying a little bait. I write to de Pise in advance, before making a great fuss of announcing I wish to take a bath. I can almost hear the servants' eyes roll in their sockets at the mention of such a frivolous afternoon luxury. I tell my maid, hoping this will be one instruction she does take in, and inform her that, despite the temperature outside, the tub must be arranged in front of the fire in my chamber and filled with hot water immediately. Since the other servants are engaged in some dreary domestic cleaning task today, it will be up to my maid to conduct the labour of fetching the pails alone. This should buy me some time.

Knowing my husband is unlikely to return for several hours, from whichever pastis-soused business meeting he is attending today, I steal up the unsightly spiral steps to my maid's little chamber, to see what I can find.

To my initial annoyance the door is locked, a fact that only serves to pique my interest further as I proceed back down the stairs. She can't have anything of value up there, so I wonder why the lock is necessary at all. From the landing windows I see de Pise's carriage has already drawn up outside.

Snatching a crewel-trimmed jacket from the chaise with an extravagant flourish, I announce that I have changed my mind and will be going out instead. I take Pépin into my arms as the girl heaves yet another pail of water into the chamber and make for the door.

'But Madame, your bathwater is ready,' she calls after me. 'I have brought it up as you requested—'

'I care not a fig,' I declare over my shoulder. 'You could have borne it up another twenty staircases and I would still be on my way out.' I pause with my back to her, unable to suppress a smile at my next unreasonable demand. 'Have the bathwater drawn again in a few hours, ready for my return.'

I sense her at the threshold of the chamber, watching open-mouthed as I make my grand sweep down the staircase to the vestibule. Unfortunately, de Pise, unaware of the deception, is already awaiting me there, and when I go to turn and creep back to my chamber, he asks loudly, 'Why are you going back upstairs, *ma chère*, have you forgotten something?'

I raise my hand, wanting to rap the guard of my fan against his idiotic cheek, but instead I bring my hand to his lips to shush him. 'I just need to find my parasol,' I purr. 'I must have mislaid it. I shall be but a moment. In the meantime,' I hand my dog to him gently, 'perhaps you would ensure Pépin is comfortable in the carriage?' I would not usually allow him to be sullied by de Pise's touch, but I don't want to take the little nougatine back inside with me and risk him giving me away. De Pise croons his acquiescence and finally adjourns to his vehicle.

When I reach the landing again, I see that the door to my chamber is now closed. With any luck, I think, that girl will not have been able to resist the lure of a warm bath and will be disrobing accordingly. Nonetheless, the scene that greets me when I kneel before the keyhole comes as something of a surprise.

My maid is not yet undressed, but is standing beside the steaming tub, holding a packet in her hand and sprinkling something small and round like sugar balls into the water. I can smell the sharp, peppery scent even from here. Mustard.

She puts the packet down and begins to remove her clothes. I draw closer to the keyhole, not wanting to miss a thing, watch carefully as she pares free her outer garments, next her stays and petticoats, and lastly her chemise. But, rather than now standing fully naked, skin glowing in the light from the fire, I note she still wears one curious garment.

It looks like some sort of bandage, bound tightly around her abdomen. She unpeels the cloth until she is free of it altogether, and for the first time I see the distinct bulge in her belly.

The girl drops the bandage to the floor like a length of fruit peel and steps into the bath. As her toes break the water with a plash, I hear voices at the other end of the passageway, so I dart back down the stairs and into the waiting carriage.

'Did you discover it?' enquires de Pise, as he signals for the driver to move off.

'Oh, yes,' I say. 'I did indeed.'

Illuminations

July, one month later

Sofi

The sun has blazed down for weeks without end. *Chopines* of sweat soak the backs of the workers and the air of the dye-house is thick with a heat that does not seem to shift from one day to the next.

I fan my face with my apron. I know I must speak to Lara today, to discuss what happened the last time I saw her, to apologise. Before she moved to the chateau, my sister and I never even went three days without talking, so it is hard to believe it has now been three months. I am not proud of this, not proud of the fact it's been easier to avoid Lara altogether than face my shame at blurting out Mama's secret. But I know I have put it off long enough. And I miss my sister's company dreadfully, uneasier though it's been in the years she has worked for the Madame.

As soon as the dinner bell rings, I head for the chateau and am crossing the forecourt when I see a carriage leave for the gates. The Madame's face lurks behind its window, a pale fish in the depths of a pond, that man de Pise in the opposite seat.

I watch the vehicle pass before proceeding up the approach to the servants' entrance, and am not far from the gravel sweep when something ahead snags my attention. There is a man, leaving a parcel of some sort on the step of the servants' door before moving off into the trees. Assuming it must be a delivery, I think little of it at first. But when I reach the door, I see exactly what the man has deposited on its threshold. A dead, wet-bodied rat. A dried daub of blood crusting the nose.

Twigs snap from the lawns behind me and I pivot quickly, determined to see who is there. A slim-set, darkly dressed man is slinking away. And this time I know very well that he isn't one of the Obersts' servants. He is Emile Porcher. The rat-catcher.

The servants' door opens suddenly and the housemaid glances between me and the lifeless animal at my feet.

'Not another,' she exclaims. 'That's about the tenth this week.'

'The tenth—?'

'Rats!' she confirms. 'We keep finding dead ones, all over the place. The chateau must be overrun with them!'

I look back to the lawns, weigh up whether I should admit what I witnessed. A vision of Porcher, peering through the crowds at the ball, flashes in my mind. That gaunt face, framed by its hanging cords of hair, set so intently on Lara. My guts squirm with apprehension.

'I must get this to a footman,' the housemaid says, picking up the rat by its tail. 'Monsieur Marchant said if any more were found he'd call that rat-catcher up from the village . . . something Porcher.'

'But I thought he left?' I say. 'Years ago?'

'He did, but he's back now, I gather.'

Before I have the chance to speak again, the maid starts down the stairs. 'If you're looking for your sister, she's up in her chamber.'

I climb the staircases towards the tower room, mind ticking over what just happened. Monsieur Marchant is about to summon that strange man to the chateau, to deal with a rat problem of the man's own making. I stop dead, understanding clanging in my skull. Of course. Porcher has been deliberately planting the rats himself to give him good reason to spend more time at the chateau, so his presence here won't seem untoward. I shudder. Could this all be a ruse, a scheme to allow himself access to my sister?

My strides lengthen on the stairs, legs swallowing two at a time as I hasten to Lara, to warn her. I swing the door open and, though the room is unlocked, it is empty. My sister is not here.

Aside from that evening after supper with our aunt, I have ventured into this chamber only once or twice before and never for long. I move to the centre of the room, finding myself enthralled by the space anew, captivated again by the scenes on the wallpaper.

A shaft of sunlight pierces the long panes of window-glass, holding in its glow the vignette of Josef flying the kite with his mother, the air before the print dancing as though infused with magical dust. It is like a chamber from a fairy tale Pa might have told me, one of fair maidens and handsome princes, misguided fathers and spiteful queens.

The sun dims for a moment and my eye is caught by an array of articles spread across the table near the window. I do not register them at first, so mundane are they, so everyday. Mind still on my daydream, I pick up the item nearest to me, a small earthenware bottle stoppered with a cork.

Absentmindedly, I run a finger over the smooth ridges of its sides, pop free the cork, and mean to replace it again when my nostrils are besieged by the stench within, by rancid wine and rotting leaves. It is certainly too vile a liquid to drink, I conclude, so it must be some sort of unguent.

I wedge back the stopper and set the bottle down again, next to several off-cuts of linen, needles and pins, a spool of cotton. Lara has been sewing and, sure enough, skirts are hanging on the pegs of the door, stays, stomachers and petticoats spread across the bed. Some lie with their side-seams unpicked, some with additional panels of fabric half-added, hanging from the garments like tongues. Under the sewing apparatus on the table is a stack of parchments, one sticking proud of the rest. Something is written on it, in my sister's hand, and I tug the paper free and read the last lines.

Next, chop & add two fresh roots of worm fern (more commonly known as Prostitute's Root). Bring to the boil, strain & drink.

I don't have the chance to take in these words before I become aware of footsteps on the stairs, a floorboard shifting near the threshold. I hastily shove the paper back beneath the others, turning to the door in expectation of it opening. But it does not.

Instead there comes a terrific series of bangs from just outside, the sound of a large object being flung from a height, to thud and plummet like a sack of wet barley. I hurry in the direction of the noise and see a figure, crumpled in a heap at the foot of the spiral, head cricked forwards.

Abundance

Lara

I hear my sister shout my name from the top of the stairs and my heart sinks. How can I possibly begin to explain to her what I've just done?

Sofi drops down beside me. 'Are you hurt? Are you able to speak?'

I slowly recover my limbs and look up. My head is ringing. I try to touch my hand to the left side of my face, which is throbbing unbearably. It must have struck a step as I fell. I wonder whether Sofi perceives what consumes me in this moment – my shock at the pain, my humiliation at being discovered, my frustration at what it has come to. This last is the strongest of all.

'Your face!' my sister exclaims. 'It is swelling, it is going purple!'

'I am not hurt,' I mutter. 'I simply tripped, was all.'

Her expression changes, as though in an instant of recognition. 'If you think you can walk, come,' she says, placing her arms around me to try to lift me from the floor as my ribs tense. 'Let us get you to bed and I will fetch some cold cloths.'

It is difficult to climb the spiral stairs with my head spinning so. The last time I felt this way was right after the wagon accident. My sister lays me down upon the coverlet and tips water from the jug to wet a length of linen.

'Is your face very sore?' Sofi asks. 'It's turning the same colour as the wallpaper!'

She is trying to make a joke, but I wince. There is no getting away from that wallpaper.

My sister gently places a cold cloth on my brow. 'There is no easy way to say this . . . ' she murmurs.

I know exactly of what she is about to speak, she does not need to carry on. 'I do not want to discuss it.'

'But you do not know what it is I mean to say.' Sofi studies my face as though trying to unknot it. 'It is typical of you,' she goes on, 'to close like a trap when there are pressing matters to discuss. Why can you never just speak out?'

My temper blackens. 'Like you, you mean? Sofi, if I behaved as you do we would have been dismissed from this place years ago.' I close my eyes. I did not mean to be harsh, but my sister is always so keen to reach for the nearest argument. 'You were about to mention *him*. De Comtois.'

Now it is Sofi's turn to close up. She doesn't move for some seconds, and I expect her to be formulating a retort, but instead she takes my hand in hers.

'I am sorry, for what happened between us last time. You are still my sister, Lara.' Her voice snags and she squeezes my fingers hard. 'But it wasn't that I was going to speak of. I know. About . . . ' Her gaze drifts to my stomach and back. 'And so will Mama before long. And everyone else, too. I cannot believe Aunt Berthé hasn't worked it out already.'

I stiffen. 'I conceal it. I am dealing with it.'

'This isn't the way,' she returns. 'Drinking who knows what to get rid of it. And now . . . today. What just happened wasn't an accident, was it?'

The taint of shame and desperation in my eyes makes me unable to bring them to hers. There is a long pause.

'I know who the father is, Lara, I saw. How could you let it happen?'

I flinch at the question. She couldn't have seen. 'Please. If you do only one thing for the rest of your days, then keep your counsel. Promise me, Sofi.' My vision of her is shrinking, my bruised left eye puffing closed.

She stills, as though weighing whether to object. But then she squeezes my hand again. 'I promise.'

I exhale slowly. The ringing in my head does not allow me to speak further, other parts of my body aching now, too.

'You are exhausted,' I hear Sofi say. 'Do you know when the Madame will return? If there is time for you to rest then you should take it. I'll watch for the carriage and wake you when it comes.'

'You . . . should be working.'

'I'm not due back until the half-hour,' she replies. 'But in any case, I shall wait.'

Sofi goes to the window and as I lie there I can hear her moving the objects on my table, shaking the bottle containing the potion I made from the ingredients on the parchment. There is the squeak of the stopper being removed, the scrape of the window opening. Through the sliver of a gap between my eyelids, I see my sister's outline at the casement, tipping what remains of the liquid outside.

My shrinking line of sight moves sluggishly from Sofi and lands on the wallpaper. It is like I am viewing each of those scenes down the barrel of a cannon. They hover distantly, circled by black.

And then, as I watch them, it happens once again. The wall-paper alters before my very eyes, each one of those scenes melting into a totally different image, an image that is so close a reflection of my life it seizes and traps me within it. The woman in the wall-paper. In every vignette her belly now swells proud as a proved loaf, round as a tight-skinned table-melon. It presses against the edge of her toilette, tips back her writing-desk to teeter on two legs. She has to stretch and strain to reach the keys of her fortepiano, and now slides down the baluster with her stomach to the ceiling. Even in the scene of her singing to her baby, her belly looks more than full enough to bear another child at any moment.

It is the fall down the stairs and the fresh knock to my head that is causing this, once more warping reality. But I remember all the other occasions I have seen myself in that paper. I remember the

335

way I have returned to this chamber to find my things disordered, not quite as I left them. And, as I bring a hand to my stomach, to the child growing inside me, a flood of awful realisation drowns the throbbing in my head.

Fine Lace Fans

Sofi

I am walking to the dye-house, my mind throwing up questions so fast their edges are raw. I did not tell my sister about Emile Porcher yesterday, didn't warn her about him as I ought to have done. The state she was in, her injuries, the rise of her belly as she lay on her bed, they ejected the matter completely from my mind. And I've told no one about Lara's condition, not even Mama. But how can I carry on this way, despite what I promised? Someone is certain to discover it soon, and concealing a pregnancy is against the law. If I do not speak out, I will be committing a crime.

I wonder if my sister can feel the baby quickening already, squirming inside her. Surely it must have happened the night of the ball, when I saw her with Guillaume in the shadows, when I saw him enter the house. Where is he now? He is a good man, he would not abandon my sister if he was aware of her plight.

I sense the other workers overtake me as I go, calling out to mock my listless pace. But I do not care. I am a pony, blinkered. There is no room in my head for anything other than Lara.

On reaching the forecourt, I see the same carriage the Madame left in yesterday, slowing as it nears the factory gates. If only her crony would take her away for good, I think. If only he would mislay her along the way and never bring her back. How much better all our lives would be.

I realise it is early for the Madame to be out and about at all. The hour that others start their work must, to a self-indulgent serpent such as her, feel like the middle of the night. At this time of day the Madame has six or seven more hours of lazing about in her satin bed-linen ahead of her, indolent as a pig in muck. Yet, behind the carriage window, I see the flickering of a fan, and I instantly know it is she.

I stare after the vehicle as it rattles down to the village. So she has kept her fine lace fans. What other baubles does she continue to presume she's entitled to, whilst those she deems beneath her toil an honest day? Whilst my sister works her fingers to the bone, fetching and carrying and satisfying the Madame's every whim, as a new life grows inside of her.

The soles of my feet land noisily on the ground, harder with every stride, and my hand drifts to my throat. That thin band of green velvet, the colour worn by the people the day the Bastille fell. The colour of hope. And then the idea calls to me, rousing and clear as the burst of a bugle.

If the Madame were no longer here, might not everything be so very different? Though the baby isn't his, I know what Josef still feels for Lara, painful though it is to acknowledge. With his wife gone, he would surely support my sister and her child. After all, he would learn the truth eventually, and Lara clearly knows full well that Guillaume is in no position to support his baby, even if Mama did not turn him away this time, like she did in Marseilles.

It is as Roux told me. There are certain men in the capital who would be very interested to learn how the Madame behaves. About her loyalties, her acquaintances, about the extravagances she maintains. The mass of factory buildings ahead of me dissolves and I see myself arriving in the city, paying Roux's man a visit. I see the Madame's name being inked onto one of his lists, in a pattern of permanent black print. I see mounted guardsmen thundering up the hill to the factory, their uniforms flaring, and I see those same guardsmen riding away, taking the Madame with them, never to be seen again.

In three days it will be a Sunday and I shall not be at work. I will do it then. I will find a way to travel to Paris. And, when it is done, it will simply be a matter of time before everything is fixed. Before I have fixed everything.

The Bird-Catcher

Somewhere outside Paris

Hortense

It is far too early to be out and about, especially on a mission such as this, but I had little choice than to be up at the cockerel's fart. If I am honest, I have found my options dwindling since the night of that wretched factory party. With the Revolution raging on, I should not have let my ire get the better of me so spectacularly.

Today de Pise collected me from shabby little Jouy to take me to see Mama. It is a privilege I'm hardly looking forward to, but for weeks Mama has pestered and harried for a meeting, and I haven't had a moment's peace. She tells me she has a brilliant plan, to remove us from the ongoing saga in the country and flee to safety. She has never much troubled herself about my safety before, and I doubt the plan is so very brilliant as she supposes.

My mother has taken refuge in her rural bolthole, as the Queen used to before France went to the dogs. She drifts about the place in her crêpes, thinking herself a sylvan maiden, but resembling not so much a shepherdess as a lump of dough wrapped in a window-net. It is to this idyll that de Pise conveys me now.

When the carriage arrives, Mama appears instantly, round and flushed and fit to burst. She totters over and grasps me to her bosoms, forgetting, as always, that I am bearing little Pépin in my arms. I scowl at her, but she is in too much of a flap to notice. In the rear parlour, a table of sugared delicacies and sparkling wine awaits.

'Plans ought to be made!' Mama is saying, over and over, seemingly unable to remain seated for a minute. She wedges her expansive derrière into a chair, only to squeak it free again seconds later and skit about the room.

'Plans, Mama? What plans?' I ask airily. At this stage it is more entertaining to feign ignorance, to watch my mother fluster awhile.

'What a question to pose!' she squawks. 'The situation in this country is perilous! Haven't you been listening to a word I've been saying? Have you not paid heed to any of my letters?'

I raise my eyebrows, simulating confusion. 'Well, Mama? It is not as though *I* can do anything, I am a married woman. In any case, why should the authorities have any interest in me?' I take a macaron from my plate and pop it in my mouth.

'Oh, pfft!' splutters Mama. 'I don't trust those rough factory labourers! What do you suppose would happen should one of them take against you? Answer me that!'

I look over at her, perfectly expressionless. The macaron is so light it melts on my tongue in a twinkling, but still I pretend to chew long after it dissolves. I shall make her wait for my answer. 'How should I know, Mama?' I say, selecting another sweet treat from the cake-stand. In truth I do not want it. It used to be that I would mind what I ate so I did not bloat towards middle age like my mother. Now I simply do not have the appetite.

To my left, de Pise's eyes widen. Clearly, he has not considered a workers' uprising in Jouy a possibility until now, even though the fate of Monsieur Réveillon's wallpaper factory in Paris was common knowledge all over Europe. Razed to the ground by the mob. And all because of a misunderstanding about a comment Réveillon made regarding the price of grain, blown up out of all proportion. These peasants have no appetite either – no appetite for the truth – they see what they want to see. We must censor every word that passes our lips now. As stifling an existence as being shut up in a factory in the arse-end of nowhere.

'If you thought a factory such a dangerous place, Mama, why allow Papa to marry me into one?'

Mama ignores this and sniffs. '*Ma petite*, the noose is tightening around our necks, nowhere is safe! And the King already murdered! Who could have predicted *that* day would ever come!' Each of my mother's statements works her into more of a frenzy, and before long she has to drop onto a chaise and summon a maid to cool her face. 'It is why I wanted to see you today especially,' she continues, flapping her hand at me. 'I want your father to take me to the Swiss border and you must come too.' Her eyes dart to de Pise. 'Oh, and you, Monsieur.'

I press flat a smile. An afterthought, I can tell.

De Pise gives an obsequious grin. 'Thank you, Marquise. It would be an honour.'

Mama turns back to me. 'And, darling – the Princesse de Lamballe, only last September! If we do not flee, the same fate will befall us, I am sure of it!'

A sickliness rises inside me, churning the undigested sweetmeats in my stomach. I know well the horrific particulars Mama is about to launch into. Pépin buries his head in my skirts as if he, also, can pre-empt what is coming.

'Poor Lamballe, thrown into that vile prison,' Mama goes on. 'Treated like a common criminal, a street woman! You heard what happened, Monsieur de Pise, did you?'

De Pise opens his mouth to answer yes, so he might be spared another lurid account of it, but Mama is in full flow now and not to be stopped.

'A great pack of them set upon her, piercing her with their pikes, bludgeoning her with their clubs, torturing her ... for hours! Such details as I cannot go into ... but by all accounts her killers were like wolves pulling apart their prey, they even tore her breasts off with their teeth! Their teeth! Poor Lamballe was hacked to pieces, even her most private parts dismembered and paraded through the streets. And do you know what happened to those remains of hers afterwards? It makes me shudder to think on it, I could not even begin to explain, suffice to say they ate her heart, fashioned belts from her entrails and made false moustaches from . . . well, it does not become me to say which of her hair they used for *that* endeavour.'

I know every word before it is spoken, having heard Mama recite this gruesome chain of events several times. Why she regularly regurgitates the tale, as though it is her first time relating it, I've no idea. I can only assume she finds some grisly melodrama in the spectacle of her acquaintance's death.

I take a sip of wine. 'I seem to recall something of it, I think,' I answer vaguely.

Mama indulges in a theatrical intake of breath. 'Really! Well, all I am saying is that the time of them showing mercy to ladies, permitting them to walk free, has long since passed. The Queen is already incarcerated. It is this savagery we must expect now, the mob have scented blood and it's ours they want.' There is a pause. 'And this contraption, the *Madame Guillotine*,' she declares with an exaggerated shiver. 'That is not the quick end they say it is. Monsieur de Pise, you'll have heard, I'm sure, of its inefficiencies?'

'I have, Marquise.' De Pise looks towards me and puts his plate down solemnly. 'Malfunctions, misaligned blades, they are not uncommon. The King himself suffered cruelly.' He speaks to me in the manner of a schoolmaster addressing a half-witted boy in his care. He needn't. Like the horrors of Lamballe's death, I am well-versed in the defects of the guillotine.

'Oh!' Mama starts, getting to her feet again. 'Savages! Barbarians!'

Now it is de Pise's turn to re-recite melodrama. It's how certain people deal with the horrors staring them in the face. They revel in them, as though rubbing salt into the healing flesh of a gash, to be thrilled by the pain anew.

'And I do, I fear,' de Pise continues, 'know of one gentleman who is certain the head remains conscious for some time after the guillotine has severed it. He has himself witnessed the signs.'

Mama shrieks. 'Mark my words, Monsieur de Pise . . . we are the hunted, we who have made this country what it is, for generations! Slain in the name of reform! But who will put things right once *we* are slaughtered? Answer me that!'

'This so-called Revolution is eating itself,' remarks de Pise.

'And I need my maids, I need my things!' Mama continues. 'Why should I be forced to live like a Puritan?'

My mother could not tolerate the monotony of her existence without her diversions any more than I. We are alike in that respect, at least. And, I have to admit, she does have a point. Why should she be compelled to change the way she lives? It is like removing a fish from the ocean, expecting it to spend the rest of its days on dry land and claiming surprise when it shrivels and dies.

I have recognised long before today the treacherous ground on which my safety rests. I am well aware of the situation, of the state of the nation. It is only a matter of time before one of the peasants working at that factory takes it into their head to spread lies about their Madame, especially given what unfolded at that wretched ball.

My parents underestimate me. They all do. For I have already resolved that it is up to me to find some means forwards now. The last time danger stalked, I did not perceive the threat until it was too late. But now I refuse to roll over and let them come for me so easily. That may be the woman's lot in the bedchamber, but not here, not this time.

As the carriage makes its way back to the factory, I angle myself towards de Pise, sugaring my voice as thickly as the *violettes confites* on my mother's cake-stand. 'I may need your help,' I say, 'very soon.' I place my hand over his, relieved that, since we are alone together in a closed carriage, nobody is able to witness it.

As I knew it would, the gesture affects de Pise like a whistle a dog. His face immediately transforms into a picture of alertness and devotion, his spine straightening to a rod. I can near see his tongue begin to loll from his mouth.

'Of course,' he says. 'Anything.'

Thinking he has given his reply I smile, hide my face coyly with my fan and turn to the window. But then he speaks again.

'You know I worship you, my dear,' he says, in a tone that makes my scalp crawl. 'Much more than your . . .' he wrinkles his nose, '*husband* ever could. What he sees in your lady's maid when the heavens have sent him a woman like you I cannot imagine. It is like comparing dog meat to a *filet mignon*.' He goes to rest a hand on my thigh but thinks better of it. 'The whole of Versailles used to talk of his disdain for you, you know. Now all they're talking about is . . .' He pauses. 'Well, I can't quite think how best to put it . . . the *delicacies* of your marriage bed.'

My hand tightens on my fan, its speed increasing. I remember the gossip, the smirks that used to trail the Queen.

'But forgive me, I have said too much.'

How has Versailles come to know of the state of my marriage, unless from de Pise himself? I want to confront him with the charge, but have little choice available to me than to keep him on side. I am suddenly incensed. How dare Josef Oberst make such a fool out of me. Is it not enough that he has traipsed after that girl all these years, behaving like a jealous lover at the ball, treating me – a marquis's daughter – as though *I* were less than *she*?

Behind the flickering half-moon of lace, icy tendrils of ire slither across my cheeks.

Billets-Doux

Jouy-en-Jouvant

Hortense

In the time it takes to journey back to the factory, my fury reaches its zenith. It is all I can do to bid de Pise farewell before, holding Pépin close, I storm into the vestibule.

'Josef Oberst!' I call. 'I demand to speak with you this instant!'

Nothing, save the ticking of a clock.

'Jo-sef!'

After far too protracted a moment the housekeeper appears, looking distinctly uneasy.

'Well, where is he?' I ask.

'I'm terribly sorry, Madame. He's down in the factory at present.'

'My maid, then. Where is she?'

'She's gone to the village, Madame. She oughtn't to be long—'

I continue up the staircase, leaving the woman wittering on behind me.

'Shall I inform the Monsieur or Mademoiselle Thibault that you wish to speak to them when they return—?'

'What?' I am hardly listening, my mind now honed as the needle of a compass. 'Yes. Actually, better than that. You can go up to my maid's room directly and unlock it for me. There are some articles of mine up there that I require immediately.'

It is a lie, but my maid is hiding something other than her

346

condition, I am convinced of it. Why else would her room be locked so religiously? It is not as though she is in possession of anything worth protecting. Most likely she has things up there given to her by Black Beard. Cheap love trinkets of some description, a salacious stack of *billets-doux*. If only my husband knew.

'Certainly, Madame. If you tell me what they are, I should be happy to fetch them.'

'That won't be necessary,' I say, pointing at the great bunch of keys she keeps tied to her waist. 'Just go there at once and unlock the door.' I do not take my eyes off the woman, daring her not to comply.

'Very well, Madame,' she mumbles at last, offering a curtsy before scuttling away.

I lay Pépin on a cushion in my chamber, then, ensuring the housekeeper is safely back below stairs, I climb the tower.

The space is simple, as I presumed it would be. Perfectly round and sparsely furnished. The commode and nightstand house an uninspiring array of everyday items, the armoire nothing more than a lot of plain garments. The shelves inside of it are all tidily stacked, but the armoire's floor is in a state of disarray, slippers and other articles lying jumbled across it. I am forced to move a stocking to close one of the doors again and, as the tips of my fingers pinch the item, I feel that it is warm. My maid mustn't long have left. I abandon the armoire, resolving to check the rest of the room. I still have the inkling there is something here to find. Some unseemly truth to reveal.

I scrutinise the bed-linens, lifting the coverlet from the mattress and, as I do, my toes stub against something underneath the bed. I bend down, careful to make as little contact with the grubby floor as possible, and see that the object is a chest. I think I have stumbled upon the very thing I came to unearth, until I prise open the lid to discover the chest is filled with nothing but drawings of flowers and landscapes and birds. Hastily, I stuff the papers back where I found them and close the lid.

Irked by the fruitlessness of my search I cross to the door, gaze skimming the space a final time. Then something gives me pause.

When I entered the room I paid no heed to the design of the wallpaper here, just assumed it to be of the sort the Obersts have peddled for years, merely taken it in as a wash of violet across the wall. But now I am quite sure I just perceived the flash of a familiar face, peering out at me. I move closer—

'What do you think you are doing?'

I cannot help but start at the words that suddenly sound from the door.

'Mademoiselle Thibault, you have an unusually deep voice today,' I say, determined not to turn around. 'And surely it must be you, since nobody else has any business to be up here, and certainly not a gentleman.'

Knowing this will annoy him, one corner of my lips lifts into a smirk. But he counters immediately.

'And certainly not *you*.'

I face him then, a single, rapid movement that sends my skirts swishing over the floorboards. 'My, husband ... it is *you*!'

'Get out.'

My eyes flick up and down him. 'I think not. Not before you have told me why it is you have crept up here, like a stoat up a tree.'

'Why do you think? Madame Charpentier told me you wanted to see me. That you'd had her unlock this room.'

I smile and tap my teeth with a fingernail, studying the apples of Josef's cheeks, the skin of them rippling over the tensing muscles beneath. 'Yes, I did want to see you, for I have something to tell you, husband. Something I thought you should know. It concerns a matter lately come to my attention.'

I recollect the small hours after the ball, the scene I witnessed from the landing window. My maid and Black Beard, huddled so amorously together on their way back to the chateau. What an intimate rendezvous must have followed, to create that bulge in her belly.

'So? What is it?'

I do not answer. Let him simmer awhile.

'Pray tell, Hortense,' Josef presses. 'Enlighten me. What is it you think you know?'

I smile again. 'There is to be a new arrival, I believe. The patter of tiny feet, here at the chateau!'

He seems confused at first, before his mouth drops open. 'But we,' he mutters, groping for his words, 'we haven't—'

I allow myself the pleasure of a few moments of trilling laughter. 'Of course we haven't. Oh no, it is my *maid* I am referring to.'

'You are insane.'

'She is with child.'

He sputters a laugh. 'No, she is not. This is another one of your schemes. A scheme to get rid of her. But she has done nothing wrong.'

'*Au contraire*, husband,' I continue. 'It is not a scheme at all, it is quite true. And if bringing a lover back here directly after the ball is your idea of her doing nothing wrong, then you are indeed a very indulgent master.'

I look at Josef who has, I mark, fallen silent.

'In fact, you met the man. At that very ball. Black beard, hands always cupped in front of himself like he doesn't know what to do with them.'

His face darkens. 'Get out!'

I carry on, undeterred. 'Come, husband, what do you make of it all? You know how I love it when you afford me a glimpse inside that head of yours.' I tap his left temple with the pad of my middle finger and expect him to fly into a rage, so I can make a mental note of his absurd, exaggerated indignation to remember later. It will keep me going through the long, boring hours of the evening. But he does not. Seeming not to have registered my dig, he merely lowers his voice, in volume, pitch and pace, and speaks quite clearly.

'Shall I tell you what goes on inside *your* head? Fear.'

It is so ridiculous a statement I go to laugh, but no sound comes.

'Your callousness, the way you mock others, it's your armour, your shell of pretty diversions. But underneath all that gold and glitter, underneath your ice and spikiness, you're afraid, Hortense. You're soft, just an unformed grub beneath its carapace. I don't know what went on in that overblown hovel where you grew up, but for God's sake, if you haven't gotten over it by now you never will.'

The unexpected cast of sadness to his voice stuns me, and I haven't the faintest notion how to respond. Furthermore, the acute and dreadful penetration of his words is utterly overwhelming, and I drag my gaze from his.

It lands on the wallpaper, on a scene that shows a woman sitting at a writing bureau, a round cage of finches at her back. I screw shut my eyes. But the unrelenting curve of the chamber remains in my vision, as though I was in that cage myself.

Determined to be rid of the sensation, I stride to the nearest join in the wallpaper and prise my nails beneath it. It lifts far more easily than I could have anticipated, and within seconds I have pulled nearly an entire length of it from the wall. Feeling an immense surge of satisfaction, I hurriedly rip the length of wallpaper into pieces and reach for the next, to do the same again, to obliterate the cage of finches next—

A howl assaults my ears, wide and fathomless, the anguish of which I have never heard in my life. Only when I turn to face him again, shreds of the liberated paper curling at my feet, do I realise the sound came from my husband, his mouth so wide a circle he might be trying to swallow the whole room.

Deceptions

August, the following month

Lara

My legs ache and I feel heavy as a cow, my ankles fat and sore. I am thankful Madame still has not noticed my condition, even though the constant deception of it is exhausting. Having to angle my body precisely so there is less chance of her marking my shape, having to bind my swelling breasts flat against my chest each morning. *I just need to continue for a few more months*, I tell myself. And in that time I must try to work out what to do.

It is morning and I have pulled straight my coverlet, tidied my things, and dressed in the low light cleaving the gaps in the shutters. But just as I'm about to cross to open them, I am again overcome by the certainty that I'm not alone. I freeze right in the centre of the space, feel the strange prickling sensation of being silently observed, as though the gaze of whomever is watching me is a sheaf of nettles across my skin. I open my mouth, intending to call out, to tell them I know that they are there, but my voice sticks in my throat.

I turn, a full circle. Nothing. Yet the sensation remains. Someone *is* here, I am sure of it. I turn a second time and as my line of sight reaches the area of wall near the hearth, I am confounded by what I see.

There is a woman, a figure just as real as I. Though her arms are outstretched, as Sid's were when she loomed from the darkness that night outside the cottage, this woman stands motionless against the wallpaper. It is like she has shaved herself completely free of the pattern.

Her height matches mine, the silhouette of her clothing mirroring my own. And perhaps this woman has not managed to free herself from the pattern after all, as I now see the fabric she wears is printed with exactly the same design as the wallpaper. Those feverish scenes mass together across her body, the violet of them deeper, accentuating its form. It is as though she is wearing a gown made entirely of the paper and nothing else, as though she is wrapped in it, consumed and submerged by the stuff, from neck to toe.

But this is not the only thing that makes my flesh chill and bristle. The face of the woman is largely lost to the shadows, save one unmistakable detail. A flat oblong is obscuring the upper part of her head, a binding at her eyes. I remember that day in the factory, the blindfolded figure appearing out of nowhere in the off-cut of wallpaper. That is why this woman's arms are extended before her. She is caught, mid-gesture, in a game of Blind Man's Buff. My heart is throbbing, erratic, a netted bird inside my chest.

Hands shaking, I throw open the shutters to flood the chamber with light and, almost through my fingers, steel myself to glance at the patch of wall by the hearth. The woman is there no longer. She has disappeared back into the wallpaper's clustering scenes, dissolving like a phantom to become one with them once more. I attempt to still my breath, implore myself to calm my thoughts, to be daunted by this room, by this paper, no longer. I have my child to think of now. But try as I might, my mind is crowded by it . . .

I hasten towards the spiral staircase, past the strip of bare plaster where the wallpaper is now missing, pink as the flesh of a dead salmon and fringed with torn fibres. An incident with Madame was how my aunt had explained the damage. It is all I can do not to finish my mistress's work and remove the rest of it, prise it from the wall and toss it into the fire. I shut the chamber door instead, twist the key fast in the lock and move, as swiftly as I am able, down the spiralling stairs.

Strange Scattered Flowers and Butterfly

Lara

When I edge Madame's door ajar to attend upon her I see that she is still asleep, dead to the world and snoring softly, her little dog curled at her side on a cushion the shade of a robin's egg. Unlike his mistress, he is not aslumber. Having observed me entering, his eyes are bug-black and wide, as though awaiting a crisis.

Madame's chamber drapes are drawn as I left them, but there is enough light coming through the shutters to reveal the peculiar display in front of me. The full expanse of floor is strewn with possessions of all kinds, cast as jetsam across the rugs. Coffee cups and fans, wigs and dyed silk blossoms, *parfum* bottles and jewels of the finest quality, all scattered like the debris of an upturned life.

It seems that Madame has spent the night removing from chests, boxes and commodes nigh on all the items she still owns. It is as though the room isn't her bedchamber at all, but the nursery of a child who has tipped every trinket from their toy chest only to tire of each in turn. My belly tightens. The baby inside me is moving again, and I have a sudden and desperate ache to hold it.

I begin to pick my way around the bed to reach for the chamber-pot below, when one object in particular catches my eye. A flash of the brightest ultramarine, rare as a sapphire, issues from a small silver-and-glass frame so deep it has the appearance of a miniature cabinet. I stoop to pick it up, tilting the item between my palms so I can better see what is inside. There, mounted on a square of dark velvet, is a large butterfly, blue and decorated as a piece of hand-painted china, wings fretted delicately as lace. It is so vibrant it might still be alive, might at any minute give a beat of its wings.

I take a step forwards but, distracted by the butterfly, I do not see the fruit fork in time. I try my best to muffle the whelp I give when it pierces the sole of my slipper. But it is too late. I am unbalanced and the floor so cluttered I cannot find free space to replant my foot. I stumble against the bedstead, my eyes flying to Madame, willing her not to wake.

Her lids bat open, drowsily at first, before focusing on me, kraken-sharp.

Bitter Fruits

Hortense

The nightmare came again last night, the creak of metal, that absolute, unrelenting circle. But this time those words my husband spoke in the tower accompanied it, rat-a-tatting at my skull like the scaffold drums.

Since it seems I can only sleep now once the sun is up, I did not wish to be disturbed for a good few hours yet. I stare at the stupid girl standing gawping at me, clutching the bed-post with one hand and some decorative object with the other.

'What are you doing?' I ask, recognising the item as my preserved butterfly.

'I beg your pardon, Madame, but I have come to see you washed and dressed.'

I close my eyes. 'Return again in two hours,' I say, thinking the words will be enough to see her gone.

'Does Madame wish me to tidy away these things while she rests?'

I raise my cheek from the pillow and fix her with a stare. 'Certainly not. They are organised like this for a reason. Come back as I instructed and I'll tell you what to do with them then.'

When the girl hesitates further, I have had enough. 'Go!' I shout and fling the nearest cushion her way. I turn back to my pillow and see it is covered with strands of white-blonde hair.

Later, when my maid returns, I am still abed, though I have not slept again. I have been thinking about what I might do. Over these past hours a scheme has come to me, and I do not know whether to vomit at its audacity or laugh until I cry.

I am aware of the girl drawing apart the drapes, swinging open the shutters, setting down the tray on the nightstand. It has been months since I've bothered to breakfast in the dining-room, Pépin's company being a far more agreeable start to the day than my husband's. At least my little dog does not seek to drink himself into oblivion before the morning has scarcely begun. Josef's behaviour, it seems, has been growing ever more unhinged since that episode in the tower when I informed him of my maid's indiscretions and he began wailing like a madwoman. But I can concern myself with the tragedian no longer. My plans are *my* priority now.

The girl starts to prepare the toilette. She orders the bottles, the pins and the powder, scents the water in the washing-bowl with drops of pomegranate extract.

'I shall not wash yet,' I tell her. 'I shall eat first.'

I select one of the *pâtés de fruits* she has brought and, continuing to mull matters over, take tiny, distracted bites around its edges, scalloping the outline. It tastes disgusting, so I feed the reshaped middle part to Pépin, but my pet has no appetite for it either. He opens and closes his mouth around the morsel several times, before spitting it out in a blob on the counterpane.

'Listen,' I announce, having by this point run every conceivable option through my mind until I become quite convinced there is no other way. 'I have a fancy to go on a trip. Though, as yet, I know not when. My trunk was too cumbersome to move further.' I nod to where I left it, balanced precariously on the chaise. 'Lift it down and pack it with the things I shall need . . . the essentials.'

My nose screws. *Essentials.* What a mean, joyless word it is.

I take another fancy from the tray, wondering if it will taste as bitter as the first. While I do, I watch my maid move the trunk. Though it isn't even that full she strains against the weight, angling it out from her belly, arms extended awkwardly in front of her middle. She is, I note, still trying to conceal her condition.

Having placed it on the floor, the girl fills the trunk gradually.

Clean stays and petticoats, stockings and top clothes, a spare pair of slippers, some small cosmetics and one or two other objects she knows me to use most regularly. She has not been occupied this way for long when she stops and regards me like a hound awaiting praise.

'I have finished, Madame,' she says meekly. 'What more would you have me do before you dress?'

I sidle from the bed with Pépin in my arms to take a closer look. Maybe she has made a fuller task of it than I imagine. But when I peer inside, I see the trunk is barely a quarter-filled. 'What is this?' I ask. 'I told you I wanted the essentials packing, did I not?'

'As you see, Madame.'

'You have barely scratched the surface,' I snort, placing Pépin on the floor. Sensing my displeasure, he beats a hasty retreat. 'Do I have to do everything myself?'

I proceed around the chamber, collecting articles as I go. 'You can add these, for a start,' I say, letting the pile of things in my arms tumble towards the girl's feet. A larger and a smaller chocolate pot, a silver fruit bowl, a pair of asparagus tongs, five Pomeranian-sized waistcoats. The components of my *carapace*, as my husband so cleverly put it.

'Madame, forgive me, but since space in the trunk is limited, surely it is wiser to keep to everyday items? Clothing and so on?'

'I beg your pardon?' I snap, incredulous at the girl's presumption. 'I've several more valises that can be packed after this trunk is filled.' I stand pondering, night-chemise billowing to settle about my body. 'No, wait a minute. There is something we will try before you continue.'

My maid hoists herself inelegantly to her feet. 'Madame?'

'Remove your clothes. I would try on your outer things,' I declare, for it is time to conduct an experiment.

Despite my order, the girl doesn't move. Hesitation and dismay murk her face. As I know girls of her class do not ordinarily fret about their modesty, it must be that she does not wish to reveal her *grossesse* by undressing before me. Little does she know that I am one step ahead of her. This time it isn't her belly I wish to examine.

'I suppose you might take your things off behind that screen, if you wish,' I add.

Still reticent, the girl vanishes behind the gilt-framed partition.

'Here,' I call. 'Pass your skirts and so on over the top. You may keep on your stays and petticoats.'

My maid does as I instruct, and I start to hold the garments up before the looking-glass. I run my thumb along the stomacher's side seams and see that pieces of a similar fabric have been patched in. She has been trying to alter their size, to accommodate her growing bulge.

It is then that I become aware of the yapping of my dog, interrupting my train of thought. I turn to the screen. 'You may come out from there now,' I say, 'and help me to secure these fastenings.'

'If you do not mind, Madame, I would much rather stay here 'til you have finished.'

There is a tremble to the girl's voice, discernible above Pépin's incessant yipping. I love the darling as though he were my own flesh and blood, but the noise is becoming grating, even to me. 'Now, now,' I soothe, stepping over the things to retrieve him.

I pry around the partition. There he is, scurrying about the feet of my lady's maid, barking like a thing possessed. My maid's face wears the same expression it might had she been caught in flagrante delicto, her arms crossed uneasily over her belly, one hand gripping the opposite wrist.

Her lower lip begins to wobble. 'I am sorry, Madame,' she gushes. 'I am very sorry.'

'Oh, you needn't worry about *that*,' I say, waving a finger at her midriff. 'Come and help me with these.'

'Madame—?' Her shock at my indifference to her condition, her relief and her misery are like a blast of air in my face. She wrings her hands, seems like she might faint. 'Please, I don't know what to do—'

I narrow my eyes. 'Do not weep,' I say, commending myself on the smoothness of my words. The offering of such sympathies would normally cause my throat to stick. Yet I begin to feel, if not sorry for this girl, a certain absurd affinity to her. I have no idea from where this unfamiliar emotion has radiated at first, before a hitherto unacknowledged notion bursts within my mind. I might once have been left in the same state as she.

'I may be able to help you with this matter, you know.' I take a breath, guiding the girl over the obstacles on the floor and towards the chaise. 'Sit, do,' I implore and so do I, not naive to the fact that it is the first time I have ever sat next to her. 'Now, I want what I am about to impart to you to be kept quiet, you understand? This is strictly a private matter. You must tell no one.'

My maid nods. 'Yes, Madame. You have my word.'

'Good,' I answer. 'So, as I have said, I find myself needing to go on a little trip. I had it in my mind to travel alone, but I see that, in your condition, some time away might be beneficial to you, also.'

The girl colours and dabs her cheeks with her knuckles.

'I plan to go abroad, to stay awhile with my ...' How best to refer to him? By his proper title? 'With the French Ambassador, in England.' Although correct, the sobriquet makes me want to laugh. To be turning to such a man. My scheme is altogether so fiendish it is outrageous, and to think my parents had not an inkling of what was going on in their *overblown hovel*.

'We will be away only as long as it remains unsafe here. Then we will return. Unless ...' I pause. 'Am I to understand you want to keep the child?'

'I did not at first,' she replies, sniffing. 'But yes, I do.'

'In that case, I should be able to make it possible. You do realise such a thing would be quite out of the question if you stayed in Jouy?'

She nods once more. We sit for a moment in silence.

'I am well aware what people think of me, you know.' I see the statement catch the girl off-guard. 'But none of them know me, not really. They never will. It is the only way, you see.'

I reach down for Pépin, who has found a path to my feet as though divining I am in need of cheer. 'I shall write to this ambassador, ask him to find you a position on his wife's estate. *His* estate,

360

now. A position that will allow you to keep the child, if it does not interfere with your duties, of course.'

I smile, knowing he will not refuse my request, not with the information I have about his predilections. 'He has always adored me,' I say drily. 'So I see no reason for him to decline.'

The girl turns her face to the light pouring through the casement.

'I shall write to him today and let you know when I have news. Now, help me out of these clothes.'

Revealments

October, six weeks later

Lara

Surely it will come soon. That single thought repeats in my mind, spiralling endlessly. *Surely today will be the day that Madame will announce she has received word from England.*

The expectation of it is appalling, exhausting. It scarce leaves space for anything else, which is a mercy, at least. When I glimpse the truth of how what I'm planning to do will betray Sofi, will hurt Mama, I am sick and want no part of it. It is a blessing, then, that this dreadful, overwhelming anticipation blanks it all out. For there is no other way.

It is late in the morning and Madame is still abed, and though I know I shouldn't – that to do so might be to tempt fate – I start to pack. I find it impossible to be still amidst this wallpaper, even now. So I make a small pile of things I will need to take with me to England, laying them out upon the table. Clothing, slippers, hairpins.

When I open the chest beneath the bed, the sight of my drawings sends a claw of sadness into my breast. I must leave them all behind, all those memories and small recollections of my life, just as Pa's things were left behind in Marseilles.

I pick up the sketch my sister made of us both that last night in the cottage, taking it over to the table to lay it atop the stack to take.

But it is too painful to see de Comtois' likeness gazing out from my own. I'm just about to replace the drawing inside the chest amongst the rest, when my grip slips clumsily and the paper drifts from my hand, sliding into the crack behind the armoire.

Slowly easing myself down, I peer into the shadows, observe that the drawing has come to rest between the armoire and the wall. I remove my slipper and try to brush the object towards me, but it does not budge, only fluttering further out of reach.

I recall the night my sister made that drawing, remember the warmth of her hand on mine as she offered it out to me. I cannot leave it discarded like this, tossed away like something unwanted, so I start to empty the armoire to make it lighter to move.

I put my foot to its base to nudge it away from the wall, straining with the effort. Lowering myself to my knees once more, I stretch for the drawing and, as I do, a chink of black catches my sight.

There is a void in the floor, I see, though at first I do not presume it to be anything more than a large space between the boards. It is only when I have retrieved Sofi's drawing and moved the armoire back into position that every last fragment of suspicion to have come to me over these past few months suddenly fuses, falling resoundingly into place.

I fling open the armoire doors and prise my fingernails around the edges of its floor. Rather than being fixed as I'd always presumed, it lifts off like a lid, the door of a trap. A perfect black square is revealed, the top step of a staircase visible just below the room's floor level, the rest swallowed by a dark and gaping chasm.

I gaze into it with both a sickening repulsion and a fresh wave of understanding. This isn't a gap in the boards at all, but a purposefully constructed passageway leading to another room. Indeed, anyone emerging from that passageway would be able to tip back the armoire's base completely silently while still inside of it, and in doing so their eyes would perfectly align with that rough hole gnawed into the bottom of the door. Through it, they would be able to see the whole room.

So I was not mistaken. Someone *was* slipping in here unobserved, just not in the manner I imagined. And all those times I felt like I was being watched in this space, I was. By unseen eyes peering through the hole in the armoire door. That is why my things were always in disarray at the bottom of it, too, no matter how many times I tidied them. It wasn't rats. It never was.

I bring a hand to my stomach, to the new life inside of me. Enough is enough.

Glancing rapidly about the chamber, my gaze lands on the night-stand. Seizing hold of it, I walk the item across to the armoire, turn it sideways to jam it inside between the floor and the bottom shelf, making it utterly impossible for anyone to access the room that way again. I slam closed its doors. For good measure, I seize a bedsheet from one of the drawers of the commode, and fling it over the top of the armoire, too.

I have only to wait a few more days, I tell myself, attempting to steady my breath. *Just a few more days before word is received from England and I shall be able to get away from this place.* I should never have doubted Madame's plan. She is as desperate to leave as I. There is not so great a difference between us, after all. But, despite my best efforts, my heart is hammering—

'Lara?'

I spin around, the combination of the suddenness of his voice and what I've just discovered sending an almost painful, surging shudder across my skin.

Josef is standing in the open door. I must have been so preoccupied with my packing this morning that I forgot to re-lock it. He takes in my expression, the way my palm cups the blatant swell of my belly, and his brows hitch, his face slackens.

'Oh, Lara . . .'

It is as though he is recognising my plight for the first time.

'Lara, listen, I know things haven't been easy for you here, but I will put them right, I swear it. You need not worry about Hortense again. I will go to Paris. I will go today – now, even. On my life, I will make things right—'

364

I cannot summon a reply, the last few minutes still churning through my mind. Driving them aside and picturing only the precious, bundled life beneath my skin, I keep my hand on my stomach and exit the room.

English Vistas

Hortense

The response from England arrives the same day as a letter from Mama. For the past week, my mother's fevered pleas for us to flee together to the border have reached new heights. She now informs me she and Papa will not leave until I join them and it's typical of Mama, I think, to shift blame for her own failings onto me. But many of our kind are doing the same, and the authorities are catching on. Her scheme is altogether too perilous, just one of the many reasons I determined months ago to find some way out of this predicament myself, even if it does mean begging favours from the French Ambassador. Jacques Antoine Marc-René du Pommier. My *darling* half-brother.

Mama uses the same erratic scrawl she did when she wrote of the Bastille, this time with added spatters of ink that litter the page like the heads of black lilies. This seems appropriate when I read the news the letter brings. The Queen's execution went ahead at midday.

With the King murdered last January and poor Antoinette arrested months ago, I suppose I should have expected this. Yet reading Mama's words, black and white upon the page, causes the morsel of sweetmeats I could manage for breakfast to rise sourly up the back of my throat. Antoinette – our sparkling, shining Queen – slaughtered.

I break the seal and read the dispatch from England next, ruminating nauseously upon its words. It is as I hoped, but not as I expected. My *dear* brother finally writes that, while he will acquiesce to my requests for passage and refuge, to introductions in England for de Pise, it is not because he has the slightest worry about the information I could share. As he so helpfully puts it in his correspondence, *an ambassador compares to a factory owner's wife as an eagle to a sparrow, and an eagle does not trouble itself with the twitterings of sparrows.*

These repellent lines and Mama's news of the Queen's murder subdue and distract me for the rest of the day. So it is hours later, as my lady's maid dresses my wig for supper, that I am able to share with her some details of the letter from England.

'I have received word,' I declare, seeing the girl's hands freeze above the comb. For the past weeks, her desperate anticipation has been impossible to miss. She is forever on edge, as though constantly checking behind herself. That makes two of us, I suppose.

I push the thought from me, the disagreeable missives of earlier once more surfacing in my mind and spurring my inclinations to spite. I am seized by the impulse to tease my maid a little, to underline the hierarchy between us with a firm hand, despite the topsy-turvy world we now inhabit.

'The ambassador has sent word. Unfortunately, there is no position available for you at present.' I am toying with her as much as the stopper of the ointment jar I roll skittishly between my fingers, and my words pop like noxious bubbles as I watch for a reaction.

'I'm sorry to hear it, Madame,' she replies, the disappointment acute and unmissable in her voice. Her countenance crumbles and she casts her eyes downwards.

I leave a lengthy and deliberate pause before continuing. 'There is, however, a position for you with his brother-in-law. It is in Dorset, quite a different area of the country, which means we will part ways when we land on English soil. They already have a French housekeeper there, as well as a number of French maids, so you can learn English from them.'

I fix my gaze on her reflection and watch her eyes transform, widening and flashing as brightly as the looking-glass itself.

'Oh, thank you, Madame, thank—'

Her hands fly to her middle. She shifts her bulk from one ankle to the other and inhales keen and sudden through her teeth, as though trying to ride the wave of sensation gripping her belly.

'What is it?' I say to her. 'Are you quite all right? You may sit, if you wish . . . For a few seconds.'

She shakes her head and, with some effort, straightens. 'Thank you, Madame, but it's nothing. Merely a twinge. It is passing now.'

We look directly at each other for a long, strange moment. Then there is a knock on the door.

'Come.'

The housekeeper enters, waffling some sort of message that has been left for me. I only hope it is cheerier than the last two.

'It's your husband,' she says. 'He departed Jouy this afternoon. He's gone to the capital, Madame. On urgent business.'

My ears prick at the news and, to my surprise, so do my maid's, as she turns to the housekeeper with an expression both of interest and concern.

'Has he indeed?' I reply. 'Did he mention when he would return?'

'He only said he expected to be gone a night or two, Madame.'

I contemplate the information. My husband's time away has come at a decidedly opportune moment, since I now have everything I need. There is only one task left to accomplish and that is to send word to de Pise, so he may prepare his carriage.

'Just a moment,' I tell the housekeeper. 'I have a message that I require to be sent immediately. Wait while I write it out and see it is delivered forthwith.'

'Madame.'

As I draw the implements towards me, my housekeeper and my lady's maid murmur together by the door. They think I am concentrating on my writing and do not hear them, but I do.

The housekeeper whispers something to the effect of, 'He left this for you.' My maid gives no response but colours uncomfortably, my eyes flicking to the mirror long enough to see her stuff a fold of paper into her pocket-bag. Another *billet-doux* from Black Beard, no doubt. Though where in that room of hers she's hiding them is anyone's guess.

'Here, then, I have finished,' I announce. 'Have this sent at once.'
'Yes, Madame,' the housekeeper answers and leaves.

I have made sure to keep the direction in my epistle brief. De Pise could not even be considered the cleverest man in a room of dullards, so the three words I've written leave him no margin for error.

Carriage. Daybreak. Tomorrow.

Autumn

Sofi

I peer from the window of my chamber, tapping a fingernail impatiently against the glass. I cannot rest tonight. Any time now they will come for that woman and it will not be a moment too soon. Everything will be resolved, I tell myself, so why do I feel so uneasy?

'Sofi!' Mama calls up the stairs. 'Have you finished that darning yet?'

The sound jolts me upright. I have not even started the task. I reach down and retrieve the work, meaning to begin, but when my eyes return to the level of the window, the linens fall back to the floor.

There is a spectre out there in the darkness, a woman's form, her lower part swallowed by shadows so she seems almost to float. I blink, lean closer to the glass and take a breath. Lara.

I tear to the door, ignoring Mama's nagging about the darning. I've hardly seen my sister of late, but I'm glad she at least looks well. She'll be better still when the Madame is gone.

On opening the cottage door, I am bewildered to see that my sister has already turned, and is making her way hastily back to the chateau.

'Lara!' I yell. 'Is that you? Stop!'

She does not slow, however, but rather increases her pace.

'Lara!' I shout again, at last drawing level with her. 'Why did you not stop? You saw the light in my chamber, did you not? What brings you here so late?'

Her mouth tenses as if she means to smile. There is an unease to her, too, tonight, which I can place no more than my own. 'You are well? It is not the baby?'

'I have had some pain, but I am well.'

'Lara!' I catch her arm, try to encourage her towards the cottage. 'Please, come inside. Sit awhile.'

My sister shakes her head. 'I am sorry, I cannot. I have to go back, I've some things to prepare for Madame.'

The mention of the Madame makes me want to spit. 'Vile woman,' I say, unable to stop myself. 'Can she not give you a few minutes' peace—?'

'Do not speak so, Sofi,' my sister cuts in. 'Her manner is just her way of dealing with adversity. You of all people should know that.'

Lara's words are pointed and my temper flares like a spark in the wind. 'What adversity has she ever known? She is every bit as bad as she seems, a true product of her class.' I force my mouth closed. Quarrelling with Lara is the last thing I want, and the Madame will get what she deserves soon enough. I'd half-thought about telling my sister what I had done when I spotted her on the track. But I could not have tolerated the argument that would have followed. I could not have borne Lara's disapproval.

My sister glances nervously back at the chateau, as though fearful the building might be closing in on her.

'Lara, is anything the matter?'

'There is something ...' She hesitates. 'Something I must tell you, Fi.'

'What is it?'

Without warning, she shoots a hand out to seize my own, pressing it to the mound of her stomach. It jerks and ripples beneath my touch.

'Oh!' I cry. 'The baby, it's moving!'

It is so genuine and extraordinary and obliterating a thrill that I cannot stop from smiling, the muscles of my face stretching almost painfully, like they haven't been used in a long time.

Lara and I stand together for many minutes, lost in the intimacy

371

of the sensation, in the vital, wondrous pulsing of it. Two sisters, one brand new life, the sharpness of the autumn night softened by the scent of woodsmoke, by the hooting of an owl overhead.

I take Lara's hand in mine. 'Do not worry,' I say. 'All will be well. I am sure of it.' There is a pause. I open my mouth to ask her what she was going to say before the baby kicked. But no words come and neither does she return to the subject.

'Goodbye,' my sister murmurs, her eyes full. She takes me in her arms and holds me fast, moved as much as I by the experience just shared. 'Goodbye, Sofi.'

'Goodnight!' I call.

The darkness palls her, and she is gone.

Unexpected Articles

Hortense

My nightmares have not come, since I have not slept a wink. Instead I lie poised, balanced on a keen blade of readiness, knowing I must soon rise and make the journey north. At my knees sits Pépin, eyes peeled and unblinking. Perhaps he, too, can sense something momentous is afoot.

As I wait for the hours to pass on this, my last night in my dismal chamber in Jouy, my mind wanders unpleasantly back to Mama's correspondence. Visions of the Queen begin to assault me, great walls of them rising from the blackness like the vignettes on the wallpaper. The mob, closing in on pale, blue-eyed Antoinette, tearing her apart, lurid sheets of crimson flooding from her neck. And I cannot tell whether it is a mob of peasants that I see surrounding her, or those chimpanzees from the Ménagerie Royale, those savages with their taste for flesh. I swoop towards the pot beneath my bed, but can retch little more into it than a few paltry strings of saliva.

I urge myself to remain calm. In one week's time, in less than that, I shall be safely in England, and this circus, this bloodbath of class and country, will be behind me for good. Should we at any point be endangered, should we be apprehended, I have given my maid explicit instructions, have told her exactly what to say and how to say it. Indeed, she can hardly refuse. If I am arrested, her little continental flit will come to nought and then what will she do about that offspring of hers?

But is it enough? As the seconds crawl by that question grows deafening. *Have I done enough?* Perhaps I have not, so I extract myself from the counterpane, light a taper and make my way to one of the armoires.

I riffle through the beautiful garments that remain inside, all the things I cannot take with me to England. Satin skirts in delicate shades nestle like rows of macarons. Expensive, lace-trim petticoats foam stark and pure as whipping cream. Crustings of silver and beads twinkle in the taper's light like sugared *chouquettes*. None will do. I could not bring myself to put so fine an array of things to such a use and, in any case, these garments are all too small for what I have in mind.

I cross to the commodes, opening and closing the drawers, beginning to think I have no choice but to stick to my original stratagem, when my eyes land on the chamber-pot I moved earlier. And that is when I remember something I assumed long forgot.

I kneel beside the bedstead and pull out from under it one of the few valises to have not been packed for England. As the clasp is released, the hideous mass of fabric balloons out at me once more, just as it did the first time. I had instructed the housekeeper to put it on the rubbish heap that day, but the insolent woman never did, and the garment found its way back amongst my belongings. The only place for such an offensive, oversized article, I decided, was in a shut valise as close to my chamber-pot as possible. I extricate the item from its case and lay it in readiness over the back of a chaise.

Now I am certain. Now I have done everything possible to ensure my scheme will work and can do no more. Through the grainy blur of blackness, the pile of luggage looms, my valises stacked solid as a prison wall. Maybe my maid was right, maybe we should not be carrying so much with us, after all.

The chamber is still dark when the girl knocks, and I immediately spring out of bed. She hands me a set of her clothes, their extra panels now removed. It is these garments I shall dress myself in now, and so I loose my night-chemise and drop it to the floor.

Heartbeat thudding, I stand before the looking-glass without a stitch to my skin, a false hair on my head or a jewel on my person, staring at my reflection for several minutes. I see a girl with a body quite white, even in the chamber's gloom. She could be anyone.

I do not bother to gauge my maid's reaction to this. I do not speak at all. I am not sure whether I can, and I'll be damned if I let anyone hear my voice falter. I slip into the girl's stays and petticoats without even asking for assistance and, rejecting the wigs, fix a plain cap over my head instead. When I am fully dressed, I turn back to the looking-glass and examine every sliver of my appearance, scrutinising my body the way a member of the authorities might. My unadorned reflection repulses me, but it is the only way.

'Now *you* must prepare yourself,' I tell my maid. 'Get undressed.'

'Undressed, Madame?'

'Come, do not dither.'

'But what am I to—'

I take up the garment from the back of the chaise. 'You will wear this.'

She stares at me aghast as the fabric settles, whispering in the silence. It is the gown my father-in-law had made prior to me coming to this place, the one smothered in the pattern of the factory wallpaper. In this pre-dawn light, the print bears even more of a resemblance to spreading mildew than it did before, crawling as it is with those horrid peasant scenes.

This isn't what I planned when the notion to flee to England initially came to me. I'd intended we would both dress the same, my maid and I, both assume the guise of humble servants. But this morning, when we leave, I shall be dressed as a maid and my maid a noble. *The topsy-turvy world we now inhabit.*

There is a half-hour left until daybreak, yet I already hear the sound of horses in the distance, navigating the bend at the bottom of the hill. De Pise's carriage is early. The time is come.

PART V

Distant Aspects

October 1793, early the same morning

Sofi

It is still dark when something jerks me from sleep and at first I am convinced it is my sister's voice. I prop myself on my elbows and listen. All is quiet, but although there is at least another hour before I must rise, I feel compelled to get up.

I open my chamber window and poke my head outside, like some early morning creature nosing the air from its burrow. The light is unusual this morning, portentous. The place where sky meets land is seeping incarnadine, as though what hangs overhead is not sky at all, but a vast cut of fabric being pulled from one of the factory's dye-baths. I shiver. I hate autumn. It is a season of endings, of withering and decay. And almost five years to the day since Pa's accident.

Knowing I will not be able to sleep again now such thoughts have found me, I decide to dress, and it is after I straighten the green ribbon at my throat that I'm once more drawn to the window. There I see them, as the first clean strip of light struggles to open the sky up to morning. A pair of unfamiliar horses waiting near the forecourt, steam jetting from their nostrils.

Could they be guardsmen's horses? Could they really have come for the Madame, at last, forced their way inside the chateau already? I press my face to the glass.

A brace of figures is moving swiftly down the end of the chateau's approach in silent concentration. Two women and a man lagging in their wake. Both of the women are carrying valises, whilst the man who is following wrestles with a trunk. The horses are driven forwards a little then, and I notice there is a carriage harnessed behind them.

I know those women. They are my sister and the Madame, the latter dressed in a truly extraordinary garment. A gown, printed with purplish splotches like the tower wallpaper, the pattern clustering darkly across the folds of its fabric. I have never seen the like of it before.

My sister, I observe, is more plainly dressed than usual and bearing a bundle of blankets in her arms. A flash of ginger. What on earth Lara is doing carrying the Madame's stupid pet, I cannot guess. Nor can I imagine where it is they are both going, at such an hour as this.

As I continue to stare, a dreadful notion reveals itself. Could the Madame be absconding, right here and now, making her flit to safety? Could she have caught wind of something I haven't, that the authorities are thundering to Jouy this very second, to see justice served?

I open my mouth to call out, to catch my sister's attention, then think the better of it for I doubt that she will hear me. I shake my head. Of course the Madame isn't leaving this way. A self-serving wretch like her would divulge her schemes to nobody and certainly not my sister. She would depart alone, under cover of blackness. The Madame instead must be leaving for Paris, taking my sister to attend upon her as she tries on yet another succession of over-priced garments she does not need.

Then something new occurs to me. By going to the capital, the Madame is heading straight for the authorities. Either she is too short-sighted to have worked this out or too arrogant to believe the danger is real. Whatever the reason, chances are she will not be coming back.

First Flight Across the Channel

Paris

Hortense

My maid and I are installed inside the carriage, each sitting rigidly erect, heads turned to opposite windows. On the seat facing us is Adrien de Pise, more soberly dressed than usual and still panting feebly from the exertion of assisting with the trunk. As planned, it is one of his family's carriages we are travelling in, one without the de Pise crest on its doors, though there was a moment when the man was foolish enough to suggest we travel in a marked vehicle.

Pépin is bundled in my arms, huddled in a coarse woollen shawl which must itch the poor mite terribly. I cannot work out whether it is me, or whether the shake about his body is more pronounced today than usual.

I shift to face my maid. I have briefed her thoroughly, warned her in no uncertain terms that if she does not do as she is bid, there will be no place for her in England. 'You remember what you are to say,' I ask, more of a command than a question. I am keeping my voice level, or trying to, but in order to conceal its wobble the tone has grown harsh. I cannot stand the sound of it inside my skull. *Craw crah-crah* it seems to be saying, like a large and annoying bird.

'Yes, Madame,' my maid replies. It has been impossible to ignore how stiff and silent the girl has grown since she stepped into that hideous gown. I've rarely seen her more uncomfortable.

De Pise raises his eyebrows. I have asked my maid the question several times already, though we cannot have been in the carriage for more than ten minutes. He attempts to take a hold of one of my hands, presumably to soothe me, but soon discovers I am not forthcoming.

'I have told you,' he says smoothly. 'If we can get past the capital, all will be well. And, even then, if we were to be stopped, it is highly unlikely anything untoward would happen.'

I feel my jaw clench, preventing a response, so go back to glaring through the window.

We pass the once-royal parkland of Versailles, both my former sanctuary and my prison, and although the roads are swarming, we are not stopped. We pass the main western thoroughfare into the capital and we are not stopped. I am almost beginning to breathe my relief, to give thanks that the worst of the danger is passing, when my nerves shatter. At the crossroads beyond, just before the river, armed guardsmen are halting the traffic. Surrounding this blockade throngs a horde of people, the nubs of their red caps bobbing ceaselessly. And, as much as I entreat myself to stay calm, as much as I know that, in reality, those shapes are just the heads of peasants, all I can see are waves, breaking on an ocean of blood.

'Say nothing, I shall deal with them if they question us,' de Pise asserts, his voice lowered.

The carriage slows to a crawl as the carts and the coaches and the men on horseback ahead are all interrogated. My maid has not spoken since we quit the house, save to answer my questions, and I now see those oyster-coloured eyes of hers are huge with dread. Ours is the next vehicle in the line.

The scaffold drums start up again, with their deafening, relentless rhythm. The same drums I've heard in my head at night for months. Then I realise it is not the drums at all, only the sound of my heart, pulsing so hard in my chest it is causing my back to throb against the seats of the carriage.

The interior of the vehicle dims as a guardsman leans towards the window, eclipsing the light. He taps the window-glass with the tip of his pike, and de Pise lowers it and flashes him a smile with more magnetism than I have ever seen him muster before.

'Good day, citizens,' the guardsman begins. 'To where are you travelling today?'

'Good day to you, Monsieur,' de Pise responds. 'A fine day, is it not?'

The inside of the carriage darkens further as a second guard appears at the other window and, like the first, signals for it to be opened. When the glass is dropped, he extends his head through the gap. I can smell his breath even from where I am sitting, the stink of the Ménagerie Royale, the fetid stench of rotten meat.

'We are on our way to the coast for passage to England,' announces de Pise. 'I am accompanying these ladies, as you see.'

'What is your business in England?'

'This lady's father is ill,' declares de Pise, following his pre-arranged script and gesturing to my maid. 'It's serious, I'm afraid, we are in a great hurry.'

'Hmm,' is all the guard's response. He turns to my maid, taking in her startling gown. 'And what is your name?'

'Lady *Merde*?' offers the second guard.

I concentrate hard on my hands, folded around the shawl in my lap, my precious Pépin concealed beneath. To have passed him to my maid to hold would have posed too great a risk to my dog and so I pray he will not move, pray they will not notice him.

'Madame Annette Dumas, Monsieur,' my maid says, adhering to her script as diligently as de Pise, with all the poise of a *duchesse* and, much to my surprise, very nearly the accent of one, too. I had not thought her capable of such. The shadow of death makes actors of us all.

'This is my companion,' she goes on, pointing towards me. 'Mademoiselle Marie Bisset.'

I manage a slight incline of the head to acknowledge my unfamiliar title.

'The gentleman is right, Monsieur,' my maid confirms. 'My father has been taken gravely ill in London. We do not know how much time he has left. You would be doing us a great kindness if you would let us go on.'

The first guard falls quiet, as though he is thinking.

The second guard chews his tongue and cranes further towards us. 'You ladies smell sweet,' he says. 'We're keeping our noses out for young ladies like you, sweet with cologne, the proper expensive stuff.'

'I'm sure you are,' says de Pise, 'but I can guarantee it is none of us you seek. Might we now pass?'

'We've arrested a number of people already today, you know,' the first guard says, as though he has only just registered the fact.

'You're doing an excellent job,' de Pise replies. 'I commend you.'

'Couple of wealthy old sots, supporters of the Queen. The name of du—'

Despite there being many people whose surnames start with these letters, I know exactly which name they are going to utter before the words are even out of their mouths. Every muscle of my body hardens, every ligament seizes, every bone locks.

'Du Pommier!' announces the second guardsman.

De Pise laughs in awkward gulps, slow and dry and ungenuine, a noise betraying far more alarm than amusement. 'Never heard that name,' he says. 'But well done. Now we have answered all your questions, I trust we can proceed with our journey.'

The guards say nothing. A man calls to them from somewhere near the rabble, causing the first guardsman to turn away. I feel the seconds slow to days and am ashamed to recognise I do not know how much more of this I can endure.

'Carry on, then,' the second guard says. 'On with your journey.' He gives the driver the nod.

'Thank you, Monsieur, thank you!' de Pise and my maid exclaim in jarring chorus, and the carriage pulls slowly away.

My maid is leaning back against her seat now, her eyes closed. De Pise is shaking, running both palms down the length of his face in an effort to compose himself. He returns my gaze. 'See, I told you—'

'Whoa there, whoa!' the driver cries, out of nowhere. The carriage again grinds to a standstill and the regained colour drains from de Pise's face, as the shapes of the same two guardsmen smother the windows for a second time.

I only recollect experiencing once before, eight years previously in Mama's salon, what I do now. Fear so high and so wide I cannot see around it.

'Forgive me, but it has slipped my mind,' the first guardsman says, with a fresh grin. 'Tell me again from where it is you have come?'

'Quite far south,' says de Pise, 'just outside Bourges.'

But the guards do not seem to be listening. One is smirking at the other through the tunnel of the carriage, as though they are sharing an unheard joke.

'It is true, Monsieur,' attests my maid.

Suddenly and simultaneously, both guardsmen erupt into laughter.

'My arse,' says the second.

'Come on, out you get,' orders the first.

'I beg your pardon—' my maid says.

'There must be some mistake—' de Pise says.

I say nothing. At that very moment, I do not think I can.

'Thing is,' the guard continues, 'one of our men saw this carriage, little more than an hour ago, pulling out of the factory at Jouy-en-Jouvant, the Oberst place. Know anything about that, do you? Only it seems funny, especially with him going there in search of the lady of that house.'

'Spent a lot of time at Versailles, have you?' says the other man, cocking his head at de Pise. 'With opponents of the Republic?'

I did not foresee this. There was always a chance of them apprehending my maid, but I never thought they might take de Pise too. They will release the girl as soon as they realise their mistake, but I doubt de Pise will be so lucky. To my dismay, my hands start shaking uncontrollably around my little dog's body, as the guards bear down on the carriage to claim their quarry.

'Out!' the first guard says, his voice raised.

They are grasping de Pise and my maid, while my heart pounds furiously, and a third guard edges my way, looking like he is about to take me too. I must do it now, there is not a second to waste.

'I'm terribly sorry, citizens,' I wail. 'I didn't want to leave this way! She made me do it! I'm a loyal friend of the Republic, you must believe me. I am one of you!' I repeat the words like a self-protecting incantation, jabbing my finger at my maid. 'It was *her*, my Madame . . . she made me do it!' All this I scream in the broad, hard accent of Marseilles, the accent of that tan-skinned factory girl. I am the greatest actor of them all.

The content and manner of my shrieking has left de Pise dumb-struck, gaping like a beached fish. Perhaps he was anticipating that I would make some admission to see him saved. But that would risk my own arrest, something I am not prepared to do.

The carriage doors crash back on their hinges, and de Pise and my maid are seized, the former about the back of the neck, the latter about the curve of her bodice. Then my skin chills with terror anew as, from under the shawl, Pépin pokes his little head and begins to yap. I try desperately to shush him, to draw the wool over him again, but I know it is too late. Those monsters have heard, and them taking my dog is too appalling a notion to contemplate.

'Why am I arrested?' howls de Pise. 'I demand to—' At his rising protestations, the guard tightens his hand on de Pise's cravat, tour-niqueting the fabric around his throat. 'Mercy, citizens! Mercy!' de Pise croaks, sweat panicking to beads on his forehead.

He and my maid are dragged from the carriage and away towards the mass of people. I see the girl clasp a hand to her belly and begin to pant.

'Her dog, too, Jean?' the second guardsman asks his comrade. 'She's got her maid holding it.'

I grip the bundle tight. The knowledge that I cannot protest – that my protestations might raise their suspicions – tortures me. What if they take my sweet pet? I could not tolerate life without Pépin, could not conceive of it. His tiny pulse is frantic in my hands.

386

'Her—?' the first guard starts and looks at Pépin, wiping his nose on his shoulder in lieu of a free hand.

I remain absolutely still, as though doing so might render me invisible. I do not even dare to breathe.

'*Non,*' the other guard decides.

At the fringes of my vision, more and more men are closing in around de Pise and my maid, and it takes but a few further seconds for them to disappear altogether. The first guardsman steps forwards then and checks inside the carriage. My face is glazed, my senses absent. I am still clutching my dog, but my hands are colourless.

'Turn around,' the guard orders the driver. 'Go back to where you came from.'

I shake my head, even though he cannot see me. I had it all planned, I can still reach the coast, even without de Pise, I can still cross to England. I lean towards the window to protest, summoning every possible drop of courage and indignation that I can.

'No, Monsieur—' In my panic, I realise I have slipped back into my natural accent. I clear my throat, attempt to correct myself quickly. 'Please, allow me to continue with my journey.' Forcing a smile, I feel the corners of my mouth quiver.

The guard peers at me, seeming not to have noticed my mistake. He grins slowly, revealing one foul tooth at a time, then breaks into a snigger. 'I'm not sure I'm following, *chérie*. You didn't want to leave, you just said so yourself. And you've no need to go to old *rosbif* land any more. Your madame's papa ain't there. He's here. In this very city. Bound and gagged by now, I shouldn't wonder.' He gives another ugly laugh.

I do not allow myself to think of my parents, of where they might be this minute and what might be happening to them. 'Monsieur, please, if you would just let me—'

'Listen, you'll be going back the way you came or you'll be going the same way as your friends. *T'as compris?*'

He slams his hand against the carriage and the driver spurs the horses into motion. I fall back against the seats, hold Pépin close and shut my eyes. The sounds of the people, the milling and the roaring behind us, ring in my ears as though I am the one surrounded.

The crowds are an ungodly entity, not human at all, but a vast, dark mob of animals. Their canines are bared and they drip with blood, all the time baying for more.

The Swing

Jouy-en-Jouvant

Sofi

I cannot seem to concentrate, to keep track of the dye mixtures, to do anything at all. It is impossible to fix my mind on anything other than that brilliant jolt of life beneath my sister's skin. I want to go to her, not only to feel it again, but to tell her that everything is going to be all right, to tell her the news.

It is a momentous day. Rumours began rippling through the workers at dinnertime, rumours about guards from the capital, seen in the village at dawn. Those same men will have found the Madame by now, will have intercepted her carriage. It is only a matter of hours before she is brought to justice, before she is gone for good.

I cannot help but imagine what my sister will make of this news, picture Lara's reaction when she realises all will be well, that she doesn't need to worry about her baby any longer. I count down the hours until I can leave work and cross to the chateau to tell her.

It is late in the afternoon when some kind of disturbance outside catches my attention. There is at least another half-hour until the end of the working day, and most people are still toiling in the factory buildings, but as I head towards the forecourt I see workers converging at the end of the track, engaged in animated discussion.

'No! . . . No!'

It is one of the *papeterie* women, her tone combining mock-outrage and undisguised glee.

'Yes, yes!' another counters and I recognise the voice as Sid's. 'Arrested!'

'Did you know? Did *you*?' a third woman is asking others in turn. 'Authorities caught up with her. Arrested this morning!'

'There she is!'

A cry goes up from the centre of the gathering and I look over my shoulder, convinced they must be addressing a woman behind me.

'Sofia Thibault! Heroine of the hour!'

This little group is almost light-footed with joy, hats off their heads and threshing the air, faces rumpled with triumph. Sid comes over and pulls me into an exuberant hug, while the rest encircle me, patting my back, shaking my hands, jerking me into a succession of enthusiastic embraces. Indeed, it seems as though they may even haul me onto their shoulders and parade me into the village. I do not understand.

'Tipped the guards off, did you, Sofi?' a man asks me. *'Très bien!'*

'What are you talking about?' I say.

'You did it, my girl!' a different woman chips in. 'Got the Madame Hortense arrested! You deserve a bloody medal!'

I frown at Sid. 'Bernadette,' she announces, 'told us Pascal had taken you to Paris a few months back, to report the Madame!'

I try to collect my thoughts. It is odd. I should be as jubilant as they, but I am not. Even as they speak, the notion chaws at me that something is not right.

'Are you *sure*?' I ask, grasping Sid's arm. 'Sure the guards have her?'

'I'm sure, all right,' a woman beside her responds. 'My son saw it all. The Madame's been taken to prison, to the Conciergerie. That's where she is now.'

The man next to her sucks the breath in through his teeth. 'Only one place she'll be going from there,' he says and his words ring out with an ominous familiarity.

I wait once more for the rush of triumph, for the strange apprehension to leave me and the mad, unbridled elation to sweep me into

390

the sky. I have done it, succeeded in having the Madame arrested, have had one of her class put where they belong. What I've longed for, for months, years, has finally happened. But the way the workers crush around me, close and frenzied, it dizzies me, and I want to be out of that press, not among it. Somehow I manage to excuse myself, trailing disconcertedly down the track towards the chateau as the group grows larger and more raucous at my back.

As I reach the forecourt I hear horses' hooves, feel the accumulating rumble of a vehicle's approach. A carriage, I see, is coming apace from the main gates, heading straight for the chateau. The same carriage I witnessed leaving at daybreak.

I turn to watch it pass. There is only one figure inside. So the Madame *has* been taken, Sid and the rest of those workers were right. The guardsmen have been scrupulous. They have listened to what I told them and served the Republic. Carried out their duty.

I wave furiously at Lara in the carriage but she must not notice me, as she does not return the greeting. My pace quickens to a sprint as I follow the speeding vehicle up the chateau's approach. I am still some distance behind it when I see the horses skid to a halt and the lone figure bound from inside the carriage and into the house. Only it is not Lara. She might be wearing Lara's clothes and cap, but I would know that pale, imperious face anywhere. It is the Madame.

The Market

Hortense

I do not wait for the vehicle to stop. Holding Pépin tight, I bolt from the miserable thing as soon as I can, like an ermine from a trap. I do not even pause to give a second thought to the luggage. The driver can unload it himself and do with the contents as he wishes. Tear the lace to threads and grind the trinkets into the earth with the heel of his boot for all I care.

I race up the front steps and into the vestibule where, to my immense frustration, the housekeeper appears. She must have heard de Pise's carriage clattering to a halt outside.

'Madame?' she asks, gaping at my drab attire.

I push past her without answering.

'Madame, are you well?'

As ever, there is no shaking the woman. I can sense her lumbering after me even as I rush up the stairs. I turn to face her, to spit a warning and drive her away once and for all. 'Leave. Me.' My words are spiked as that guardsman's pike at the carriage window. Final as the swipe of the guillotine.

I concentrate all my energies on reaching my chamber. I shall lock myself inside of it, before anybody else has the chance to observe me. Then a new plan jostles to formation in my mind and, rather than stopping at my chamber door, I hurry down the passageway to the tower, pivoting its stairs in a breathless orbit. I need some time to make a plan, a place in which to do it where nobody will think to find me.

Inside my maid's chamber, I thank the Lord the girl had the foresight to leave the key in the back of the door, knowing she would not be returning. The notion makes me freeze a second. I cannot deny that I was serving myself by taking my maid with me, using her to create a self-shielding smokescreen, but I was trying to help her, too. Can I really be sure the authorities will release her when they discover they have the wrong person? Pépin wriggles in my arms, pushing this unpalatable chain of doubts from my mind. Placing him gently on the bed, I entreat him to stay quiet.

I twist the key hard in the lock with a dull clunk and remain motionless at the door, listening for movement on the floors below, praying none of the servants have heard me come up here. But a locked door alone is insufficient. I must move something against that door to make absolutely certain nobody will get in.

I draw myself straight to glance about the chamber, then stop dead, my blood congealing in my veins. From the opposite wall, a large object looms. Sheeted white and twice my own height, it could almost pass for Mama's great birdcage—

I steel myself, edging towards it and snatching away the shroud. It is just an armoire. If I could somehow push it across the room to block the threshold, *then* I could rest assured that I was safe.

I take a hold of the armoire, but am seconds from attempting to move the thing when I see a commode, much nearer to the door. I shall move this instead, I decide, then I might stack other objects on top of it to form a makeshift barricade.

Once I have heaved it into place I look around, assessing what else I can move, stack the chair on top of the commode, and grasp anything else to hand to add to the pile. When I stop to recover my breath, I see the barricade I've made not only obscures the door, but a large section of the vile wallpaper, too. But it does not conceal enough.

My gaze comes to rest on a vignette I had not noticed the first time I came up here. It shows some kind of repulsive market, at which round cages are stacked, one atop the other. Birds are crowded within these cages, beaks parted and pushed between the bars as though gasping for air.

There are two figures in the print also, the men operating this ghoulish enterprise. One seizes the captured creatures, holding them fast on his lap before passing them to his comrade who, axe raised high, decapitates each in turn. Headless birds scurry at their feet.

These are the figures from the paper in my chamber at Versailles, I recognise them instantly, for it is impossible to mistake those faces, warped as they are by such cruel delight. I saw them again today, made flesh, blotting out the windows of de Pise's carriage.

My hands fly to cover my face, to extinguish that horror, and I stifle a scream. I want to launch every object my maid has left behind at that loathsome pattern, watch as the paper nicks and rips and comes free of the wall. But I cannot. The noise would alert someone to my whereabouts and my game would be up.

I cannot make a new plan with this peasant's cap itching my head and I have had enough of the unsightly article, so I tear it off and toss it to the floor. The pads of my fingers seek out the long hairs at the edges of my near-naked scalp and I pluck.

The sound of my name being shouted thunders from the forecourt.

Love Leads Them Away

Sofi

For some moments I find I cannot move, that the soles of my feet have sprung roots and lashed themselves to the gravel. I must have been mistaken, there isn't a chance the Madame would be dressed so plainly, sullying herself with clothes such as those.

As I stand staring at the doors, I become aware that the group of workers from the track has swelled further, and now stretches right across the forecourt and up towards the chateau. Handfuls of people are even making their way to the edges of the gardens, to tie lengths of coloured calico and wallpaper around the vast old sycamore, transforming its branches into the ribboned tails of a kite. I recall that Josef was found at the top of that tree hours after his mother's death, and the sight of the workers crowding its trunk stokes the unease in the pit of my stomach.

'Liberty! Liberty!' Their declarations reach me on the wind. 'It's a Liberty Tree!' Then they break into song, the Marseillaise. *'Allons enfants de la Patrie ... The day of glory has arrived!'*

Paring my attention away from them, I hasten to the servants' door, past the luggage the carriage driver has heaped like rubbish on the ground. Inside the chateau, everything is perfectly silent and still. I must find my aunt, ask her what is happening and where my sister is.

I eventually come across Aunt Berthé descending the servants' stairs to the lower floor, dressed like she might be heading out.

'Sofia! My, what a day. Such a lot of goings-on. And what with Monsieur Oberst in the capital with Monsieur Guyot, there's—'

'I came to ask if Lara had returned?' I interrupt. 'I saw the Madame, but not—'

'Returned?' Aunt Berthé replies distractedly.

'She went out. With the Madame. I saw them, very early this morning.' I cast my mind back to first light, realise with a ripple of dismay that it must have been my sister I'd seen clad in the swarming pattern of that wallpaper gown, and not the Madame. 'I thought Lara would be back here by now, I thought—'

'Lord, whatever is all that noise?' Aunt Berthé stands on tiptoes to peer through one of the passageway's high windows. A pony and gig have drawn up near the entrance. 'Ah, that's here for me,' she says, nodding at it, 'and I'm late, I'm afraid. I'm sure your sister will show up soon enough, Sofia. Madame's probably just had her go to the village—'

'So the Madame *is* here?'

'Oh yes, dear. Upstairs. Well, then. *Salut!*'

I watch my aunt leave, unsure whether to follow or tear up the stairs and confront the Madame instantly. Seeds of panic sprout and bud inside of me, and I dash along the passage, meaning to fetch Aunt Berthé back even though I can already hear the gig moving off in the direction of the gates. Nevertheless, I increase my stride, taking the steps to the servants' door two at a time, not seeing the familiar silhouette blocking the entrance until I am nearly upon it.

'Oh!'

The man turns.

'Guillaume? What on earth are you doing here?'

Despite my heightening alarm I'm immediately happy to see him, even though his pose is awkward and his countenance discomfited and unfathomable. As he turns towards me, I notice he is worrying something between the tips of his fingers. A small object, glinting and golden. He hurriedly slips it into the top left pocket of his waistcoat.

I crane to look over his shoulder, but the pony and gig bearing my aunt have long gone.

'Sofi, is something the matter? You do not look well. Here—' He holds the crook of his arm out to me, but I do not want it.

Around us, the workers are surging still further, their numbers massing on the approach, the Madame's name blaring between them. And that is when the seedlings of panic in my belly seize me fully in their grip and I finally understand. It feels like my stomach is spilling through the soles of my feet.

'Sofi?' Guillaume says. 'What is it?'

I try to respond, but am muted by dread.

Guillaume takes my arm. 'Please, can I fetch you anything? Let me help in some way.'

'It is Lara,' I manage at last. 'I saw her leave. Very early this morning. With the Madame.'

'Indeed?'

'She's not here!' In vain I try to align mind to breath to tongue and teeth, but the din in my head is as overwhelming as the noise surrounding us. 'The Madame has returned. Lara has not.'

'So she might soon be back?'

I shake my head wildly. 'You do not understand. I saw the Madame clearly. She returned dressed in my sister's clothes. What if—' The panic constricts me, tightens my chest. 'What if there has been some mistake? Listen, the workers are celebrating, right now. Crowing of the Madame's arrest. But the Madame has not been arrested, she is upstairs. So that must mean Lara . . . '

I look at Guillaume, my vision swimming, and see my own anguish reflected back at me. The name those workers threw around as though it was a mere pleasantry I now say out loud. 'The Conciergerie.' Roux's voice snakes into my ears. *To be tried from there . . . nothing more than a formality.*

'We must go there directly,' Guillaume replies. 'My horse is at the gates.'

He takes my hand, or maybe I take his, and together we sprint down the hill and force a way through the workers thronging in the forecourt. Even though they do not seem to mark us, some of them are saying my name, confirming it was I who got the Madame arrested. Their words catch me like poisoned darts.

'Here.' Guillaume gestures to a tethered grey mare, almost the

397

same colour as the horses he drove for Pa, another lifetime ago. He mounts and extends an arm to me, and I pull myself up behind him, flinging my hands around his waist.

At our backs the groups of workers expand and merge, every one of them preoccupied by the same topic. Their words echo tens, hundreds, thousands of times.

Madame Hortense will go to the guillotine.

Fountains and Animals

Paris

Sofi

The horse is barely across the bridge when I skid from its hot, mud-spattered flank. Jumping down after me, Guillaume leads the animal to the nearest drinking trough as I stand and cast frantically about. The streets are teeming even here, on this island in the middle of the Seine, and I haven't the first idea in which direction we should be heading.

'Do you know the place?' I call to Guillaume, not knowing why he would. Then I stiffen. Down the street and to my right, an enormous building looms.

With its pale facade and elegant towers, the river curving around it like a moat, the Conciergerie might almost be mistaken for a vast chateau. But it is not what it seems. The Queen herself was confined to one of its cells before being taken to the guillotine. What if Roux and that man at the factory were right? What if there *is* only one destination for prisoners from here?

I grab Guillaume's arm and pull him up the steps towards the massive arching entrance, to the doors dense with bars thicker than my ankles. 'We are looking for a woman brought here this morning,' I say to the guard and give my sister's name.

'You might know her as Hortense Oberst or Hortense du Pommier,' adds Guillaume.

The guard examines us suspiciously. 'Can't remember every prisoner off the top of my head, can I? What do you want with her?'

'There has been a mistake,' I say. 'The woman you have here is not who you think she is.'

The guard scans my face. 'Isn't she, now?'

I go to speak again, but feel Guillaume's hand on mine.

'We should like to see her, citizen,' he says. 'We would be grateful if you could tell us where we will find her.'

The guard's face eases from indignation to indifference. He goes inside and reappears some moments later, gesturing with his pike to the opened door. 'Take the steps at the end, turn left and tell the man at the bottom which prisoner you're here for.'

Leaving Guillaume to thank the guard I start inside, knowing there isn't a second to waste. But the dinginess of the building, the stench of it, the rats that scurry along in the stains and the shadows, they have the effect of wearying my pace. I dig my nails into my palms, hope defiantly that the woman in that cell will not be Lara. With each step I force down a heightening, stomach-pitching certainty too terrible to contemplate.

In the passageway of the lower floor, a second guard is slumped against the wall, probing a callous on his hand with the prong of his belt-buckle.

'Please, we are looking for Hortense Oberst,' I say.

'That one,' he grunts, tilting his head without looking up.

As a third guard pushes open the door of the cell, I realise I am shaking uncontrollably. I blink in the half-light as a waft of air hits me square in the face. It is frigid and damp, thick with the stinks of previous inmates.

I step tentatively inside. There is a shape in the corner, hunched and indistinct, but when my eyes adjust to the lack of light I see it is a woman, crouched on all fours, head dipped to her chest. The shape of her clothing indicates her to be someone of means, but she is wheezing, producing an unearthly groan, a noise not genteel but bestial. Dear Lord, it cannot be. 'Lara?'

The head moves, the woman's face slanting upwards to the door.

It *is* her, my beautiful sister, her countenance contorted with, consumed by, pain.

'Lara!' I rush over and crouch at her side, my knees seeping wet from a puddle on the floor.

'Sofi,' my sister says, breath ragged on my face. 'The baby . . . it's coming.'

'Ten minutes,' shouts the guard.

I look to the door, where Guillaume is standing aghast.

The guard raises his voice. 'Ten minutes. *Vous comprenez?*'

'Impossible!' I cry. 'We must stay with her, do you not see the state she is in?'

'Ten minutes.'

Guillaume stops the other man by the sleeve. With his free hand, he removes some coins from his jacket and presses them into the guard's fist. 'More time would be appreciated, citizen.' He is trying not to let the tremor in his voice show, for Lara's sake, but it rises nonetheless.

Pocketing the money, the guard nods. 'An hour, that is the most I can allow,' he mutters, and the door thuds closed.

I take my sister by the shoulders. 'Breathe, breathe,' I implore her, as though I have seen many babies born. But it is a sham. I've only ever attended one delivery before, with my mother when I was a child, and I have hardly a clue what was done.

'I cannot,' Lara gasps, her face twisting and tightening as she is seized by another upsurge of pain. 'It's too early. It will not live, it is not yet eight months, it's too early—'

'You must not think so,' I say. 'Only breathe!' We squat upon the floor, gripping each other's hands, and take great breaths of air together. In . . . Out . . .

It is then that I notice what Lara is wearing, recognising the gown I'd seen earlier, the gown I had presumed was clothing the Madame. Like the factory's wallpaper, the fabric of it is alive with clustering scenes and it is uncanny, even in this dire moment in this squalid cell beneath the city, how my sister appears to be covered in wallpaper from head to toe. Wallpaper with a pattern now distorted by blood, a print now blurred by water.

Guillaume hovers against the sodden wall of the cell, not knowing where to look.

'What can I do?' he pleads. 'How can I help?'

'Your brothers and sisters . . . do you know how it was done when they were born?'

'I . . .' Guillaume's face falls. 'No. Only my sisters were permitted to attend.'

His words are punctuated by my sister's strangled wails, and we start to breathe together again, Lara and I, unsteadily, effortfully, as time slows to an agonising drip.

There is a clinking at the door and the guard reappears, though it seems like no more than a handful of seconds since he left. As he is back so soon, I presume the man has come with help. But I am wrong, too stupidly expectant. He has not.

'Right,' the guard says, motioning to Guillaume and me. 'Time's up. You two are going to have to leave.'

'We cannot!' I cry. 'This woman is giving birth, do you not see? She cannot be left alone!'

The guard sniffs slackly. 'Babies have been born here before. We just follow the orders.'

'Look, I am telling you, and you *must* believe me . . . this isn't Hortense Oberst,' I plead, my exasperation soaring now. 'This woman's name is Lara Thérèse Thibault. She is my sister, she is Hortense Oberst's lady's maid. You have arrested the wrong person.' I cannot believe that a man so shortsighted, so disinterested, could possibly be a servant of the Republic. It doesn't make sense.

The guard takes in Lara's gown, dirtied as it is with prison filth and the gore of childbed. He looks sceptically between the two of us and shrugs. 'You don't look like sisters. Anyway, I wasn't the one who arrested her.'

'Please,' I implore. 'Who is in charge here? Tell the Governor we wish to speak with him urgently. Something has to be done!'

Guillaume steps forwards. 'Citizen—' he begins and feels inside his jacket. He has some money left, by the sounds of it, but not much.

'I cannot take any more of your coin,' the guard says, pushing Guillaume away and moving to the door.

A beat of silence.

'Wait!' Guillaume calls. He removes an object from the top left pocket of his waistcoat, the object I'd seen him with earlier at the chateau door. A beautiful, polished ring, too slim to fit his own fingers. 'Here,' he says, voice lowered. 'Real gold. We wish to speak with the Governor personally, as soon as possible, to explain the situation. Please, see what can be done.' He passes the ring to the other man.

The guard pinches the gold with thumb and forefinger, tests it between chipped teeth. 'I'll do what I can,' he replies, once he seems satisfied. Then he leaves.

My sister cries out again.

'Breathe, just breathe through it,' I say. I check under her skirts and gasp. 'Lara, keep going! I can see the head!'

Not one hour later, the baby glides into my arms. A tiny miracle, purple and floured with white. 'A boy,' I tell Lara, shaking once more. 'Oh, thank heavens. A baby boy.'

I am just about to pass the child to my sister when I realise he is completely still, completely silent. Perhaps Lara was right, perhaps he will not live. It was not like this when I entered the world, Mama has decried, a hundred times. I arrived screaming raw lungfuls of air, announcing my existence for all to hear. This baby, too, should be making noise.

'Is something wrong?' Lara pants, registering the alarm on my face.

Then I see what has happened. The milk-yellow cord is wound about the baby's neck.

'Quickly, do you have a knife?' I urge Guillaume, praying that he carries one as faithfully as Josef.

'What is it?' Lara presses, her panic surging.

Guillaume swiftly produces a pocket-knife from his jacket and passes it to me. I cut through the spiralling, glutinous rope and quickly untangle it from the baby's head. There is a hollow, deathly silence.

'Sofi?'

As I wonder how I could even begin to explain any of this to my sister, the baby at last makes a noise, a bald, urgent cry like the screech of a raptor chick. He starts to move, too, little limbs working as though trying to swim through the air and into his mother's arms.

'It's nothing,' I tell Lara, giddy with relief. 'Everything is fine. He is strong and healthy.'

While my sister lies against the wall, her face drained and ashen, I cut a strip of her skirts to serve as a cloth. Hurriedly, I spit on the fabric and clean the baby's head, removing my shawl from under my cloak and tucking him inside of it as though wrapping a loaf. When I place the child at Lara's breast and she sees the small, crinkled face of her son for the first time, pinked mouth spreading wide, chest working like miniature bellows, it is as though she has been injected with an elixir.

Guillaume and I help Lara onto the low stone platform meant to serve as a bed, and take our places either side of her, flanking her like the twin shells of a nut, my sister, in turn, encasing the baby as though he was the precious kernel inside. The cathedral bells peal out at intervals across the river. One in the morning. Two. More time than I expected, but still not enough.

The noise the guard makes on his return has both Guillaume and me springing to our feet. But when I mark how the man's eyes are fixed upon his boots I know he does not bring good news.

'The Governor says there is nothing to be done. Not tonight.'

'Did you even try to explain the situation?' I say, heart thumping. 'As much as I could.'

'Please, can we not see the Governor ourselves?' asks Guillaume.

The guard shakes his head. 'He's retired for the night. But he said to tell you this prisoner's to be tried in the morning. If there has been a mistake, it will be righted. Justice will be done.'

'A trial—?' 'But, he cannot—' Mine and Guillaume's words gush together.

The thought of my sister on trial is too wretched to bear. And yet, hasn't the Revolution so far been just? Hasn't progress been made?

I have to believe justice will be served tomorrow, that the mistake *will* be realised. That the Madame will be captured, at last, and my sister freed.

Despite the fact it has not bought us what he promised, the guard does not offer Guillaume his ring back and Guillaume does not ask for it. That object, I think, bartered us perhaps one extra hour. Yet it might have been priceless, a family heirloom. And then the realisation hits me. It was meant for my sister. That is why Guillaume appeared at the servants' door earlier, he was looking for Lara. He had found out, somehow, that she was carrying his child. He was going to ask her to be his wife. I had been right all along.

'I swore to Lara I would never tell, but—' I seize Guillaume's arm. 'Your son . . .' I say, my grasp tightening with every word. 'He *is* your son.'

405

The Sun and the Darkness

Lara

The minutes slip and evaporate, as if they were mere fractions of fractions of a second, my attention entirely fastened on the bundle of new life in my arms. Every moment that passes I marvel at this tiny being anew, this innocent, helpless miracle. I am utterly consumed by love, by a blinding, shimmering, all-encompassing ball of it, huge as the sun and huger still. I did not think such a love was possible. But there is hardly any time left at all.

I hear the cathedral bells chime two, just as I did the parlour clock the night of the *Bal de Printemps*. Their weighted, dolorous knells echo against my sister's words, and that is when I recognise exactly what she is saying to Guillaume and know I must speak. I drag my gaze from my child and, taking in Sofi's terrible anguish, I knock her arm from Guillaume's and draw her to me.

'Sofi,' I murmur. 'I have tried to tell you, over the past months—'

'I already knew. That Guillaume is the father.'

Hearing his name and perhaps sensing something of what is to follow, Guillaume gets to his feet, quietly assuming a position near the door.

'No, Fi. You are mistaken.' I will myself on. 'It is not Guillaume who is the father ... It is Josef.'

I have always tried to protect my sister, to conceal those things I knew would hurt her, even if it meant making life more difficult for myself. But there is no time for that now, no minute for pause. Sofi

406

arcs her head wildly, threshing my revelation away as though it were a betrayal. I hold her tighter.

'Sofi, listen. It is not how it looks.' I did not want to tell her like this, but the time we have left together is spilling fast. 'Josef, he . . . he *forced* himself on me. The night of the ball.' I swallow hard, the awful words ringing from the walls of the cell like the cathedral bells.

My sister's expression twists and plunges, from disbelief to horror. For the briefest instant I glance at my hand, grasping Sofi's fast. The sleeve of my gown, with its wallpaper pattern, seems to swallow my forearm like a snake its prey, and I wonder whether I should tell Sofi the rest. But there is no time to explain.

'Now, Fi, please, you *must* do as I say,' I continue hastily. 'You must take him, the baby. Everything will be all right. I promise—'

I have not seen my sister cry since before Pa died and, though she is not crying now, I feel her body convulse once, as if a single sob had escaped it. Her arms encircle me so hard I fear both our bones will snap.

'It will not be for long, you will be with him again soon,' Sofi whispers shakily, her voice barely there, and presses her forehead to mine.

There is a shout from the door. 'No mucking about,' the guard barks. 'You've had your extra time. Now leave. *Tout de suite.*' Three others step into the cell behind him.

In those last, snatched seconds it comes to me and I cannot fathom why I did not think of it earlier. I clutch my sister harder. 'The baby's name, Fi,' I say, my mouth right on the shell of her ear. 'I want to name him . . . '

The guards bear down on Guillaume. His voice is rising and there are hands then on my sister, too, prising her from me, her own taking the baby. Feeling his weight in my arms one moment and nothing the next, it is like my ribs have been wrested asunder and my heart pulled free of them. An absence wider and deeper than anything I have known.

Paris by Night

Sofi

Outside the prison walls the baby bawls at my chest, as Guillaume and I trudge dazed along the street, my legs wanting to buckle with every step. It is impossible to believe that not twenty-four hours have passed since I got out of bed to see Lara leaving the chateau with that woman. It is impossible to believe any of it.

My feet suddenly lock. The bundle in my arms has stopped bawling and is peculiarly still. I grab at the shawl, pull it free fearing the worst. With a gurgle, the baby's face puckers and relaxes and I'm flooded with relief. It takes some seconds for me to hear my name being repeated.

'Sofi . . . Sofi, can you mount?'

I nod at Guillaume, holding the baby securely in my arms as he lifts me onto the horse. 'Where are we going?' I ask, my voice seeming unreal, distant and small. 'The trial . . . I need to be here in the morning. We cannot go back to Jouy.'

'We will go to my sister's family, where I am lodging, to get some rest. She will be able to help with the child. It's a mile or so north. Could you manage that?'

I make a sound I mean to be a yes, so Guillaume mounts the mare, behind me this time, and spurs the animal on.

We have almost reached the house of his sister when the thought breaks biliously. *Josef.* The new wrongness of his name is like a boulder launched through glass. I had been looking at Josef through that glass, seeing him flawed but perfected, seeing him all wrong. It is as

408

though his skin had been an exquisite layer of paper, paper that has now peeled from the wall to reveal the cracks beneath. How could he have done that to my sister?

I force the thought away, try to focus instead on the fact that Josef is in Paris, at Monsieur Guyot's chateau, as my aunt told me. The authorities will listen to him, I am certain of it. If Josef tells them they have arrested the wrong person, then we will be able to stop this.

And so I know I must find him. Even though it is the last thing I want to do.

Leda

Lara

I am lying balled on the stone platform of the cell, arms folded tight against my empty belly. I try to block out the ache in my body, to concentrate only on my baby, on Sofi, but admitting to her what happened takes me right back to it, to the night of the *Bal de Printemps*.

The air of the tower chamber was charged strangely. I felt it as I stared at my reflection in the small oval looking-glass on the wall, whilst the light from the candle I held revealed the paper's pattern, curving in on either side of me as if it were an opened mouth.

I was only peering into the mirror as I had meant to undress. To remove myself from the discomfort of my ball clothes and unpin the forget-me-nots from my hair. So when he appeared silently behind me, his reflection materialising over my shoulder, I startled.

When I spun to face Josef, the first thing I marked was how bizarre his expression was, how disconnected, stiff with trepidation. A sheen of determined intent misted his pale eyes. I knew immediately that he must have observed Guillaume and me, talking so secretively only minutes before, and my heart sank.

For a moment, I said nothing. I felt the flowers tickling my hair and suddenly wanted to tear them out and flatten them underfoot. I wanted to make myself plain, unadorned, to twist my face in such a way he would not desire me. I was ashamed of being clad in those fine garments, my hair dressed and curled. I was ashamed of seeming wanton.

As he took a step towards me, the candle made the grey satin he was wearing deepen and echo with his eyes. It was strange how, in that instant, I noted the proportions of his countenance and that shamed me too. His full mouth, the slight cleft to his chin, the clean cut of his jaw. I could almost see why my sister was so taken with him, but it was always much more than that for Sofi. It was the gap he filled. It was his matching pain.

'Why have you come?' I asked, pressing the words through my teeth.

'How could I not.'

A statement, not a question. He moved nearer, so we were standing very close together, and I could smell the sour drink upon him and see the set of his brows, hard and honed. Absent was his customary demeanour, the manner of a long-lost child.

He reached a hand to my face, buried his nose in my neck and inhaled, the action resolute and long. I remembered I was wearing the lavender cologne he gifted me, on his birthday all those years before.

Aside from the stench of drink, his face on my skin, his touch at that point had not been unpleasant, and I disliked the fact I thought so more than I disliked what was happening.

It was when his head rose from my neck that he kissed me properly. At first his lips wavered on mine, as they did when he kissed me in the woodstore. Then his ardour grew faster, harder. He gripped me by the arms, pulled me towards the bed. My legs and feet seized, heavier and more rigid than ever, the toes of my slippers scuffing the floor as he dragged me on.

I knew I must speak, else he would think I was compliant, that I wanted this as much as he. My mind began to dredge up words, my tongue almost immovable in my mouth. 'You have—' I forced. 'You have lost your senses.'

But he just smiled, a smile I had never seen him give before. 'Apprehensive? I think we both are.'

He had not even heard what I said, had mistaken its meaning, had not listened, had not understood. And I knew then it was too late. He fell back onto the bed, taking me too.

Hanging helplessly over him, I felt my hairpins loosen and in vain my fingers flew up to try and stay them. But the sight of this only impelled him further and his hands grasped my upper arms so purposefully I could not move. 'Like a tent,' he commented, when my hair fell to drape either side of his head. 'How I have wanted this.'

Hastily, Josef swapped our positions so that he was on top, hands running over my body with an urgency that seemed just as uncomfortable to him. Perhaps he comprehended, some part of him at least, that this was not right, yet he said nothing, and neither did he stop.

A forget-me-not, the flower-head smooth and cold, was crushed between the coverlet and my forearm. I suspected, even then, that before he left he would pick it off the mattress and take it with him, that it would end up with those other things he must have taken without my noticing. The hairpin I dropped in the meadow on my first morning in the factory. The cap that came free during our game of Blind Man's Buff. The comb that went missing after Sofi told me he'd ventured into our chamber. The jacket button that fell off when I steadied him as he staggered drunkenly through the darkness outside the cottage. And finally, the pen he must have lifted from my crate when I moved into the tower. Little, inconsequential pieces of myself that I had never seen again.

My mind began to shift peculiarly then, to swim upwards as though freed from its moorings. I tried to find words, to speak once more before the sensation overwhelmed me and rendered me senseless.

'No ... no ... NO!'

He thrust me flat against the mattress, his weight pinning me. I could feel his hands on my skirts, drawing them higher and higher, and my mind did the same. It rose until it had drifted, airily, all the way up to the cross-beams, sensing below it some strangled sound, a steadfast creaking increasing in volume and rhythm. And the figures surrounding us in the wallpaper looked mutely on, the minutes slipping and evaporating, just as they are now.

The recollection of that night brings me back to Sofi. I am glad I told her, glad I found the strength. This, at least, gives me some peace. And I am finally away from that place, away from the wallpaper. In a strange way, I am almost free.

Attributes

Sofi

Benoît Chastain appears at the door to his lodgings dressed in his shirt. I am only half-aware of what happens next, of Guillaume explaining to his brother-in-law why we are arriving at his house at such an hour. Of Guillaume's sister materialising at her husband's side, cooing and lifting the baby gently from my arms.

'My, he's light as a sparrow's feather!' Agathe murmurs, as she loosens her chemise. It is nothing, I think I hear her tell me, her youngest is still feeding at her breast.

'Do you have writing things?' I say groggily, as though I was the one roused from sleep. 'I must write a letter. There is no time to lose.'

Guillaume guides me into a chair. I open my mouth, vaguely intending to explain to him that Josef must be found. But I find I cannot say his name.

'First things first,' Agathe begins, as the baby suckles softly. 'We must get you a drink.' She nods to her husband, who rubs the sleep roughly from his face and pours from a pitcher.

I look at them in disbelief. I want to leap from the chair, to clutch the fronts of their nightshirts and shake them, insist they fetch me ink and parchment at once.

Benoît puts a cup of wine in my hand. I peer at the dark liquid and see only a measure of blood. Nausea churns my stomach and I press my fingers to my mouth. I cannot drink it.

'Please,' I say, with effort, trying to get them to understand. 'I must write a letter. To Jo— To Monsieur Oberst. It is urgent.'

414

'There is no need,' Guillaume replies and for a second I think him mad. 'I shall ride to Jouy and fetch him.'

I push the cup of wine away. 'He is not in Jouy. He is in Paris. At the Maison des Peupliers—'

'The Guyots' chateau?' Guillaume asks, to my astonishment. 'I know it. The forge I work at made a delivery there, not two months ago. If I leave now, Monsieur Oberst should still be abed.'

Guillaume wants to do everything within his power to save my sister, of course he does. Though he admitted nothing in that cell and has not spoken of her since we left it, his torment is impossible to miss.

'I will go with you,' I say. 'What if Monsieur Oberst does not believe you are speaking the truth? He will listen to me.'

Guillaume's face shadows. 'You should stay here, with the little one. Get some rest. When Monsieur Oberst hears what has happened, he will come.'

I glance to the baby at Agathe's breast.

'I shall find the Monsieur and return with him as soon as I can,' Guillaume says, coming to me and taking my hand in his. 'You have my word.'

I nod, too exhausted to reply.

'What time does the trial begin?' asks Agathe.

'Nine.' Guillaume answers for me.

Benoît rests a hand on my shoulder. 'Do not worry, Mademoiselle. He will fetch the man. They will be back before you know it.'

The Palace of Justice

Sofi

The night races past and Guillaume does not return. I watch the dawn's light widen in the sky. I watch Benoît leave for work, Agathe rouse her children and rekindle the fire. Any moment, I pray, I shall hear Guillaume's horse in the street, the sounds of a second beast accompanying it. And then Josef will dismount and tell the authorities they have made a dreadful mistake. But still there is no sign of either of them. If it wasn't for Lara's baby I would feel more alone than I ever have in my life.

At seven in the morning, I have no choice but to venture to the Palais de Justice by myself. I kiss the baby's small head before I leave him with Agathe, take in the scent of this piece of my sister, his smells of sweet milk and of bread.

The centre of the city, when I reach it, looks larger than ever before. Yet Paris is choked with hostility now, with a blood lust that crackles off every surface. The capital's edges are sharpened and, though the sun is up and shining, the air is cold as the belly of an eel.

I arrive at the Palais early, but the front of the building is already aswarm. There is nothing to do but wait, to pass each agonising minute furiously scanning the crowds, hoping that at any moment I shall see them, striding towards me. Guillaume gave me his word. Even if the journey to Monsieur Guyot's house took longer than he expected, surely he and Josef should be here by now?

Time seeps as I stand there, powerless to do anything save climbing the courthouse steps for a better view of the street. As I do, a vehicle approaches and figures are bundled out of it and into the Palais. A shout goes up, intense with hate, and I know those figures were the prisoners, brought from the Conciergerie next door. That Lara must be among them. So where is Josef? Where is Guillaume? Time is running out.

I shield my eyes and continue my frantic watch. And just when I think I can bear it no longer, just when I resolve to stand on these steps and shout his tarnished name until the noise engulfs the whole city, I spot him. Josef is here already, amidst these hundreds hankering for blood. I would know that posture, that waved blond hair anywhere, despite the unfamiliar revulsion it now arouses in me.

I raise onto tiptoes and strain over the heads of the crowds. 'Josef!' I yell, so loud my ears pop.

But he makes no acknowledgement as, at that moment, another man taps him on the elbow. Josef swivels unsteadily and the stranger engages him in conversation, words flowing between them. He cannot have heard me. He cannot know. Otherwise he would already be racing up the steps towards the Palais entrance.

'Josef!' I am screaming this time, an ugly, unseemly noise that burns my throat.

Surely he must have heard, be able to see my hands thrashing the air? He moves forwards, at last, as though about to push in the direction of the building. Then he hesitates once more, allowing the stranger to sling an arm around his shoulders. What is he waiting for?

'Call for the trial of—' comes a loud voice from the courthouse door. I turn to look. A clerk is there, squinting at the sheet of paper he is holding and reeling off names. The Marquis du Pommier and his wife. Adrien de Pise, the Madame's crony. The last of them is hers.

'Hortense Oberst neé du Pommier.'

Inked onto one of their lists, in permanent black print. Except it is not the Madame who is answering to that name, not the Madame who is answering to her crimes. It is my sister.

I spin back to the crowd, but he is gone. 'JOSEF!' I scream again, a cry as accusing as it is desperate. 'JO-SEF!' I twist this way and that, craning my neck to try to locate him. I attempt to dart forwards, to descend the steps so I might find him, but the throng at the Palais is shoving inside now. After struggling against it, in vain, for a few moments more, I allow it to take me.

The trials have already begun as I reach the courtroom, a vast space crammed with people, their commotion echoing the hectic ornamentation of the walls. High in a box, below a ceiling that dips in points like drawn spearheads, sits the Judge, listening to a clerk addressing another man, the Public Prosecutor. Though I believe there should be some, I see no lawyers. A paltry handful of men sits in the jury. This is not a trial, I want to shout. This is a farce.

Bringing the first man's trial to an end not minutes after it starts by declaring him guilty, the Judge calls for the guards to usher in the next prisoner.

'Madame Hortense Oberst!'

The joy, the relief that would envelop me if the Madame was to reveal herself now, from the middle of this group of the condemned. But it is Lara who emerges, to be positioned roughly before the Prosecutor. My heart plummets anew at the sight of her, submerged by the pattern of that gown, her face unwashed, her golden hair hanging limply down her back. But most affecting of all is her expression, the weary resignation of it. I want to tell her to fight, to keep faith.

'That woman is not Hortense Oberst!' I shout.

The spectators, having fallen silent at the sight of my sister, begin to murmur. Lara looks over at me and smiles weakly.

I open my mouth to shout the same again when the Judge turns to Lara, demanding, 'Madame, what is your name?'

'She is Madame Hortense Oberst,' the Prosecutor interjects. 'Born Hortense Amandine Alouette Louise du Pommier. I have it here.' He presses his finger to the papers before him as though he was holding the word of God.

'Your name?' the Judge asks again.

'I . . . I am Lara Thibault.'

A hush, before the murmurings of the spectators grow louder.

'She is Lara Thibault!' I repeat.

The Judge appraises my sister impatiently. 'Very well, let us re-solve the matter. Bring out the other prisoners.' A clerk looks at him, confused. 'The other two,' the Judge hectors. 'The Marquis and his wife.'

My head sweeps left and right, searching for the prisoners the Judge is referring to. And then I realise and my heart gallops with hope. The Madame's parents. Josef may not be here, but they will confirm my sister is not who everyone thinks she is. This is a court of the law – they have to.

Duplicities

Lara

The noise of the crowd flows and ebbs, swells and recedes, as if my sense of hearing was being honed and blunted like a blade, though each time dulled a little more. I observe my sister, there amongst the onlookers. She is wracked by torment, pale and thin and fraught.

Was it really less than a day ago when, in the dank bowels of the Conciergerie, that little swaddled and helpless thing of mine was taken from my arms? I feel it as though it is happening even now, the profound, unbearable wrench of it, of Sofi lifting him away. My breasts seep under my stays, and I bring my arms across my front to try to conceal them.

I suddenly remember the letter my aunt passed to me, the day before Madame and I left in the carriage. It remains in the pocket-bag tied beneath the skirts of this gown, his words tucked away, still, concealed even through childbirth.

As Madame's mother and father enter the courtroom, Sofi's face radiates with hope. I have seen them a handful of times before, but they look so different now. The Marquis is unwigged, the remaining hair on his head a soft white and cropped close. There is a streak of black on the bridge of his nose and his jowls hang loose, like they have had the air let from them. The Marquise is without her wig, too, its absence giving her the look of a smeared dessert dish that Madame might have eaten from, missing its cream-ice topping. Her bodice is grubby and she is dabbing at the corners of her eyes with the pad of her ring finger.

'Marquis,' says the Prosecutor. 'There is a matter we wish to be settled. Look around this room and tell me ... do you see your daughter Hortense here?'

I hold my breath. The Marquis looks surprised by the question, but the Prosecutor's words immediately cause his wife's whimpering to cease. She glances tentatively about, her eyes sliding over me at first, before sticking on my face, two green clasps.

The Marquis, however, is staring at the Prosecutor as though he had posed a trick question.

'Well?' bellows the Judge. 'The enquiry is simple enough. Can you or can you not see your daughter?'

The crowd quietens and the Marquis swallows noisily. 'No,' he says. 'No, I cannot.'

I exhale so forcefully my vision speckles. There are gasps from the room, declamations of shock. Spectators nudge one another and remark, 'Not his daughter! That's not his daughter!'

'Quiet!' shouts the Judge. 'This is most untoward.'

'I will ask you again,' cuts in the Prosecutor. 'Are you quite sure that what you are saying is correct and you cannot see your daughter in this room?'

'Monsieur, if I might speak,' the Marquise starts, her voice growing in confidence. 'My husband will be the first to admit that his eyesight is not what it was. Our daughter is indeed in this room. She is over there.' She extends a shaking finger in my direction.

There are more gasps from the gallery, more cluckings of thrilled disbelief.

'Liar!' cries my sister. 'That is not true, she's lying! It is second nature to the likes of them!'

'Control yourself or leave, Mademoiselle!' the Judge warns her. 'A simple question has been asked, Marquis. Is that woman over there your daughter, or is she not?'

'Come now, you must tell the truth,' says the Prosecutor. 'We have a lot of people to get through today.'

A hush falls. The Marquis hesitates, he cannot look at me, cannot meet my eyes. His wife grasps the blue delta of his wrist, sinking in her fingernails. There is a moment of utter silence that seems to last a lifetime. Then the Marquis utters, 'She is, she is,' and hangs his head.

'Our daughter!' shrieks the Marquise. 'Oh, *ma petite*, our youngest girl!' She begins to weep again, and this time, it seems, her tears fall freely. She has lied to protect her child and, I ask myself, would I not have done the same? I wonder whether she pities me, feels any guilt at all.

'Stay there,' the Judge instructs her. 'I shall do you next. And this one . . .' He nods from me to the guards. 'GUILTY!'

Before I know it there are hands upon me, bearing me out of the courtroom. My sister's voice roars in my ears.

The Wolf and the Lamb

Sofi

'No!' I shout, over and over. 'She's lying! No!'

A thicket of hands reaches for Lara, pulling her away until she is swallowed completely by a mess of bodies rushing to one of the doors.

'Get her out, for God's sake!' a man in the courtroom calls.

Hands are on me, too, then, and for a brief misguided moment I wonder if it is possible that Lara and I have swapped places, somehow, that they are delivering me to the scaffold instead of her. *You deserve it*, a small voice in my head whispers, *you know you do.*

I fight against the guards with all that I have. Surely there is something more that I could say, to show those men how wrong they are. To prove my sister's innocence. I thrash and I kick, but they only hold me faster, haul me back outside.

'Leave her!' a voice barks when we near the entrance, gruffer and louder than I've ever heard it. It causes the guards to drop me to the ground and quickly disperse.

Guillaume offers me his hand and I get up, looking around disoriented, expecting Josef to be with him. But he is not. Guillaume is alone.

'I am sorry, Sofi,' Guillaume says. 'I could not find Monsieur Oberst. I searched everywhere. He wasn't at the Guyots' house. They hadn't heard from him since last night.'

My mouth has gone dry. Had I really seen him in the square before the trial, or was it nothing more than a trick of my eyes, my own wishful thinking conjuring the scene? I cannot work out what to say, what to do. Everything has fallen away.

'I am so sorry.'

Guillaume and I hover on the Palais steps, mute and impotent, knocked and jostled by the crowd.

'They called that a trial,' I moan. 'It was a farce.' I want Lara suddenly and the urge of it is overwhelming. I want to hold her once more, to feel the warmth of her touch and see her easy smile.

Guillaume's jacket emits an unexpected burble and only then do I notice the way the garment bulges at the front, seeming to move of its own accord.

'Here,' he says, revealing what is inside. 'Agathe met me in the square. She thought he might bring you some comfort. He's had his feed.'

I lift the baby from Guillaume's arms, rock and shush him, feel his warmth penetrate my chest like a small sun. 'Thank you.'

'Let us leave now,' Guillaume says, after another moment has passed. 'Let us return to Jouy and decide what is to be done. There is no good in staying.'

I shake my head. 'I *will* stay,' I insist, my voice breaking. 'I must. You do not have to if you cannot, but I owe my sister this much. If she can at least know I am with her when . . .' The sentence hangs there.

Guillaume does not answer but places a hand at my back and gently guides me north, in the same direction as the whistling, chanting hordes. To the square in which the opponents of progress are dispatched. The Place de la Révolution. The name appals me. Up ahead, the tocsin bell begins to toll.

When the wooden structure staging the awful contraption comes into view I can hardly bear to look. I hug the baby to me, encircle the little form as Lara did in her prison cell and will myself to keep moving.

Guillaume stays my arm. 'Might this be far enough?'

'I want to go closer,' I tell him, pushing on. 'We must be near the front.'

424

'Are you sure?' he asks repeatedly. 'You do not have to witness this.'

Again and again I answer yes, I want to be as close to Lara as possible. I owe it to her. I think of watching the murder of the Governor de Launay outside the Bastille. How I believed his life was owed a witness. I think of Lara's words to me that evening before I left for the meeting in Paris. *Just as many lives lost as lives improved.* The remembrance of it makes me want to vomit, but I focus on pressing forwards with every last drop of stamina I can muster.

We push all the way to the front, to the guards that surround the platform, their faces nothing more than ovals of blank ignorance. Behind us the square swells to bursting point, spilling the crowds into the surrounding *rues*, all the way to the banks of the river.

We haven't been at the scaffold long when a cry rises in the distance, brutal and ugly, building to a roar. The tumbril must be approaching, its progress through the baying throng agonisingly slow. The first time I see it is when it jolts to a standstill, Lara's face coming into view simultaneously, her gaze instantly meeting mine. She gives me the same smile she did in the courtroom, weary and resigned.

I do not take my eyes off her, do not watch the boy or the Madame's mother meet their ends in the guillotine's jaws, do not register the deafening cries from the crowd. *'VIVE LA FRANCE! VIVE LA FRANCE!'* I simply take in all that I can of Lara, like a man treasuring desperately the last seconds of a vanishing world, only recognising its value the very moment before it is gone for good.

They pull my sister out of the tumbril, the shredded fabric of that wallpaper dress splaying behind her like pleading fingers, a plain cap sitting tight against her head. No hair escapes from beneath it and her neck is red and bare. Her head must have been shorn, and the thought of that being done to her is almost sadder and more horrible to contemplate than the thought of what will happen next.

Before the length of cloth is tied against her eyes, I unswaddle my sister's baby from my cloak and turn him tenderly so she might see his face one last time. She smiles at me again, for the slimmest second more, and then her eyes are covered.

A pair of guards guide Lara roughly into the clamping lunette of the guillotine and she fumbles unseeingly forwards, unable to use her bound hands to aid her. It is like watching a terrible game of Blind Man's Buff. The executioner prepares himself.

Although it is nearly impossible to drag my gaze from what is unfolding in front of me, a paper shoved towards Guillaume abruptly snatches my attention. A single inked name leaps blindingly from its stark white plane.

Hortense Amandine Alouette Louise Oberst
(neé du Pommier)
A traitor of the Republic

Yes, it is she who is the traitor and not my sister, not Lara. Terror and shame and misery and despair surge from a place deep inside of me and I scream at the men on the scaffold, shout at them to stop, that Lara's name isn't even on that paper, that they have the wrong person entirely. But I know it is futile. That what is about to happen cannot be changed.

As the *déclic* is pulled, the contortion of sound coming from my mouth suddenly stops, mid-word, as though the action swipes it clean away, tears the scream from my throat. The blade falls sickeningly from the sky, metal catching sunlight as though winking at me. I cannot move.

Scenes in Black Ink

Lara

Something extraordinary has just happened and I cannot wholly believe it. One minute my head is caught in the guillotine's lunette as though snared, the next I am in the tower chamber once more, head caught in reflection in that oval looking-glass instead, just as it was in Madame's silver tray. Head and looking-glass together are as a kite now, suspended, the scenes from the frantic violet wallpaper hovering and overlapping behind it, gathering like fast clouds in a busy sky.

The vibrations of light from the candle I am holding seem to animate the paper unnaturally, making the figures populating those printed scenes look as though they are dancing across the wall, memories across a closed eyelid. The same candle also illuminates the room's shape, as it has done before, the stripe of light reflected in the mirror a bright tongue, thickest darkness either side of it. I think I am on the verge of being swallowed up whole by this chamber now, of becoming part of that dense, infinite blackness forever. I am so tired it might be a mercy. I have never liked this room.

My unanchored mind trails the space, circling the wallpaper in a spiral as though I am shut up in an exquisitely lined box. It is airless, each finger-width of wallpaper inundated by those haunting, repeating scenes, suspended in time. They seem to murmur together, their noise building, the same figure in every scene turning to peer out from the pattern at once. Madame Justine. The woman in the wallpaper.

There she is, kneeling below the sycamore, taking a picnic beneath the dining table. And there again, skimming stones by the river, sitting at her toilette, her writing desk, her fortepiano. Shopping at the market.

The longer I take them in, the more the vignettes of Madame Justine's life flicker strangely, melting into altogether more familiar scenes. There is the woman in the wallpaper seated high on a wagon, the surface of a horse-pond shimmering expectantly in the distance. There she is again, standing in a meadow, the cuts of paper before her spread like a giant display of butterfly specimens. There again, flat upon a mattress, her fichu spread at her back in wings. And there once more, within a city courtroom, charged with offences against her country. *Her whole life . . . there in the wallpaper.*

On and on they go, scene after scene speeding together, a spiral narrowing, tightening to the point of a screw. It is like the bottom has been smashed from an hour-glass and the sand is draining. Time is spilling, falling away. Time is running out.

Suddenly comes the last scene of all. A Parisian square, a sunny sky. A scaffold, a lunette, a towering instrument of death. A young woman about to meet her end. A child about to lose his mother. But the woman in the wallpaper now is not Madame Justine. The woman in the wallpaper is me.

Then I understand what is happening, why I am back in the tower again, back before that wallpaper. Those scenes, flickering incessantly through my mind as memories across a closed eyelid, are the scenes of my own life. A life that is about to end.

I am not in that tower room at all, I am here on the scaffold. The blade has fallen and I am experiencing those final, precious moments of consciousness before the last scene of them all fades, and everything tips and furs into oblivion.

The explosions of the cannons, the firing of the pistols, my ears ringing.

VIVE LA FRANCE! VIVE LA FRANCE!

My sister's voice, calling my name.

They say that hearing is the last thing to go.

The shouting begins to dim. The sounds lessen and dip.

How precious everything is. How fragile. Breath inside a bubble, held within the thinnest, frailest skin. It might burst at any second.

My mind whirrs and churns no longer. It is over. A blanket of calm settles, soft as still-falling snow.

Sensation floods, collapses under its own weight. A dying star, shrinking to a pinprick.

The little dot, all that remains of a scene, of a life, hovers there ... then vanishes.

Consumed ...

by ...

black.

Discardings

Sofi

I'd intended to turn away when Lara's head was displayed to the crowd, but when the time comes I find I cannot summon any part of my body or my mind into motion. My lovely sister is lifted into the air, her cheeks the purest white, bright crimson falls at her neck, the sky above flashing an extraordinary blue, just for a second. The three colours of the *cocarde* pinned to my cloak. It burns the skin beneath it like a cup of acid.

The blindfold tied about Lara's eyes falls away, and I am shocked to see her face once more. Her eyes are open and, in the seconds her head is held aloft, it seems to me that her expression changes, from shock to recognition to sadness. Then she appears to look right at me, and I could almost believe she was smiling.

As my sister's head is placed back in the basket at the foot of the guillotine, a rectangle of paper is borne by the breeze and comes to rest at the platform's edge. The front rows of onlookers surge forwards, white kerchiefs held high, fluttering eagerly as tickets to be cashed. The kerchiefs are dipped in the blood dripping between the planks of the scaffold. The crowd's souvenirs of the day, the dead's lurid autographs.

I rush forwards too. I snatch up that rectangle of paper before anyone else can and tuck it under my clothes, safe behind the baby. The action causes him to stir, to open his mouth, and when he does every other sound fades. The cry of a parentless child is the only thing I hear, echoing loudly in a world empty of my sister. I shush

430

the baby, rock him. I touch my forehead to his, soft as the skin of an apricot, and imagine he is Lara.

Guillaume and I cling to each other then and, when we part, I pass him the baby and unpin my *cocarde*. I drop it to the ground, to be trampled into dust.

Papier

Sofi

I am so tired, I realise, my body as heavy as if it were weighted by chains. Nothing makes sense any more. Not Agathe Chastain in her high-backed chair by the fireplace, nursing my sister's baby at her breast. Not Guillaume sitting next to me, hands intertwined on the tabletop, leaning so low his nose is almost touching his knuckles. Not the Chastains' gaggle of children, animating their toy guards-men into action across the rug, the miniature figures disgusting to me.

My eyes linger on the rectangle of paper, laid on the table like a place-mat. It is not so white as it was, a rust-red smudge now cross-ing the top of it. The baby clicks his lips and the clock ticks, and the sight of that red smear fills the room like a wound, newly slashed.

Without taking my eyes off the paper before me, a word escapes my lips. 'Mama.' My voice is unfamiliar, the syllables too noisy in my head, too noisy in the room, despite barely being there at all. I have not uttered a word since we returned from the square.

'That from your ma, love?' says Agathe, inclining her head to the letter.

Her voice takes an age to reach me, even though she is sitting just a few paces away. 'No,' I reply, slow and distant. 'I only thought . . . that my mother doesn't know what has happened.' My speech is monotone, my face leaden, expressionless.

The baby gurgles and, with a rasp of linens, Agathe wipes milk from his tiny, pursing mouth.

'It is addressed to my sister,' I say. 'It's in the Monsieur's hand.'

'Monsieur Oberst?' Guillaume asks.

'Yes.' I dip my head. 'I cannot open it.'

I cannot bear to read that man's words. I drag my vision from the smudge of scarlet to the bundle in Agathe's arms. Just as I saw no trace of de Comtois whenever I looked into my sister's gentle face, I see no resemblance to anyone other than Lara in her baby, in the sweetness of his expression, new to the world though it is.

'I can help, you know,' Guillaume says to me quietly. 'Help support the baby.'

My gaze snaps to his and there is a pause as Agathe glances between us. 'Might be best if we let you have some privacy awhile,' she says, getting to her feet. 'The little ones and I have some organising to do. *Allez, mes enfants*, let us tidy the chamber.'

'I am not little, Mama,' one of her boys protests.

'I shall take this package with me too,' Agathe says, nodding at the small round face poking up through the gap in the shawl. 'He's full now so I'll lay him down for a nap. He'll be no trouble.'

'Oh ... yes, thank you,' I murmur, hearing neither Agathe and her children exit, nor the sound of Guillaume dragging his chair closer to mine. We sit in silence for a while, him staring at his empty hands, me at that letter, as though into the blackness of a chamber in the blank-eyed moments before waking from a nightmare.

'I saw you,' I say, a hopeless burst of anger widening in my chest. 'On the night of the ball.' He was there, with Lara, just before Josef ... He must have been.

Guillaume's brows arc into two questioning marks. 'You saw me?'

'With Lara. On the approach to the chateau. I saw you both, going inside together.'

He looks half-blank, half-shamed. The same expression he gave when I happened upon him at the servants' door, before we left for the Conciergerie.

'I overheard Lara that night, saying the pair of you had something to discuss.'

There yet again, that same look of unease. 'I did wish to speak

433

to your sister about something. Since I knew I could not raise the matter with your mother.' His hand moves to hover, momentarily, over the top left pocket of his waistcoat. 'But it is not how it looks. I did not even set foot inside the chateau that night.'

If only he had. If only things *had* been how they looked. What Josef had done . . . it might never have happened.

'I came to the chateau yesterday afternoon to find you, to ask—' He hesitates.

I close my ears to whatever might come next. I cannot listen to it, not now. The thought that whispered to me in the courtroom earlier digs its way determinedly into my brain like a maggot, fat and unwelcome. That this might be my fault, that it was I who reported the Madame, I who wanted her gone, that it was *my* actions that led to my sister—

'I loved her!' I say, firing the words at him as though he had just disputed the fact. 'I know what people think . . . that I'm sulky, ill-tempered, too headstrong for my own good. That I was jealous of my sister. But I loved her.' A multitude of sobs are backed up in my throat, and I have to close my mouth to lock the rest of it away.

'I know you did, Sofi.' He puts his hands over mine. 'And she loved you. Very much.'

I want to run, to clamp my hands to my ears and shut everything out. I shake away Guillaume's touch and clamp my hands around that still-sealed rectangle of paper instead, jumping to my feet.

'I need to go back. Right away. I need to tell Mama.'

'Let me come with you—'

'No,' I say, crossing to the fire. 'I will do this myself.'

He looks injured. 'But, how—?'

I leave Guillaume's words hanging in the air, knowing exactly what I must do. I must retrieve my sister's baby and find transport back to Jouy. I must get out of this city and I must do so immediately.

The Madame arrived back at the chateau alone, little more than a day ago, in her consort's carriage. I saw her with my own eyes and she must be there still. Her parents are dead now and de Pise too. She has nobody left to turn to. Where else could she possibly be but there?

I was wrong earlier, my thoughts tumbling too quickly. This isn't my fault, it is hers. And this time, I will make sure that justice is delivered myself.

I uncurl my fingers and release the paper into the flames.

Lavender Fields

Jouy-en-Jouvant

Sofi

By the time we reach Jouy, night has fallen. The freezing air casts blurred rings around the moon, and the stars are so bright the sky is a great spill of the darkest, blackest ink against them.

I peel back my cloak to check on the baby. He is silent at last, sleeping beneath it. For most of the journey he bawled. Perhaps he could sense how each turn of the wagon's wheels bore him further from his mother.

I found the drayman on the main street near the Chastains' house, heading south-west. I direct him along the track to the cottage now, ask him to wait a moment while I climb down and retrieve a coin from inside for his trouble.

As the man spurs off his horses, I close the cottage door. The house is quiet and still, but a fire, I see, is smoking in the hearth. Mama must already have returned from the factory.

'I might ask where you've been.' The voice cuts at my back. 'S'pose you heard about the Madame and went galloping to the capital to watch her head come off.'

Appearing from the yard at the rear, Mama busies herself with the fire awhile, her words suspended between us. She has not noticed the bulge at my breast and drops into a chair as though there was nothing more to say.

'Mama,' I announce, moving towards her. 'This is your grandson.'
I lower the baby into her arms, instantly marking the void he leaves
in my own. Then I watch, as her face spreads and lapses to shock.

'My—?'

'He will need a wet nurse as soon as possible.'

Mama's expression clouds, and it does not take long for her face to
re-assume its usual veneer of disapproval. 'What in the Lord's name
have you done?'

Her ignorance is so outrageous that I almost laugh. 'He's not
mine, Mama. He is . . . ' My voice wants to rip. 'He is Lara's.'

'*Lara's?*' Mama's tone sours. 'I might have known. And where on
earth is she now, pray?'

I straighten and squeeze my hands into fists, nails gouging palms.

'You were right, Mama, I did go galloping off to the capital yesterday. For something dreadful happened. It wasn't the Madame
who was executed . . . ' I force a breath. 'It was Lara. It was a terrible
mistake. There was a trial – a farce – and nothing could be done. I
tried to stop it but I could not. I failed.'

As the words bleed from me, I keep anticipating that Mama will
interject, will claim that I am lying. But she does not.

'She is dead.' I fight to steady my voice. 'Lara is dead.'

Mama's face gains twenty years in twenty seconds, her mouth
opening so wide a hand might have reached in and taken her
tongue. I remember how she always treated my sister, carping
and picking and belittling her at every turn. Sucking the joy from
Lara's life, just as she does from her own. *Her manner is just her
way of dealing with adversity.* Lara had said it about the Madame,
but it may as well have been Mama she was referring to. How out-
landish that two women so far removed should both clutch at the
same shield.

'Do you have anything to say, Mama?' I ask, stepping closer.
'Because I do.'

The baby whimpers and shifts inside the shawl.

'I know. About Lara's father. Lara told me herself, in fact.'

I hear the echo of Lara's words to me the day of the meeting

437

in Paris. How she told me it was the likeness I'd drawn of her the night before she moved to the chateau that made her realise what our mother was hiding. I recall that day in Pa's workshop, when de Comtois arrived dressed head-to-toe in the pale blue of a pearl, the exact shade Lara wore to the ball. How Mama herself had remarked on it. *Done up like a lady and in his colours, too ... I really am surprised you didn't see the resemblance.* I bring to mind how Lara's finely sloping chin ended in the same delicate point as de Comtois'. How their eyes were that same rare shade of grey.

My mother's broken countenance meets mine, her chin loose, her brows collapsing together. It is a pitiful expression and I do not want to pity her. I have to concentrate very hard in order to go on.

'What did you think you were doing, Mama, lifting your skirts for de Comtois? Did his looks turn your head? Did you believe you understood him, better than anyone?'

The words spew from depths I do not understand. Am I talking about my mother or myself? Did I believe I understood Josef, better than anyone, a man capable of— I move to the door. I will go to the chateau. I will finish this now.

Behind me, the baby starts to cry, a quiet, unearthly noise. But as I reach a hand out to leave, I realise it is not the infant at all and I freeze, incapable of turning. I have never heard Mama weep before, just as I have never really heard her laugh. It has all been shuttered away, behind her mask of scorn and censor. The sound at my back affects me strangely, makes me think of my sister and crushes my heart. I wish I had chosen my words more carefully, spoken more softly. It's what Lara would have done.

'It happened at the factory.'

For a second I presume she means this factory, but then I understand. She is referring to the soap factory, where she worked in Marseilles, and alarm rakes over me. What if the same, dreadful thing happened to Mama as to Lara, a pattern repeated?

'Yes, our eyes met and yes, I thought I was in love with him,' she says, as if to clarify the question. 'I also thought he felt the same.'

I want to tell her she was a fool, in that case, but again it feels wrong, somehow, too close. I might easily have spoken those same words about Josef.

'That's what he told me, every time we were together,' Mama goes on. 'That, despite our differences, he wanted to marry me. That he was going to ask his parents. I should've known it would never happen. By the time I found out I was expecting, he had already gone elsewhere.'

I ask myself if de Comtois knew about my sister. The way he scrutinised her when he came to increase Pa's rent, not with lust but recognition. He must have known. I bet the man has offspring scattered across the whole of Marseilles.

Mama drops her head to the baby's and starts to weep again, and suddenly I see it. The fact that she wanted to leave Marseilles. Her disgust at the scent of lavender. Her words when Lara first went to work for the Madame. *Not so humble as they suppose.* Her muttering about the objects in my father's workshop being the property of de Comtois. *Just like everything else*, were the words she had added, lost against the racket of my own thoughts at the time.

I realise that Mama is utterly consumed by shame. Shame that she had fallen for such a man's lies. Shame that she hadn't been a better judge of character. Shame that de Comtois had got her with child. And shame that, at one point, she actually loved him. Her humiliation had twisted her, every year a little more, like a high and lonely tree continuously lashed by the wind.

Crossing to where she sits, I slowly bend towards the baby and kiss his downy head. My face lingers there awhile, my gaze finding Mama's. Her eyes would usually flick from mine at such closeness, but tonight they do not. A large tear tracks down her cheek.

I look at her a hair's breadth longer, then slowly place a kiss in the centre of her forehead. There is absolute silence. I do not wait to watch for her reaction, even though it is impossible to recall the last time I kissed my mother. I simply move back to the door.

At the top of the approach, the chateau's pale facade coalesces through the darkness, shouldering a heavy sky. In the time I've been inside the cottage, dense, ominous clouds have gathered to stifle the stars. A vengeful gale whips at my clothes. A storm is coming.

There are no lights showing from the building, but the closer I get the more obvious it becomes. There is the faintest glow in the window of the tower room. My sister's chamber. So faint it is hardly there at all.

As my pace quickens, something slides free of my clothing and lands on the gravel. A small, silvered thing, catching the fading moon's light. Guillaume's knife. I never gave it back.

She-Wolf

Sofi

I am no more than a few steps from the chateau when a figure suddenly liquefies from the blackness. I stop dead, peering through the massing gloom at the slender form before me.

The man freezes also, cowering a little. I take in his slim silhouette, his lank scraps of hair. Emile Porcher. Loitering again at the chateau, creeping about in the dark, just as he did the night Madame Justine was found—

'You!' I shout, my blood surging. 'I know why you're here, why you're always here – you're looking for my sister!'

Porcher recoils as though struck.

'I know what you've been doing. I've seen you. Planting dead rats around the place to get close to Lara. You're lucky I didn't tell my aunt what you were up to months ago – you'd have been dismissed!'

There is an ominous pause, filled by the wind beating up around the building's walls, the first icy thrashings of rain. Porcher wavers, avoiding my eyes and glancing into the distance. Any moment, I think, he will pick up his pace and flee. But instead, he turns slowly to face me.

'That would have been a small price to pay.'

I had forgotten how peculiar the man's voice is, high and fretful, and his reply throws me.

'I heard about Madame Hortense's death,' he continues.

A lump swells in my throat.

'That is why I came tonight. With the Madame gone, I fear your sister is in greater danger than she was before.'

'The Madame gone!' I lob out the words, each one hard as a pebble. 'It isn't the Madame—'

'I saw her,' he cuts in. 'At the ball. Your sister.'

I cast my mind back to that night, to Lara dressed in those fine clothes. Beautiful, though just a little out of date, making her look like she belonged to another age entirely. My stomach stiffens. 'What do you mean?'

Porcher lowers his head, spine hunched like he is working up the courage to continue. 'That ball,' he starts uneasily, 'was ten years to the day since the last one. Since . . .' His eyes penetrate the night, and I am certain they have found the spot where the old sycamore stands, that silent witness of a decade earlier. 'I felt I had to be there. And when I saw your sister . . . That was when I knew.'

'Yes, ten years since Madame Justine's death,' I respond. 'Which *you* had something to do with!'

'That isn't true!' Porcher spits, 'I would never—' His thin, dark lips press together. 'Justine was a friend. I met her at the Maison des Peupliers. She used to tutor Monsieur Guyot's children. This was well before that other man ever came on the scene—'

'Monsieur Wilhelm?'

He nods. 'I was a *garçon d'écurie*, looking after the family's horses. One day, when Justine was on a break from her duties, we began talking.' He hesitates, eyeing me defensively. 'I'm not stupid. I knew there was no chance a girl like her would ever be interested in the likes of me. But she always had a kind word when no one else ever did, and from time to time she'd come to the stables . . . we'd walk together. One day, in the woods near the chateau, we heard this horrible noise, the kind that chills your blood. It was a wolf, caught in a snare, the rope cutting right into its neck.'

I flinch at this last part, the clamping lunette, the appalling wink of the guillotine's blade flashing in my skull.

'The wolf was in pain, petrified, its teeth bared. Then I heard

442

Justine saying it was a she-wolf. The animal's teats were swollen. I hadn't even noticed.'

My memory flickers back to the story Pa used to tell us. *Le Petit Chaperon Rouge.* The starving wolf, struggling to provide for her cubs.

'Even in her state, that she-wolf was so strong. And Justine went right up to her. No fear. She cut through the snare with my pocket-knife while I held the animal. Once freed, the wolf loped away, calling softly, and it felt like Justine and me were the only other creatures in the world. A second later, there was this small flash of grey in the brush. A cub.' His voice dips to barely a murmur. 'Justine said, with its parent saved, it still had a chance at life . . . '

His last sentence overcomes me momentarily. I think of Pa again.

Porcher sniffs. 'I've never forgotten that day and never will.'

'And that is why you visit Madame Justine's grave? Why you drew a wolf on her headstone?'

His small amber eyes glint sadly.

'And also why you came to Jouy in the first place? Since Madame Justine was here?'

'No,' he returns. 'I loathed that man for marrying her, but . . . I cannot deny she seemed happy.'

'But you ended up in Jouy regardless? Even though you knew she was content without you?'

Porcher winces as though the question was a blade. 'That was pure chance. Ma grew ill. She'd moved to Jouy some years before. I only came here for her. I never saw Justine, never told her I was here. I never went up to that chateau once. Not until the night word reached the village she was missing.' He tenses, clutching handfuls of his jacket. 'I couldn't just sit there and do nothing.'

'Yet you were the one who found her?'

'I separated off from the rest of the party was all, to cover more ground. Though I know how it looks. At first, when I saw the shape on the earth over there . . . ' he raises a finger to the edge of the gardens, 'I thought it was a heap of linens . . . '

'The shape on the earth *over there*? What do you mean?'

'I mean over there. Under the sycamore.' Porcher's voice clogs in his throat. 'God help her. I couldn't stand to see her in that state. I pulled down her skirts. And when I did, I saw those marks . . . on her neck.'

Deep lines. Cutting right into the skin. The Madame's face was purple.

'God help her,' the man repeats. 'She, of all people . . . she didn't deserve that.'

'So why weren't you arrested?' I ask, trying to steady my voice. 'When you found her that way?'

'I was. They came upon me the exact moment I was covering her up. I was carted off straight away. Rat-catcher living alone with his mother? I'm well aware what people think of me.'

'And yet you were released?'

'Plenty of people were willing to swear I hadn't been anywhere near the chateau that evening. I'd been working 'til late . . . '

I glance up at the tower, the vague haze of light showing at its window. The woman responsible for Lara's death is up there, still, and for a moment I have no idea why I am standing here, in the gathering storm, listening to this man.

'I came to your cottage all those years ago as I always thought it was Justine's husband who killed her. I was going to warn you about him, warn you that your sister wasn't safe at the chateau . . . But, like I say, once I saw her at that ball, with Monsieur Wilhelm dead. Well, then I knew I'd been wrong. I knew it was—'

My flesh creeps. 'You think it was Josef.'

Another strange pause.

'Monsieur Josef's not right—' says Porcher. 'Folk think *I* was the oddity, for living with my ma. But you tell me *he's* not, when your sister's been in his house all this time . . . dressed exactly like *her*, the absolute spit of his mother!'

My mouth drops open. I force the image of Madame Justine to mind, attempting to summon her exact likeness from the tower wallpaper. I do not see the resemblance, not one bit. Lara is Lara. I have never seen anybody in her except herself, the sister I knew and loved. Perhaps I was seeing it wrong.

444

'I'm sorry,' Porcher mutters. His voice is quieter now, the peculiar whelp-like pitch of it lower. 'If I scared your sister. I only wanted to ensure she came to no harm. But please tell her that, with Madame Hortense now dead—'

'It's not Madame Hortense who's dead,' I shout. 'It is Lara. You're too late.'

Leaving him hovering there, the rain falling harder by the half-second, I swing open the servants' door and hasten inside.

The Dancing Lesson

Hortense

When I heard the village bells this morning, I imagined it was the sound of the tocsin and a sickness rose in my throat. With the house quiet, I girded myself into motion, moving my barricade away from the door and bringing everything up to this dismal room. Aside from a blanket for Pépin and my writing things, there was precious little left worth conveying up those depressing, winding steps at all.

I am still wearing my maid's clothes, itchy and unpleasant as they are, but I dare not remove them. I dare not let anyone pry beneath my disguise. I've forced that cap of hers back on my head again, also. I swear I can smell some cheap cologne upon it. Lavender.

On the table before me lies a stack of newly written correspondence ready for dispatch. Letters to every possible contact I've been able to recall. The stack is not very large. But if I can locate someone trustworthy and pay them enough to take me to the coast, there might still be hope. The arrest of my maid has bought me some time, but the noise in the forecourt yesterday was impossible to ignore. 'Hortense du Pommier has gone to the guillotine!' the workers chanted. A hundred cheers followed, so loud there might have been a hundred thousand. They dispersed, but could return at any minute. I do not have long.

In order that I might see my pen upon the page, I have been forced to light a taper. I've tried to shield as much of its glow as possible, have nudged the table to the side of the window to make it less visible from outside. Perhaps I should close the shutters. But being locked in this curving, dome-capped space – this room that so resembles a birdcage – is abominable enough as it is. And now, in these most desperate of times, balanced at the unseen precipice between danger and safety, life and death, the events that occurred all those years ago finally confront me in full and frightful detail.

I could not bear to acknowledge them before, but that is the thing about being followed by death, to check how close it is you have to look behind you, and when you do you see every dark and hidden part of the way you have come. The episode took place at Versailles. A July, exactly four years before my wedding day. I had just turned fourteen.

My dear Mama declared she wanted her rooms renewed. That everything had to be refreshed, the old wallpapers stripped, the mouldings repainted, the drapes and soft furnishings replaced with new. So the servants moved every piece of furniture in those rooms away from the walls, covering it all up with vast sheets of linen.

Due to the upheaval to her precious apartments, Mama decreed that she and Papa would travel abroad for the duration of the work. Papa told me it was imperative that I stay behind and continue with my lessons in manners and deportment, though in truth he was loath enough to take one female with him, let alone two. And so I was abandoned at the palace like an unwanted parcel, while my parents did what they always did and pleased themselves.

Mama flapped over the renovations for weeks, planned the whole enterprise precisely, convinced something would go awry in her absence. As luck would have it, my half-brother was at Versailles for the summer, and Mama gave him instructions to liaise with my nursemaid, to come in at intervals to oversee the work. *Frère Jacques*. He wasn't the French Ambassador to England then, of course.

Like my first meeting with the Obersts, it happened in Mama's salon. My nursemaid had sent me in there to retrieve something, but I became distracted by the silhouettes of the birds, flickering restlessly beneath the linen cover of my mother's great walk-in birdcage. I hadn't heard my brother enter the room behind me.

'Wouldn't it be interesting to see what was under here?' Jacques said.

447

I thought he meant the birdcage, even though his hand was skimming the back of my skirts. Jacques lifted the linen and the movement caused the birds to twitter, their wings pulse and thrum.

'Shall we get into this together?' he asked.

The door groaned shut, the wretched shriek of metal-on-metal passing straight through me, the bolt secured behind us so that nothing would fly out.

We watched awhile, as the little birds darted through the vines, observed how the mirror that curved around the inside of one half of the cage reflected the linen sheet covering it, making it look like we were surrounded by a barred white sky.

Then Jacques sat upon the love seat with the mirror behind him and stretched, as though limbering up for a ride. 'Come,' he said and patted his knee. 'I need your assistance with something.'

My handsome, smiling, grown-up half-brother was asking for my help and, as I had always been instructed not to make a fuss, to remember my lessons in politeness and etiquette, I went to sit down.

'The other way,' he told me, taking my hand and turning me to him.

I climbed onto his lap and he seized a handful of my hair, holding me there so I was facing the mirror. I used to dress more plainly then and the sight of my unpainted face, my unwigged hair and my unbejewelled body was almost as repulsive to me as the recollection of my reflection in that mirror, bobbing up and down like a dove. Almost as repulsive as the increasing frenzy of those finches, as the structure's never-ending curve, the fastness of its bolt, those unrelenting bars.

I now glance down at Pépin, who is lying at my feet. He came into my care exactly one month after the episode, a placatory gift from Mama, who seemed not to have a clue why my demeanour had altered so drastically in the time she'd been away. And my dog has been my little comforter ever since, taking nothing from me except what I wish to give. I could not go on without him.

With the wind beginning to rage outside, I resolve to write one more missive and then extinguish my light. I dip my pen into the inkpot. '*My dear—*' I begin, but before I can go any further, a noise on the stairs makes me jump. The line of my pen veers wildly from the last word, leaving behind it a black laceration. *Calm yourself,* I think, *it is most likely one of the housemaids returned, all I need do is remain silent and she will go away.* But then the most terrific hammering starts up on the outside of the door. I bring a hand to my mouth and my eyes snap to my dog.

'Shhh,' I beseech him. 'Hush, now.' But Pépin is already up, spitting at the door, his peg-teeth glinting, tiny ears flat.

The hammering stops and I pray the perpetrator has gone. But as I wonder whether to replace my barricade, there is a shout from the landing.

'I know you are in there, open this door!'

I don't fully recognise the voice at first, that of a rough young woman, evidently. My cheeks flood with irritation. What a pity it is that I am forced to lie low, else I would have no hesitation in flinging the door open and slapping the insolent woman's face for her.

'Open this door!' the voice shouts again. 'Or I shall open it myself!'

I wonder whether this woman has a key, but my thoughts are quickly answered. Out on the landing, she begins throwing her full weight against the door, sending the whole thing quaking and thundering as though on the brink of fracture. I shall have to open it now, who knows how many others might be summoned by this commotion.

'Very well,' I hiss, my teeth clenched. 'Stop your noise!' I go to the door, turn the key and edge it ajar. 'What is it you want—?'

At once a foot appears in the gap, preventing me from closing it again, and the door is pushed with such force the action momentarily knocks me sideways. I right myself and regard the girl opposite me, my mouth open. A bolt of lightning illuminates the entire room and when I recognise the interloper, my stomach turns.

'Surely you know who I am?' she says. 'I am Sofi Thibault, the sister of your maid. The one sent to the scaffold this morning in your place. The one *you* sentenced to death!'

449

The one you sentenced to death. Surely she is wrong? There is no way the authorities would have executed a maid. Why should they? Yet I find myself unable to breathe, my whole body stiffened by guilt. What have I done?

Pépin is up from his blanket now, darting to and fro at the intruder's feet, yapping and snarling. The Thibault girl does not hesitate, she lashes out a foot in his direction and Pépin scrambles to avoid it. His paws skew across the bare boards.

'Leave him!' I shout, recovering my senses and incensed by the deed. I see her pat her bodice, as though checking for something, and in a single sweep she withdraws the object. A knife. She clamps both hands around the handle and points it at me. 'How dare you!' I declare. 'I've a good mind to have you arrested!' I can tell the girl is as tense as I, we are each of us trying to anticipate what the other will do next. The scene is becoming a pantomime, ludicrous.

She laughs, an arid, uneven sound. 'Have me arrested? And how will you do that? I am sure the workers would be very interested to learn that Madame Oberst is still alive and well!'

In the centre of that round room we circle one another like wary partners, eyeing each other up. She takes a step forwards, I two back. We are as dancers, struggling to remember our steps against the percussion of the rain on the window-glass. All the while, the knife remains brandished between us, plated blade glinting in the taper's light.

'What happened to your sister,' I begin. 'I did not mean—'

'I know well what you mean,' she interrupts. 'You care for nothing but your own wants.' Her grip tightens at the knife's hilt, fingertips reddening. 'The way you have treated my sister, had her slave for you, even knowing her condition these past months. You did not deserve her.'

I can tell the girl is making an impossible effort to keep her words steady. All I must do is remain calm myself. Out-manoeuvre her. But, in that moment, the meaning of what she has just said strikes me. *The baby.* Did my maid's baby die too? Of course it did. My actions brought an end to not one but two lives today. I close my eyes. Before me, the factory girl is still ranting and raging.

450

'He was never worthy of her, either!'

There is a beat, no more. She has given too much away, not realised her words have just handed me what I need. 'Ah yes,' I murmur. 'My husband, of course.'

The factory girl lowers her eyes and this is my opportunity. I take her in as another bolt of lightning blasts the chamber. I know I must snatch that knife from her hand, somehow. By provoking her to lunge forwards, perhaps? But I am shorter than her, and she is sinewed, determined. Could I do it?

I reset my face with disdain, re-assume my usual sneer. 'That is what this is *really* about, is it not? My darling husband is damaged, you know. Set to fester, I'll wager, the minute his mother expired. He needs lancing, like an abscess. Like a poisoned, yellow-topped boil!' Despite the danger before me, the accidental analogy makes me laugh.

The girl's face shadows curiously, as if registering something familiar.

'In any case, I am surprised at you. Here you are, bemoaning the fact the man you love hardly knows you exist, when your sister's corpse is not yet cold.'

It happens quickly then, more quickly than I could have foreseen. The girl shoots forwards, the blade coming before her. I leap to my left, reaching out, as I do, to grab at the handle of the knife, but the action is judged a moment too precipitously and I miss. We are in front of the window now and my dearest dog is back, as though springing to my defence, jumping and barking at our feet, seeming to sense that the situation is escalating, is becoming irreversible.

The Fall

Sofi

I stare hard at the Madame. The gall of her, standing in Lara's chamber, wearing Lara's clothes, her own possessions strewn about as though the space was a pleasure-house for her exclusive enjoyment.

I recognise her trick right away. She was trying to reach for the knife. But she missed. The confrontation, our heightened senses, they have set our movements off-kilter. With the Madame still distracted, I see my chance. I dip a hand to the floor and seize the scruff of that idiotic dog's neck, raising it into my arms. There I hold it and I will not let go. My elbow forms a vice around its body, restraining it in such a way that it cannot wriggle free or spiral its head to reach my flesh with its jaws. With my other hand I bring the knife to its throat. The dog whimpers. I can feel its heartbeat against my chest, so wild and so fast it echoes my own.

How have I been brought to this? I could never do it, I realise, never hurt this animal or any other, and the knowledge confounds me, cleaves me in two. When all's said and done, I do not even have the courage to take a pointless dog's life in place of my father's, in place of my sister's. How could I ever take the Madame's? What a coward I am, not an avenging angel at all, but gutless, pathetic. The draughts from the window come cold at my back.

When the Madame observes what I have done, her countenance cycles from outrage to fury to despair. She thinks I am about to hack the creature's head clean off its shoulders, an eye for an eye. The noise she makes next I have never heard the like of before. It is something between a roar and a howl, something primal and hideous. She bares her teeth and charges forwards, straight at me. I tense. Then everything dissolves into the blur of our two bodies. Scratching, wresting and wrangling, an auburn shape caught somewhere in between. The knife clangs to the floor.

I become conscious that I am no longer holding the dog, either. It must have leaped away in the struggle, concealed itself somewhere out of reach. Still the two of us move back and forth, slippers scuffing floorboards, neither of us making any exclamation at all. Then, suddenly, we part. One minute I am tangled with the Madame and the next I am not.

I look up. There she is, staggering backwards past the armoire towards the window, the dog wide-eyed at her breast, aware of its mistress flailing and teetering. I see it all in a terrible, exaggerated motion.

Her balance finally lost, the Madame tips backwards, clawing at the walls, tearing away a strip of the paper. Her skirts splay wide as wings as she smashes through window-glass and frame alike, the sound an explosion. The storm gushes in through the gap like a hungry beast.

For the briefest second, grotesquely elongated though it is, a scene from long ago seizes my vision. The precious rag-doll Pa had given me – with its yellow-wool hair and gentlewoman's clothing – plummeting from the cottage window.

Wings

Sofi

As I rush towards what remains of the tower casement there is no sign of the Madame. I can see only a dark oval of sky, velvet like an open mouth, a thunderclap the roar issuing from that mouth, the splintered glass surrounding it a set of jagged teeth.

I throw myself to the floor and squint into the void of night, the wind blasting my hair, rain stinging my face like flung handfuls of gravel. I call the Madame's name, my voice swallowed by the storm, then discern the merest flicker of movement below. Something pale is beating at the blackness, a bird with a broken wing. I draw myself to the brink of the casement. The Madame's petticoats, only a little below me, flapping wetly in the wind.

'Please!' Her voice is foreign suddenly, absent of scorn or contempt and loaded with fear. 'Please, help!'

She hones into focus through the elements then and I see what has happened. The Madame is dangling from the window of the tower, frantically clutching a fractured piece of casement with one hand, gripping her frozen, panicked dog with the other. Her feet are scrabbling desperately, slippers clawing against the tower wall, seeking purchase.

The backwards plunge has snatched off the Madame's cap, and the top of her head is visible for the first time, devoid of wig. The hair that once covered it is almost gone, replaced by merging patches of baldness, her scalp dotted with scabs. The sight of it shocks me more than what has just happened, more than the fact she is now clinging on for her life.

454

'If you can, pass me your dog,' I urge. 'Then I'll pull you up.'

Her face is strained, her grip slipping, yet she is reluctant to part with the animal, even now.

'Quickly,' I command, 'do as I say!'

Perhaps knowing she has no choice, the Madame strives fiercely to raise her left elbow, edging the dog up and towards me, body shaking.

'That's it!' I jerk the animal from her, fast as I can, and place him on the floor behind me. 'Now, reach up and give me your hand.'

As the Madame wrenches herself towards me, I become aware of a noise on the approach. A horse's hooves, proceeding apace to the chateau. There is no time to see who is coming and there is certainly no time to wait for them to help. Bracing myself against the wall, I heave upwards with all of my strength.

The woman and I gradually manage, by degrees, to close the seemingly unbridgeable gap between us, until she is at last able to find a foothold and, with one huge and final pull, we tumble inside. The momentum of the action causes us both to smack into the armoire as we go, our movements heavy and reckless. As a result, the piece of furniture is almost toppled, rocking forwards to settle in a new position on the floor.

I stare at the armoire's base, at first not believing what I see. A cavity has appeared beneath it, a cavity that must have been totally concealed when the armoire was in its usual place. Before I can make sense of what it means, the dog's small russet backside swiftly vanishes down into the gap.

'Pépin!' the Madame calls, voice frenzied anew by the disappearance of her pet. 'Pépin! Where have you gone? Come back!'

I take in the opening utterly aghast, put my weight to the armoire to shove it forwards as much as I can. I step back and examine the chasm that is revealed, evaluate the missing square of floor, the steps sinking into a tunnel of blackness. A secret passageway.

I remember the way I hid in this armoire that first night I stole up here, how its floor creaked and gave under my weight. I remember what Pascal said, about the lights coming straight out of the wallpaper. And then I remember my sister. That this was her chamber, her private space. And, slowly and sickeningly, things start to add up—

'So-fi!'

A voice sounds from the gravel below, knotting tight my throat, swelling and melting through the howling wind. I spin from the hole in the floor to face the window.

Josef is motionless at the front of the chateau, gazing dumbfounded at the tower. He is yelling my name, hair plastered to his head, while his horse paws the earth at his side. He must have seen everything, I realise. Despite the storm, the candle burning in this room would have lit the scene unfolding at the window like a vignette on the wallpaper.

'So-fi! Are you hurt?' Josef shouts slowly. 'Is Lara hurt? Dear God!'

It takes me a moment to understand. He saw me with the Madame, a woman almost the same height as Lara, and wearing Lara's clothes.

'No, that is not—' I stop myself.

At my back the Madame is calling for her dog, attempting to entice it from the hole in the floor.

'One moment!' I shout to Josef, then drop beside the woman, gripping her arm.

'Listen to me,' I say, expecting instinct to take over and her to shake me away. But she does not. 'That is Josef outside. If you want to live, you must go and go now. Otherwise ... well, you won't escape the guillotine twice.'

She nearly laughs. 'Don't you think I've tried? Go where, pray? I have nowhere to go—'

'Anywhere,' I interrupt. 'As far from here as you can. As far from *him* – from Josef – as you can.'

She registers my expression as I spit Josef's name to the air and there is a flash of recognition in her eyes. 'Listen, I will call down to him, get him to come up here. While you ... go down there.' I point at the black square of missing floor. 'As quickly as possible. I'll follow.'

Leaving her crouched by the abyss, I return to the window. Josef is still on the gravel below, one hand raised impotently to the tower as though hailing a carriage.

'Josef!' I shout, the word painful on my tongue. 'Can you come up here?'

The Madame's gaze flicks between me and the shattered casement for a half-second longer. Then she scrambles into the floor, murmuring her dog's name.

Josef is gone from the gravel now, the place where he stood taken by thrashing waves of rain. I strain my ears above the tempest. I can just make out a set of footsteps on the lower floor, a tread of boots on tiles across the vestibule.

'Josef, up here!' I cry again, at the top of my voice.

'Sofi?'

His answer echoes from the landing below, his stride widening and accelerating, closing in on the spiral steps to the tower.

I call out to him once again, and am almost at the hole in the floor when a scene in the wallpaper hooks my attention as it never has before. I stare at it a moment longer, then hurl myself into the secret passageway after the Madame, having not the first idea where it will lead us.

Second Flight from Jouy

Hortense

I climb into the floor calling Pépin's name, trying to coax the dear thing out from wherever he has gone. He is most probably as undone as I by everything that has happened tonight, he's never usually so disobedient. Up in the tower chamber the girl again shouts to my husband, trying to lure him up the main stairway to the room. Then she dives down the secret steps and into the passageway behind me, hurrying me along.

'Pépin?' I murmur. 'Pépin, where are you? Come to *Maman*!' I stoop to negotiate the winding staircase in the pitch dark, sweeping my hands through every part of the space, expecting to make contact with the flossy coat of my dog at any moment. The Thibault girl is right behind me now, urging me to move more quickly still, telling me that Josef is almost inside the tower room, that our time is running out.

Suddenly, I flounder into a hard wooden wall. The passageway has ended.

'Why have you stopped?' the girl asks. 'There must be a way through.'

But I am hardly listening to her, preoccupied by the notion that if this *is* the end of the passageway, then my little dog must still be in it somewhere, or else found his way back up to the tower. There is nowhere else he could have gone. I hesitate, weighing whether I should retrace my steps, already hearing my husband circling above.

The girl nudges me aside and stealthily but firmly puts her shoulder to the wall. Eventually the wood gives, a room opening dimly before us. We move into it, as the storm outside reaches another crescendo.

I call to my dog again, hoping he can hear my voice above the wailing winds, wondering if there is some other opening he could have squeezed himself through, to bring him out here. Upstairs, Josef's footsteps cease abruptly, and he shouts the Thibault girl's name. His voice is different. Impatient, insistent. The girl freezes her strides when she hears it.

'Come on,' she insists, taking hold of my arm once more. This time I shake her off.

'I'm not going anywhere without my dog—' I pause, only then realising which chamber we have come out in. I recognise its bare and whitewashed walls, the silhouette of the bedstead rising like a rib cage from the dark, the shape of that curious rosewood box hunched on the nightstand. 'This,' I say, 'is my husband's chamber.'

The girl's face assumes a peculiar twist of dismay and loathing as she considers the statement. I recall the look in her eyes when she spoke Josef's name earlier, noted how her voice contorted around the word. She proceeds to the door. 'You do what you want. I'm leaving.'

'There is not a chance I shall be going anywhere without my dog,' I repeat, more weakly than I intend. I persist in calling out his name, my anguish rising. Why does he not come?

'Suit yourself,' the girl replies, silently edging the chamber door ajar.

No light spills in from the landing, which remains cast in a thick shroud of gloom. The servants must still be elsewhere, celebrating my demise. The place is deserted and, save a very faint glow from the vestibule, all the sconces unlit.

Instead of making a dash out onto the landing, the girl turns back to me. 'If you know what's good for you, you will leave immediately,' she utters. 'You don't understand what—'

'And neither do you,' I cut across her, my voice as low as hers. 'You

459

think Pépin my toy, nothing more than an accessory. What you fail to see . . . is that he is my only friend in the world.' My voice cracks and I cannot stop it.

A narrow beat passes. A beating of rain at the casement and thunder overhead.

'Listen carefully,' the girl says. 'You don't know what your husband is capable of. My sister tried to warn me about him. He . . . did something awful to Lara, and I have reason to believe he did something awful to his mother as well. He'll have seen by now that the armoire in the tower has been moved and who knows what that might make him do. You heard the tone of his voice just then. Stay if you like. I really don't care. But I'm getting out.'

I hesitate a second further, hearing Josef pacing upstairs again like a caged bear, moving to the opening in the tower room floor, moving onto the hidden staircase. And so I follow the girl. I have no choice. As I cross the landing, my heart contracts as if someone had driven their great fists into my chest to wring it like a rag. There is still no sign of Pépin.

The Thibault girl darts through the blackness to a hinged section of panelling in the wall. 'Door to the servants' stairs,' she says, closing it behind me.

We hasten down the square descent, lower and lower into the murk, my agony intensifying with every step, until finally, the stairs end. We have reached the chateau's lowest recesses, the servants' floor. A whole working world I was totally oblivious to, until now.

The Thibault girl beckons me up a last set of stairs and opens the door in front of her, the servants' entrance. An almighty eruption of wind swipes the door clean from her grasp, smashing it back on its hinges and nearly knocking us off our feet.

'Keep to the shadows,' she says. 'Near the walls of the house. Where you won't be seen from the upstairs windows.'

As she heads to the gravel sweep at the front of the building, I start to shiver. I do not halt to question what she meant before, about what my husband could have done to her sister or his own mother. I can think of nothing but my dear Pépin. If he follows us

460

out here he will be drenched, will be blown into the skies by this furious, vengeful wind.

A dark mass sways from the blackness ahead of us. My husband's horse, endeavouring to shelter itself in the curve of the tower. The girl reaches out to its reins and glares at me.

'Well?' she says. 'Get on. Leave.'

We stare directly at each other for a moment, just as we did the first day I arrived in this accursed place. Then I insert a foot into the stirrup, meaning to raise myself side-saddle like a gentlewoman, before thinking the better of it and swinging my entire leg over the back of the horse.

'I shall make enquiries,' I say, trying hard not to cry and failing dismally. 'About my dog. If he is found I shall have him brought to me.' But I already know that the danger here is such, and my options so diminished, the reality is I most likely will never be re-united with my sweet pet again, never hold his warm form in my arms, nor feel his small puffs of breath upon my face. And I do not know how I shall ever bear it, an absence wider and deeper than anything I have known. A pain that wrenches me in two. A sob escapes my lips.

The girl studies my expression, her brows knitting together. She removes the cap from her head and passes it up to me. My fingers awkwardly find my scalp, only realising now that it has been uncovered since my fall from the window.

I pull the girl's cap over my bare, wet head and attempt a smile. She does not reciprocate but nods once, as though acknowledging my gratitude to her gesture.

'Go,' she says, and smacks the horse's hind-quarters to drive the beast into motion.

The animal canters down the hill, into the village, out of the village, on and on and on. I ride and I ride, not knowing where it is I am going or what will become of me. The tears on my cheeks are colder and more endless than the rain.

After a while, the scene at the horizon suddenly arrests my gaze. Despite the storm still roaring behind me, the distant sky, I see, is clearer. It is clustered with diamonds, and it seems there is no longer anything between myself and that infinite expanse of jewels, nothing barring me from touching the moon's white gown. She dazzles brightly as the sun, calling me to her.

The Arts

Sofi

From the lee of the building I watch the Madame ride away, her receding shape abolished by the elements.

When I go to move, a rapid flare of lightning reveals something beneath my foot. I bend down and peel the object from the gravel. A soggy strip of paper with a violet print, that piece of wallpaper the Madame tore as she staggered backwards through the tower window. I edge closer to the front of the building, to the little light coming from the vestibule. Printed on the wallpaper is a fragment of the scene depicting Josef and his mother at the market. Due to the way it is torn, the figures have been left behind on the wall, and so all the scrap shows is a round cage, a songbird liberated from its opened doors.

I let the Madame go free. I would never have thought I was capable of such, but during those last moments with the woman in the tower, I'd heard only my sister's voice in my ears. *Just as many lives lost as lives improved. Where does it end?* Lara was right. She always was.

I told the Madame that I was going to leave, too, but that was a lie. Lara couldn't get away from Josef, so I'll be damned if I'll run away from him now. I will stay. For I know exactly what I am going to do next. All my life I've charged in like a bullock, outraged and steaming, and it has been a mistake. And, although I know Josef must be made to face what he has done, this time I will not charge in at all.

As I threw myself down the hole in the tower room floor after the Madame, a vignette flickered into life in the light from the taper on the table. Josef and his mother, flying the kite. A sudden realisation had come into being then, too, a conviction formed from a host of familiar scenes, exactly like the pattern of the tower wallpaper. I'd just never put them together before.

Josef and I playing cat's cradle, how uneasy he became when the strings caught around my finger. What Aunt Berthé told us at supper, of the winds that blew up in the hours before Madame Justine's untimely death. How Bernadette spoke of the marks on the woman's neck. *Deep lines. Cutting right into the skin. The Madame's face was purple.* Emile Porcher, revealing he found Madame Justine's body beneath the very tree depicted in the wallpaper.

These memories had all melded together, repeatedly returning to that same printed scene. Josef and his mother, flying their kite near the vast old sycamore. Yet, when I gazed at it in the moment before plunging into the secret passageway, I had, for the tiniest fraction of a second, not seen Madame Justine in that vignette at all. I had seen Lara.

Of all the vignettes in that paper, I cannot help but think it is the one of Josef and his mother flying the kite that carries some hitherto unrecognised significance. That it holds the key to what happened to Madame Justine that night, and in turn what happened to my sister.

Instead of going back to the cottage, desperate to hold Lara's child again though I am, I hunker against the driving rain and advance to the dye-house. Lifting the bar free of the door I go inside, snatching a candle and striker from the box by the entrance. I make my way to the tables where the leftover colours are kept, and lift the lids on the pails. Red madder inside the first, indigo blue in the second. A start, but not enough. Several tables away I find some of the pale wash used to prime the paper. Into the bucket of madder, I pour this white primer and, lastly, the indigo. Red, white, blue. The colours of the *cocarde*, of the Revolution. Red and blue for the citizens of Paris, white for the aristocracy. I stir the mix until a violet-purple is formed. The same shade as the tower wallpaper.

And then, I do nothing. I do not tear impetuously to the Oberst house. I sit and I wait. I wait for an hour, for two. I wait until I am sure that Josef will be asleep. And then, with the storm still rioting through the factory, I calmly replace the lid on my pail, take up a brush and make my way to the chateau.

The Woman in the Wallpaper

Sofi

The world halts, the last four years narrowing to this moment like the point of a spiral, the end of a pin. Everything is set.

I quietly clamber down into the tower floor once more, tiptoeing along that hidden passageway, the unfamiliar clothes that sheath my body making me shudder.

When I reach his chamber, I silently open the door. The form on the bed is immobile, unstirring.

'Josef?' I whisper. 'Jo-sef.'

At first, there is nothing. Then, the faintest shifting of the mattress.

'Jo-sef?'

He slowly raises himself as I watch closely, not moving a hair. The candle I am holding I keep firmly behind my back, ensuring my face is in darkness, so all that can be seen of me is the new shape of my silhouette, the outline of my cap and clothes.

'Jo-sef?'

He shocks forwards then, as though seized by a fit. 'Is it you?' he pleads. 'Is it?'

I give no reply, but silently turn and disappear into the passageway, scrambling back up the stairs and into the tower chamber. The shutters have been drawn against the storm now, so I put my candle down amidst the handful of others I've placed around the room, and I take up my position.

It isn't long before the floorboards start to creak and shift, fluctuating towards me as though an invisible entity was walking across them. Did my sister ever mark this too? Did she know it was caused by Josef, pulling himself up those concealed steps beneath the armoire? Or was she simply terrified by the sight of it?

He must have been making his way up to this chamber for years, I realise, perhaps always using that secret entrance, that rat-run. *It was almost like the light had floated straight out of the wall of its own free will.* Not a *feu follet* at all, as Sid had imagined, but a lost soul nonetheless. Josef, bearing a candle. A motherless boy grown into a man so damaged he'd—

Observing the armoire door edge noiselessly ajar, I am seized by the certainty that he must have crept upon Lara this way the night of the ball, and waves of anger and nausea threaten to overwhelm me. As he unfolds himself from the bottom of the armoire, his expression is not sly but rather hopeful, eager. Then he sees me properly, and his expectation shatters.

'Sofi?' he says, embarrassment abutting anger. 'Where is your sister? I came up here to direct her to a drier room for the night.' He pauses, his gaze darkening. 'And why . . . are *you* wearing *that*?'

I glimpse my reflection in the oval looking-glass on the wall and my gut ripples queasily. I could not look more different from Lara, from Madame Justine, yet all I now see in that looking-glass is the woman in the wallpaper, glancing anxiously back at me. Josef's mother resurrected. Free, not only of the wallpaper, but of death itself.

For I have dressed in the very same clothes Lara wore to the *Bal de Printemps*. The same clothes Josef's mother wore exactly a decade before her. A fine cutwork fichu and cap, stomacher and skirts the pale blue of a pearl.

'Take those things off.' Josef strides towards me, not registering the indecency of the command. 'Put them back as you found them.'

'You were in Paris today,' I tell him, ignoring his instruction. 'I saw you. Outside the Palais de Justice.'

My words appear to fluster him, make him momentarily forget his irritation that it should be *me* up here and dressed this way, and not my sister.

'Well ...' he begins. 'If you must know, I was. I was on my way to Hortense's trial when I ran into someone I knew.'

'But you did not attend the trial?'

'What is all this—' His lips screw and he exhales, exasperated. 'No. We went back to the man's apartments, watched the executions from the far end of the square.'

'And before that—?'

'Listen, Sofi, I don't know what this is all about—'

'Guillaume tried to find you last night,' I push on, returning the interruption. 'He rode to Monsieur Guyot's house.'

'What business did he have with me?' Josef snaps, the muscles flexing along his cheekbones. 'I was out with an acquaintance, though again I don't see what concern it is of his. Or yours, for that matter.'

So that is where Josef had been when Guillaume was seeking him, drunk in some Paris tavern. My hands tighten. 'You have no idea, do you?'

He makes an indecipherable noise, sighs. 'About what?'

'About Lara.'

His countenance shades, for the minutest second, clears. 'Where is she? At the cottage?'

'She's ...' I cannot say it suddenly, my mouth is parched, the pain of a knife at my throat. But I have to go on. I must. 'She's dead, Josef.'

He takes in my expression. Then he laughs. 'Impossible.'

'It is true. There was a dreadful mistake. Lara was arrested instead of your wife and ... it was *her* they took to the guillotine, not the Madame.'

'Ridiculous!' he sputters. 'I watched the blade fall myself. Look, I don't know what you're up to, Sofi, or why you're here, wearing that. It seems like you might have gone mad.'

It was my sister he watched die on that scaffold, but he cannot see it. He only sees what he wants to see. He always has. I give a slow, deliberate shake of the head, regain my composure.

'Fine, let us suppose this fantastical notion of yours is the truth. If

468

Hortense wasn't killed, then why isn't she here? She has nowhere else to go. Her parents are dead, de Pise, too. Where is she?'

'I don't know.' It is the truth. I have no idea where the Madame has gone. I only wish my sister had also been given the chance to flee to safety. His indignation, his disbelief, catch my temper. 'Why would I lie to you about Lara? What reason would I possibly have for lying about such an appalling thing? My sister is dead, Josef. Lara is dead. She went to the guillotine in place of your wife. She was running away with her, trying to escape. Trying to escape all this.' I splay my arms towards the wallpaper. 'Trying to escape *you.*'

There is a moment of silence as Josef fixes me with a direct and searching stare. I can see the blood pounding in his neck, under the curl of hair at his temple. Then his gaze loses its focus and he begins to shake, pressing the heels of his hands to his brows. 'It cannot be,' he mutters, 'it cannot.'

'Lara was with child,' I spit, her name choking me. 'Surely you knew?' I search his face. For shame, for guilt or disappointment, but his pallid eyes show nothing.

'Get out.'

I take a step forwards. 'I know what you did. To Lara. How could you?' The wind rages behind my words.

He does not reply.

'I asked you a question, Josef. And I want an answer. *That* is why I have come here tonight. That is why I am dressed this way. To make you see what you have done. To ask you why.'

A boom of thunder, loud as a cannon. Rain battering what remains of the window-glass like a hail of musket fire.

I step closer still. 'How could you?'

'I told you to get out!'

He is shouting now, bearing down on me. But I do not flinch. I will not. Instead, I reach for my pail and toss its lid aside.

'Very well.'

Lunging the brush into the bucket I cast great, unwieldy swathes of dye across the wallpaper, watching as its scenes dissolve behind

469

the running, spattering tracts of purple liquid, watching as it obliterates them.

At my back Josef is crying out wildly, screaming for me to stop, attempting to get a hold of my bodice, my waist, grabbing at my skirts. The realisation that I am wearing the same garments Lara was when he forced himself on her suddenly assaults and incenses me, spurring me on. I begin flinging the contents of the pail at the walls, the dye streaking to the floorboards, the pale blue of my dress vanishing beneath slashing spills of purple.

There is the slightest second more before I become aware that Josef's hands are no longer on me and, out of breath, I spiral to face him.

His legs have buckled. He has sunk all the way to the floor and is covering his head with his hands. I notice how small he looks amongst the desecrated patches of wallpaper. A boyish crumple of a man.

I lay down the pail and brush, wipe my hands on my stomacher and wait. Minutes go by.

'I loved her,' he murmurs, at last.

I detect the echo of my own voice, declaring the same thing to Guillaume in the hours after Lara's death.

'What you did to my sister. Dressing her like your mother, spying on her, invading her privacy, her life . . . ' I gesture to the armoire, to the passageway concealed below it, stretching from this room to his. 'Violating her . . . ' I have to pause. 'That is not love, Josef. None of it.'

When he speaks again his voice seems very young. 'It is . . . my fault,' he stammers. 'I killed her.'

A bolt of fear shoots through me as the wind screams at the casement. Emile Porcher was correct.

'You did, didn't you? You killed your mother? Strangled her with the strings of your kite?'

Josef stares at me as though I had spoken an atrocity. 'I . . . no! I did not mean—' His face contorts hideously, head coming to rest against the wall. 'It was late one afternoon, I was eleven. The wind was getting up, a storm threatening. It was already growing dark.

But I was desperate to try out my new kite. Mama didn't want me to at first, she said it was too late, but I . . . I ran outside anyhow, and she had no choice but to follow. We tried to fly the kite for a while, but the wind changed, became so strong I couldn't keep hold of it. It got tangled. In the sycamore.'

It is an agony listening to his story, the story I have incited him to tell. It is like waiting for a man to give confession. A man, in turn, waiting for his own absolution. His throat tightens with every syllable.

'I climbed the tree, but couldn't reach the kite. So my mother tried, but then . . . well, the branches were slippery, and she lost her footing and . . . ' Josef rubs his face with both hands, so hard he might be trying to dislodge flesh. 'She got caught in the strings as she fell. They tangled . . . around her neck.' He pauses. 'I couldn't do anything. It was impossible to untangle the strings with her weight . . . pulling them down . . . And I had forgotten my pocket-knife. If only I'd had it, I could have cut the strings. I could have saved her. If only I hadn't insisted we go out to play with the kite that day, if only . . . '

I look to my feet, floored by the horrifying tragedy of it all.

'It was my fault.'

I try to make sense of the awful details he's just conveyed to me. The way he carries a pocket-knife so faithfully, the swiftness with which he cut through the strings trapping my fingers when we played cat's cradle. The marks on Madame Justine's neck, so deep due to the weight of her body. Yet Emile Porcher said he discovered her upon the ground. 'But your mother . . . she was found—'

Josef gives a single, miserable nod. 'The strings . . . they snapped eventually and she fell. Her skirts . . . well, the speed of the fall caused them to lift.' He presses his face to his palm. 'In any case, it was too late by then.'

I screw my eyes closed but can still picture the horrible scene. Madame Justine, her neck caught up in the kite strings, struggling for her life. I wonder if that's what Josef sees, too. Every time he closes his eyes.

'My aunt said nobody could be sure how she died. Surely they saw the kite?'

He shrugs. 'It blew away in the storm. Maybe my father did know. But he never spoke of it, or her, again.'

Josef sits stock-still, his attention drifting to the ceiling trusses before returning to my face. 'You don't believe me.'

'It isn't that I—'

'You asked me earlier why you would lie about such an appalling thing as your sister's death. Well, why would *I*? Why would I kill my own mother? Why would I do that? I was eleven, Sofi. She was everything to me.'

Josef's wide lips shrink together, his chin weakens. He lowers his head, dull hair falling forwards to obscure his face. I have been wrong about him so often, but I know, in this moment at least, that he is speaking the truth.

Thinking again of what he has just told me, I briefly imagine crossing to where he sits, to put my arms around him. Then I think of what happened to my sister, of what he did to her, and I turn away from him instead.

'Goodbye, Josef.'

'Sofi?' he croaks. 'I truly am sorry—'

I draw the door to the tower room closed behind me and descend the stairs, unknotting the green ribbon Josef gave me all those years ago from my throat. I had expected that my reckoning tonight would be with the Madame. But it had been with him.

When I reach the vestibule, I see that most of the candles in those huge, sun-like chandeliers have burned themselves out. The space is in semi-darkness. But it is not quite so dark that I cannot make out a strange ball in the entranceway, utterly dwarfed by the two front doors.

'Where on earth have *you* been?' I whisper, overcome by sadness for the little creature, now quite alone in the world. Madame Hortense's pet dog. I slip my hands under his body and raise him into my arms. I wonder if he remembers that it was I who, only a few hours ago, pressed a blade to his throat?

472

I slide to the cold floor, my legs seeming to drain of all strength, and nestle the small dog on my lap. It is nice to have his warmth and weight for comfort. Although only hours have passed since I last cradled him, I already miss having my nephew in my arms. I crave his smell, the reassuring bundle of him, and want to return to the cottage at once, but the exhaustion sucks at me so much I cannot move. That baby, the remaining piece of my sister. I bury my face in my skirts. Nothing will ever be the same again.

I do not mark the hours that go by while I remain there in the vestibule, the winds storming the chateau's walls, surging over the roof, revolting through the trees. As the first feeble light slips through the lunette windows and onto the floor at my feet, I finally drift into sleep. At one point, I imagine I hear something. But when I open my eyes again the room is still empty and everything silent. The storm has passed.

473

The Offering to Love

Sofi

A weight falling, a cacophony of feverish shouts. *'VIVE LA FRANCE! VIVE LA FRANCE!'*

I wake suddenly, gasping stale breaths, then look down at myself, startling anew. I am still wearing the clothes from the previous night, still dressed as the woman in the wallpaper. Wide stains of purple have bled and dried across the blue silk overnight, as though the paper itself had seeped right off the wall and under my skin.

I go to stand, to return to the cottage and change, but my body is stiff, chilled to the bone by the coldness of the floor tiles. I rub my neck, pausing a moment. There is a noise, emanating from somewhere high and far away. It is insistent and inhuman, a harsh, repetitive yowl. I squint and look around. It feels as though I have been asleep for no time at all, but the sun is higher now, imbuing the pale squares of floor around me with a fuzzed orange glow. When the noise comes again, slightly louder this time, I realise the little dog has gone.

I get inelegantly to my feet, proceeding to the floor above as the barking worsens, contorting to an urgent howl. Maybe the animal is hungry, I think. Maybe he is lonely. My pace increases on the stairs.

The upper floor is as deserted as the rest of the building and, though the dog's howling is even louder up here, it reaches me from a higher location still. There is, I know, only one place that creature could be.

The spiralling stairs to the tower room creak under my feet, the air growing more frigid as I climb. When I reach the door to my sister's chamber, I see it is ajar.

The dog rushes through the small opening towards me and makes a yap, his large eyes imploring. I try to calm him, try to calm myself, to stay my breath and shivering hands. I push the door wider and that is when the smell hits me. Sweat and damp and fumes of alcohol, all cut through with the tang of ammonia. Something else, too. Something I had smelled up here last night and supposed to be lavender. The ghost of a scent from my sister's cologne, the cologne Josef had given her.

I move inside. There he is, in the very centre of the room. Suspended by his neck and swinging gently from a rope thrown across one of the rafters. I dash towards him, tripping over the chair cast aside near the door. I wonder whether I should clutch at his legs, bear his weight so he might breathe. But when I reach out and touch his hand, his flesh is shockingly cold.

The shutters have been opened again and Josef's body is soaked from the rain that has come hammering in through the smashed casement. His body is dripping, hair stuck to his forehead. But his light eyes are wide, parted lips set in an odd expression of relief.

As I drop to my knees, my fingers brush against something. It is that drawing I made of Lara, all those years ago. I hold the torn parchment in my palm and remember the stab of pain it gave me when I saw it that night outside the cottage. It must have been *this* Josef was looking at when the end came, it must have slipped from his hand as it slackened. He was thinking of Lara. Despite it all, the last thing he saw was her. And yet—

I bring the drawing closer to my face, look between my sister's portrait and the remaining vignettes on the wallpaper. Only in comparing the two so directly like this do I see it. How alike Justine Oberst and Lara look in these images. My vine and bead decoration encircles Lara's profile just as the lunette window does Madame Justine's. They are as two matching cameos, rare and precious. I had never perceived it before.

In that second, all becomes clear. A distant landscape sharpening into focus, a vista revealing itself at dawn. And though there is no excuse for what Josef did to my sister, I recall the way in which he always looked at her, as though she'd returned from another realm, was an angel, a ghost. He looked at her with that same desperate intensity with which I looked at him. As if she could make everything right.

'For thee and I, dilly dilly, now all are one, And we will lie, dilly dilly, no more alone.'

The horror of what Josef witnessed happen to his mother, the removal of her things, the depth of her absence, it had coloured everything, rendered his actions obsessive, perverse. It had been the reason for his infatuation with my sister, had led to him recreating those precious, printed moments of his childhood with Lara, the moments immortalised in the paper's pattern.

By staging each of those moments as deliberately as a play, with my sister their unknowing player, Josef had been re-enacting his memories of his mother, shoring and strengthening them so they would not be lost, like water through fingers, just as I feared my memories of Pa would be lost when we left Marseilles. But what Josef never came to see was that he'd been keeping his mother alive in the wrong way, fixed like a dye only on the corrupting pain of her loss, never recollecting the joy of her existence.

In the end, that wallpaper and the woman in it consumed him entirely. And Lara's death, I realise, has ended the awful repetition of those scenes, closing off the pattern once and for all.

I glance to the window and notice something different about the view. The glass is not the only thing missing. Out at the edge of the lawns, there is a gap where the sycamore once stood, the tree that bore Josef's marks. Two jagged letters, freshly cut. *J. O.* The J not for Josef, but Justine. He hadn't carved his own initials in that tree, I think, but engraved a tribute to his mother.

The workers had called it the *Liberty Tree*. Yet now it lies felled across the grass, uprooted by the storm. The ribbons of calico and coloured paper that had been tied around its branches are gone.

Love Triumphant

Sofi

The day blurs by. I think of Lara, of Josef, of what I might have done to save them. Of whether I really could. I think of Lara's little boy, that new life, alone in the world. How he needs me. How I need him. I think of my mother, of Guillaume. Of my own wretched guilt in reporting the Madame and prompting my sister's arrest. Of how it will haunt me for the rest of my life. Of how I deserve nothing less.

I watched my Aunt Berthé return earlier, saw my mother wail at her breast, her sister cosseting her like a child. I watched as the other servants returned, too, to cut down Josef's body and lay it out on the bed in his chamber, gently as a babe in a nursery. I once thought it would be impossible to leave his side, but when the time came it was easy.

As I turned from him, I caught sight of a pretty box on his nightstand, the polished wood veined red, its lid open. I looked inside, expecting to see a stack of letters, some kerchiefs or bottles of men's cologne. I did not distinguish the items within at first – a hairpin, a woman's linen cap, a blue jacket button, a comb, a pen. I believe the thing that finally stunned my mind into recognition was the smallest item of them all. A pressed flower, faded blue petals clustering around centres of pale yellow. A dried stem of forget-me-nots, the flowers my sister had worn in her hair to the ball.

I stared at that strange collection of my sister's possessions for a while, then added the likeness of Lara that Josef carried with him and closed the box's lid. These things were not Josef's, they never were. They belong to Lara's child now, are pieces of his mother that he can touch and hold.

When I reached the cottage, where a wet nurse from the village stood by, I took that baby back in my arms and rocked him. Watched his little face pout and settle. Now, as the afternoon passes, I find myself in the tower chamber again, amongst the remains of my sister's things, absorbed by my solitude. There is a strange peace to the chateau today that I have never known before. The absolute stillness after exhaling. I look around, move across the room at a mourner's pace, stroking my hands over Lara's possessions. I bring the fabric of her clothing to my nose and inhale the scent of her, insert my hands into a pair of her gloves and feel her touch once more.

It happens so suddenly then. My mouth falls open and a cry escapes it, then another. I drop to the bed as grief floors me, makes my eyes brim and spill, and I cry in great gulps for it all. For Lara, for Pa, for what has been lost, for the mistakes I have made. For once, I do not try to swallow down or shake the tears away, I allow them to come. For the first time since Pa's death, I am strong.

When I recover myself a little, I notice that the afternoon light has grown weaker, thinning and greying beyond the casement. My eyes find the patch of wall near the hearth, the only area of the paper left unspoiled by the runs of dye. Yet it almost looks like extra colour has been added there also, the violet of those scenes deeper, somehow, accentuating their form.

I rub my eyes and let out a long and ragged breath, go to stand when my toes catch against something beneath the bed. Crouching down, I drag the thing towards me, tilt back its lid. A chest, full of papers.

They are Lara's drawings and I had no idea there were so many. I remove stack after stack of them, lost in their beauty. It has been so long since I looked at her work. Maybe I never have properly. How exquisite it is. Foliage and flowers, beetles, butterflies and birds. Creatures of all kinds, captured so realistically they might at any moment fly or scuttle or sprout from the page. Each one of them is alive, rendered in meticulous detail. Pa would have been so proud of her.

I only now understand why he treated Lara as he did, why he praised her so, lavished her with attention and love. He knew she was not his. He was not favouring her, but making her feel wanted. Something else I'd never seen properly until now.

There, amongst the other work, my own face catches my eye. The drawing I made of myself and my sister the night before she left for the chateau, now decorated with butterflies and flowers in her own hand. She had kept it all this time, stored it as carefully as the rest, despite the pain it must have caused her. I recognise a number of sketches towards the bottom of the pile as the drawings she did in Marseilles, the rest of them more recent. Lara continued to make art long after she left her job in the factory, that much is clear. My sister always wanted to see her work turned into something lasting, her designs made manifest.

I resolve to ask in the print-house about Lara's drawings as soon as I can, to take a selection of pages with me, enquire whether the designers might be interested in using them. But anxiety froths in my stomach. The print-house, the factory. What will happen to it all, now that Josef is gone? I had not considered—

Out on the landing, a man coughs gently. I spring from the floor to see who is there and my face lights. 'Guillaume!'

'Apologies, I did knock. Your aunt said I might find you here. But I can leave if you are busy.'

I rush to the door and throw my arms around him without checking myself. 'Not at all.'

Guillaume awkwardly thumbs his cuffs when we part, not knowing what to do with his hands, so I take one of them and usher him inside. 'How is it you are here?'

He shifts his weight from one foot to the other. 'I came to see you. And your mother. To see if you needed anything.' Guillaume's hand starts to his jacket pocket, withdrawing from it a folded piece of paper. 'I also came to give you this.'

As soon as I see my sister's name inked in that distinct, looping hand, I know. It is Josef's letter, the one that came free from my sister's skirts on the scaffold. The smear of red on it is so faint now it's hardly visible at all, and I wonder if Guillaume, knowing it would distress me, has tried to clean it away.

'You do not have to read it,' he says. 'But I thought . . . well, that you went to burn it so hastily I was worried you might come to regret it. I don't know, destroy it again if you want to . . . nevertheless, I thought you should have it.'

I recall my hands, numbed and rigid in the hours after we returned from the square, shaking as they cast that paper into the Chastains' fireplace. 'But how did you—?'

He colours slightly. 'It landed clear of the flames. I took the liberty of removing it straight away. I do not think you saw.'

Burning a letter. I could not even get that right. I press the paper between my palms. 'Thank you.'

Observing the concern crossing his face, I feel the texture of the parchment and imagine my sister's touch upon it. I look at it a second more, take a deep breath and prise the seal apart.

It throws me at first, to be confronted by so many lines in Josef's hand, one over the other. But I tell myself to read slowly, to start from the beginning. I want to know what he had to say to my sister. Guillaume is right, I would have come to regret destroying this letter without reading it.

'If you would rather, I can leave,' Guillaume says.

'No, stay,' I murmur. 'Please.'

Josef starts the letter with an apology, repeatedly begging Lara's forgiveness. The words disgust me and I must force myself to read on.

'Oh.'

I drop onto the bed, smooth the pages across my lap as I take in their words.

'Sofi?'

'I am fine.' But my pulse is thumping. *I killed her.* It wasn't his mother Josef had meant when he uttered those words in the tower last night. It was my sister. 'It was him all along.'

Guillaume looks at me, puzzled.

481

'All this time, I thought *I* was the one who had gotten Lara arrested. I travelled to Paris, months ago, to report the Madame to the committee.'

'You reported the Madame?' There is surprise in his voice and disappointment in his countenance. Just a trace, but unmistakable. I cannot bear to mark it.

'And I am sorry for it,' I say. 'Truly. It was wrong. But I was so blinded by hatred for her, for her class. I couldn't see past it, couldn't see anything else at all.' I exhale deeply and point to the letter. 'Josef states here that he was going to Paris the day before my sister's arrest to report the Madame himself. I suppose he finally accepted responsibility for his actions and wanted her gone. So he might support Lara.'

'He did?'

I study Guillaume, unable to detect any hint of jealousy in his tone.

'Josef *did* know my sister was carrying his child, he says so in this letter. He admits . . .' I continue, swallowing hard, 'his *mistakes* and swears that he was going to make things right.'

Guillaume nods gravely. 'I hope it has eased your mind a little.'

'Wait, there is more—' I grip the paper tighter. 'Josef mentions a will. He not only went to Paris to report the Madame, but also to see to his will.' I read the lines that follow once, then twice more to ensure I'm not mistaken. 'In the event of his death, he leaves everything to Lara, to her baby. He legally recognises the child as his.'

I stare ahead of me, dumbfounded. I remember Josef's face the previous night, his blank eyes when I told him Lara had been pregnant. He must not have been aware that the baby had come early and lived. He must have assumed it had died with my sister.

'Thank you, Guillaume,' I say. 'For retrieving this from the fire, for bringing it to me. If you hadn't, well, then I should never have known.'

He frowns thoughtfully. 'If the factory, the chateau, if . . . all this . . .' Guillaume gestures into the air. 'If Monsieur Oberst willed everything to Lara, to the child, then … does it not now fall to your care, as his guardian? At least until your sister's baby is older?'

'I … I don't know. I suppose—'

Guillaume crosses discreetly to the wall, where he busies himself examining what remains of the wallpaper. In the scene directly before him, Josef and Madame Justine spin each other in joyful delight at the *Bal de Printemps*.

'He never got over her death,' I tell him. 'Josef – his mother, I mean. She died tragically when he was a child and it distorted his entire life. That's her in the paper.'

Guillaume's eyes widen. 'You know, she looks a little like—'

'Yes,' I reply. 'Like Lara.' And although I still do not see an exceptional similarity between Madame Justine and my sister, I do see the way in which Josef's, Monsieur Wilhelm's and even Emile Porcher's losses had coloured their perspectives of her.

'I really am sorry,' Guillaume says in a rush of words. 'Not just about your sister, but Monsieur Oberst, too. You cared for him a great deal, I think.'

'I did,' I reply and the words feel odd. 'Or I thought I did.' Mama's voice repeats in mine.

When did I think I had fallen in love with Josef? Was it when he returned my rag-doll? No, it was that first night in Jouy, when we took supper with Aunt Berthé. It was when she told us of his mother's tragic death, and I'd leaped on the news like a starving man on a crust of bread, convincing myself that Josef and I could be the ones to save each other.

Guillaume gives a quiet hum, as though weighing the information. 'So, this was your sister's chamber?'

'Oh … yes.' The thought crosses my mind that I should give him something of Lara's. I search through the papers once again and pull out my sister's drawing of the marketplace back in Marseilles. 'Here,' I say, offering it out to him. 'She would have wanted you to have something of hers.' I think carefully before uttering the next part. 'I know you loved her.'

There is a long pause before Guillaume sighs. I expect him to take the drawing and have to look away, to hide the catch in his throat as he thanks me for it. But he simply clasps his hands in front of himself as he always does and mumbles. 'It was you, Sofi.'

Taking in the earnestness of his gaze, I try to determine what he might mean.

'It was always you.'

Self-consciously and without thinking, I raise a hand to my head, pat the coils of coarse hair poking from my cap. It is impossible.

'Everyone always preferred Lara to me. She was the beautiful one. She was the one who was gentle and good.'

'Not everyone.'

A silence. At once, my mind rakes up a multitude of questions, things I cannot make sense of. 'Did Lara know?'

He nods solemnly. 'I told her a few days before I heard you were moving to Jouy. That's why she left me the address of the factory. So I could find you again.'

'She did?'

'I had someone write here on my behalf, several times,' he adds. 'The letters must have gone astray.'

I recollect the words I spewed at my sister, years ago, and my cheeks burn with embarrassment. *If he did have someone write to you, Mama would always get to his letters first.* It was me the letters were for, not my sister. I anticipate the flash of anger in my chest, at what Mama must have done to those pages, but it does not come. She was just trying to protect us, her actions clouded by what happened with de Comtois.

'But why wait so long? To find us?' I flush anew. 'To find *me*?'

'My mother died, very suddenly of the fever, not long after you left. My younger siblings needed me.'

'Oh.' I could kick myself for the crassness of the question. 'I'm so sorry.'

'They relied on my wage. I had employment with my uncle, in Marseilles.'

'Of course.' A moment passes. 'But the night of the ball? I saw you and Lara together—'

484

'After the incident with the Madame, I could not find you. I thought you must already have gone home.'

I think of returning to the cottage that night, of my mother's revelations snaking through the darkness. I realise I hadn't stopped to listen to her then, not really. I wish I had been calmer, been able to find a little more empathy.

'So I waited to speak to Lara,' Guillaume goes on. 'Asked if I could talk to her about you, before I made a fool of myself.' His eyes come to rest at his feet. 'She invited me into the chateau, to talk in the servants' hall, but I did not think it appropriate. If Monsieur Oberst had found out ... well, I didn't want her to get into any trouble on my account.'

How stupid I was. I had only ever seen the servants' door close, heard the lock turning from within. My sister, locking up for the night. It was as Guillaume told me in Paris. He never even went inside. He must have cut through the trees on his way back to the factory gates.

'Lara and I were friends, but I came to the ball to see *you*, Sofi.'

He had, of course he had. He had found me at the *Bal de Printemps* before he found Lara, just as I was on my way to dance with Josef, had held and calmed me as the Madame erupted.

'You came to the house, back in Marseilles, just before we left,' I say, remembering the scene I witnessed from my chamber window. 'You spoke with Mama, and I thought you were asking about Lara ... but you were actually asking about *me*?'

'I was.' He pauses, uneasy. 'I sought to ask your mother's permission to ...' His voice trails away. 'Unfortunately she thought I was attempting to make promises I couldn't keep.'

The gold ring he handed to the guard in the Conciergerie. Everything crystallises before me in a vast sweep of comprehension. Once again, I'd been looking at it all wrong.

'Your ring!' I exclaim. 'It was for me?'

He lowers his head again. 'It was. It was my mother's.'

'You were going to ask *me*—'

'Yes. I'm sorry.'

485

'Don't be sorry.'

I think of that ring, exchanged for one extra hour with Lara. One extra hour that Guillaume bought for Lara to spend with her child. How that time was far more precious than the metal. Yet the item is lost to him now, all the same.

I move to the window, where a robin is calling outside, throwing his song to the autumn sky. 'Why did you work for my father? When you knew he could not pay you?'

'Is that not obvious?' Guillaume answers. 'Though I liked your father very much. He was a good man.' He crosses to join me.

'Lara gave him a name, you know. Her baby. She whispered it to me in the cell, before . . . ' My throat stiffens, but as I form the letters of the word, my hope, my love for my sister and for that perfect little piece of her soars. 'She named him Luc. Short for Luqman.'

'After your father.'

'After our father.'

We turn towards the view through the still-broken casement at the same time. The sun has lowered, and the buildings of the factory are silhouetted in the distance, the air cool and steady. In that moment, there does not seem to be any need to speak again, for I know that in a while I shall take Guillaume back to the cottage. We will gather at the fire and begin to find a way to continue, to not let what has happened warp and consume us. To honour the lives of Lara and my father, to honour their memory and have them live on.

Guillaume and I watch together, as the last blush of light dips below the horizon.

Epilogue

Jouy-en-Jouvant, 1794, ten months later

In the spire of the little church, the bells are about to be rung. The nave is heady with the scent of wild olive blossom, brought especially from the south, and the whole village is lit clean by summer sunshine. Among the garlands and the flowers, and among the amber candles, the congregation is gathering. In another half-hour the entire workforce of the Oberst wallpaper factory will be there, to watch their mistress marry, to celebrate the union of:

Sofia Eleonore Thibault & Guillaume Christophe Errard

The bride is about to leave her house for the church. She is dressed in a smooth ivory gown, the finest she has ever worn, purple blooms of thyme studding the dark curls of her hair. She embraces her mother, who links arms with another woman, the bride's aunt, and together the sisters begin their walk to the village to join the congregation.

The bride scoops up the small infant playing at the foot of her toilette, a baby boy who has been making a rag-doll bob merrily along the rug, watched attentively by a small auburn dog. It is a curious juxtaposition; the well-dressed young master of this chateau, being so entertained by such a simple thing. With the child in her arms and the doll in his, the woman makes her way to the waiting carriage.

Beyond it, a gap in the line of trees bordering the gardens catches her eye, the place where the ancient sycamore once stood. The woman pauses to observe that gap, remembering the events which followed the storm that felled it.

A few months before Christmas, the grave of Wilhelm and Justine Oberst was opened to allow their son to rest beside them. The manner of his death would usually deny him a churchyard burial, but the community had made an exception. Josef Oberst's name had been added to the burial-stone beneath those of his parents, carved by the village mason.

The craftsman had also chiselled a second stone, to be erected at the edge of the same cemetery, in a quiet spot overlooking a meadow, washed by blue forget-me-nots in the spring. This stone bears an ancient family name of its own.

L. THIBAULT

The bride will take the infant back to the churchyard, in several days' time, to lay a posy on these monuments to his parents, to discuss and remember them, just as she does every week.

Oberst, Thibault & Co., as the factory is now known, has been modernising its processes. Old printing blocks, used for twenty years and more, are wrapped and crated and securely stored in vaulted cellars. New metal printing rollers have been manufactured, engraved with the more modern designs of a whole, fresh range of wallpaper. They are populated not only by groups of figures in Marseillais landscapes, captured like cameos, but by beautiful flora and fauna. The surfaces of these patterns teem lush with foliage, with jumping fishes and bobbing birds, with bees and beetles and olive blossoms. The factory's output is, once more, a commemoration of a rare and special bond between two people. Once Wilhelm and Justine Oberst, now Sofia and Lara Thibault, for these new designs are the joint work of two sisters, and in them the elder lives on; her talent memorialised, unforgotten.

The business is growing, the workers paid well. The man hovering nervously at the altar today, dark hair and beard trimmed neatly for the occasion, is also responsible for its success. He has been the one to design and craft the new metal plates and rollers, the secret to the factory's crisp, desirable patterns. The wallpaper is attracting customers almost daily, shops in European capitals requesting, in weekly increasing numbers, that they too might stock these modish, modern wares.

Several months ago, for example, a Venetian businessman visited the factory. Signor Maggiolini. He brought with him his wife, an olive-skinned, mahogany-haired, exquisitely dressed woman with a musical voice. A woman carrying a little pet dog. But it wasn't this woman or her husband that caught the eye of the bride at the time. It was Signora Maggiolini's lady's maid. It was the familiarity of her face; the way her almond-shaped eyes glinted like peridots; the recent growth of white-blonde hair beneath the cap on her head. It was the way the maid's expression lit whenever she was passed her mistress's small dog.

Back inside the chateau itself, things are changing, too. Furniture is being rearranged, rooms stripped of their old decor, paintwork refreshed. A hidden passageway, constructed when the chateau was built and modelled on the house that inspired it, is blocked-up. The paper that has hung for decades is peeled away from the walls and in its place are pasted rolls of the factory's newest designs. But these refurbishments will not just benefit the family who now lives there, for the function of the building is shifting, its rooms being repurposed. Several months from now, a new kind of drawing school will open at the chateau, run by its mistress, the bride herself. It will be a place where female students can come to study and sharpen their skills. A real place of progress.

When blocks bearing the factory's old wallpaper designs were put to storage in the chateau's vaulted cellars, another set of printing blocks, long-presumed lost, was unexpectedly found. Together, they form the scenes of a love story, vignettes from a childhood. A boy and his mother enjoying an unusual picnic, the mother and her boy playing the fortepiano as one. Though the blocks do not look so old as they might. Perhaps they are copies, made under the previous master's orders, and not the originals at all.

With everyone at church, a single factory worker remains. This amber-eyed man, thin laces of hair reaching to his collar, makes a bonfire. He piles on kindling, stacks on logs, then adds the wallpaper lately stripped from the tower. Observing the man work in the moments before the bride steps into the carriage, the baby's mouth suddenly starts wide. The child emits a gurgle, more formed than his usual murmurings. Indeed, this time the noise could almost be mistaken for a word.

'*Ma-man.*'

The baby jabs a chubby finger into the air and the woman holding him looks to where he points, gaze lingering on the old tower wallpaper, spattered with purple. She sees, for the first time, one scene in particular that she has never noticed before. There, amongst the tumbles of flora and fauna, suspended in time, is the chateau's old mistress, Madame Justine. She is blindfolded, hands extended before her, light hair swept beneath a newer style of cap. The woman in the wallpaper is playing a game with her son, but he looks older now, watching enraptured as she fumbles towards him.

The paper catches. Flames lick through the middle of the scene, spreading to its edges. The bride shakes her head. She is mistaken, for has she not studied that pattern innumerable times? Has she not identified every one of its scenes? She has. The pattern has not changed.

Cradling the child close, the woman climbs into the carriage and the driver steers the ponies towards the village. Soon, the scene will open up before her – the church glowing ochre in the sunshine, the well-wishers and the swirling ribbons – as the carriage rounds the corner.

Historical Note

Women and the French Revolution

An aspect of the French Revolution which has always intrigued me, but which I knew nothing about before writing this novel, was the role and advancement of women. Did the Revolution offer real change and opportunity for women in the country? Or did the progress it ushered in only benefit its male citizens?

Women took part in some of the most important events of the Revolution, including the 'Women's March' on Versailles in October 1789 to demand bread from the King. They formed their own political clubs and societies during this period of constitutional turmoil, publishing newsletters and pamphlets to put forward their thinking. It was, however, repeatedly rejected by France's (male) politicians.

Perhaps the most famous feminist of the time was Olympe de Gouges. Her 1791 *Déclaration* argued for a woman's equal right to education, property, employment, suffrage and free speech. Following the September Massacres of 1792 (during which the Princess de Lamballe and thirty-five women and girls from the Salpêtrière Hospice were brutally murdered), de Gouges began to vocally condemn the spiralling violence: 'Blood, even that of the guilty, if shed cruelly and profusely, sullies revolutions forever.' Unfortunately, her words angered a number of Paris's most powerful men, who branded her immoral. She was summarily guillotined for her trouble in 1793.

As the Revolution wore on, it started to become clear that it would not usher in the changes women had hoped for at its start. Women were denied both suffrage and property rights, and the opportunities for them to gain an education remained very limited. In 1795, following a street protest about food shortages, women were banned by parliament from attending political meetings altogether, and gatherings of more than five women were made illegal.

The new Constitution defined a good citizen as a 'good son, good father, good brother, good husband'. It seems that, ultimately, the Revolution brought neither liberty, egality or fraternity to the majority of French people.

'Lucid' Decapitation

The invention of the guillotine in 1792 – a device famed for its swiftness of dispatch – prompted a fascination for how long it was possible for a victim to stay conscious after decapitation. It's another aspect of the French Revolution that has always fascinated me (albeit rather morbidly). As a result, I was keen to somehow include 'lucid' decapitation in this novel, which is the reason why Lara's story does not immediately end the second the blade drops.

Reports of the period, detailing strange occurrences after the moment of execution, were numerous. Some described heads being presented to the crowds with moving lips, a wandering gaze or, perhaps most chilling of all, a change in facial expression – from shock to terror to, in some cases, acceptance.

One of the more famous anecdotes of supposed consciousness following execution by guillotine is the story of Charlotte Corday, beheaded in 1793 after assassinating the radical political journalist Jean-Paul Marat. Legros, a carpenter overseeing the execution, allegedly took hold of Corday's head post-decapitation and slapped it across the face. Spectators were adamant that, in reaction to this insult, Corday not only blushed but displayed an expression of 'unequivocal indignation'. Legros was imprisoned for three months for the episode.

As interest grew in such post-mortem anomalies, scientists began conducting their own experiments. Many of those condemned to die were asked to blink for as long as possible after the guillotine's blade had fallen. Whilst some did not flicker their eyelids at all, others, such as the chemist Antoine Lavoisier, who met his end at the guillotine in 1794, purportedly managed to blink for between fifteen and twenty seconds.

A Dr Séguret took things further still, subjecting a number of guillotined heads to a series of experiments by exposing their eyes to sunlight, observing that they 'promptly closed, of their own accord, and with an aliveness that was both abrupt and startling'.

As for King Louis XVI himself: whilst there are no records of the royal eyelids moving after his head was severed, eye-witnesses reported that, rather than cleanly bisecting his neck, *Madame Guillotine*'s blade cut through the back of his skull and into his jaw instead. This made the King's execution perhaps the most famous example of the guillotine's failings, and certainly not the quick end its inventor had intended.

Egality, Fraternity and Historical Liberties

I'd like to emphasise that *The Woman in the Wallpaper* is first and foremost a work of fiction, written solely for the entertainment of its readers. As such, I've taken a number of historical liberties throughout the text, creating an overall flavour of a French Revolutionary setting, rather than a dogged referencing of historical fact.

The details of Lara's execution were inspired by possibly the most famous beheading of the time; that of King Louis XVI himself. As such, these scenes in the book are rather more heightened than an 'average' execution would have been (the kerchiefs being dipped in blood to act as souvenirs, for example). Louis was guillotined in the Place de la Révolution (now the Place de la Concorde), but of the over 2,400 people who met their ends in the guillotine during the Revolution, only around half were actually executed in this square. And although, in my Prologue, two women and a seventeen-year-old boy meet their makers in the jaws of *Le Rasoir National*, relatively few women were executed this way compared to men, and even fewer children. Soberingly, however, the youngest victim of the guillotine during this period was just fourteen years of age.

Bernard-René Jordan de Launay, Governor of the Bastille, was not murdered by the crowds directly in front of the prison, but taken north-west and killed at the Hôtel de Ville. But, for the purposes of this story, it made more dramatic sense to keep events unfolding in one place. Similarly, the baker, Desnot, the man whose crotch was on the receiving end of de Launay's unfortunate kick, was not the man responsible for decapitating the Bastille's Governor. That gruesome task actually fell to a butcher named Mathieu Jouve Jourdan.

Le Roucas Blanc is another artistic liberty taken. In 1788, I believe this area of Marseilles was populated by the bourgeoisie, rather than the upper-classes. However, the symbolism of having the most privileged inhabitants of a city dwell on the 'Roucas Blanc' (the white rock) – following the white of the *tricolore* representing the aristocracy – seemed too good to pass over.

The red, white and blue cockade was a slightly later invention than I have implied in this novel, and wouldn't have appeared at the storming of the Bastille. Most likely neither would the phrase 'Liberté, Égalité, Fraternité'.

In reality, the Revolution was a long and complex period of history, not quite the clear-cut uprising of peasants overthrowing nobles that I have perhaps insinuated it was within these pages. Being a noble per se was never illegal, though while some high-profile nobles were indeed executed, and many more came under suspicion, a great number fled the country. Others, by contrast, merely elected to sit tight, waiting and hoping for the tide to turn.

I also have taken some artistic licence with the factory's dyeing processes. Plantstuffs and steeping likely wouldn't have been used as a method of colouring wallpaper, being reserved for fabric dyeing. Rather, powdered pigments mixed with oil or water would have been used instead.

For any other particularly offensive historical inaccuracies, I most humbly apologise.

Acknowledgements

Though penning a novel hardly constitutes a day at the coalface, writing this book – a process that has spanned five years, two bouts of chronic illness and long Covid – has been one of the biggest challenges of my life. I always thought I was a giver-upper, ready to throw in the towel at any opportunity, but the various problems I've encountered on this journey have proven to me that I am, in fact, a cockroach, able to survive a writing apocalypse and totally unwilling to die.

Given a succession of drafts of this novel, plus around 150K other related words, have been forever consigned to various recycling bins, that this book now exists is nothing short of a miracle. And so my heartfelt appreciation is due to anyone who has helped make its existence possible along the way.

My thanks go to my agent, Rachel Neely, and the rest of the team at Mushens Entertainment, as well as my editor, Rosanna Forte, and everyone at Sphere and Little, Brown.

Thanks to Melanie Clegg, who gave me some invaluable French Revolution pointers early on in the process.

Thanks to Sally O-J, who read a very early version of this manuscript and offered the verdict: 'the first chapter's excellent, but after that it goes totally tits-up'. That's when I knew I was in trouble. And also when I knew I had to work hard to try and put it right!

Thanks to the many friends who have encouraged me along the way (especially fellow writers Marie-Louise Plum, Anna Mazzola, Jessica Hatcher-Moore, Kirsty Smith . . . and too many others to list here!). And extra thanks to Lindsey Fitzharris, the source of much inspiration, support and wise advice.

Thanks to everyone who has cheered me along on social media for years, people I'm now lucky enough to call friends. To the kind and generous authors who offered quotes. To you, the reader, for taking the time to pick this book up in a busy, noisy world.

Thanks (and this is one for anyone else currently struggling to find a way into traditional publishing) to the agents and novel competitions who rejected my work, for giving me the rocket fuel to press on, in the shape of fresh supplies of indignation and downright bloody-minded stubbornness.

Thanks to my Mum, Paula, for her support throughout this process and beyond, and for listening to my regular diatribes, which always began: 'I just can't write a novel'. To my Grandad, Derek, my Nana, Joyce, and to my great-grandparents Hilda and Bill for the stories.

Thanks to my gentle and constant companions Huxley and Harris.

Thank you to Barry, without whom this book could not have been written.